GIANT DAYS

VOLUME FOUR

BOOM! BOX

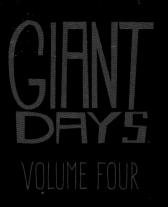

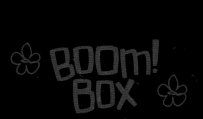

Ross Richie CEO & FOUNDER
Matt Gagnon EDITOR-IN-CHIEF
Filip Sablik PRESIDENT OF PUBLISHING & MARKETING
Stephen Christy PRESIDENT OF DEVELOPMENT
Lance Kreiter VP OF LICENSING & MERCHANDISING
Phil Barbaro VP OF FINANCE
Bryce Carlson MANAGING EDITOR
Mel Caylo MARKETING MANAGER
Scott Newman PRODUCTION DESIGN MANAGER
Irene Bradish OPERATIONS MANAGER
Sierra Hahn SENIOR EDITOR
Dafna Pleban EDITOR, TALENT DEVELOPMENT
Shannon Watters EDITOR
Eric Harburn EDITOR
Whitney Leopard ASSOCIATE EDITOR
Jasmine Amiri ASSOCIATE EDITOR
Chris Rosa ASSOCIATE EDITOR

Alex Galer ASSOCIATE EDITOR
Cameron Chittock ASSOCIATE EDITOR
Mary Gumport ASSISTANT EDITOR
Matthew Levine ASSISTANT EDITOR
Kelsey Dieterich PRODUCTION DESIGNER
Jillian Crab PRODUCTION DESIGNER
Michelle Ankley PRODUCTION DESIGNER
Grace Park PRODUCTION DESIGN ASSISTANT
Aaron Ferrara OPERATIONS COORDINATOR
Elizabeth Loughridge ACCOUNTING COORDINATOR
Stephanie Hocutt SOCIAL MEDIA COORDINATOR
José Meza SALES ASSISTANT
James Arriola MAILROOM ASSISTANT
Holly Aitchison OPERATIONS ASSISTANT
Sam Kusek DIRECT MARKET REPRESENTATIVE
Amber Parker ADMINISTRATIVE ASSISTANT

BOOM! BOX

GIANT DAYS Volume Four, February 2017. Published by BOOM! Box, a division of Boom Entertainment, Inc. Giant Days is ™ & © 2017 John Allison. Originally published in single magazine form as GIANT DAYS No. 13-16. ™ & © 2016 John Allison. All rights reserved. BOOM! Box™ and the BOOM! Box logo are trademarks of Boom Entertainment, Inc., registered in various countries and categories. All characters, events, and institutions depicted herein are fictional. Any similarity between any of the names, characters, persons, events, and/or institutions in this publication to actual names, characters, and persons, whether living or dead, events, and/or institutions is unintended and purely coincidental. BOOM! Box does not read or accept unsolicited submissions of ideas, stories, or artwork.

A catalog record of this book is available from OCLC and from the BOOM! Studios website, www.boom-studios.com, on the Librarians page.

BOOM! Studios, 5670 Wilshire Boulevard, Suite 450, Los Angeles, CA 90036-5679. Printed in China. First Printing.

ISBN: 978-1-60886-938-1, eIBN: 978-1-61398-609-7

MAR 16 2017

939

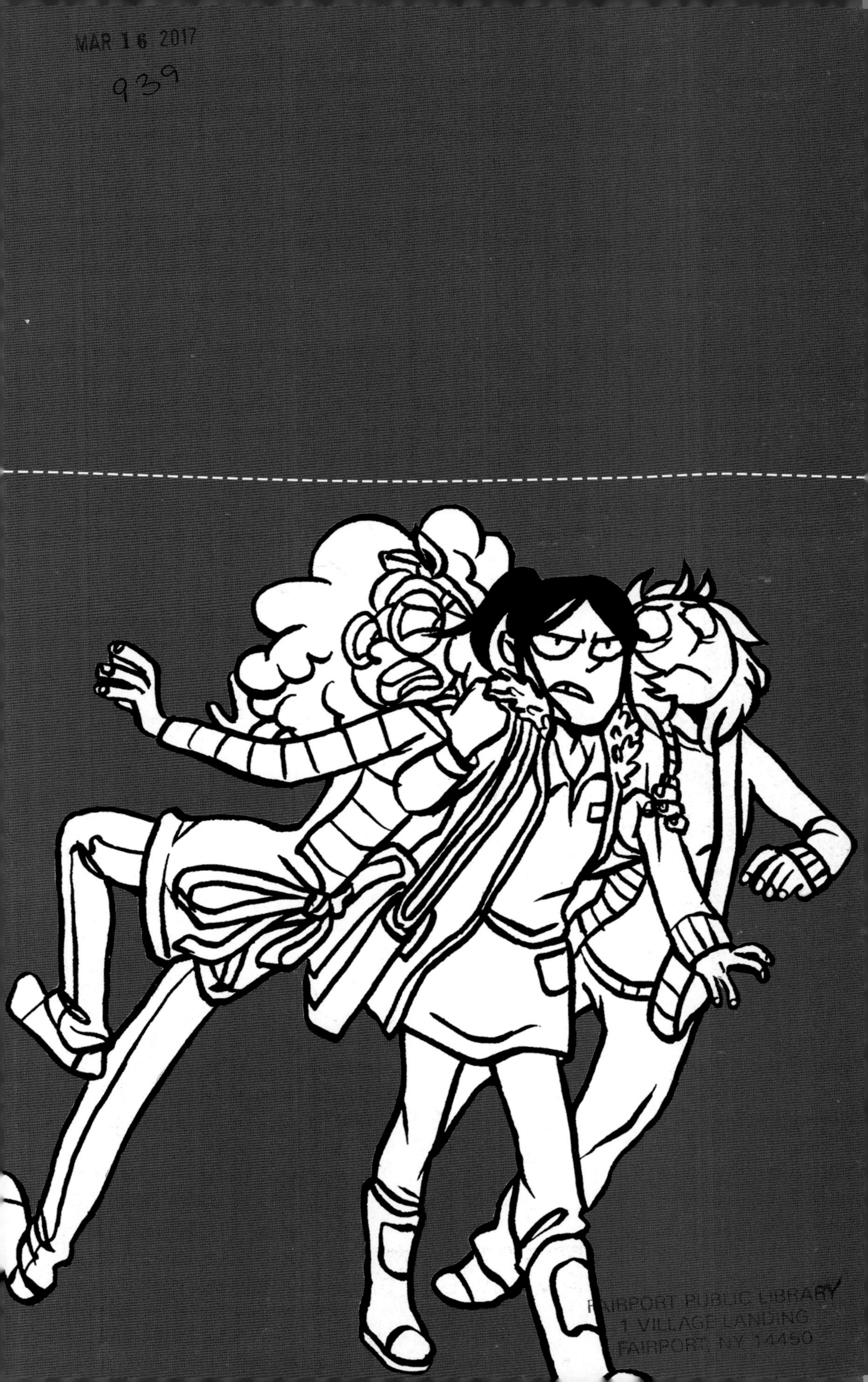

GIANT DAYS

CREATED & WRITTEN BY
JOHN ALLISON

ILLUSTRATED BY
MAX SARIN

INKS BY
LIZ FLEMING

COLORS BY
WHITNEY COGAR

LETTERS BY
JIM CAMPBELL

COVER BY
LISSA TREIMAN

DESIGNER
MICHELLE ANKLEY

ASSOCIATE EDITOR
JASMINE AMIRI

EDITOR
SHANNON WATTERS

CHAPTER THIRTEEN

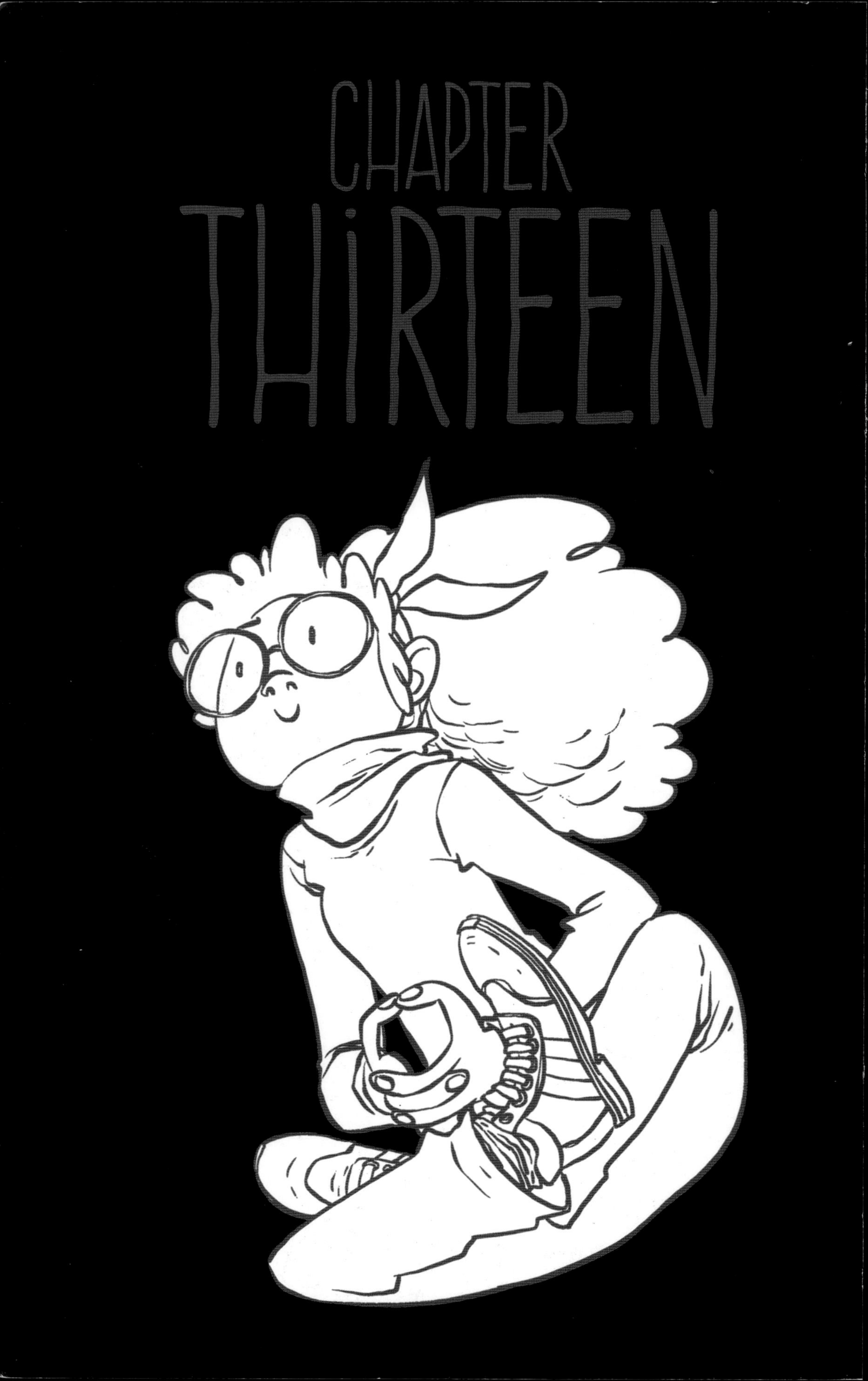

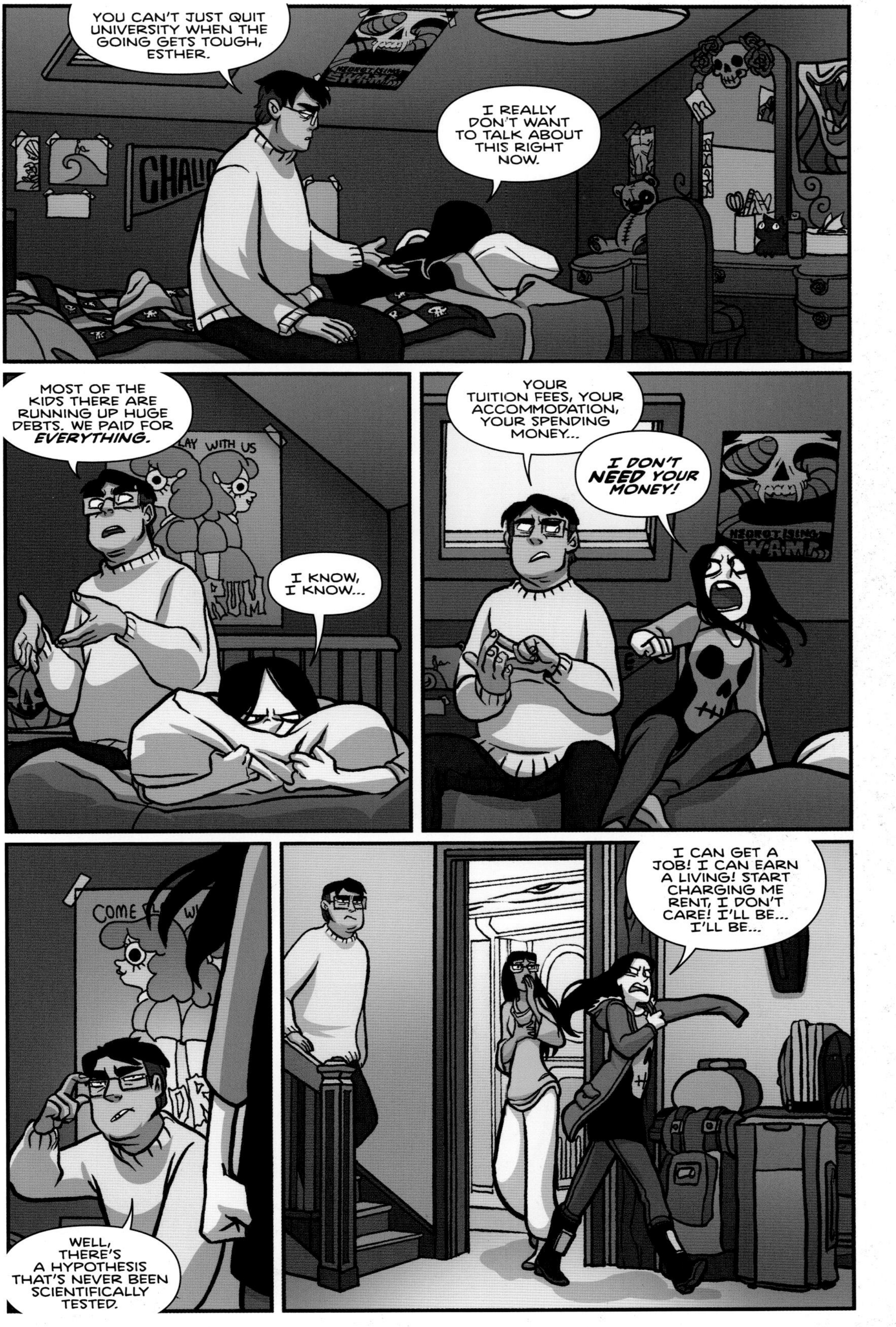
YOU CAN'T JUST QUIT UNIVERSITY WHEN THE GOING GETS TOUGH, ESTHER.
I REALLY DON'T WANT TO TALK ABOUT THIS RIGHT NOW.
MOST OF THE KIDS THERE ARE RUNNING UP HUGE DEBTS. WE PAID FOR ***EVERYTHING.***
I KNOW, I KNOW...
YOUR TUITION FEES, YOUR ACCOMMODATION, YOUR SPENDING MONEY...
I DON'T NEED YOUR MONEY!
WELL, THERE'S A HYPOTHESIS THAT'S NEVER BEEN SCIENTIFICALLY TESTED.
I CAN GET A JOB! I CAN EARN A LIVING! START CHARGING ME RENT, I DON'T CARE! I'LL BE... I'LL BE...

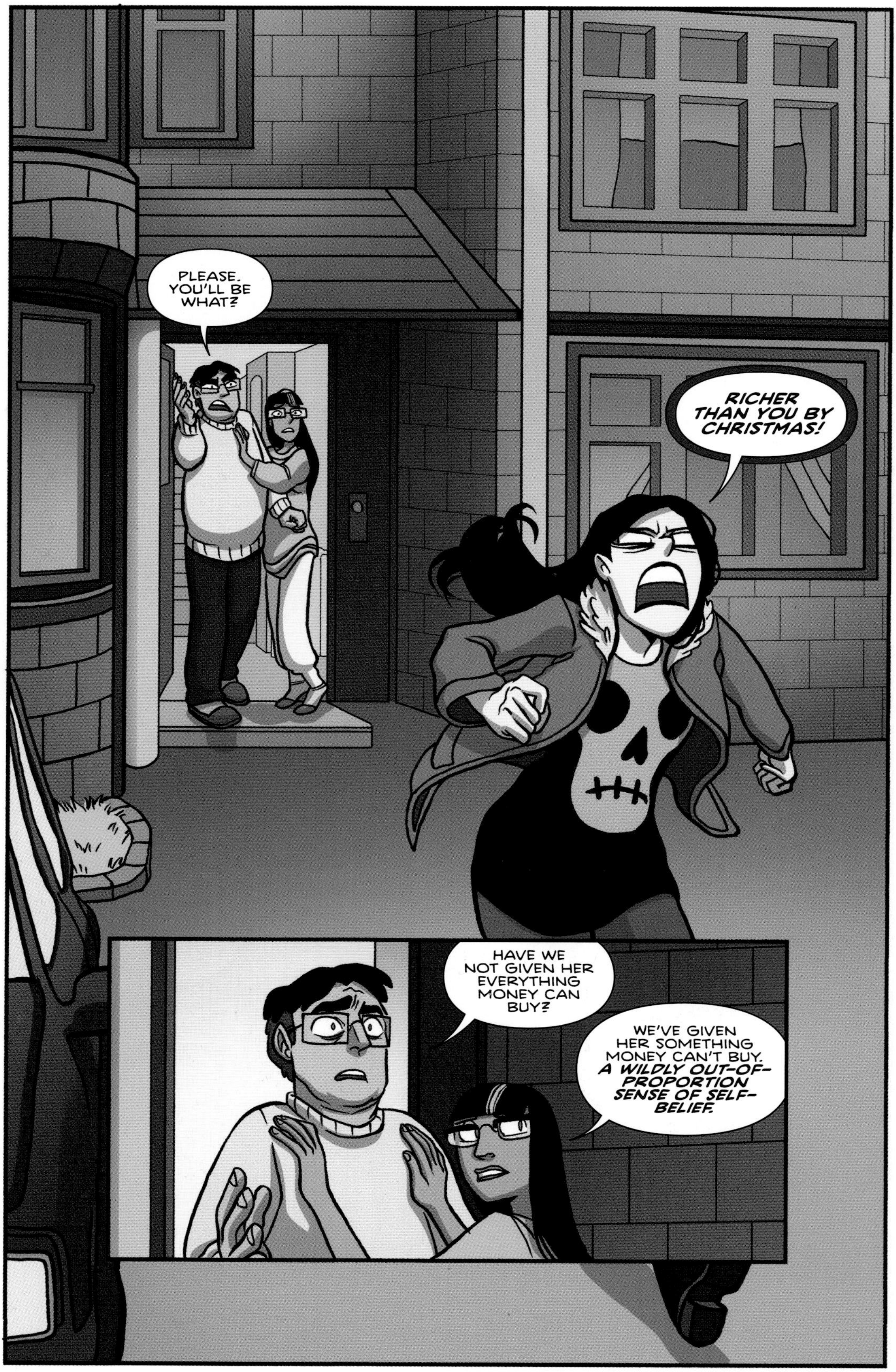
PLEASE. YOU'LL BE WHAT?
RICHER THAN YOU BY CHRISTMAS!
HAVE WE NOT GIVEN HER EVERYTHING MONEY CAN BUY?
WE'VE GIVEN HER SOMETHING MONEY CAN'T BUY. A WILDLY OUT-OF-PROPORTION SENSE OF SELF-BELIEF.

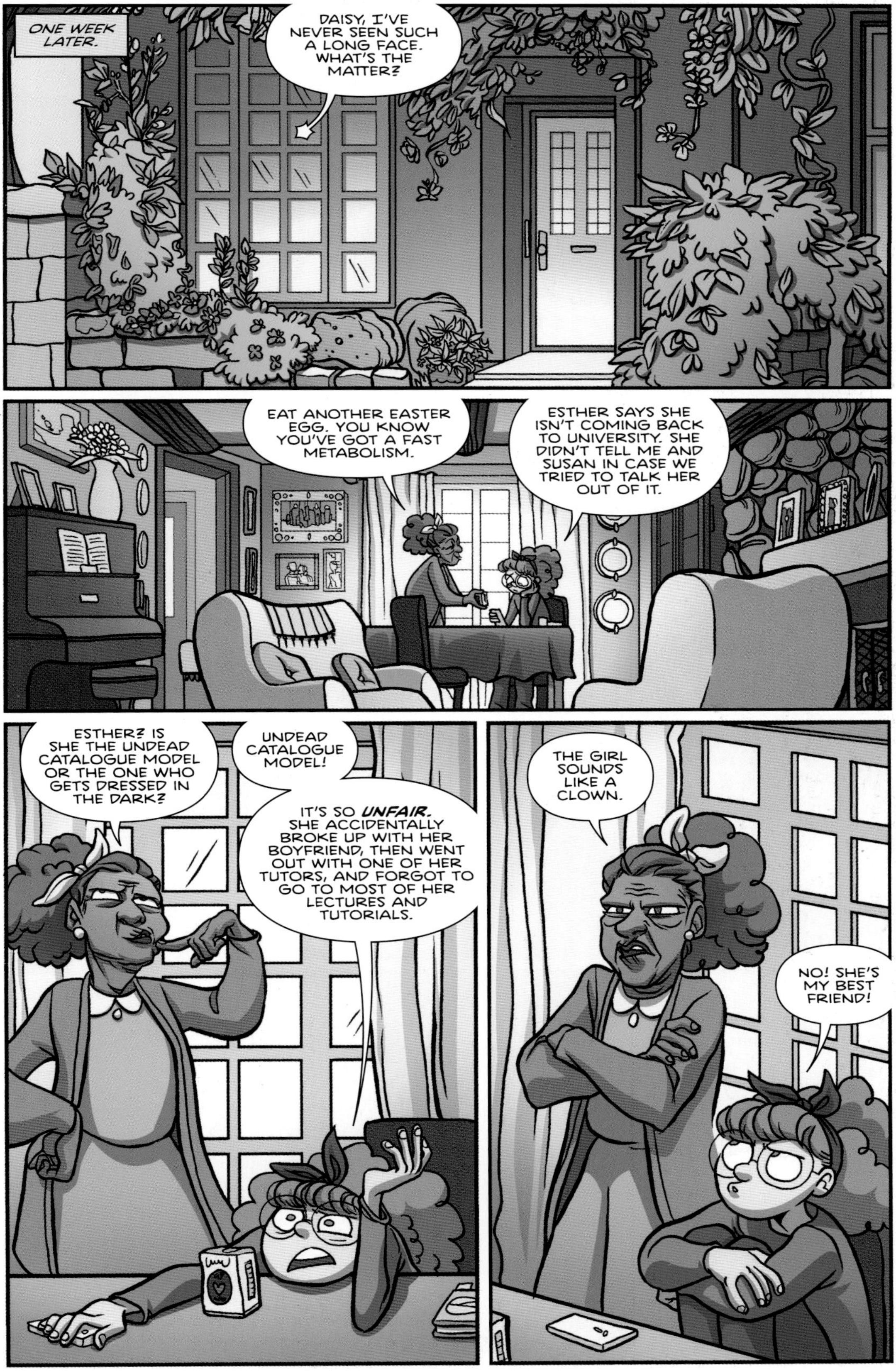
ONE WEEK LATER.
DAISY, I'VE NEVER SEEN SUCH A LONG FACE. WHAT'S THE MATTER?
EAT ANOTHER EASTER EGG. YOU KNOW YOU'VE GOT A FAST METABOLISM.
ESTHER SAYS SHE ISN'T COMING BACK TO UNIVERSITY. SHE DIDN'T TELL ME AND SUSAN IN CASE WE TRIED TO TALK HER OUT OF IT.
ESTHER? IS SHE THE UNDEAD CATALOGUE MODEL OR THE ONE WHO GETS DRESSED IN THE DARK?
UNDEAD CATALOGUE MODEL!
IT'S SO *UNFAIR.* SHE ACCIDENTALLY BROKE UP WITH HER BOYFRIEND, THEN WENT OUT WITH ONE OF HER TUTORS, AND FORGOT TO GO TO MOST OF HER LECTURES AND TUTORIALS.
THE GIRL SOUNDS LIKE A CLOWN.
NO! SHE'S MY BEST FRIEND!

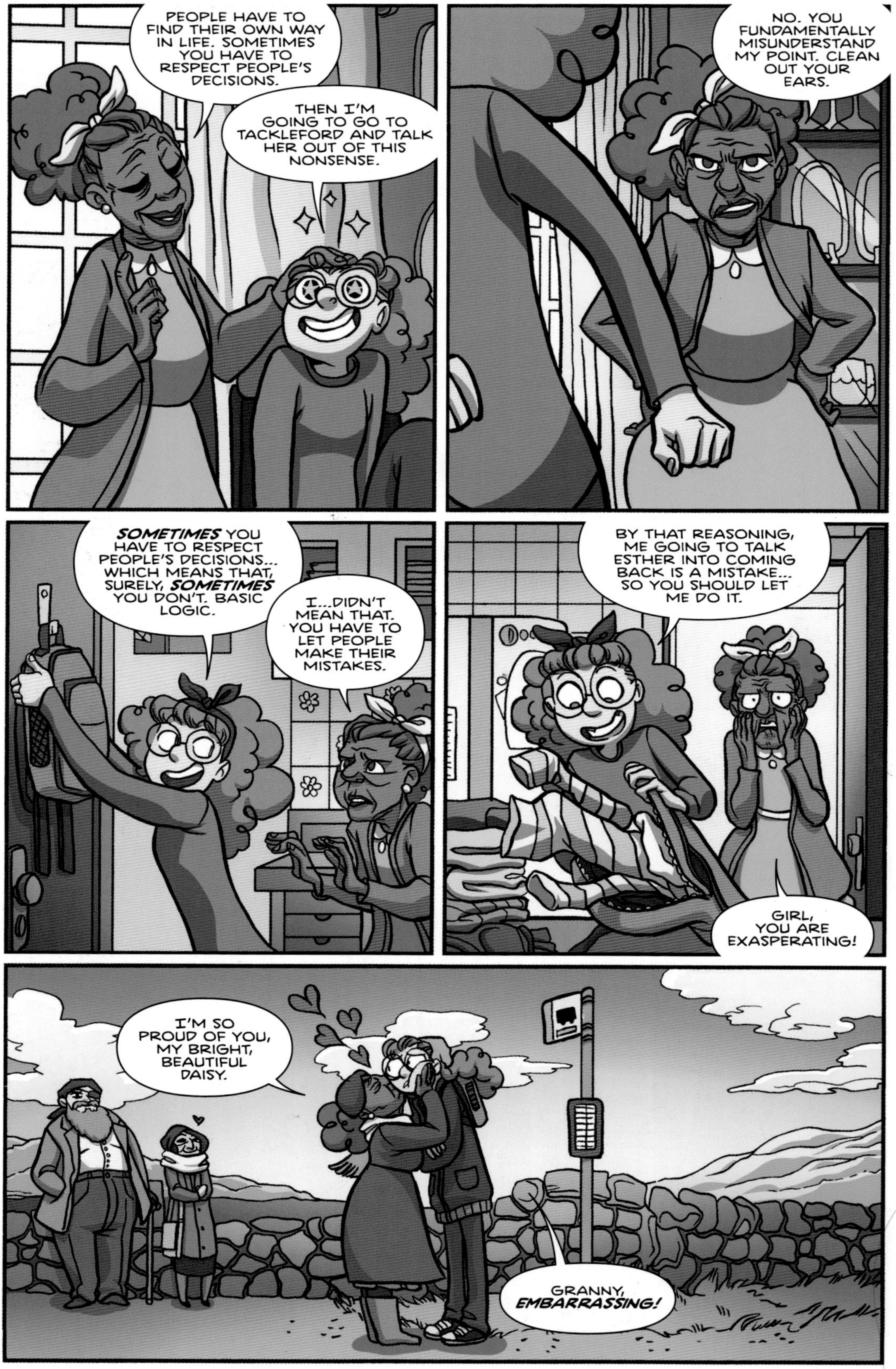
PEOPLE HAVE TO FIND THEIR OWN WAY IN LIFE. SOMETIMES YOU HAVE TO RESPECT PEOPLE'S DECISIONS.
THEN I'M GOING TO GO TO TACKLEFORD AND TALK HER OUT OF THIS NONSENSE.
NO. YOU FUNDAMENTALLY MISUNDERSTAND MY POINT. CLEAN OUT YOUR EARS.
SOMETIMES YOU HAVE TO RESPECT PEOPLE'S DECISIONS... WHICH MEANS THAT, SURELY, SOMETIMES YOU DON'T. BASIC LOGIC.
I...DIDN'T MEAN THAT. YOU HAVE TO LET PEOPLE MAKE THEIR MISTAKES.
BY THAT REASONING, ME GOING TO TALK ESTHER INTO COMING BACK IS A MISTAKE... SO YOU SHOULD LET ME DO IT.
GIRL, YOU ARE EXASPERATING!
I'M SO PROUD OF YOU, MY BRIGHT, BEAUTIFUL DAISY.
GRANNY, EMBARRASSING!

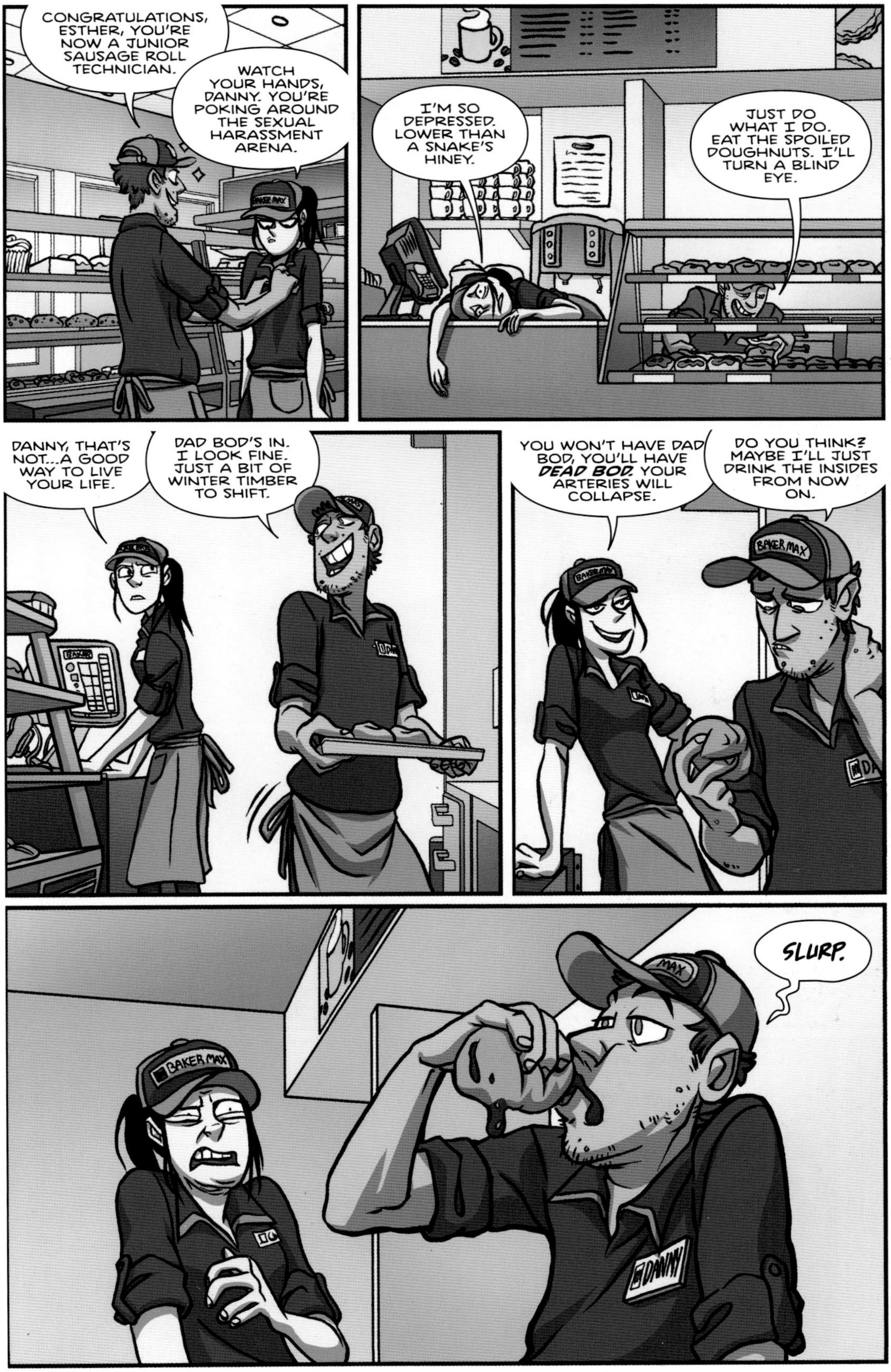
CONGRATULATIONS, ESTHER, YOU'RE NOW A JUNIOR SAUSAGE ROLL TECHNICIAN.
WATCH YOUR HANDS, DANNY. YOU'RE POKING AROUND THE SEXUAL HARASSMENT ARENA.
I'M SO DEPRESSED. LOWER THAN A SNAKE'S HINEY.
JUST DO WHAT I DO. EAT THE SPOILED DOUGHNUTS. I'LL TURN A BLIND EYE.
DANNY, THAT'S NOT...A GOOD WAY TO LIVE YOUR LIFE.
DAD BOD'S IN. I LOOK FINE. JUST A BIT OF WINTER TIMBER TO SHIFT.
YOU WON'T HAVE DAD BOD, YOU'LL HAVE DEAD BOD. YOUR ARTERIES WILL COLLAPSE.
DO YOU THINK? MAYBE I'LL JUST DRINK THE INSIDES FROM NOW ON.
SLURP.

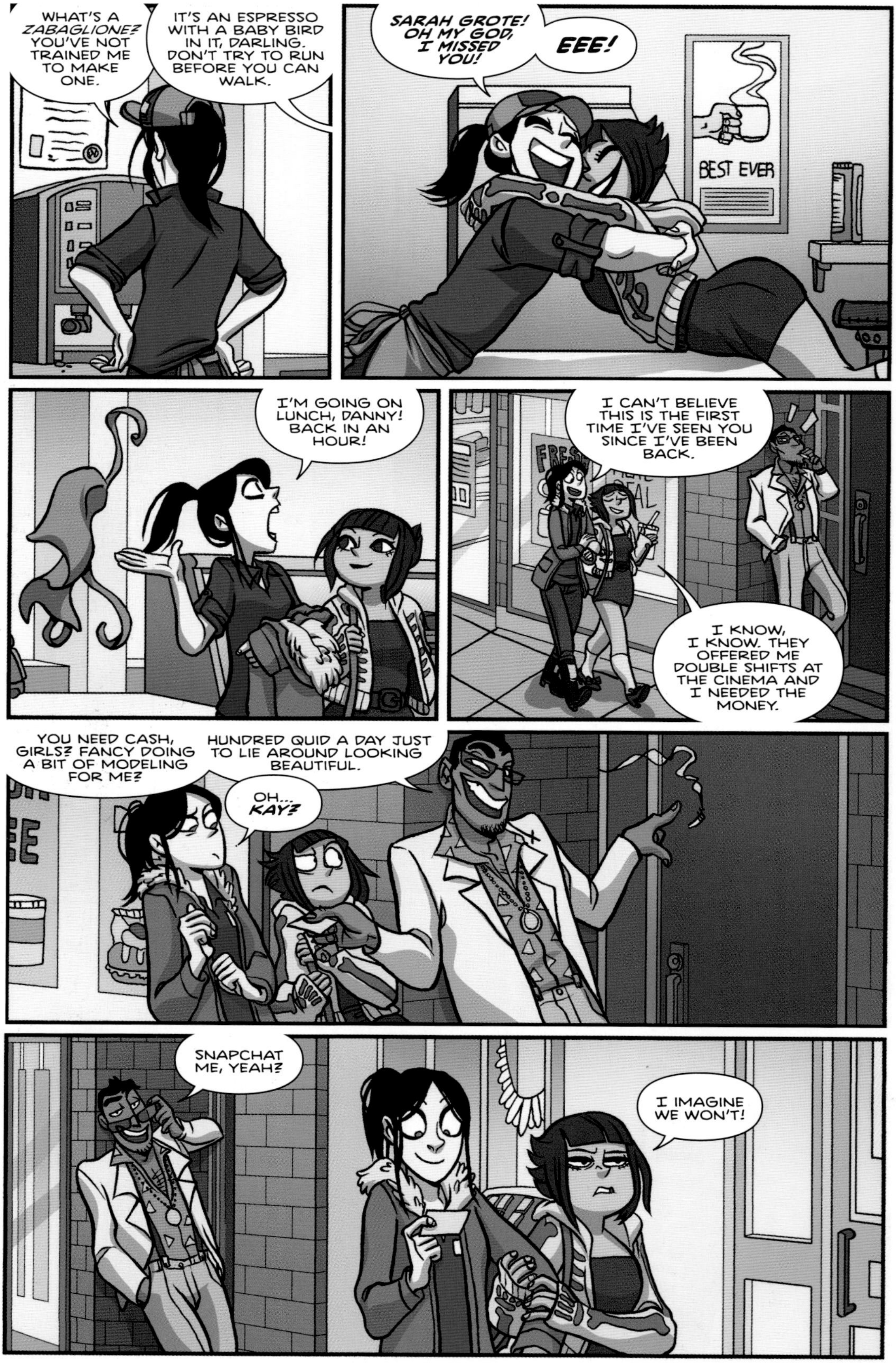
WHAT'S A ZABAGLIONE? YOU'VE NOT TRAINED ME TO MAKE ONE.
IT'S AN ESPRESSO WITH A BABY BIRD IN IT, DARLING. DON'T TRY TO RUN BEFORE YOU CAN WALK.
SARAH GROTE! OH MY GOD, I MISSED YOU!
EEE!
BEST EVER
I'M GOING ON LUNCH, DANNY! BACK IN AN HOUR!
I CAN'T BELIEVE THIS IS THE FIRST TIME I'VE SEEN YOU SINCE I'VE BEEN BACK.
I KNOW, I KNOW. THEY OFFERED ME DOUBLE SHIFTS AT THE CINEMA AND I NEEDED THE MONEY.
YOU NEED CASH, GIRLS? FANCY DOING A BIT OF MODELING FOR ME?
HUNDRED QUID A DAY JUST TO LIE AROUND LOOKING BEAUTIFUL.
OH... KAY?
SNAPCHAT ME, YEAH?
I IMAGINE WE WON'T!

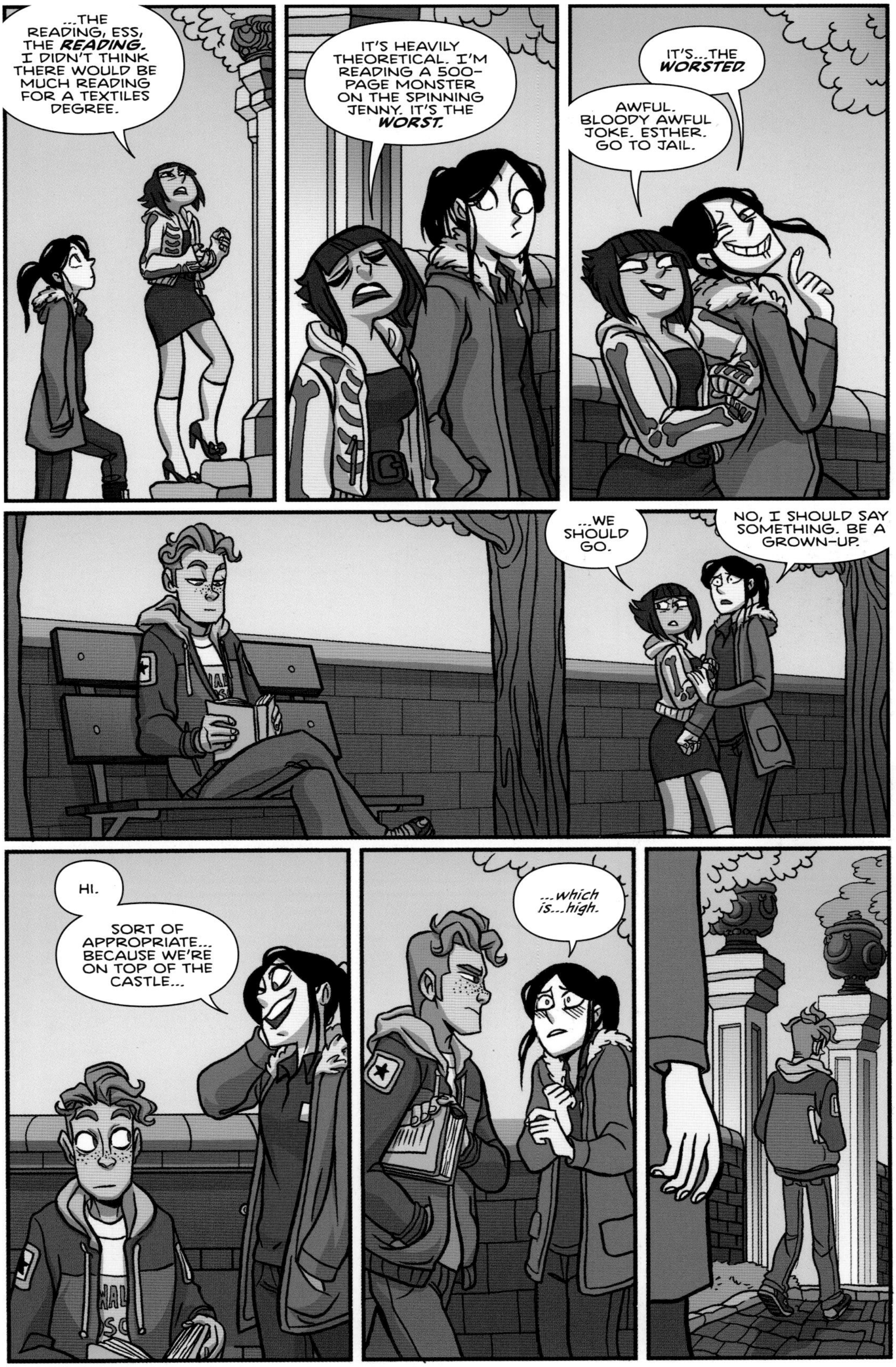

...THE READING, ESS, THE *READING.* I DIDN'T THINK THERE WOULD BE MUCH READING FOR A TEXTILES DEGREE.
IT'S HEAVILY THEORETICAL. I'M READING A 500-PAGE MONSTER ON THE SPINNING JENNY. IT'S THE *WORST.*
IT'S...THE *WORSTED.*
AWFUL. BLOODY AWFUL JOKE. ESTHER. GO TO JAIL.
...WE SHOULD GO.
NO, I SHOULD SAY SOMETHING. BE A GROWN-UP.
HI.
SORT OF APPROPRIATE... BECAUSE WE'RE ON TOP OF THE CASTLE...
...which is...high.

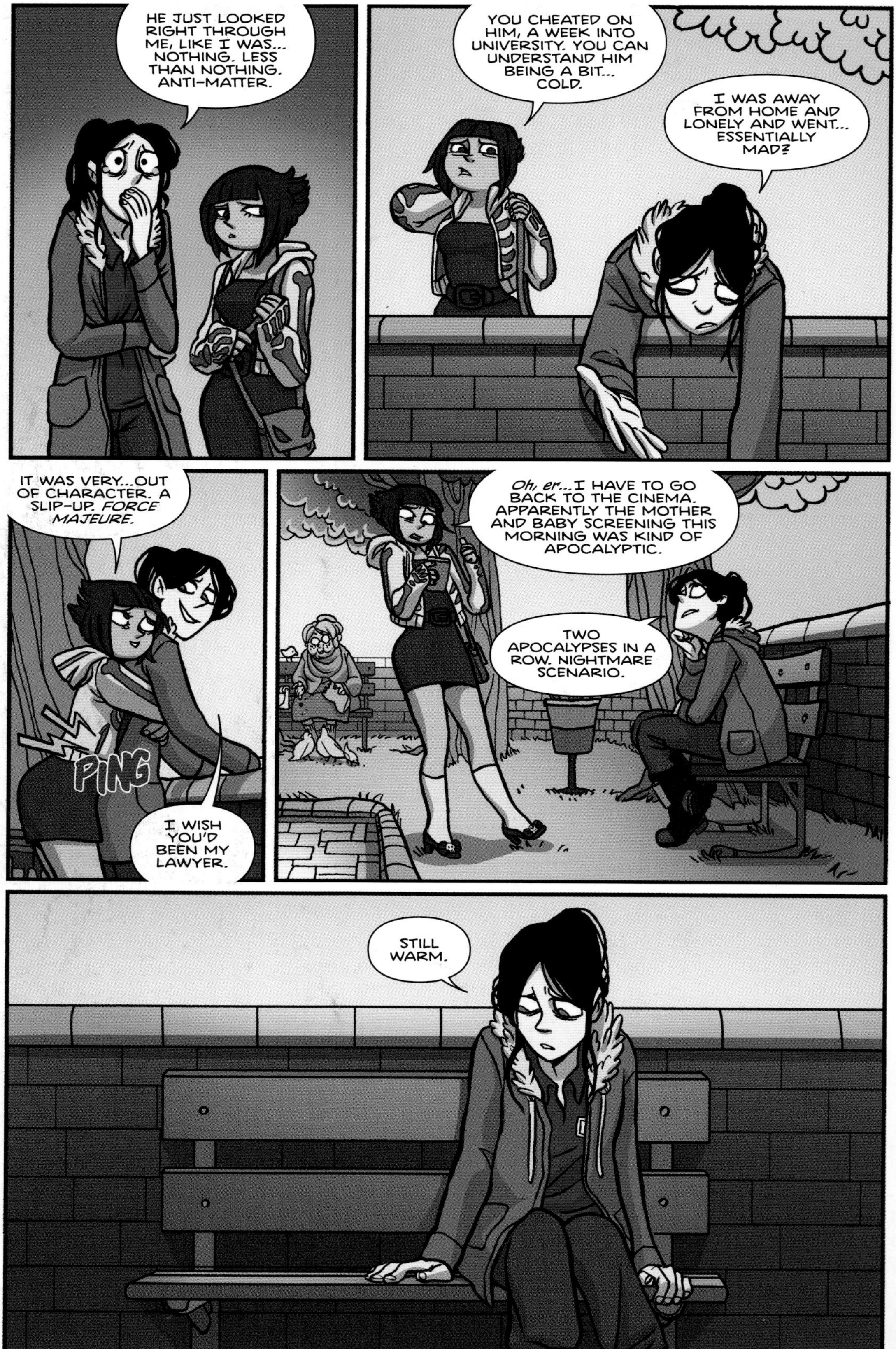
HE JUST LOOKED RIGHT THROUGH ME, LIKE I WAS... NOTHING. LESS THAN NOTHING. ANTI-MATTER.
YOU CHEATED ON HIM, A WEEK INTO UNIVERSITY. YOU CAN UNDERSTAND HIM BEING A BIT... COLD.
I WAS AWAY FROM HOME AND LONELY AND WENT... ESSENTIALLY MAD?
IT WAS VERY...OUT OF CHARACTER. A SLIP-UP. *FORCE MAJEURE.*
PING
I WISH YOU'D BEEN MY LAWYER.
Oh, er... I HAVE TO GO BACK TO THE CINEMA. APPARENTLY THE MOTHER AND BABY SCREENING THIS MORNING WAS KIND OF APOCALYPTIC.
TWO APOCALYPSES IN A ROW. NIGHTMARE SCENARIO.
STILL WARM.

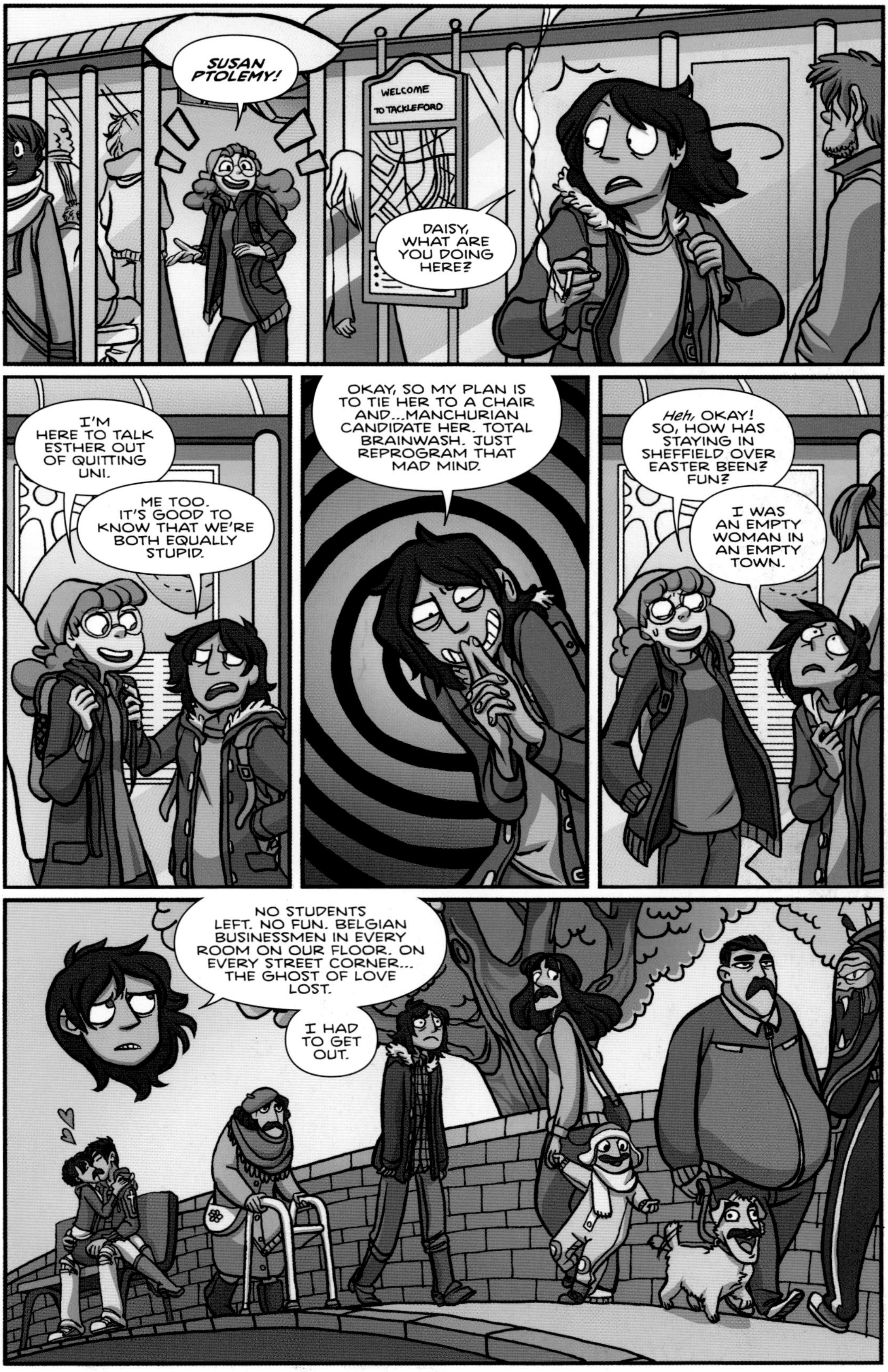
SUSAN PTOLEMY!
WELCOME TO TACKLEFORD
DAISY, WHAT ARE YOU DOING HERE?
I'M HERE TO TALK ESTHER OUT OF QUITTING UNI.
ME TOO. IT'S GOOD TO KNOW THAT WE'RE BOTH EQUALLY STUPID.
OKAY, SO MY PLAN IS TO TIE HER TO A CHAIR AND...MANCHURIAN CANDIDATE HER. TOTAL BRAINWASH. JUST REPROGRAM THAT MAD MIND.
Heh, OKAY! SO, HOW HAS STAYING IN SHEFFIELD OVER EASTER BEEN? FUN?
I WAS AN EMPTY WOMAN IN AN EMPTY TOWN.
NO STUDENTS LEFT. NO FUN. BELGIAN BUSINESSMEN IN EVERY ROOM ON OUR FLOOR. ON EVERY STREET CORNER... THE GHOST OF LOVE LOST.
I HAD TO GET OUT.

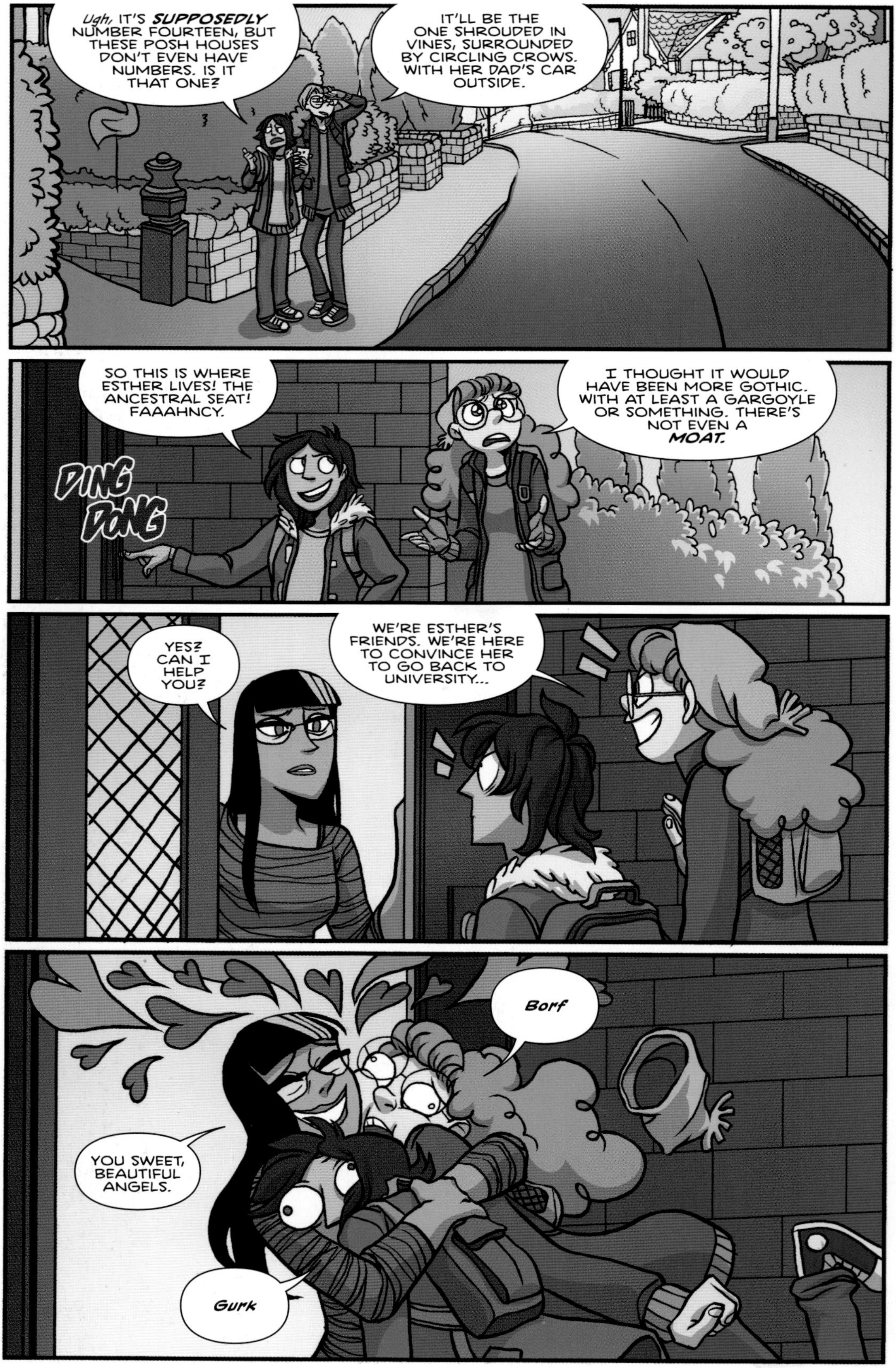
Ugh, IT'S SUPPOSEDLY NUMBER FOURTEEN, BUT THESE POSH HOUSES DON'T EVEN HAVE NUMBERS. IS IT THAT ONE?
IT'LL BE THE ONE SHROUDED IN VINES, SURROUNDED BY CIRCLING CROWS. WITH HER DAD'S CAR OUTSIDE.
SO THIS IS WHERE ESTHER LIVES! THE ANCESTRAL SEAT! FAAAHNCY.
I THOUGHT IT WOULD HAVE BEEN MORE GOTHIC. WITH AT LEAST A GARGOYLE OR SOMETHING. THERE'S NOT EVEN A MOAT.
DING DONG
YES? CAN I HELP YOU?
WE'RE ESTHER'S FRIENDS. WE'RE HERE TO CONVINCE HER TO GO BACK TO UNIVERSITY...
Borf
YOU SWEET, BEAUTIFUL ANGELS.
Gurk

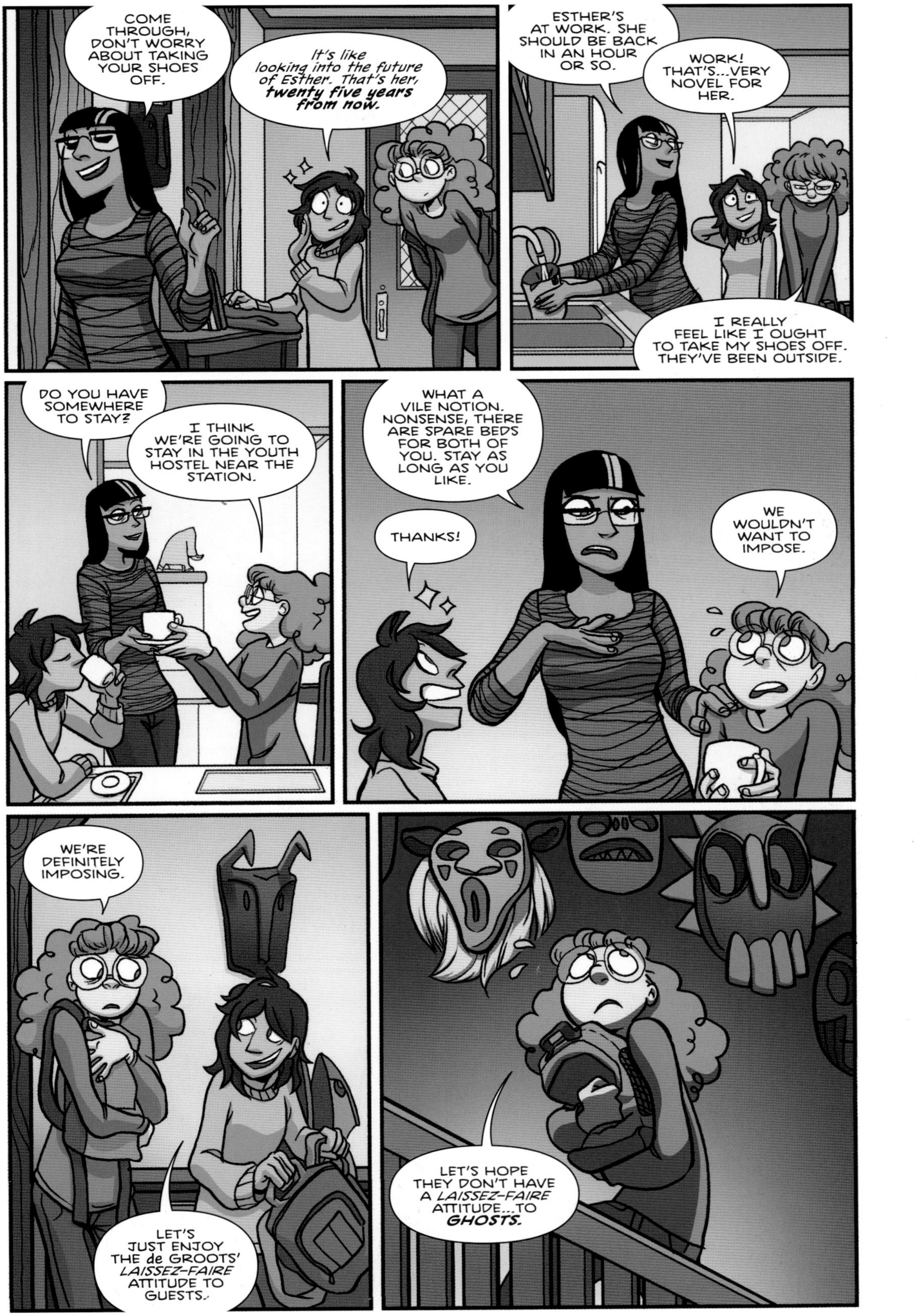
COME THROUGH, DON'T WORRY ABOUT TAKING YOUR SHOES OFF.
It's like looking into the future of Esther. That's her, twenty five years from now.
ESTHER'S AT WORK. SHE SHOULD BE BACK IN AN HOUR OR SO.
WORK! THAT'S...VERY NOVEL FOR HER.
I REALLY FEEL LIKE I OUGHT TO TAKE MY SHOES OFF. THEY'VE BEEN OUTSIDE.
DO YOU HAVE SOMEWHERE TO STAY?
I THINK WE'RE GOING TO STAY IN THE YOUTH HOSTEL NEAR THE STATION.
WHAT A VILE NOTION. NONSENSE, THERE ARE SPARE BEDS FOR BOTH OF YOU. STAY AS LONG AS YOU LIKE.
THANKS!
WE WOULDN'T WANT TO IMPOSE.
WE'RE DEFINITELY IMPOSING.
LET'S JUST ENJOY THE de GROOTS' LAISSEZ-FAIRE ATTITUDE TO GUESTS.
LET'S HOPE THEY DON'T HAVE A LAISSEZ-FAIRE ATTITUDE...TO GHOSTS.

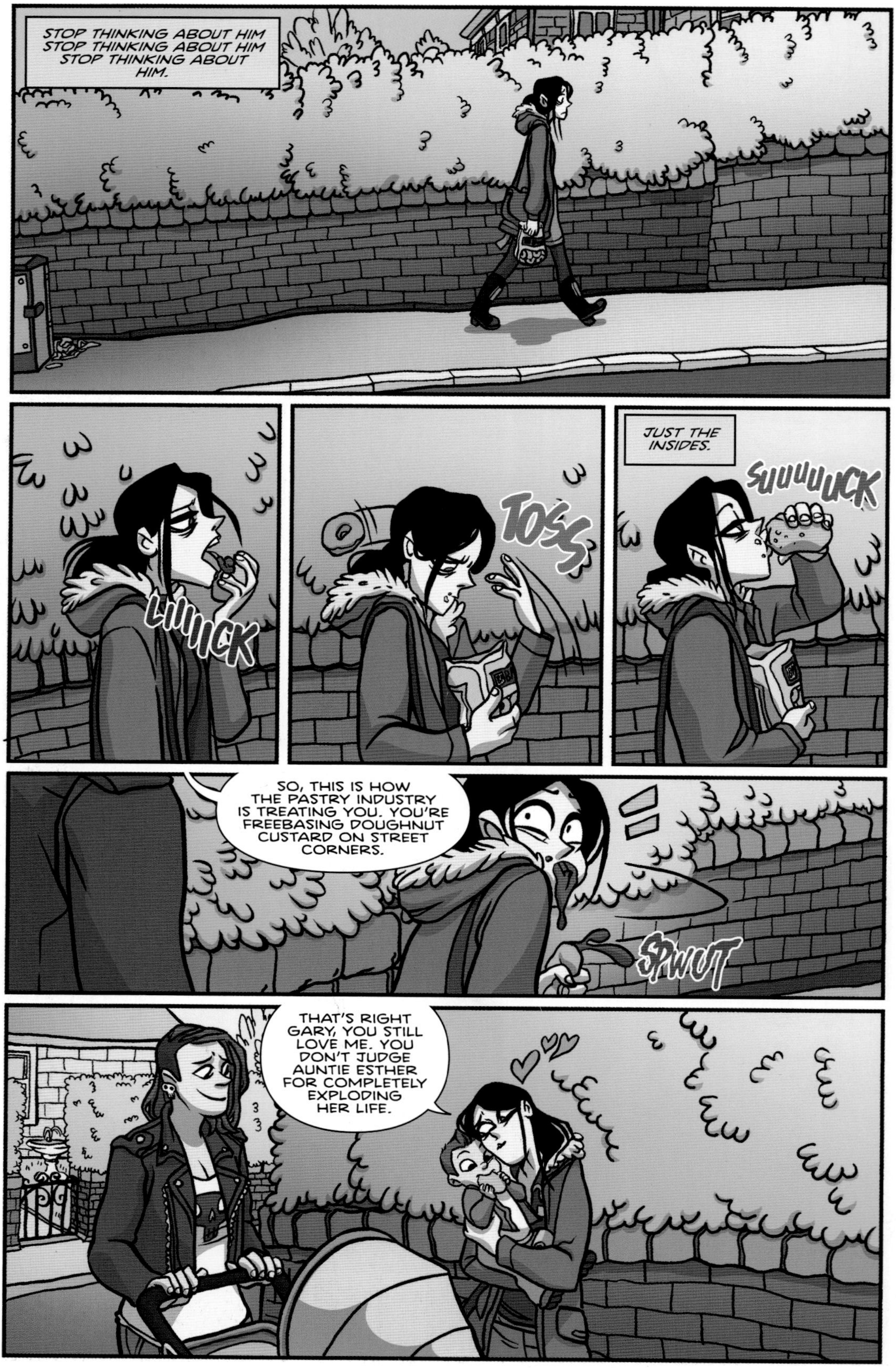
STOP THINKING ABOUT HIM STOP THINKING ABOUT HIM STOP THINKING ABOUT HIM.
LIIIICK
TOSS
JUST THE INSIDES.
SUUUUUCK
SO, THIS IS HOW THE PASTRY INDUSTRY IS TREATING YOU. YOU'RE FREEBASING DOUGHNUT CUSTARD ON STREET CORNERS.
SPWUT
THAT'S RIGHT GARY, YOU STILL LOVE ME. YOU DON'T JUDGE AUNTIE ESTHER FOR COMPLETELY EXPLODING HER LIFE.

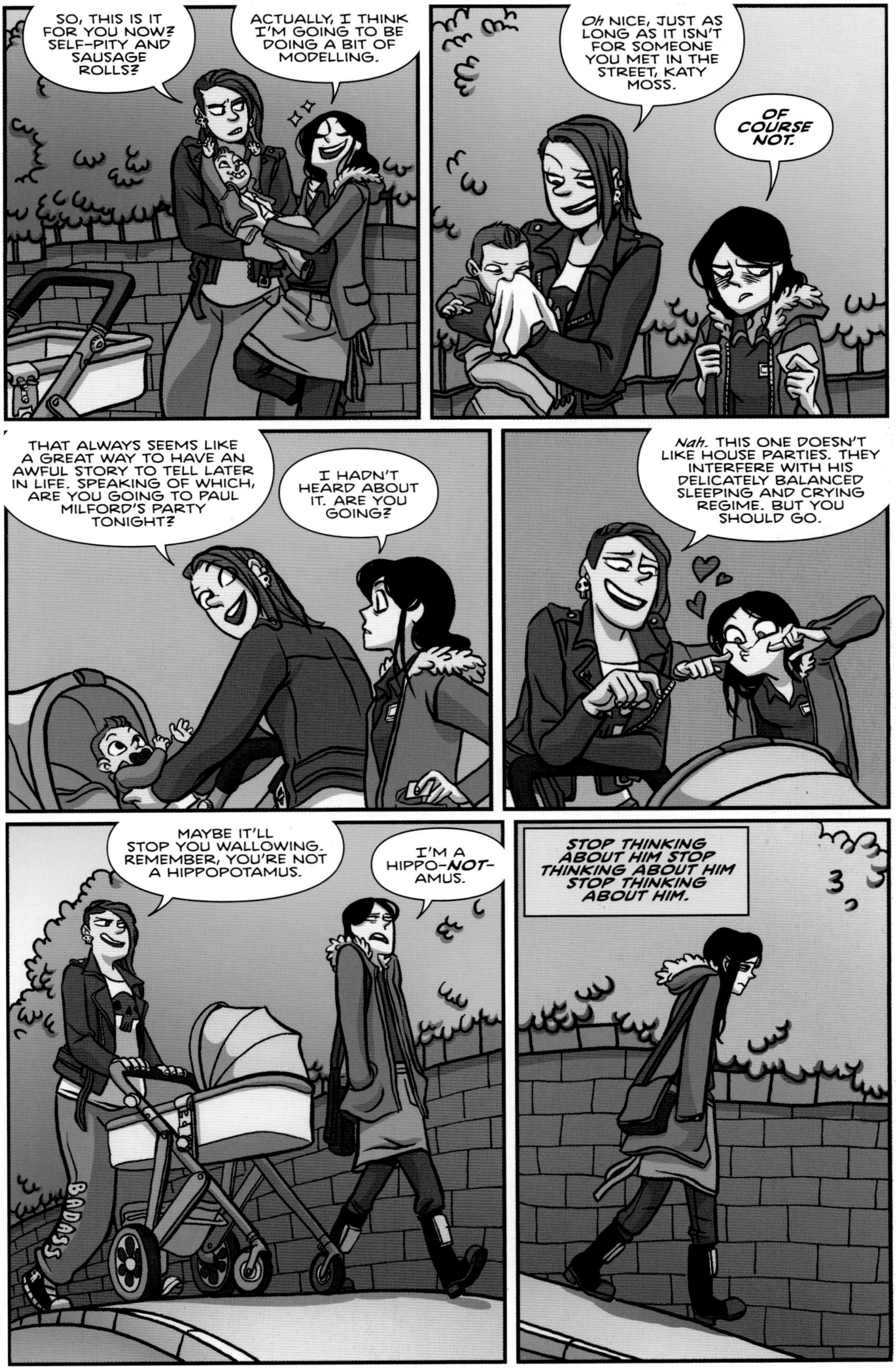
SO, THIS IS IT FOR YOU NOW? SELF-PITY AND SAUSAGE ROLLS?
ACTUALLY, I THINK I'M GOING TO BE DOING A BIT OF MODELLING.
Oh NICE, JUST AS LONG AS IT ISN'T FOR SOMEONE YOU MET IN THE STREET, KATY MOSS.
OF COURSE NOT.
THAT ALWAYS SEEMS LIKE A GREAT WAY TO HAVE AN AWFUL STORY TO TELL LATER IN LIFE. SPEAKING OF WHICH, ARE YOU GOING TO PAUL MILFORD'S PARTY TONIGHT?
I HADN'T HEARD ABOUT IT. ARE YOU GOING?
Nah. THIS ONE DOESN'T LIKE HOUSE PARTIES. THEY INTERFERE WITH HIS DELICATELY BALANCED SLEEPING AND CRYING REGIME. BUT YOU SHOULD GO.
MAYBE IT'LL STOP YOU WALLOWING. REMEMBER, YOU'RE NOT A HIPPOPOTAMUS.
I'M A HIPPO-NOT-AMUS.
BADASS
STOP THINKING ABOUT HIM STOP THINKING ABOUT HIM STOP THINKING ABOUT HIM.

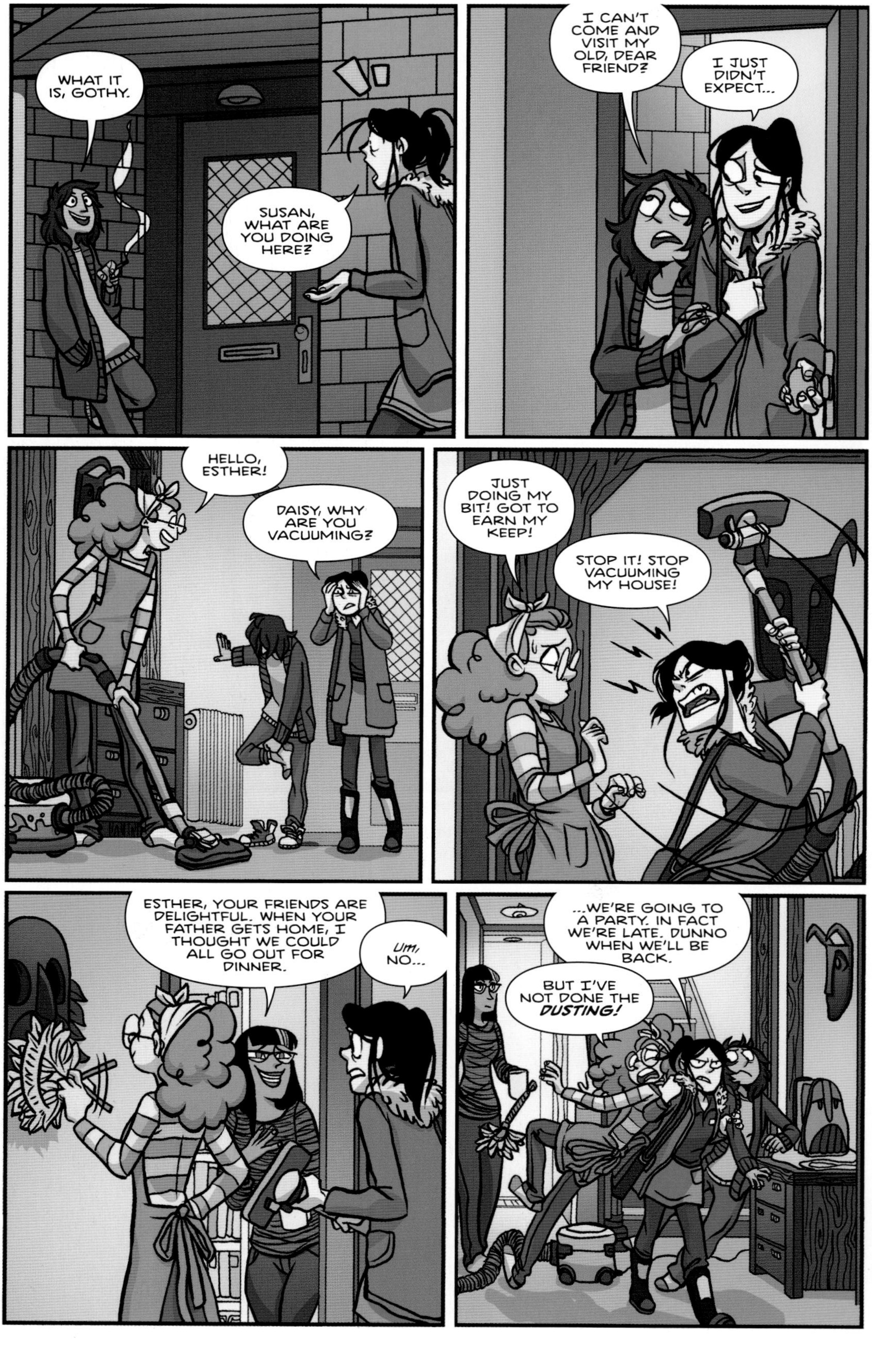
WHAT IT IS, GOTHY.
SUSAN, WHAT ARE YOU DOING HERE?
I CAN'T COME AND VISIT MY OLD, DEAR FRIEND?
I JUST DIDN'T EXPECT...
HELLO, ESTHER!
DAISY, WHY ARE YOU VACUUMING?
JUST DOING MY BIT! GOT TO EARN MY KEEP!
STOP IT! STOP VACUUMING MY HOUSE!
ESTHER, YOUR FRIENDS ARE DELIGHTFUL. WHEN YOUR FATHER GETS HOME, I THOUGHT WE COULD ALL GO OUT FOR DINNER.
UM, NO...
...WE'RE GOING TO A PARTY. IN FACT WE'RE LATE. DUNNO WHEN WE'LL BE BACK.
BUT I'VE NOT DONE THE *DUSTING!*

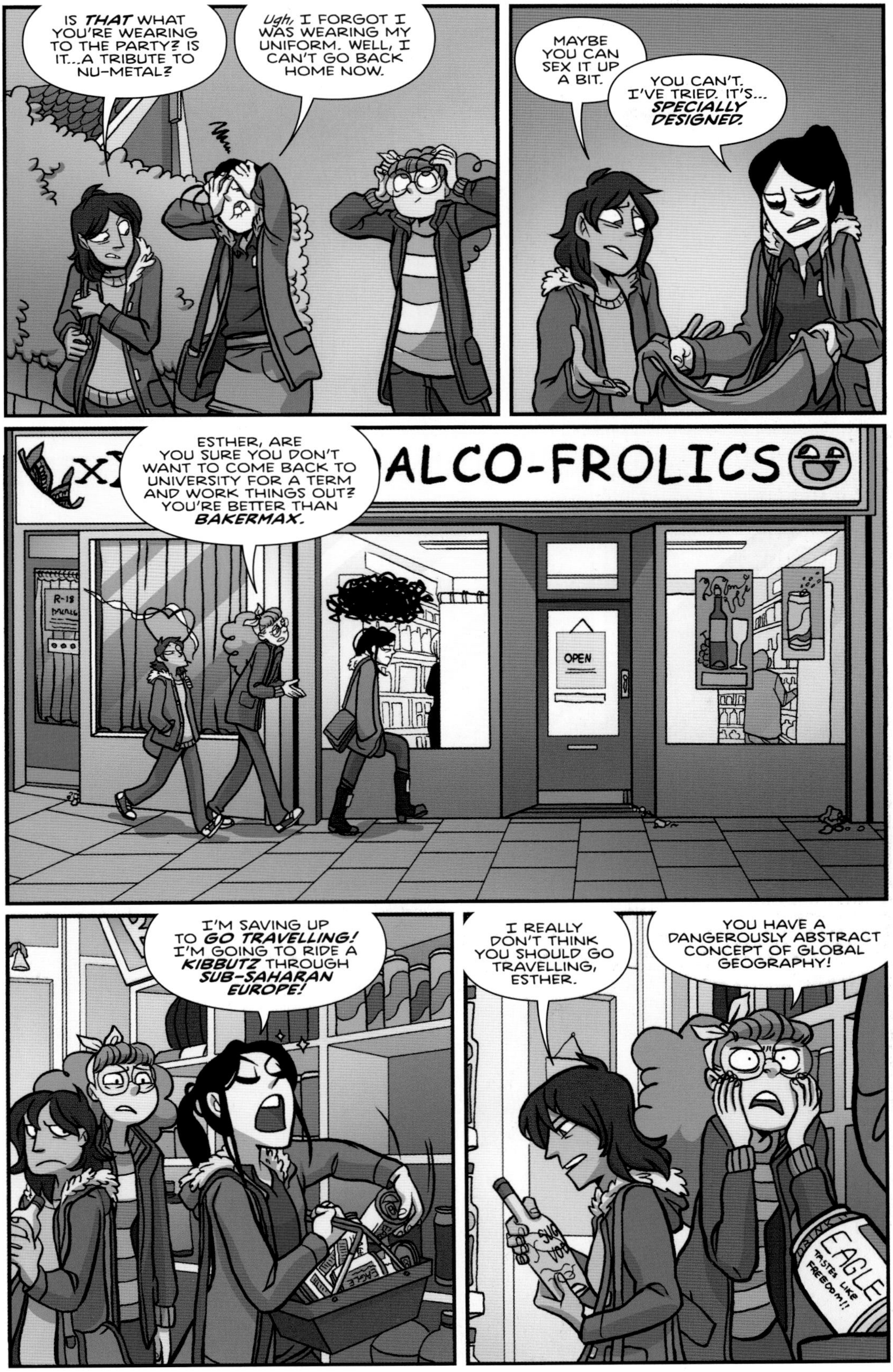
IS *THAT* WHAT YOU'RE WEARING TO THE PARTY? IS IT...A TRIBUTE TO NU-METAL?
Ugh, I FORGOT I WAS WEARING MY UNIFORM. WELL, I CAN'T GO BACK HOME NOW.
MAYBE YOU CAN SEX IT UP A BIT.
YOU CAN'T. I'VE TRIED. IT'S... ***SPECIALLY DESIGNED.***
ALCO-FROLICS
ESTHER, ARE YOU SURE YOU DON'T WANT TO COME BACK TO UNIVERSITY FOR A TERM AND WORK THINGS OUT? YOU'RE BETTER THAN ***BAKERMAX.***
OPEN
I'M SAVING UP TO ***GO TRAVELLING!*** I'M GOING TO RIDE A ***KIBBUTZ*** THROUGH ***SUB-SAHARAN EUROPE!***
I REALLY DON'T THINK YOU SHOULD GO TRAVELLING, ESTHER.
YOU HAVE A DANGEROUSLY ABSTRACT CONCEPT OF GLOBAL GEOGRAPHY!
EAGLE
TASTES LIKE FREEDOM!!

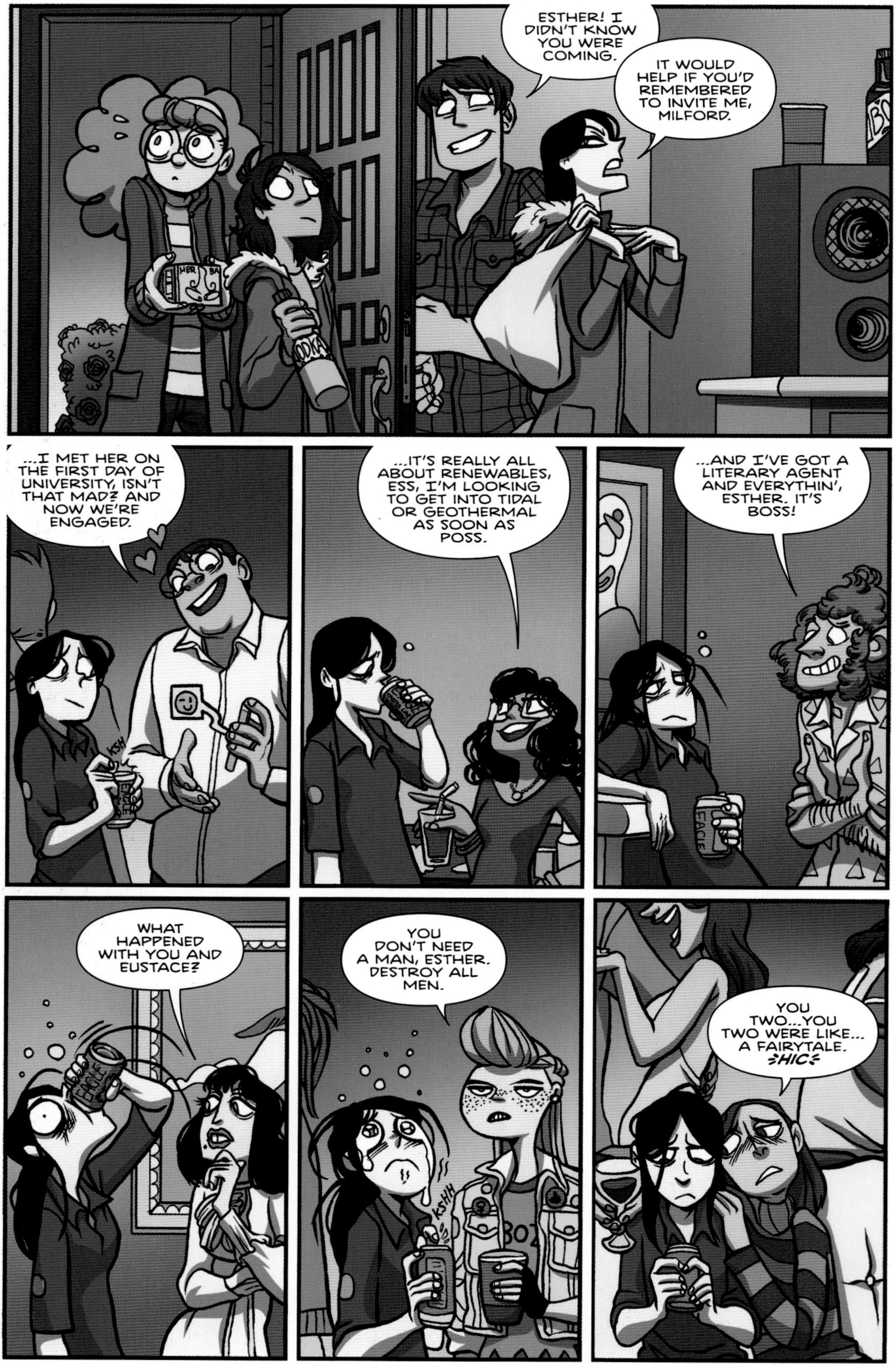
ESTHER! I DIDN'T KNOW YOU WERE COMING.
IT WOULD HELP IF YOU'D REMEMBERED TO INVITE ME, MILFORD.
...I MET HER ON THE FIRST DAY OF UNIVERSITY, ISN'T THAT MAD? AND NOW WE'RE ENGAGED.
KSH
...IT'S REALLY ALL ABOUT RENEWABLES, ESS, I'M LOOKING TO GET INTO TIDAL OR GEOTHERMAL AS SOON AS POSS.
...AND I'VE GOT A LITERARY AGENT AND EVERYTHIN', ESTHER. IT'S BOSS!
WHAT HAPPENED WITH YOU AND EUSTACE?
YOU DON'T NEED A MAN, ESTHER. DESTROY ALL MEN.
KSHH
YOU TWO...YOU TWO WERE LIKE... A FAIRYTALE.
HIC

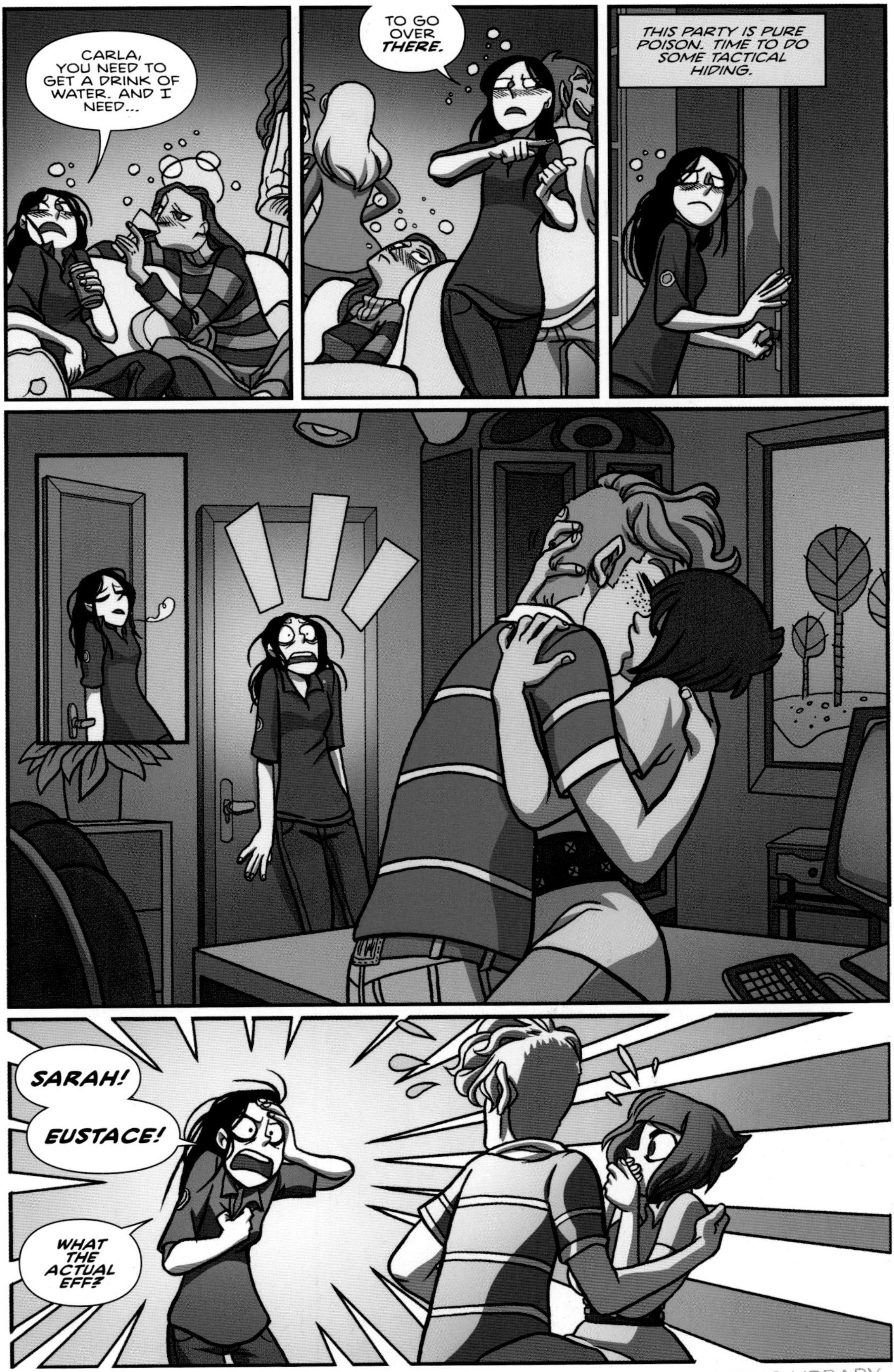
CARLA, YOU NEED TO GET A DRINK OF WATER. AND I NEED...
TO GO OVER THERE.
THIS PARTY IS PURE POISON. TIME TO DO SOME TACTICAL HIDING.
SARAH!
EUSTACE!
WHAT THE ACTUAL EFF?

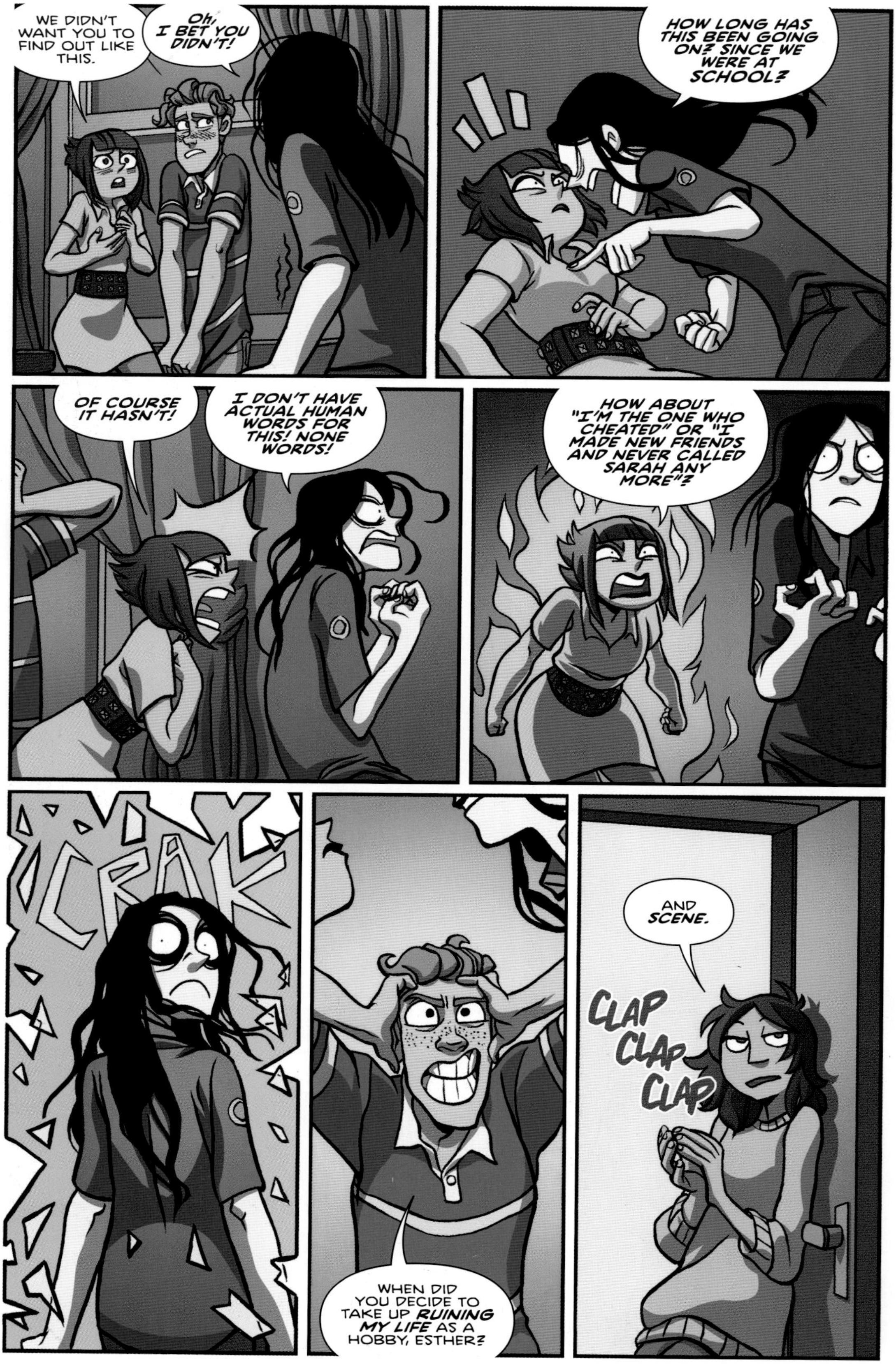
WE DIDN'T WANT YOU TO FIND OUT LIKE THIS.
Oh, I BET YOU DIDN'T!
HOW LONG HAS THIS BEEN GOING ON? SINCE WE WERE AT SCHOOL?
OF COURSE IT HASN'T!
I DON'T HAVE ACTUAL HUMAN WORDS FOR THIS! NONE WORDS!
HOW ABOUT "I'M THE ONE WHO CHEATED" OR "I MADE NEW FRIENDS AND NEVER CALLED SARAH ANY MORE"?
CRAK
WHEN DID YOU DECIDE TO TAKE UP RUINING MY LIFE AS A HOBBY, ESTHER?
AND SCENE.
CLAP
CLAP
CLAP

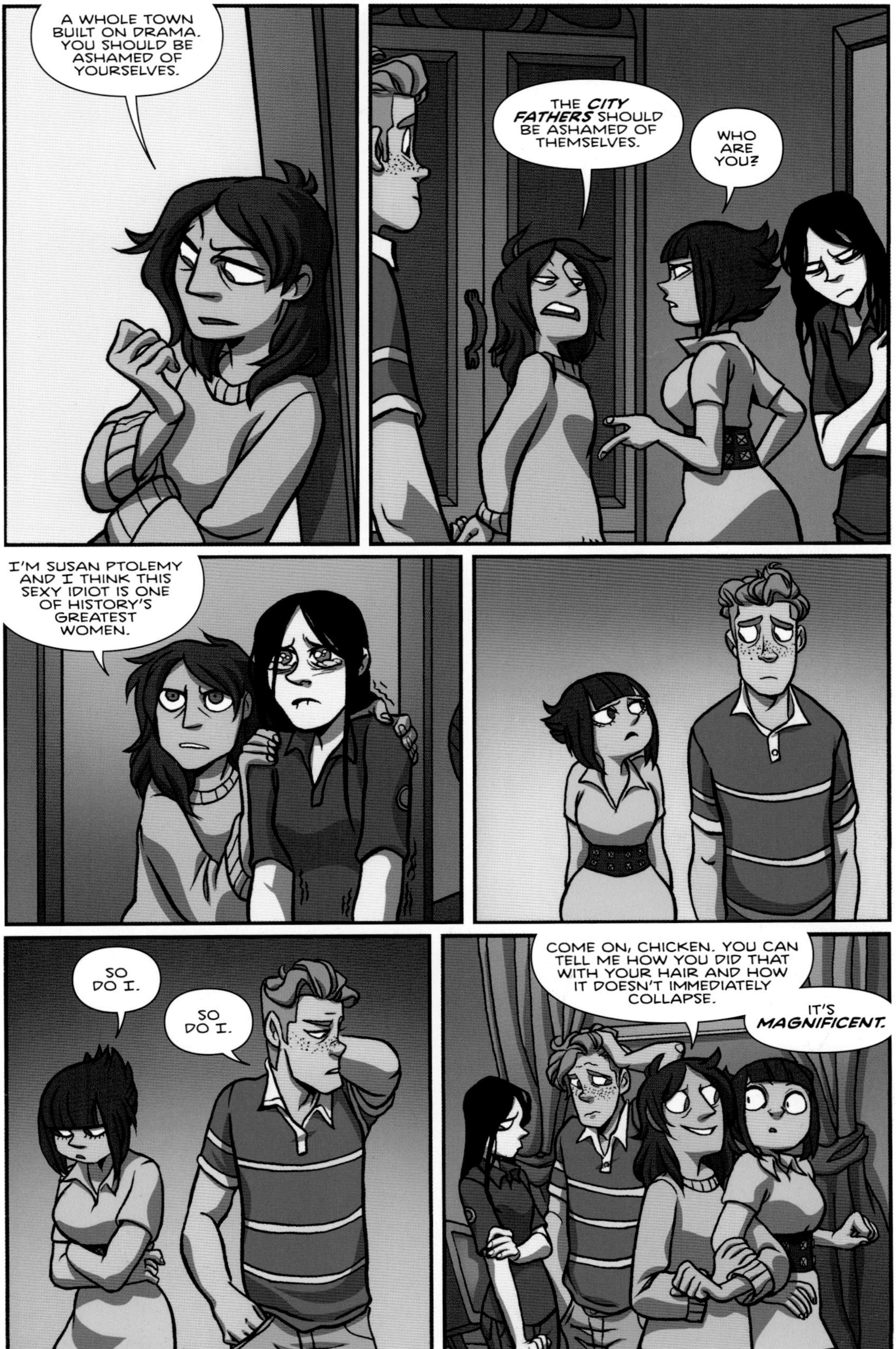
A WHOLE TOWN BUILT ON DRAMA. YOU SHOULD BE ASHAMED OF YOURSELVES.
THE *CITY FATHERS* SHOULD BE ASHAMED OF THEMSELVES.
WHO ARE YOU?
I'M SUSAN PTOLEMY AND I THINK THIS SEXY IDIOT IS ONE OF HISTORY'S GREATEST WOMEN.
SO DO I.
SO DO I.
COME ON, CHICKEN. YOU CAN TELL ME HOW YOU DID THAT WITH YOUR HAIR AND HOW IT DOESN'T IMMEDIATELY COLLAPSE.
IT'S *MAGNIFICENT.*

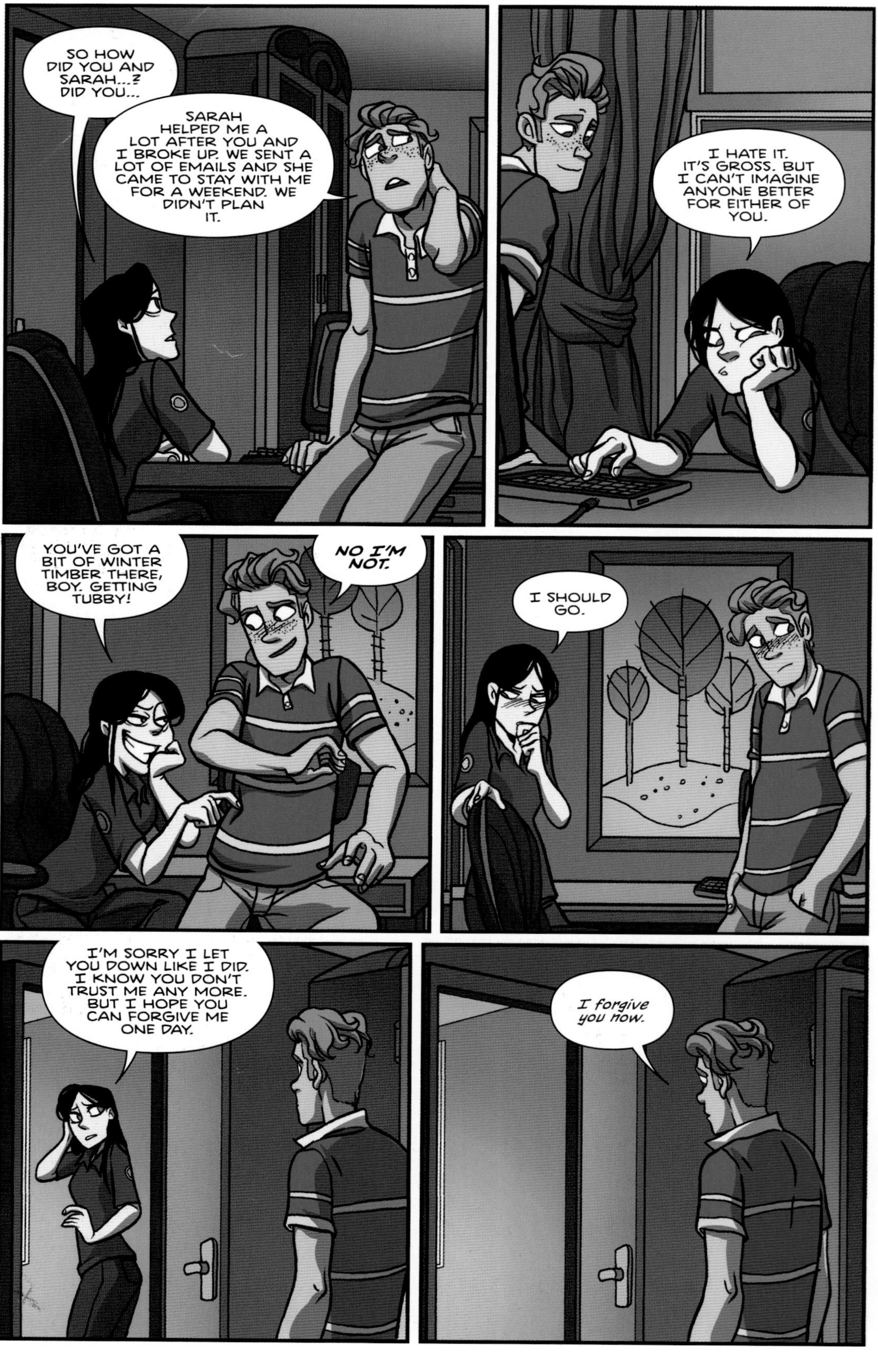
SO HOW DID YOU AND SARAH...? DID YOU...
SARAH HELPED ME A LOT AFTER YOU AND I BROKE UP. WE SENT A LOT OF EMAILS AND SHE CAME TO STAY WITH ME FOR A WEEKEND. WE DIDN'T PLAN IT.
I HATE IT. IT'S GROSS. BUT I CAN'T IMAGINE ANYONE BETTER FOR EITHER OF YOU.
YOU'VE GOT A BIT OF WINTER TIMBER THERE, BOY. GETTING TUBBY!
NO I'M NOT.
I SHOULD GO.
I'M SORRY I LET YOU DOWN LIKE I DID. I KNOW YOU DON'T TRUST ME ANY MORE. BUT I HOPE YOU CAN FORGIVE ME ONE DAY.
I forgive you now.

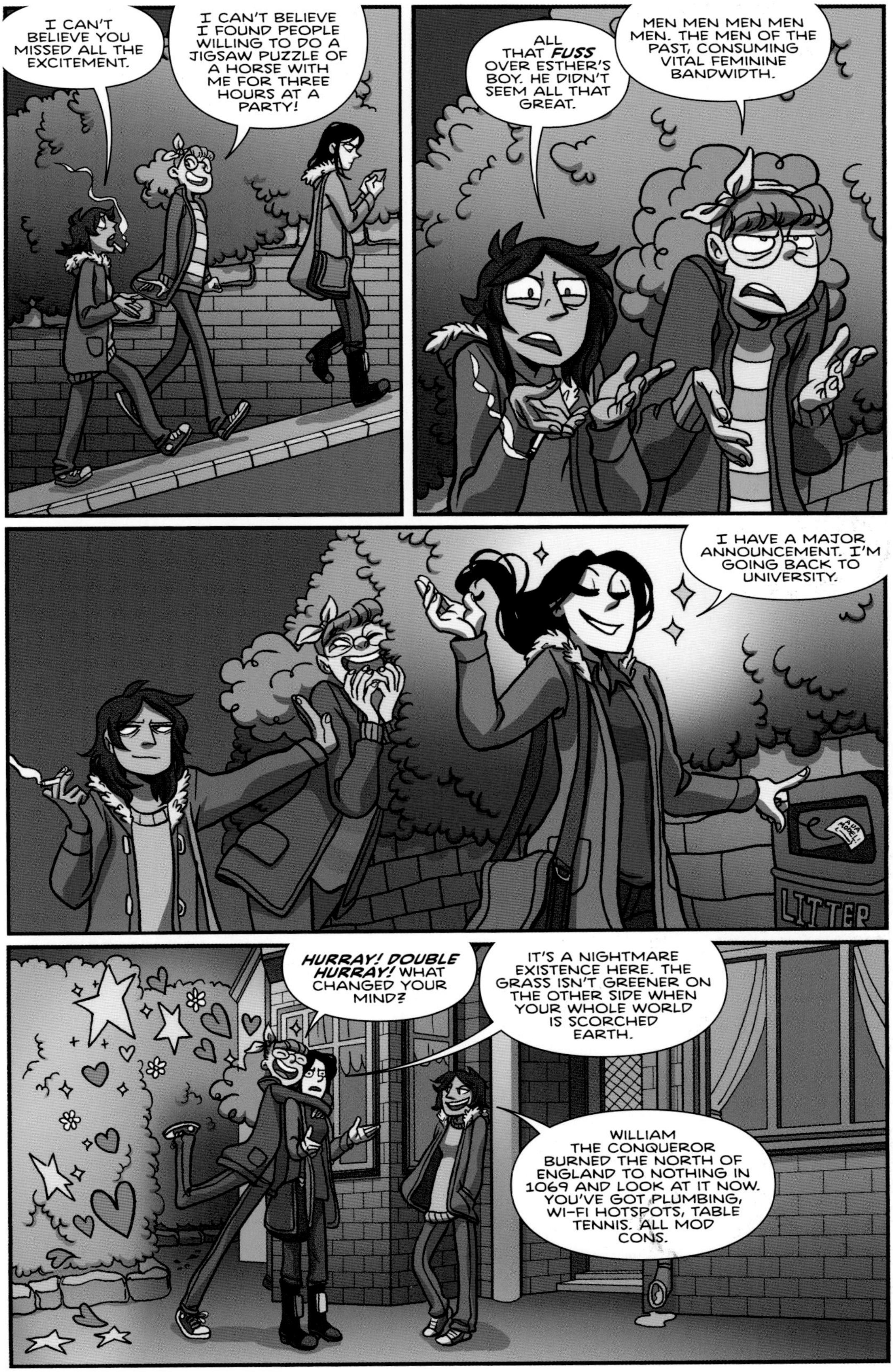

I CAN'T BELIEVE YOU MISSED ALL THE EXCITEMENT.
I CAN'T BELIEVE I FOUND PEOPLE WILLING TO DO A JIGSAW PUZZLE OF A HORSE WITH ME FOR THREE HOURS AT A PARTY!
ALL THAT *FUSS* OVER ESTHER'S BOY. HE DIDN'T SEEM ALL THAT GREAT.
MEN MEN MEN MEN MEN. THE MEN OF THE PAST, CONSUMING VITAL FEMININE BANDWIDTH.
I HAVE A MAJOR ANNOUNCEMENT. I'M GOING BACK TO UNIVERSITY.
LITTER
HURRAY! DOUBLE HURRAY! WHAT CHANGED YOUR MIND?
IT'S A NIGHTMARE EXISTENCE HERE. THE GRASS ISN'T GREENER ON THE OTHER SIDE WHEN YOUR WHOLE WORLD IS SCORCHED EARTH.
WILLIAM THE CONQUEROR BURNED THE NORTH OF ENGLAND TO NOTHING IN 1069 AND LOOK AT IT NOW. YOU'VE GOT PLUMBING, WI-FI HOTSPOTS, TABLE TENNIS. ALL MOD CONS.

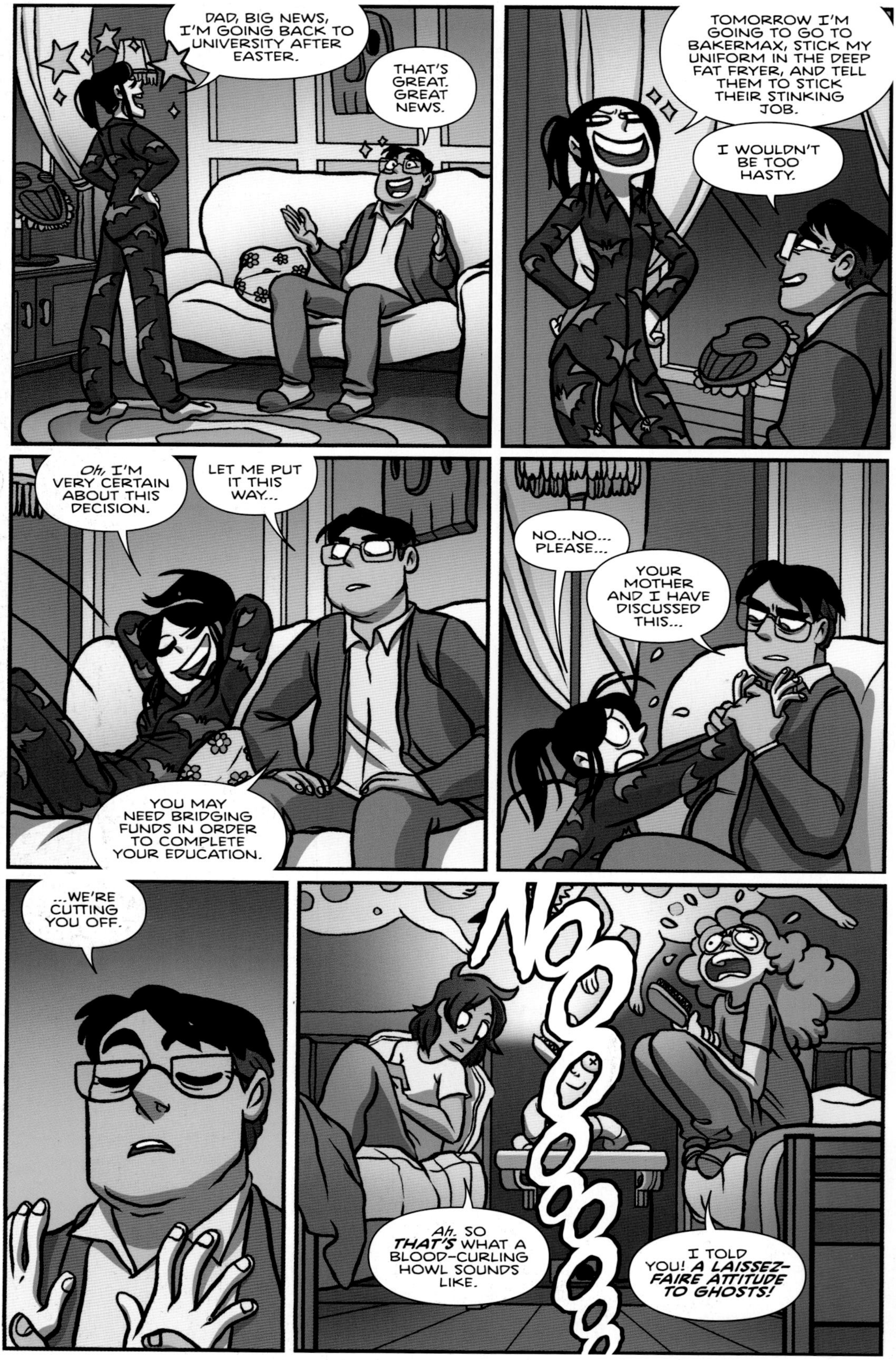
DAD, BIG NEWS, I'M GOING BACK TO UNIVERSITY AFTER EASTER.
THAT'S GREAT. GREAT NEWS.
TOMORROW I'M GOING TO GO TO BAKERMAX, STICK MY UNIFORM IN THE DEEP FAT FRYER, AND TELL THEM TO STICK THEIR STINKING JOB.
I WOULDN'T BE TOO HASTY.
Oh, I'M VERY CERTAIN ABOUT THIS DECISION.
LET ME PUT IT THIS WAY...
YOU MAY NEED BRIDGING FUNDS IN ORDER TO COMPLETE YOUR EDUCATION.
NO...NO... PLEASE...
YOUR MOTHER AND I HAVE DISCUSSED THIS...
...WE'RE CUTTING YOU OFF.
NOOOOOOOOOOO
Ah. SO ***THAT'S*** WHAT A BLOOD-CURLING HOWL SOUNDS LIKE.
I TOLD YOU! ***A LAISSEZ-FAIRE ATTITUDE TO GHOSTS!***

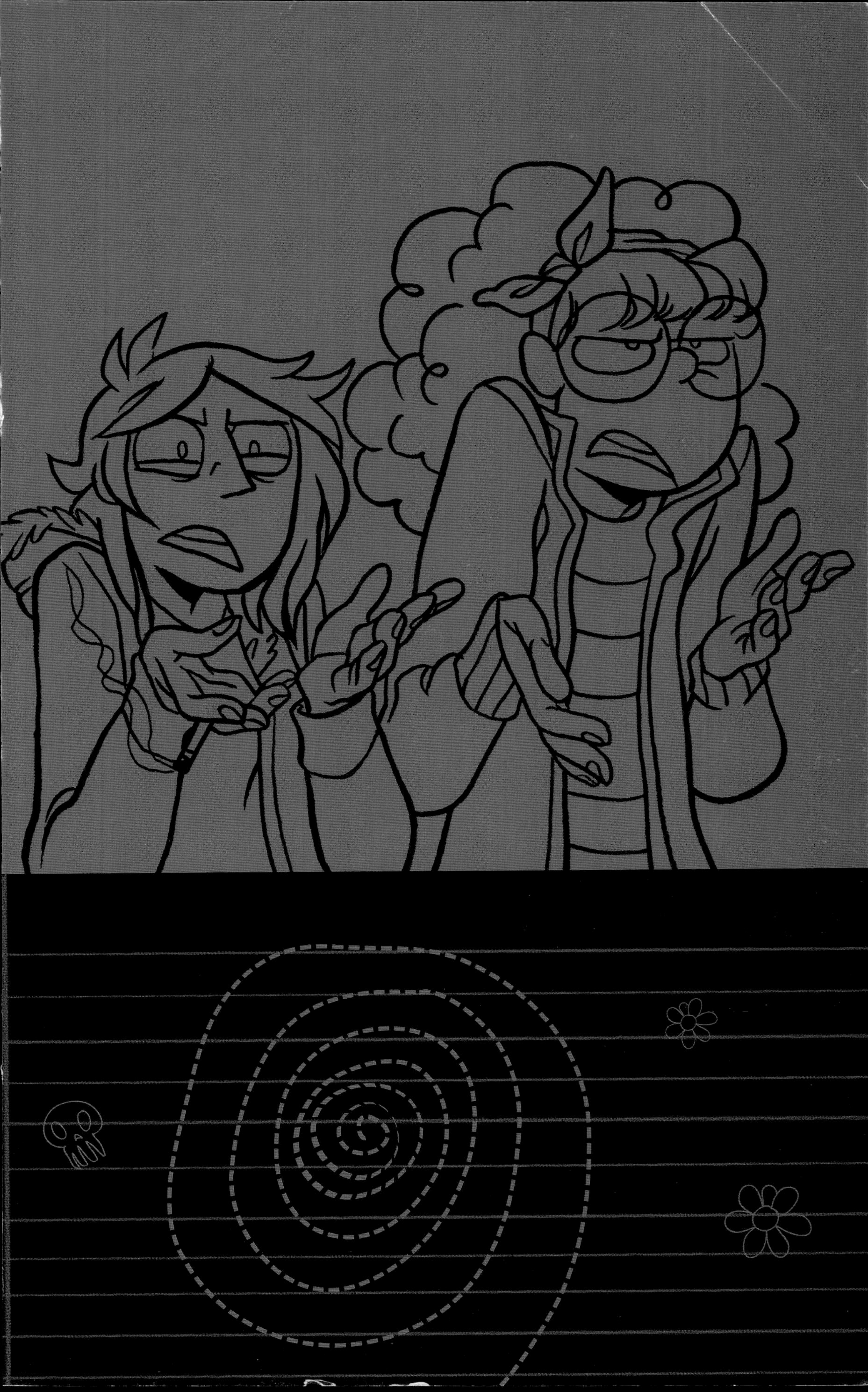

CHAPTER FOURTEEN

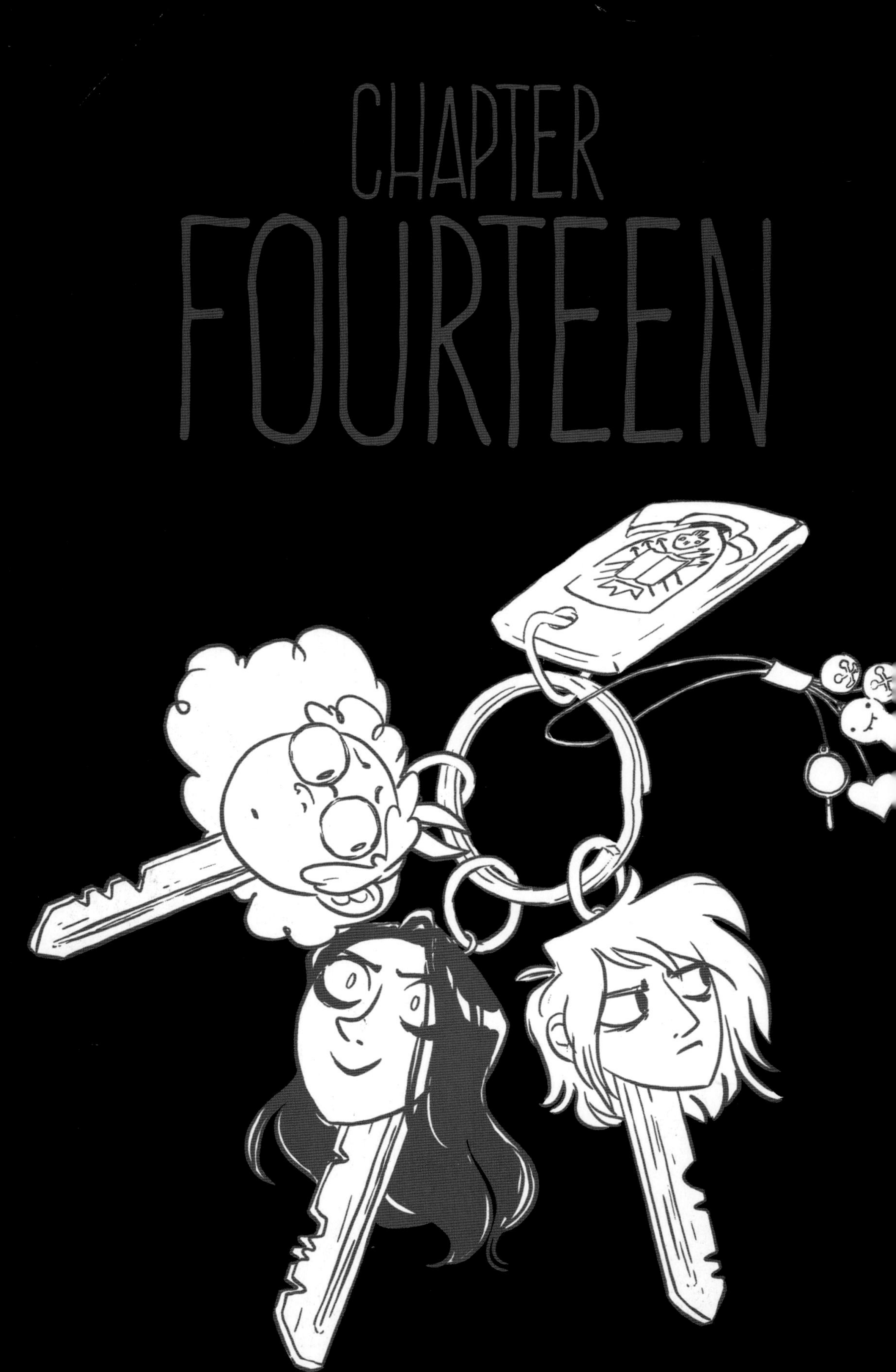

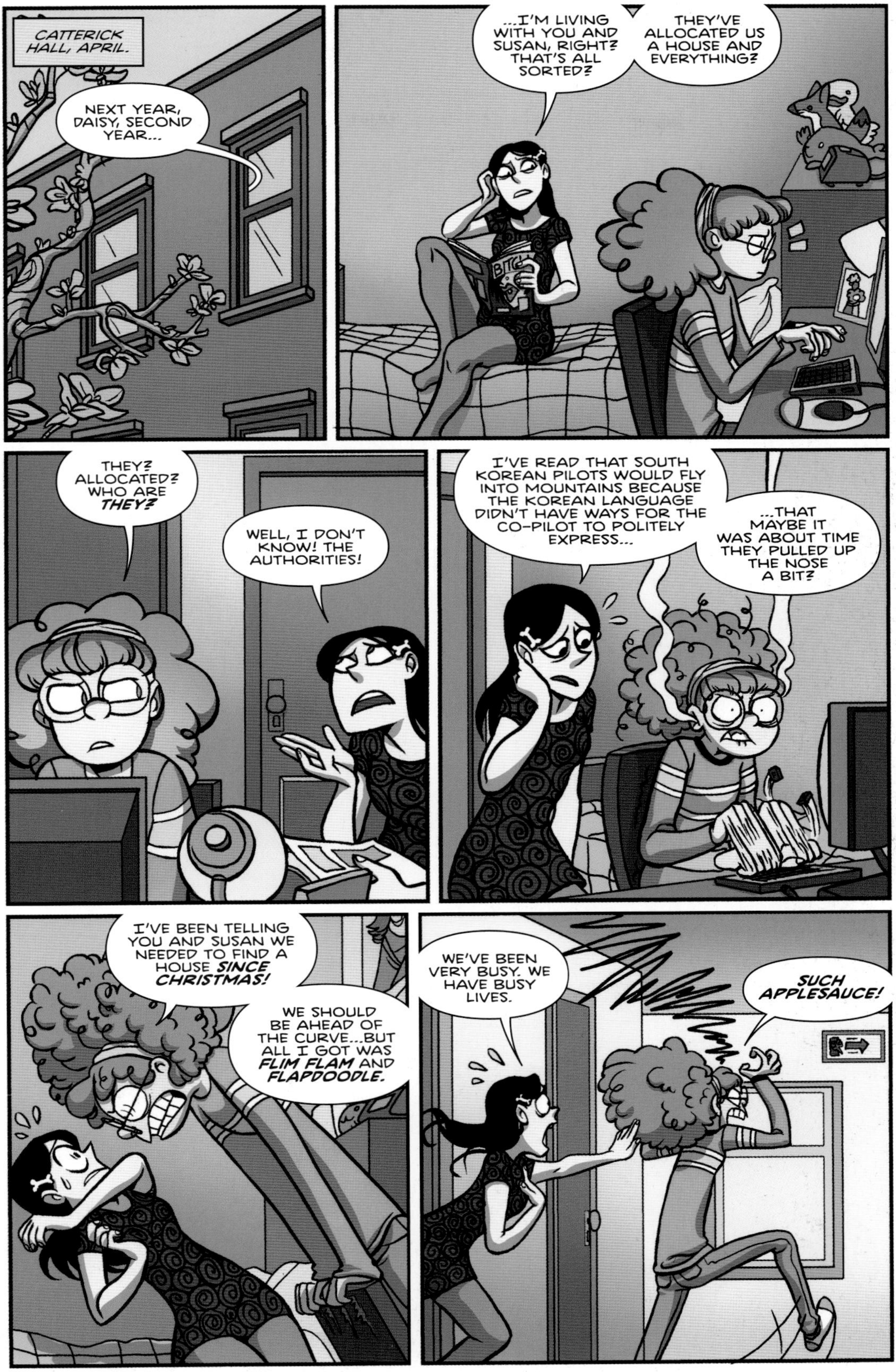
CATTERICK HALL, APRIL.
NEXT YEAR, DAISY, SECOND YEAR...
...I'M LIVING WITH YOU AND SUSAN, RIGHT? THAT'S ALL SORTED?
THEY'VE ALLOCATED US A HOUSE AND EVERYTHING?
THEY? ALLOCATED? WHO ARE THEY?
WELL, I DON'T KNOW! THE AUTHORITIES!
I'VE READ THAT SOUTH KOREAN PILOTS WOULD FLY INTO MOUNTAINS BECAUSE THE KOREAN LANGUAGE DIDN'T HAVE WAYS FOR THE CO-PILOT TO POLITELY EXPRESS...
...THAT MAYBE IT WAS ABOUT TIME THEY PULLED UP THE NOSE A BIT?
I'VE BEEN TELLING YOU AND SUSAN WE NEEDED TO FIND A HOUSE SINCE CHRISTMAS!
WE SHOULD BE AHEAD OF THE CURVE...BUT ALL I GOT WAS FLIM FLAM AND FLAPDOODLE.
WE'VE BEEN VERY BUSY. WE HAVE BUSY LIVES.
SUCH APPLESAUCE!

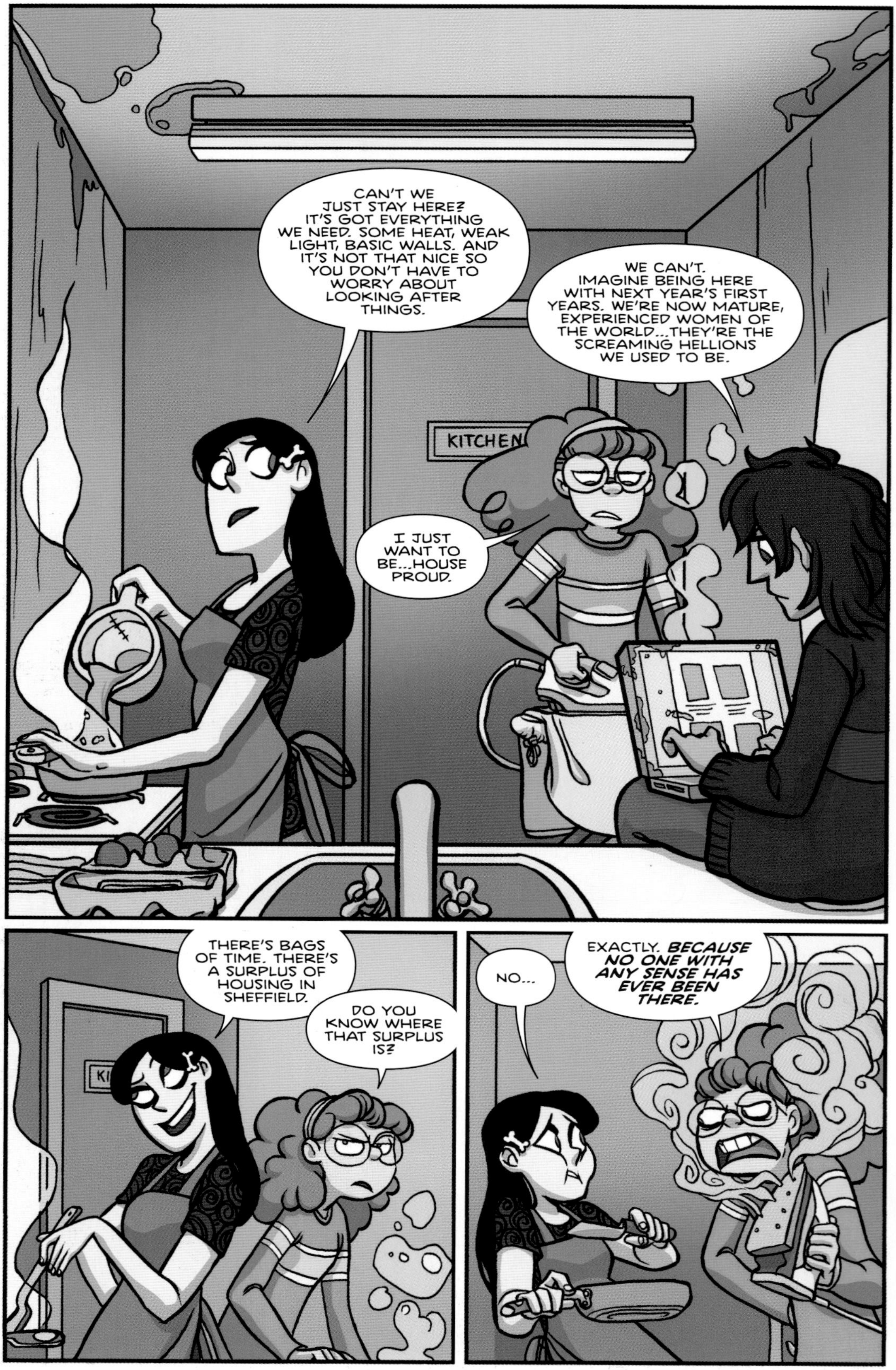
CAN'T WE JUST STAY HERE? IT'S GOT EVERYTHING WE NEED. SOME HEAT, WEAK LIGHT, BASIC WALLS. AND IT'S NOT THAT NICE SO YOU DON'T HAVE TO WORRY ABOUT LOOKING AFTER THINGS.
WE CAN'T. IMAGINE BEING HERE WITH NEXT YEAR'S FIRST YEARS. WE'RE NOW MATURE, EXPERIENCED WOMEN OF THE WORLD... THEY'RE THE SCREAMING HELLIONS WE USED TO BE.
KITCHEN
I JUST WANT TO BE... HOUSE PROUD.
THERE'S BAGS OF TIME. THERE'S A SURPLUS OF HOUSING IN SHEFFIELD.
DO YOU KNOW WHERE THAT SURPLUS IS?
NO...
EXACTLY. ***BECAUSE NO ONE WITH ANY SENSE HAS EVER BEEN THERE.***

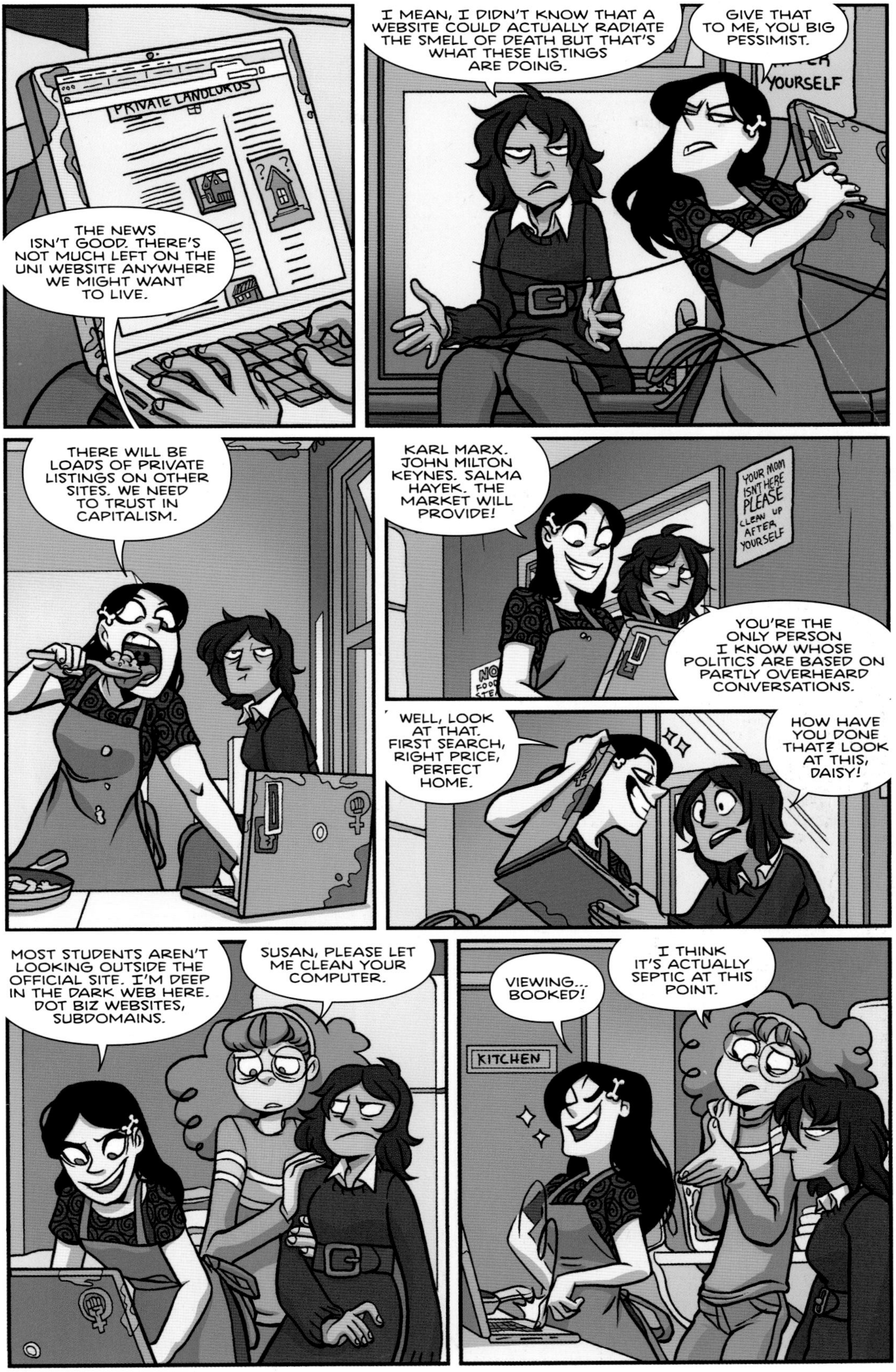
PRIVATE LANDLORDS
THE NEWS ISN'T GOOD. THERE'S NOT MUCH LEFT ON THE UNI WEBSITE ANYWHERE WE MIGHT WANT TO LIVE.
I MEAN, I DIDN'T KNOW THAT A WEBSITE COULD ACTUALLY RADIATE THE SMELL OF DEATH BUT THAT'S WHAT THESE LISTINGS ARE DOING.
GIVE THAT TO ME, YOU BIG PESSIMIST.
YOURSELF
THERE WILL BE LOADS OF PRIVATE LISTINGS ON OTHER SITES. WE NEED TO TRUST IN CAPITALISM.
KARL MARX. JOHN MILTON KEYNES. SALMA HAYEK. THE MARKET WILL PROVIDE!
YOUR MOM ISN'T HERE PLEASE CLEAN UP AFTER YOURSELF
YOU'RE THE ONLY PERSON I KNOW WHOSE POLITICS ARE BASED ON PARTLY OVERHEARD CONVERSATIONS.
WELL, LOOK AT THAT. FIRST SEARCH, RIGHT PRICE, PERFECT HOME.
HOW HAVE YOU DONE THAT? LOOK AT THIS, DAISY!
MOST STUDENTS AREN'T LOOKING OUTSIDE THE OFFICIAL SITE. I'M DEEP IN THE DARK WEB HERE. DOT BIZ WEBSITES, SUBDOMAINS.
SUSAN, PLEASE LET ME CLEAN YOUR COMPUTER.
KITCHEN
VIEWING... BOOKED!
I THINK IT'S ACTUALLY SEPTIC AT THIS POINT.

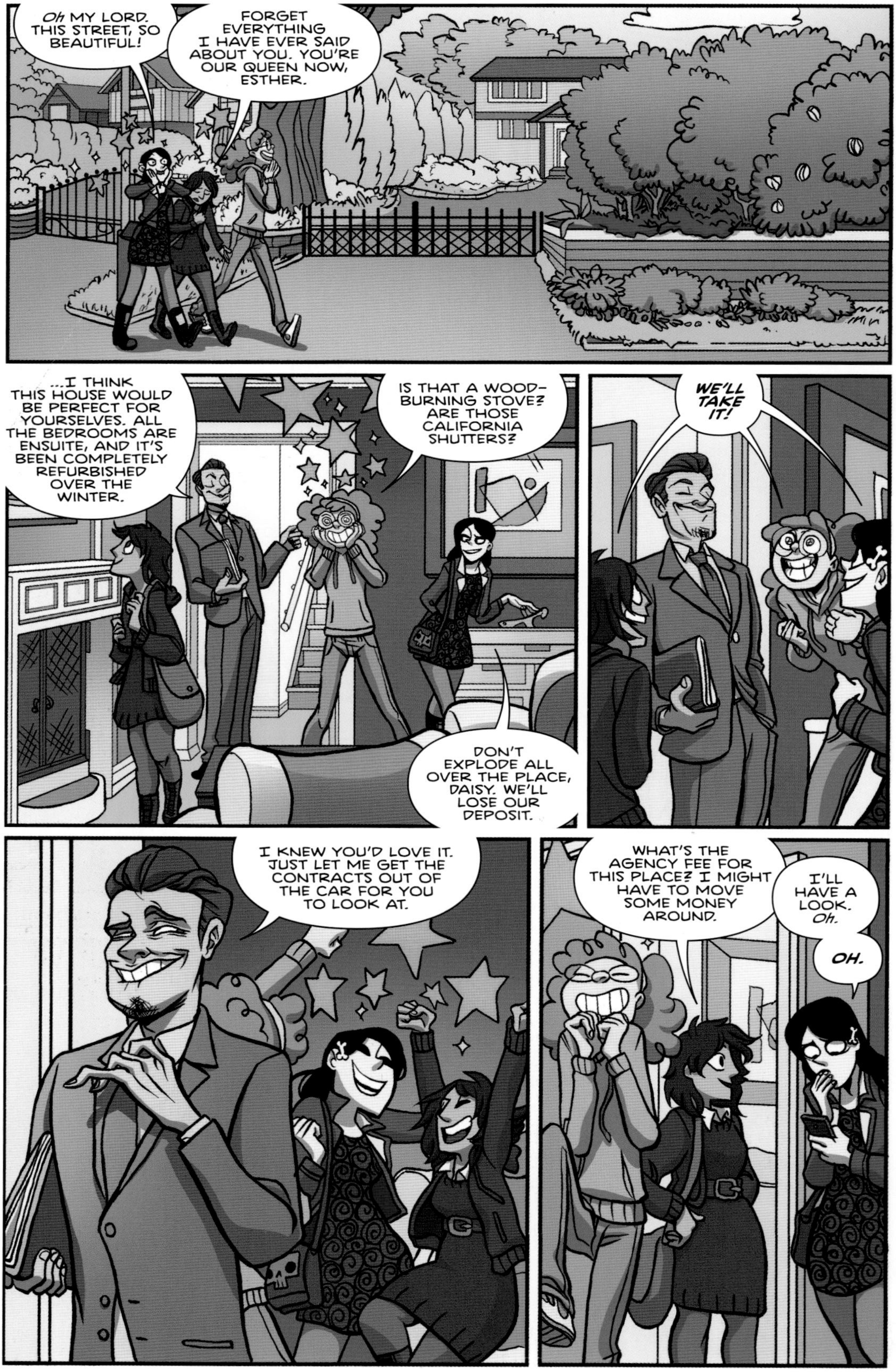
Oh MY LORD. THIS STREET, SO BEAUTIFUL!
FORGET EVERYTHING I HAVE EVER SAID ABOUT YOU. YOU'RE OUR QUEEN NOW, ESTHER.
...I THINK THIS HOUSE WOULD BE PERFECT FOR YOURSELVES. ALL THE BEDROOMS ARE ENSUITE, AND IT'S BEEN COMPLETELY REFURBISHED OVER THE WINTER.
IS THAT A WOOD-BURNING STOVE? ARE THOSE CALIFORNIA SHUTTERS?
DON'T EXPLODE ALL OVER THE PLACE, DAISY. WE'LL LOSE OUR DEPOSIT.
WE'LL TAKE IT!
I KNEW YOU'D LOVE IT. JUST LET ME GET THE CONTRACTS OUT OF THE CAR FOR YOU TO LOOK AT.
WHAT'S THE AGENCY FEE FOR THIS PLACE? I MIGHT HAVE TO MOVE SOME MONEY AROUND.
I'LL HAVE A LOOK. *Oh.*
OH.

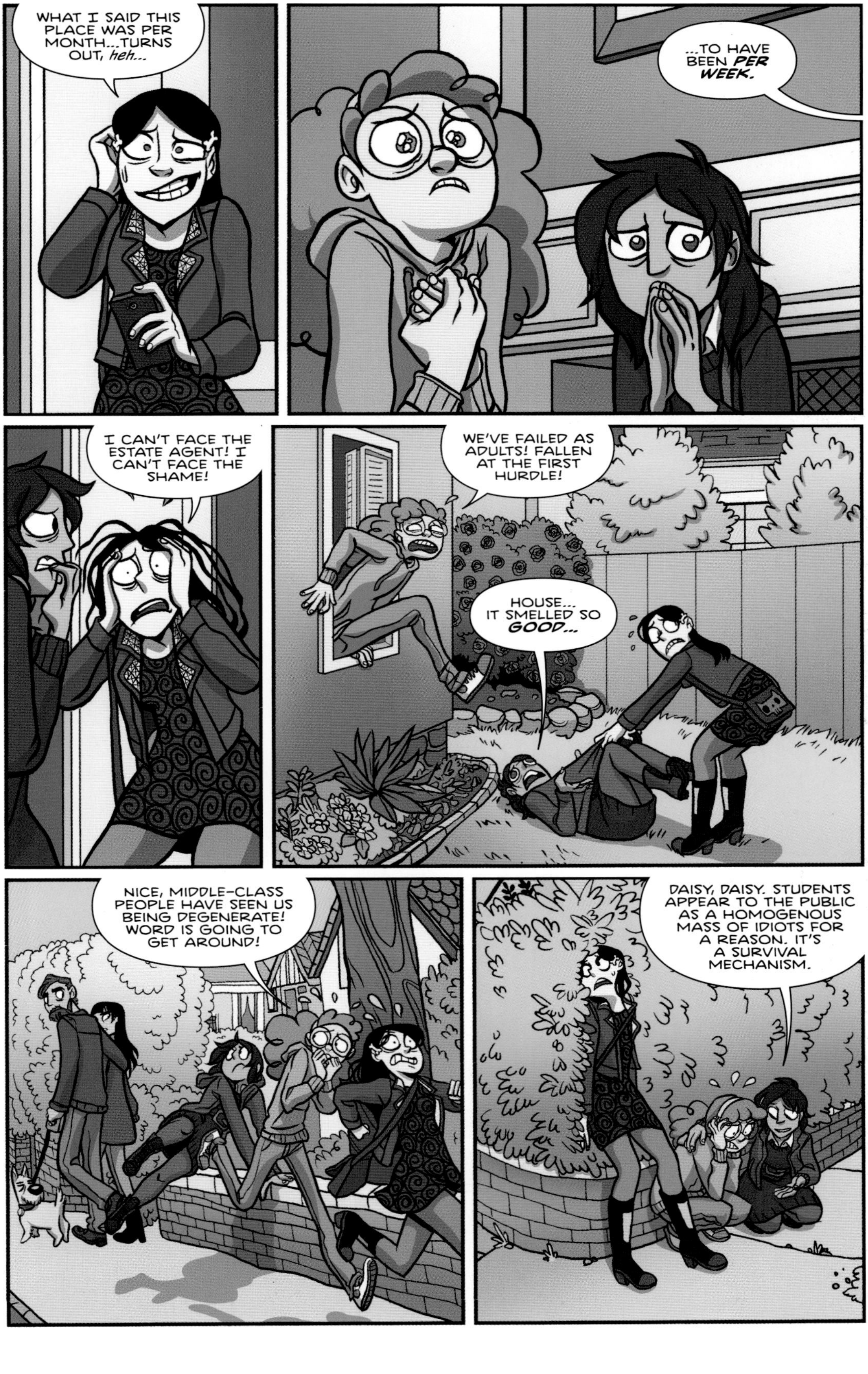
WHAT I SAID THIS PLACE WAS PER MONTH...TURNS OUT, *heh*...
...TO HAVE BEEN ***PER WEEK.***
I CAN'T FACE THE ESTATE AGENT! I CAN'T FACE THE SHAME!
WE'VE FAILED AS ADULTS! FALLEN AT THE FIRST HURDLE!
HOUSE... IT SMELLED SO ***GOOD...***
NICE, MIDDLE-CLASS PEOPLE HAVE SEEN US BEING DEGENERATE! WORD IS GOING TO GET AROUND!
DAISY, DAISY. STUDENTS APPEAR TO THE PUBLIC AS A HOMOGENOUS MASS OF IDIOTS FOR A REASON. IT'S A SURVIVAL MECHANISM.

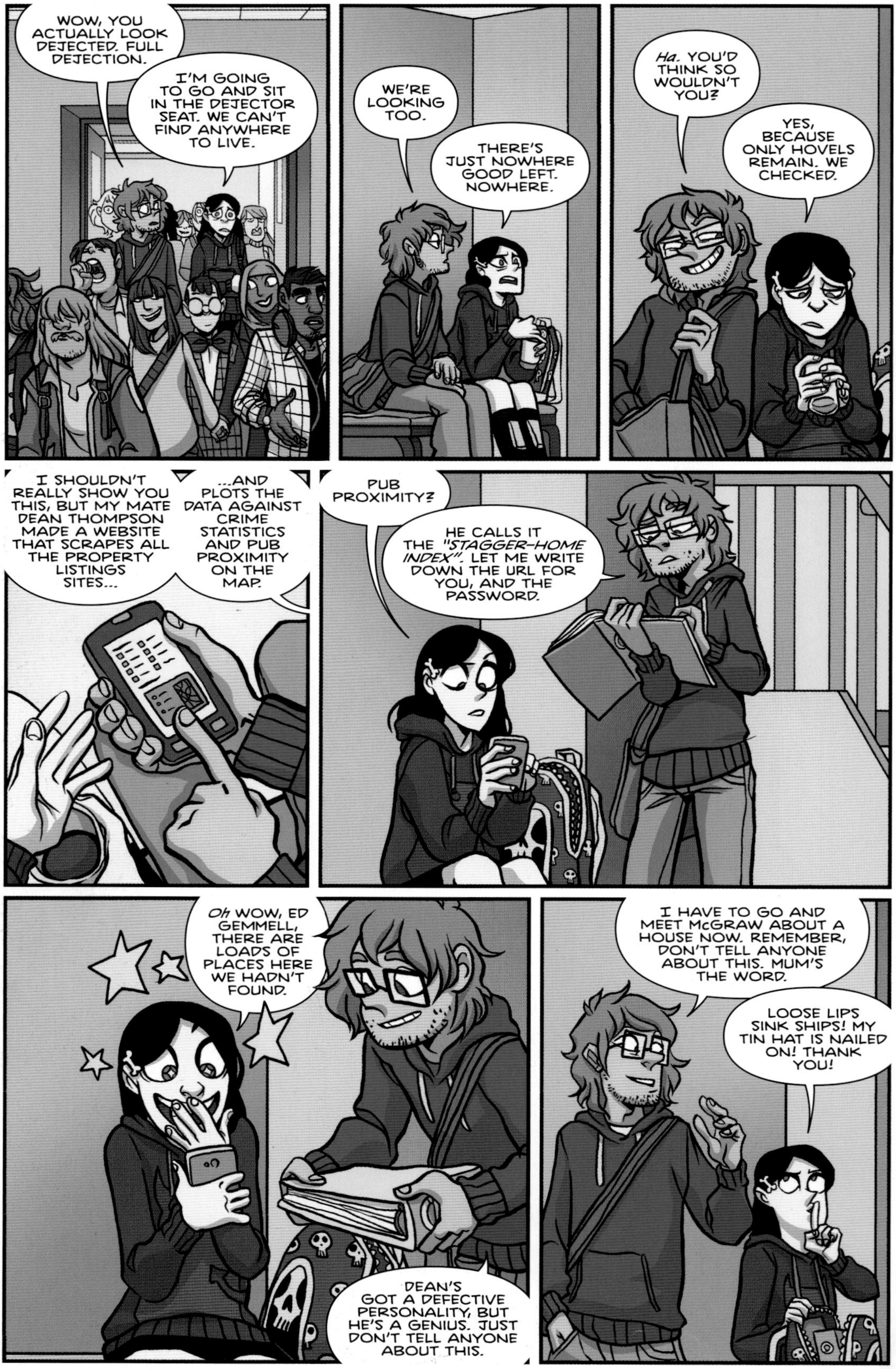
WOW, YOU ACTUALLY LOOK DEJECTED. FULL DEJECTION.
I'M GOING TO GO AND SIT IN THE DEJECTOR SEAT. WE CAN'T FIND ANYWHERE TO LIVE.
WE'RE LOOKING TOO.
THERE'S JUST NOWHERE GOOD LEFT. NOWHERE.
Ha. YOU'D THINK SO WOULDN'T YOU?
YES, BECAUSE ONLY HOVELS REMAIN. WE CHECKED.
I SHOULDN'T REALLY SHOW YOU THIS, BUT MY MATE DEAN THOMPSON MADE A WEBSITE THAT SCRAPES ALL THE PROPERTY LISTINGS SITES...
...AND PLOTS THE DATA AGAINST CRIME STATISTICS AND PUB PROXIMITY ON THE MAP.
PUB PROXIMITY?
HE CALLS IT THE *"STAGGER-HOME INDEX"*. LET ME WRITE DOWN THE URL FOR YOU, AND THE PASSWORD.
Oh WOW, ED GEMMELL, THERE ARE LOADS OF PLACES HERE WE HADN'T FOUND.
DEAN'S GOT A DEFECTIVE PERSONALITY, BUT HE'S A GENIUS. JUST DON'T TELL ANYONE ABOUT THIS.
I HAVE TO GO AND MEET McGRAW ABOUT A HOUSE NOW. REMEMBER, DON'T TELL ANYONE ABOUT THIS. MUM'S THE WORD.
LOOSE LIPS SINK SHIPS! MY TIN HAT IS NAILED ON! THANK YOU!

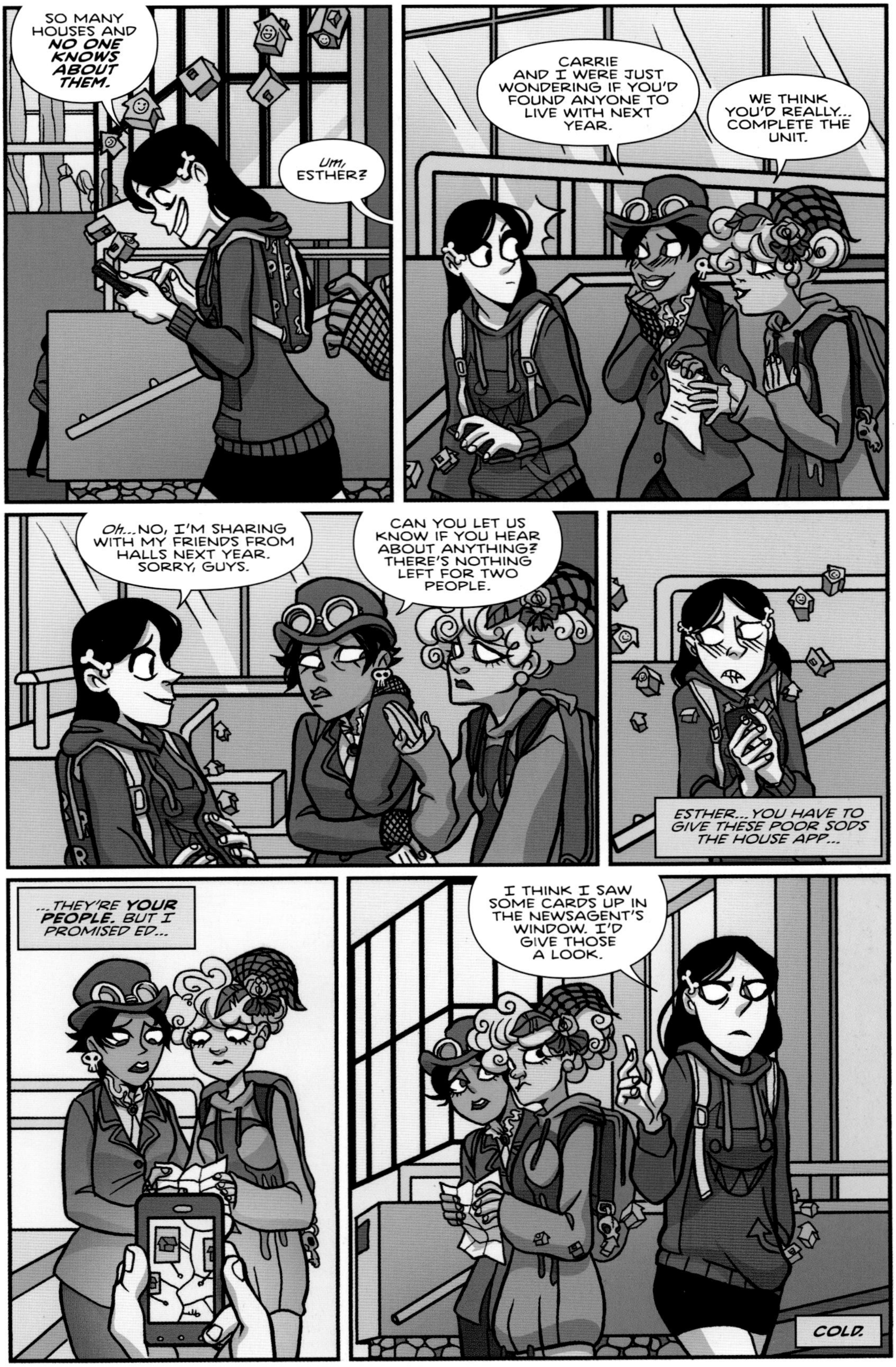

SO MANY HOUSES AND NO ONE KNOWS ABOUT THEM.
UM, ESTHER?
CARRIE AND I WERE JUST WONDERING IF YOU'D FOUND ANYONE TO LIVE WITH NEXT YEAR.
WE THINK YOU'D REALLY... COMPLETE THE UNIT.
OH... NO, I'M SHARING WITH MY FRIENDS FROM HALLS NEXT YEAR. SORRY, GUYS.
CAN YOU LET US KNOW IF YOU HEAR ABOUT ANYTHING? THERE'S NOTHING LEFT FOR TWO PEOPLE.
ESTHER... YOU HAVE TO GIVE THESE POOR SODS THE HOUSE APP...
...THEY'RE YOUR PEOPLE. BUT I PROMISED ED...
I THINK I SAW SOME CARDS UP IN THE NEWSAGENT'S WINDOW. I'D GIVE THOSE A LOOK.
COLD.

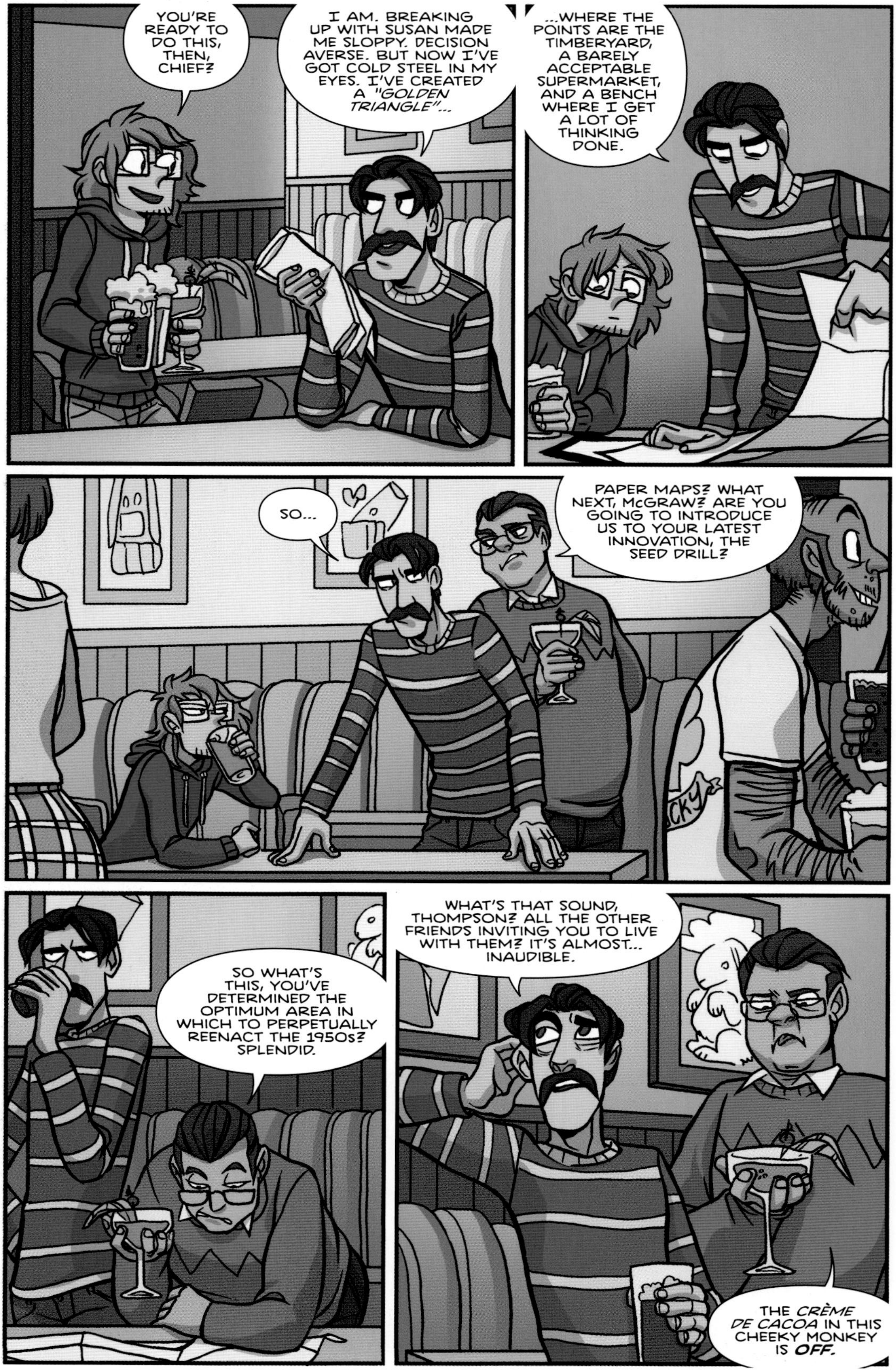
YOU'RE READY TO DO THIS, THEN, CHIEF?
I AM. BREAKING UP WITH SUSAN MADE ME SLOPPY. DECISION AVERSE. BUT NOW I'VE GOT COLD STEEL IN MY EYES. I'VE CREATED A *"GOLDEN TRIANGLE"*...
...WHERE THE POINTS ARE THE TIMBERYARD, A BARELY ACCEPTABLE SUPERMARKET, AND A BENCH WHERE I GET A LOT OF THINKING DONE.
SO...
PAPER MAPS? WHAT NEXT, McGRAW? ARE YOU GOING TO INTRODUCE US TO YOUR LATEST INNOVATION, THE SEED DRILL?
SO WHAT'S THIS, YOU'VE DETERMINED THE OPTIMUM AREA IN WHICH TO PERPETUALLY REENACT THE 1950s? SPLENDID.
WHAT'S THAT SOUND, THOMPSON? ALL THE OTHER FRIENDS INVITING YOU TO LIVE WITH THEM? IT'S ALMOST... INAUDIBLE.
THE *CRÈME DE CACOA* IN THIS CHEEKY MONKEY IS ***OFF.***

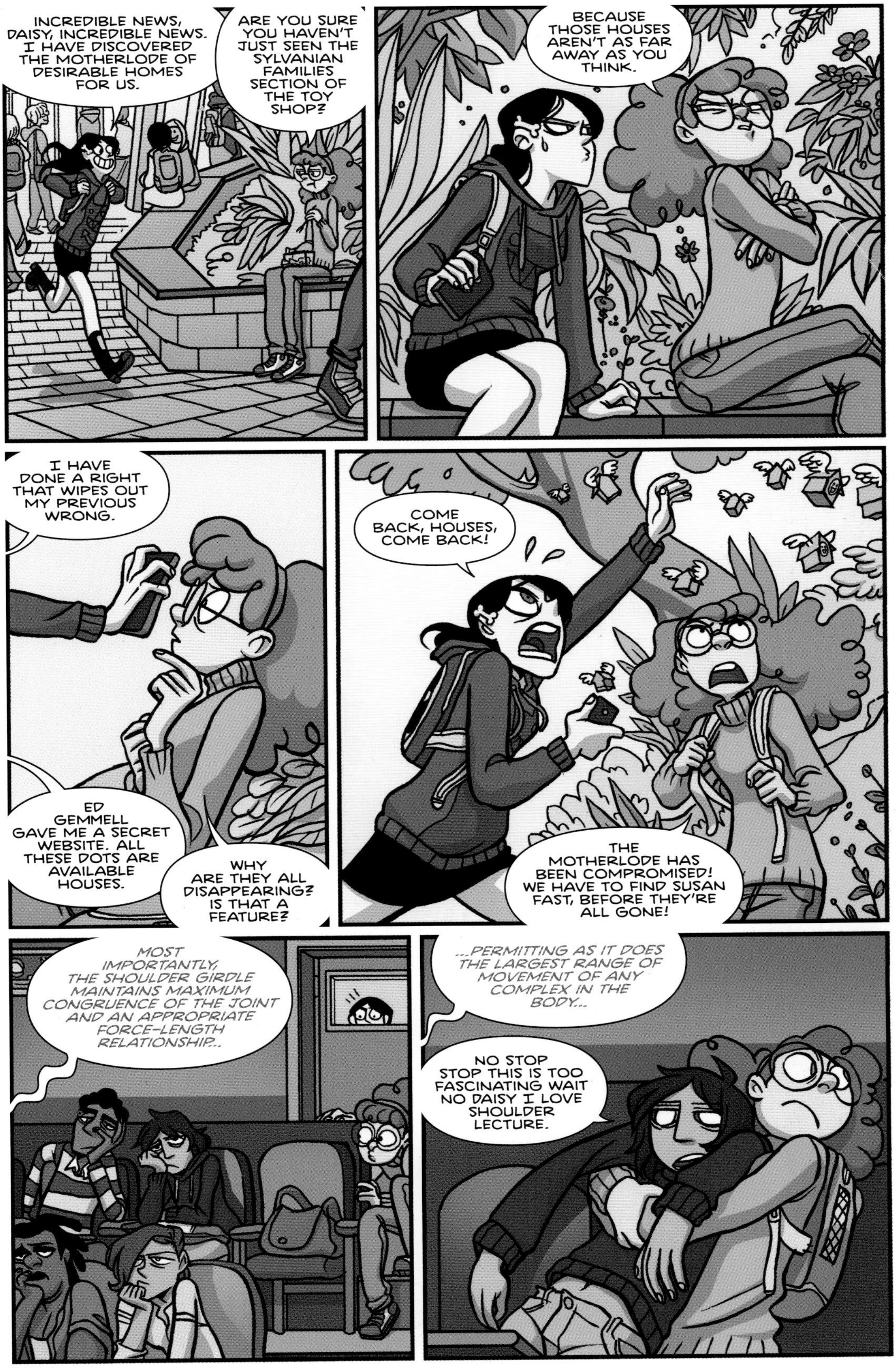
INCREDIBLE NEWS, DAISY, INCREDIBLE NEWS. I HAVE DISCOVERED THE MOTHERLODE OF DESIRABLE HOMES FOR US.
ARE YOU SURE YOU HAVEN'T JUST SEEN THE SYLVANIAN FAMILIES SECTION OF THE TOY SHOP?
BECAUSE THOSE HOUSES AREN'T AS FAR AWAY AS YOU THINK.
I HAVE DONE A RIGHT THAT WIPES OUT MY PREVIOUS WRONG.
ED GEMMELL GAVE ME A SECRET WEBSITE. ALL THESE DOTS ARE AVAILABLE HOUSES.
WHY ARE THEY ALL DISAPPEARING? IS THAT A FEATURE?
COME BACK, HOUSES, COME BACK!
THE MOTHERLODE HAS BEEN COMPROMISED! WE HAVE TO FIND SUSAN FAST, BEFORE THEY'RE ALL GONE!
MOST IMPORTANTLY, THE SHOULDER GIRDLE MAINTAINS MAXIMUM CONGRUENCE OF THE JOINT AND AN APPROPRIATE FORCE-LENGTH RELATIONSHIP...
...PERMITTING AS IT DOES THE LARGEST RANGE OF MOVEMENT OF ANY COMPLEX IN THE BODY...
NO STOP STOP THIS IS TOO FASCINATING WAIT NO DAISY I LOVE SHOULDER LECTURE.

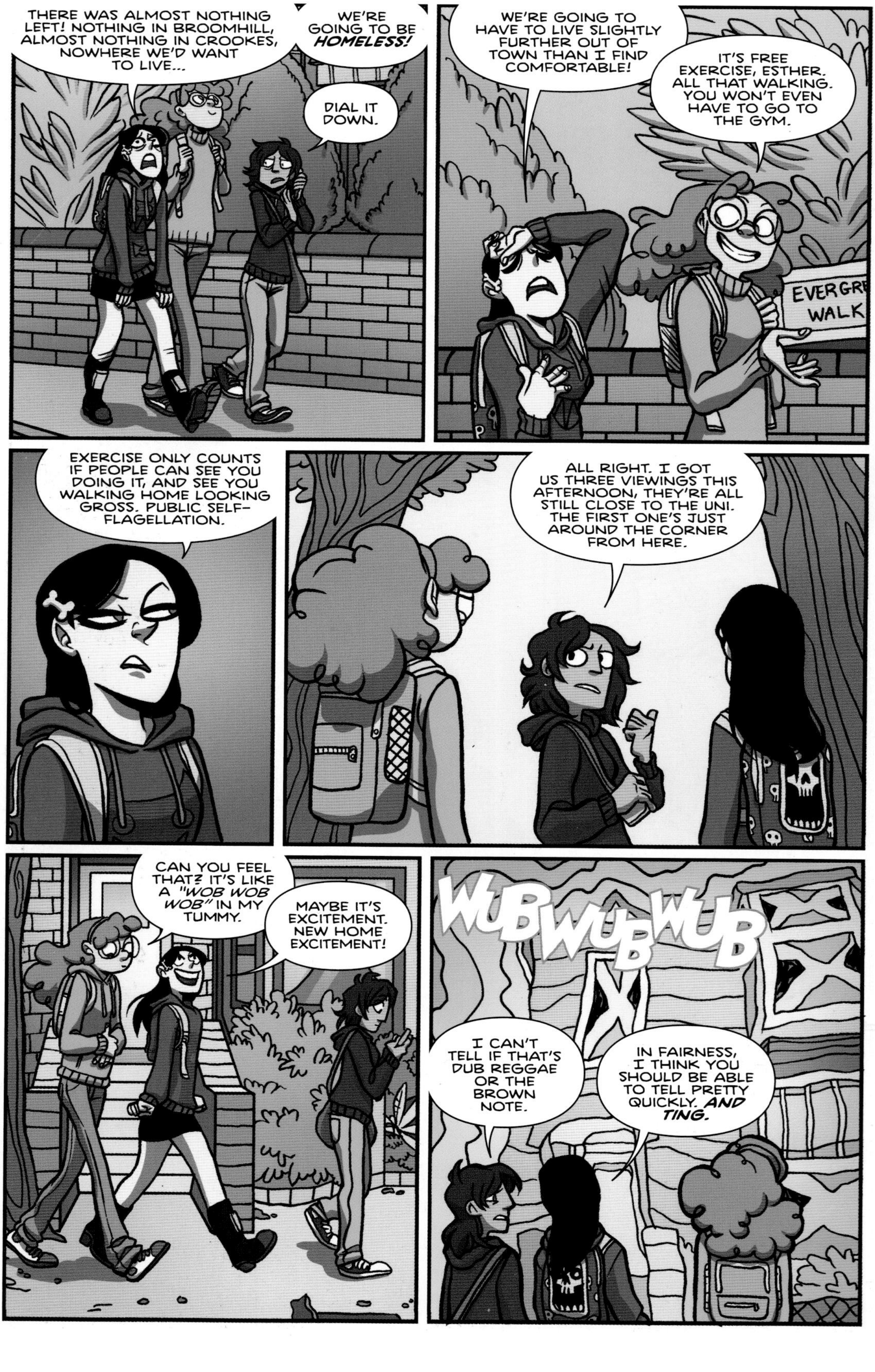

THERE WAS ALMOST NOTHING LEFT! NOTHING IN BROOMHILL, ALMOST NOTHING IN CROOKES, NOWHERE WE'D WANT TO LIVE...
WE'RE GOING TO BE *HOMELESS!*
DIAL IT DOWN.
WE'RE GOING TO HAVE TO LIVE SLIGHTLY FURTHER OUT OF TOWN THAN I FIND COMFORTABLE!
IT'S FREE EXERCISE, ESTHER. ALL THAT WALKING. YOU WON'T EVEN HAVE TO GO TO THE GYM.
EXERCISE ONLY COUNTS IF PEOPLE CAN SEE YOU DOING IT, AND SEE YOU WALKING HOME LOOKING GROSS. PUBLIC SELF-FLAGELLATION.
ALL RIGHT. I GOT US THREE VIEWINGS THIS AFTERNOON, THEY'RE ALL STILL CLOSE TO THE UNI. THE FIRST ONE'S JUST AROUND THE CORNER FROM HERE.
CAN YOU FEEL THAT? IT'S LIKE A *"WOB WOB WOB"* IN MY TUMMY.
MAYBE IT'S EXCITEMENT. NEW HOME EXCITEMENT!
WUB WUB WUB
I CAN'T TELL IF THAT'S DUB REGGAE OR THE BROWN NOTE.
IN FAIRNESS, I THINK YOU SHOULD BE ABLE TO TELL PRETTY QUICKLY. *AND TING.*

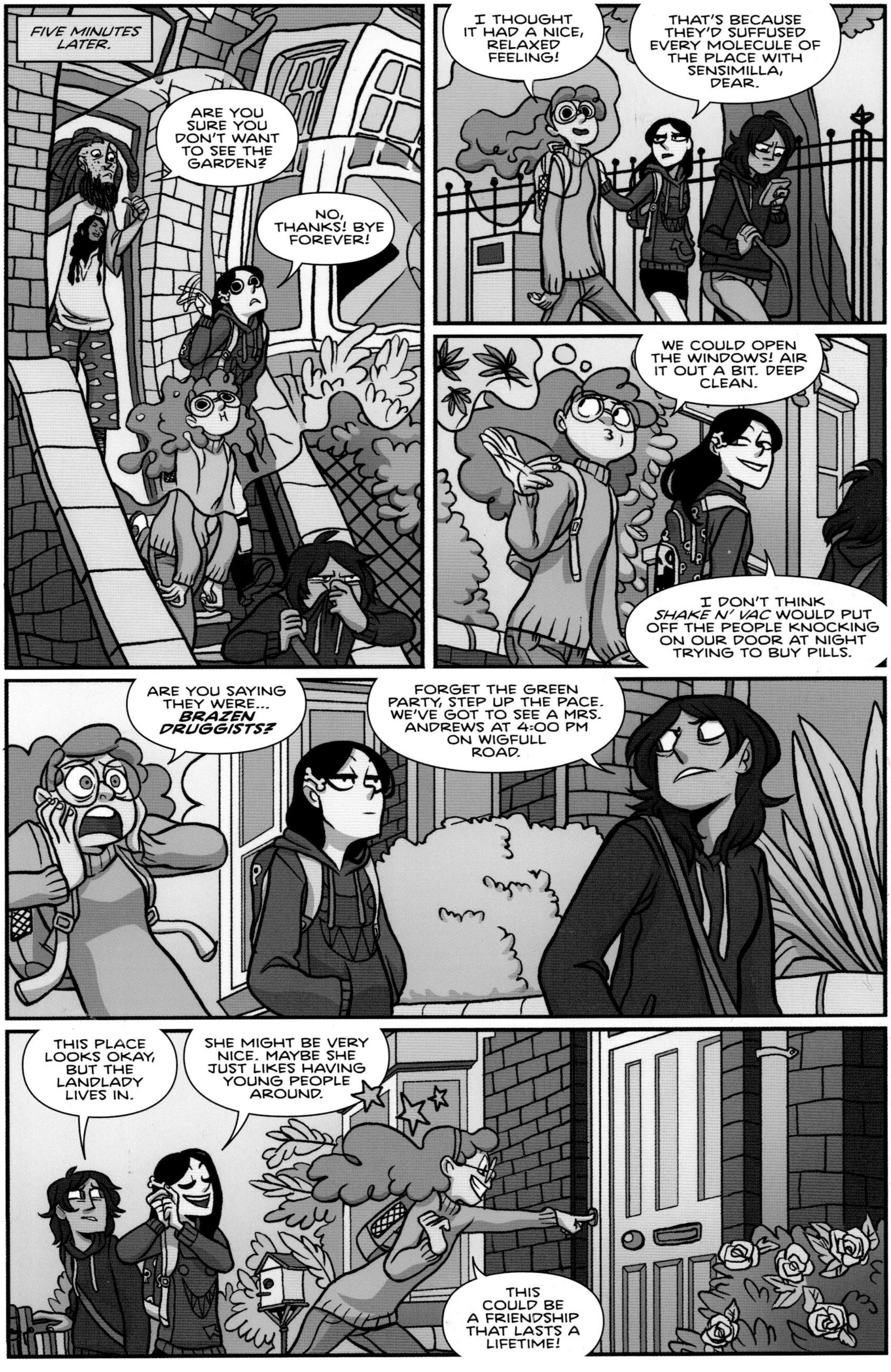
FIVE MINUTES LATER.
ARE YOU SURE YOU DON'T WANT TO SEE THE GARDEN?
NO, THANKS! BYE FOREVER!
I THOUGHT IT HAD A NICE, RELAXED FEELING!
THAT'S BECAUSE THEY'D SUFFUSED EVERY MOLECULE OF THE PLACE WITH SENSIMILLA, DEAR.
WE COULD OPEN THE WINDOWS! AIR IT OUT A BIT. DEEP CLEAN.
I DON'T THINK SHAKE N' VAC WOULD PUT OFF THE PEOPLE KNOCKING ON OUR DOOR AT NIGHT TRYING TO BUY PILLS.
ARE YOU SAYING THEY WERE... BRAZEN DRUGGISTS?
FORGET THE GREEN PARTY, STEP UP THE PACE. WE'VE GOT TO SEE A MRS. ANDREWS AT 4:00 PM ON WIGFULL ROAD.
THIS PLACE LOOKS OKAY, BUT THE LANDLADY LIVES IN.
SHE MIGHT BE VERY NICE. MAYBE SHE JUST LIKES HAVING YOUNG PEOPLE AROUND.
THIS COULD BE A FRIENDSHIP THAT LASTS A LIFETIME!

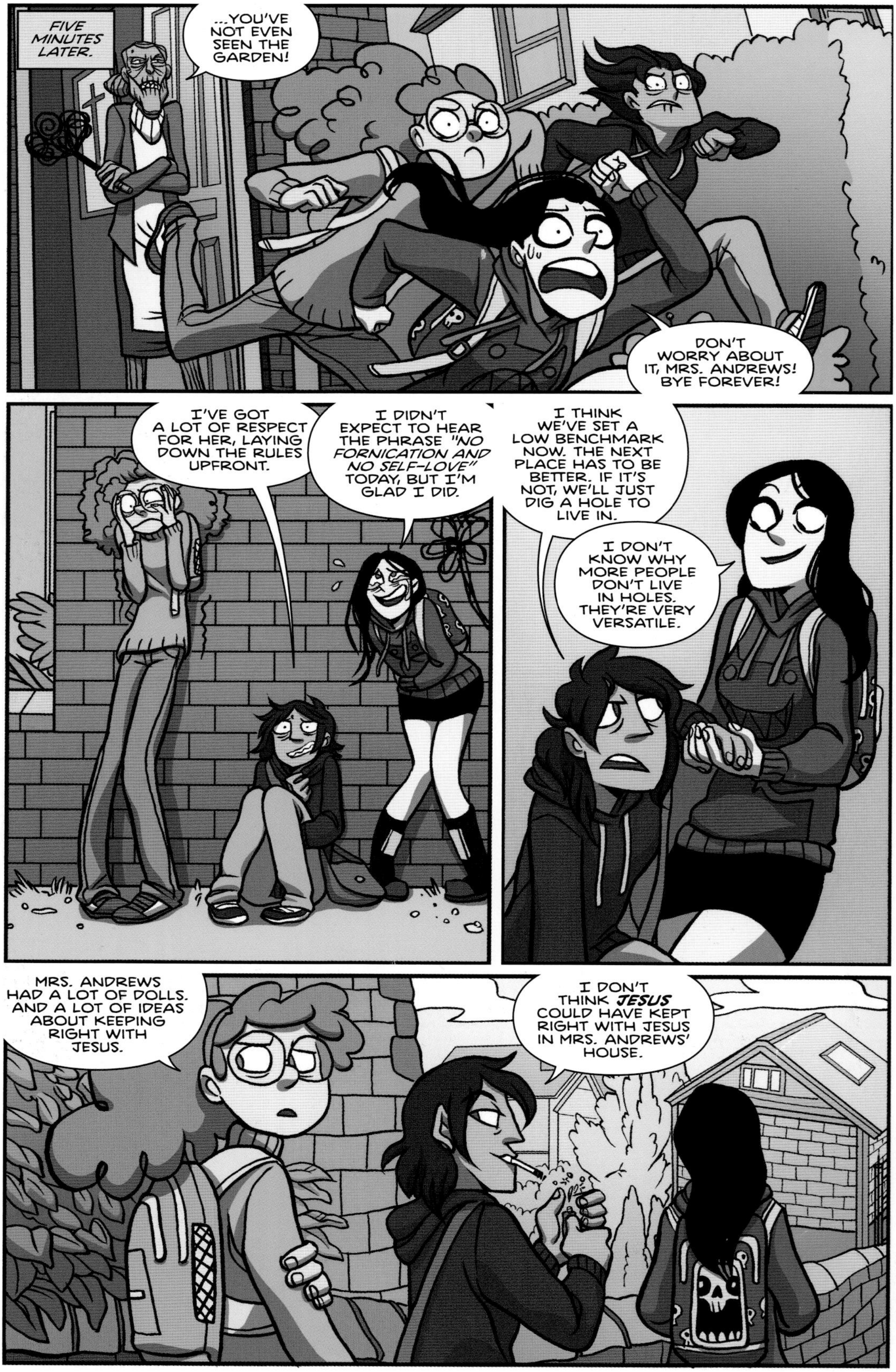
FIVE MINUTES LATER.
...YOU'VE NOT EVEN SEEN THE GARDEN!
DON'T WORRY ABOUT IT, MRS. ANDREWS! BYE FOREVER!
I'VE GOT A LOT OF RESPECT FOR HER, LAYING DOWN THE RULES UPFRONT.
I DIDN'T EXPECT TO HEAR THE PHRASE "NO FORNICATION AND NO SELF-LOVE" TODAY, BUT I'M GLAD I DID.
I THINK WE'VE SET A LOW BENCHMARK NOW. THE NEXT PLACE HAS TO BE BETTER. IF IT'S NOT, WE'LL JUST DIG A HOLE TO LIVE IN.
I DON'T KNOW WHY MORE PEOPLE DON'T LIVE IN HOLES. THEY'RE VERY VERSATILE.
MRS. ANDREWS HAD A LOT OF DOLLS. AND A LOT OF IDEAS ABOUT KEEPING RIGHT WITH JESUS.
I DON'T THINK JESUS COULD HAVE KEPT RIGHT WITH JESUS IN MRS. ANDREWS' HOUSE.

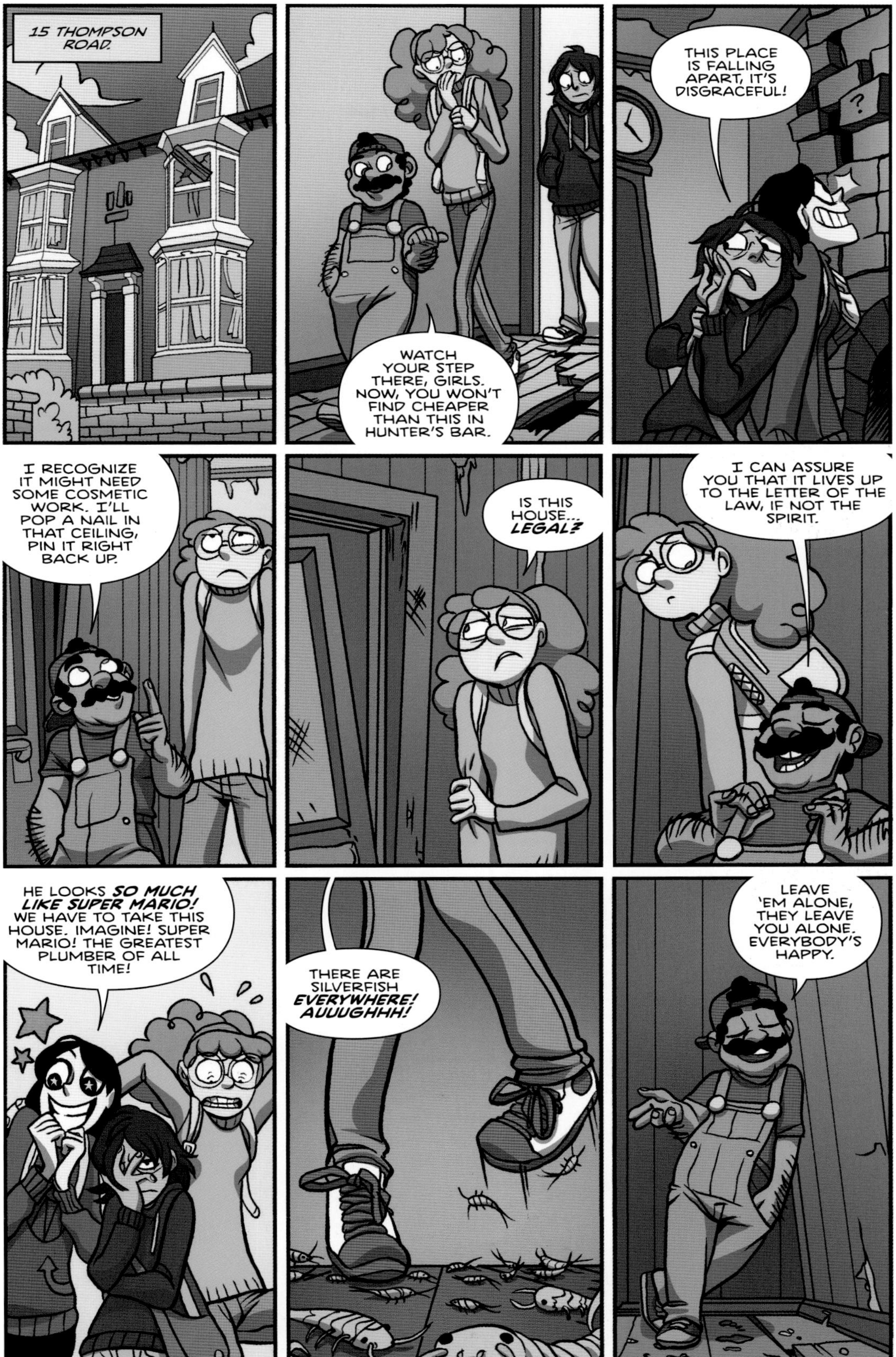
15 THOMPSON ROAD.
WATCH YOUR STEP THERE, GIRLS. NOW, YOU WON'T FIND CHEAPER THAN THIS IN HUNTER'S BAR.
THIS PLACE IS FALLING APART, IT'S DISGRACEFUL!
?
I RECOGNIZE IT MIGHT NEED SOME COSMETIC WORK. I'LL POP A NAIL IN THAT CEILING, PIN IT RIGHT BACK UP.
IS THIS HOUSE... ***LEGAL?***
I CAN ASSURE YOU THAT IT LIVES UP TO THE LETTER OF THE LAW, IF NOT THE SPIRIT.
HE LOOKS ***SO MUCH LIKE SUPER MARIO!*** WE HAVE TO TAKE THIS HOUSE. IMAGINE! SUPER MARIO! THE GREATEST PLUMBER OF ALL TIME!
THERE ARE SILVERFISH ***EVERYWHERE! AUUUGHHH!***
LEAVE 'EM ALONE, THEY LEAVE YOU ALONE. EVERYBODY'S HAPPY.

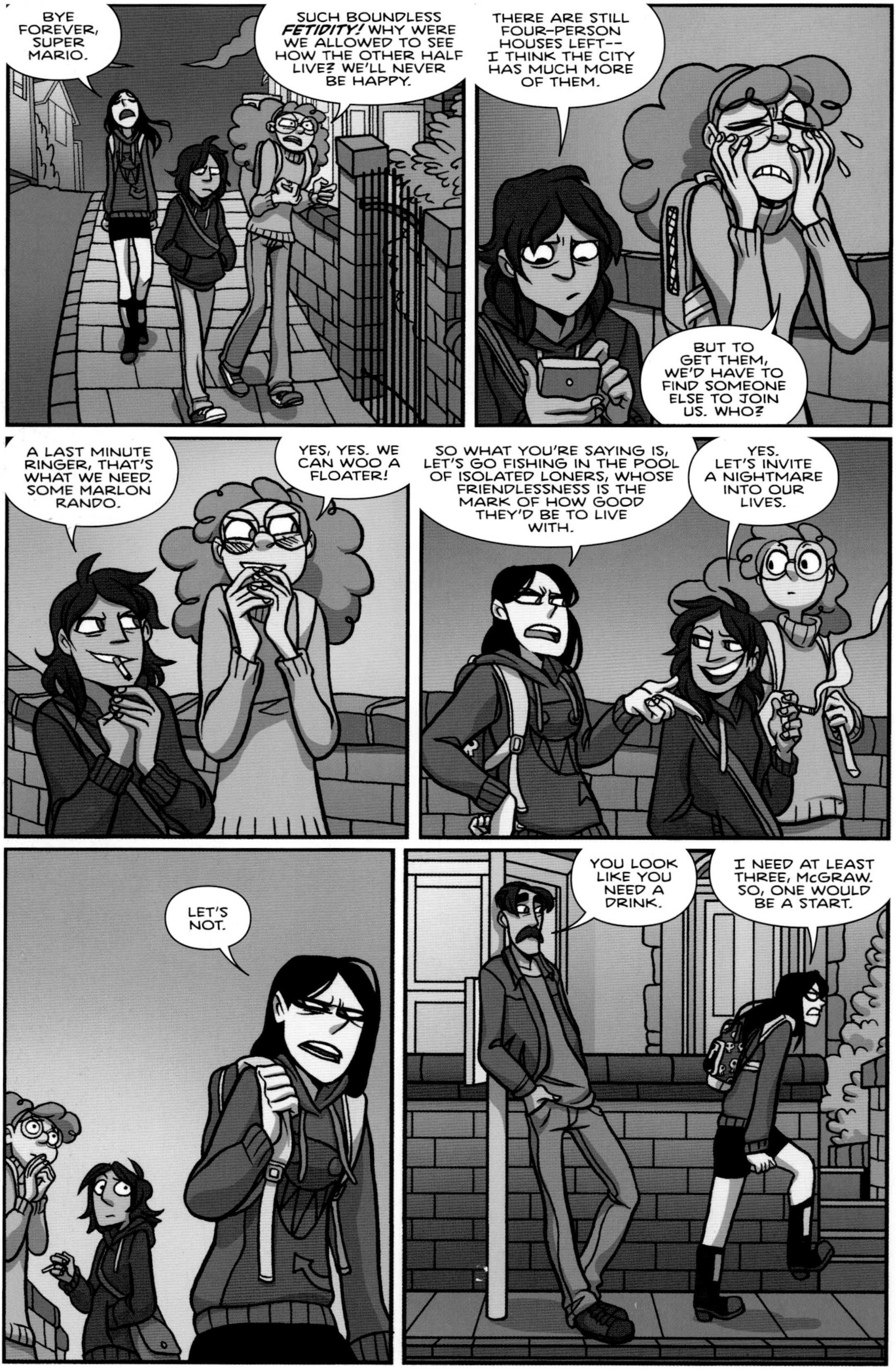
BYE FOREVER, SUPER MARIO.
SUCH BOUNDLESS FETIDITY! WHY WERE WE ALLOWED TO SEE HOW THE OTHER HALF LIVE? WE'LL NEVER BE HAPPY.
THERE ARE STILL FOUR-PERSON HOUSES LEFT-- I THINK THE CITY HAS MUCH MORE OF THEM.
BUT TO GET THEM, WE'D HAVE TO FIND SOMEONE ELSE TO JOIN US. WHO?
A LAST MINUTE RINGER, THAT'S WHAT WE NEED. SOME MARLON RANDO.
YES, YES. WE CAN WOO A FLOATER!
SO WHAT YOU'RE SAYING IS, LET'S GO FISHING IN THE POOL OF ISOLATED LONERS, WHOSE FRIENDLESSNESS IS THE MARK OF HOW GOOD THEY'D BE TO LIVE WITH.
YES. LET'S INVITE A NIGHTMARE INTO OUR LIVES.
LET'S NOT.
YOU LOOK LIKE YOU NEED A DRINK.
I NEED AT LEAST THREE, McGRAW. SO, ONE WOULD BE A START.

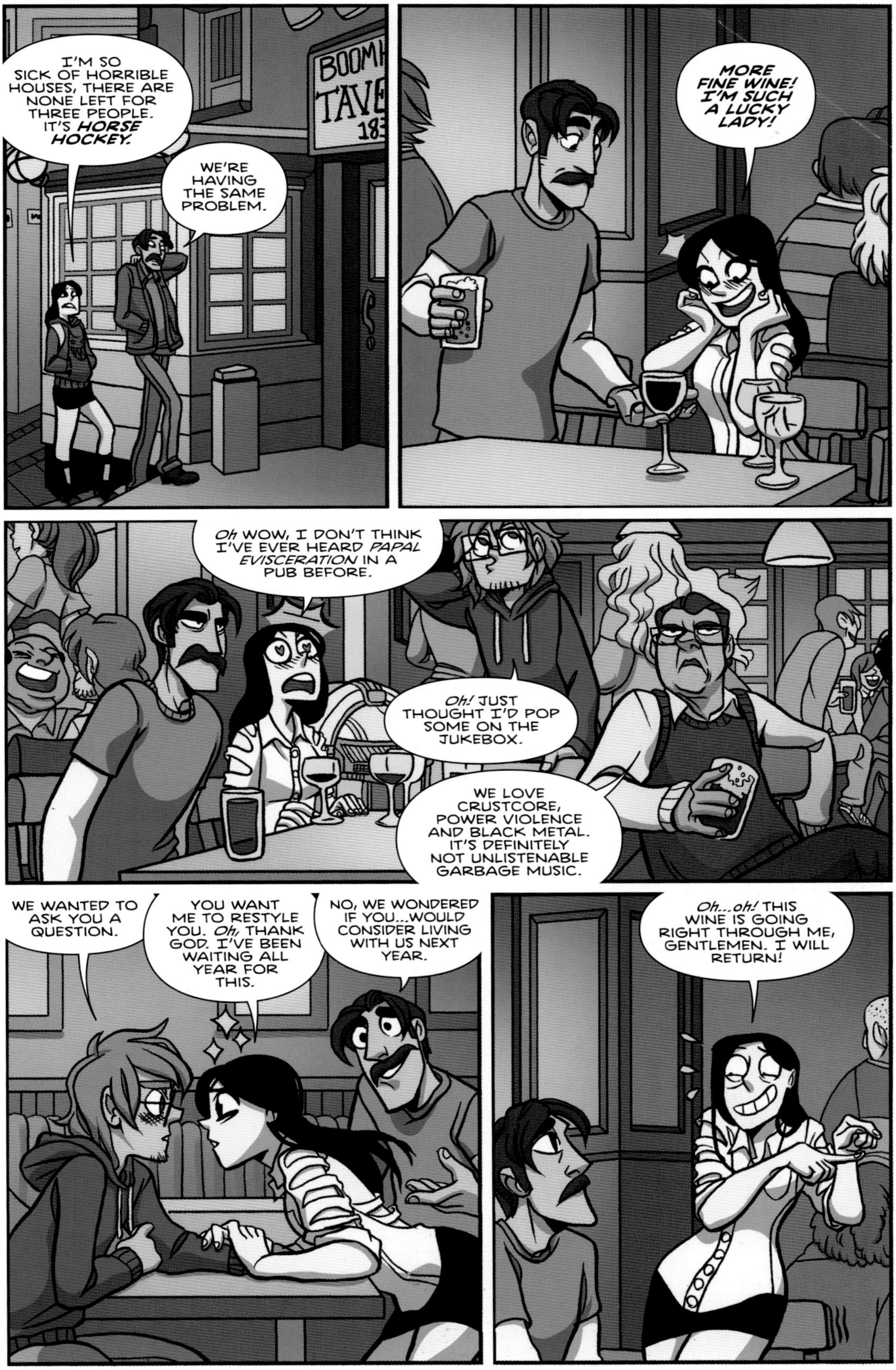
BOOMH TAVE 183
I'M SO SICK OF HORRIBLE HOUSES, THERE ARE NONE LEFT FOR THREE PEOPLE. IT'S *HORSE HOCKEY.*
WE'RE HAVING THE SAME PROBLEM.
MORE FINE WINE! I'M SUCH A LUCKY LADY!
Oh WOW, I DON'T THINK I'VE EVER HEARD *PAPAL EVISCERATION* IN A PUB BEFORE.
Oh! JUST THOUGHT I'D POP SOME ON THE JUKEBOX.
WE LOVE CRUSTCORE, POWER VIOLENCE AND BLACK METAL. IT'S DEFINITELY NOT UNLISTENABLE GARBAGE MUSIC.
WE WANTED TO ASK YOU A QUESTION.
YOU WANT ME TO RESTYLE YOU. *Oh,* THANK GOD. I'VE BEEN WAITING ALL YEAR FOR THIS.
NO, WE WONDERED IF YOU...WOULD CONSIDER LIVING WITH US NEXT YEAR.
Oh...oh! THIS WINE IS GOING RIGHT THROUGH ME, GENTLEMEN. I WILL RETURN!

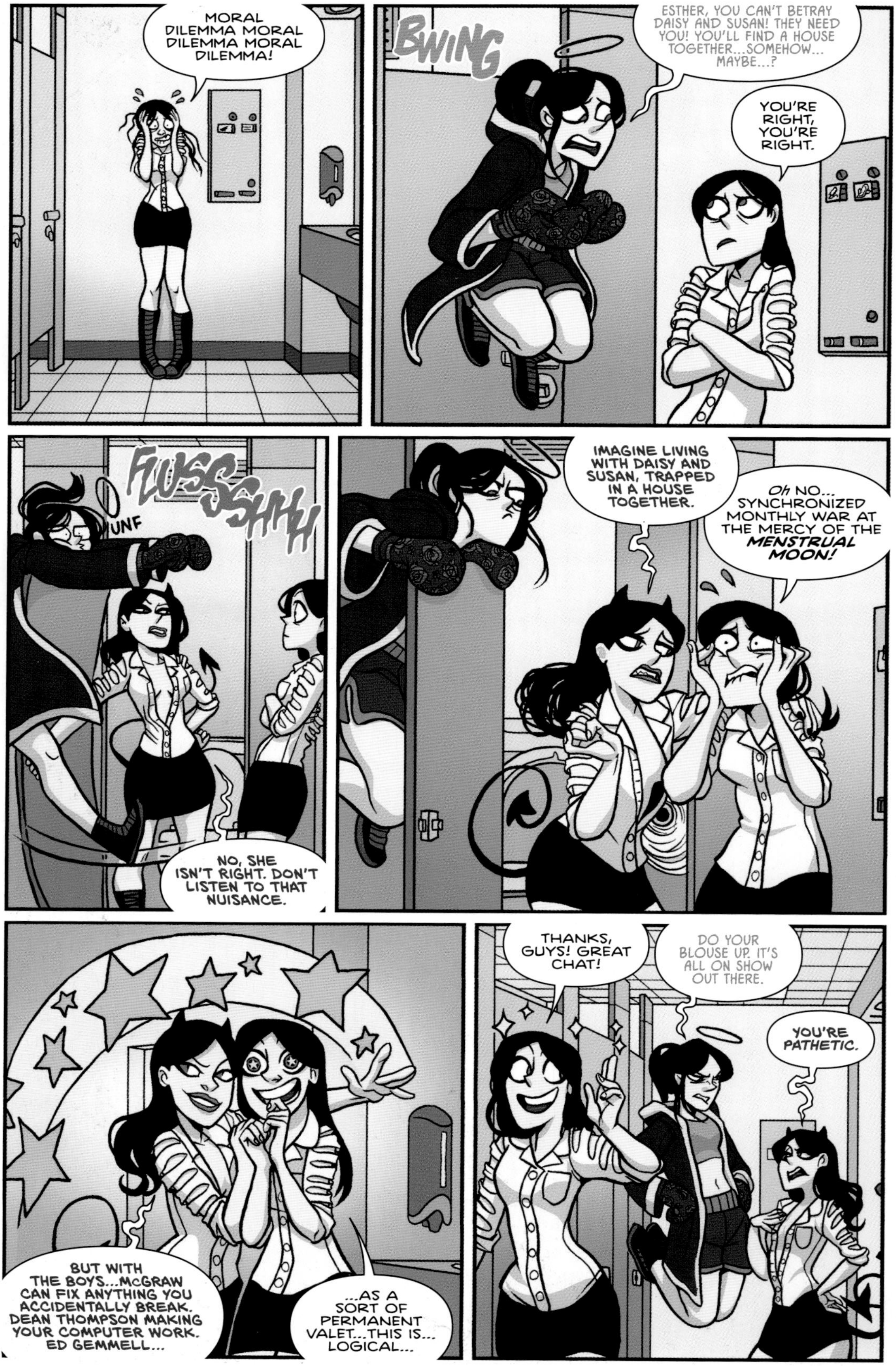

MORAL DILEMMA MORAL DILEMMA MORAL DILEMMA!
BWING
ESTHER, YOU CAN'T BETRAY DAISY AND SUSAN! THEY NEED YOU! YOU'LL FIND A HOUSE TOGETHER...SOMEHOW... MAYBE...?
YOU'RE RIGHT, YOU'RE RIGHT.
FLUSSSHHH
UNF
NO, SHE ISN'T RIGHT. DON'T LISTEN TO THAT NUISANCE.
IMAGINE LIVING WITH DAISY AND SUSAN, TRAPPED IN A HOUSE TOGETHER.
Oh NO... SYNCHRONIZED MONTHLY WAR AT THE MERCY OF THE ***MENSTRUAL MOON!***
BUT WITH THE BOYS...McGRAW CAN FIX ANYTHING YOU ACCIDENTALLY BREAK. DEAN THOMPSON MAKING YOUR COMPUTER WORK. ED GEMMELL...
...AS A SORT OF PERMANENT VALET...THIS IS... LOGICAL...
THANKS, GUYS! GREAT CHAT!
DO YOUR BLOUSE UP. IT'S ALL ON SHOW OUT THERE.
YOU'RE ***PATHETIC.***

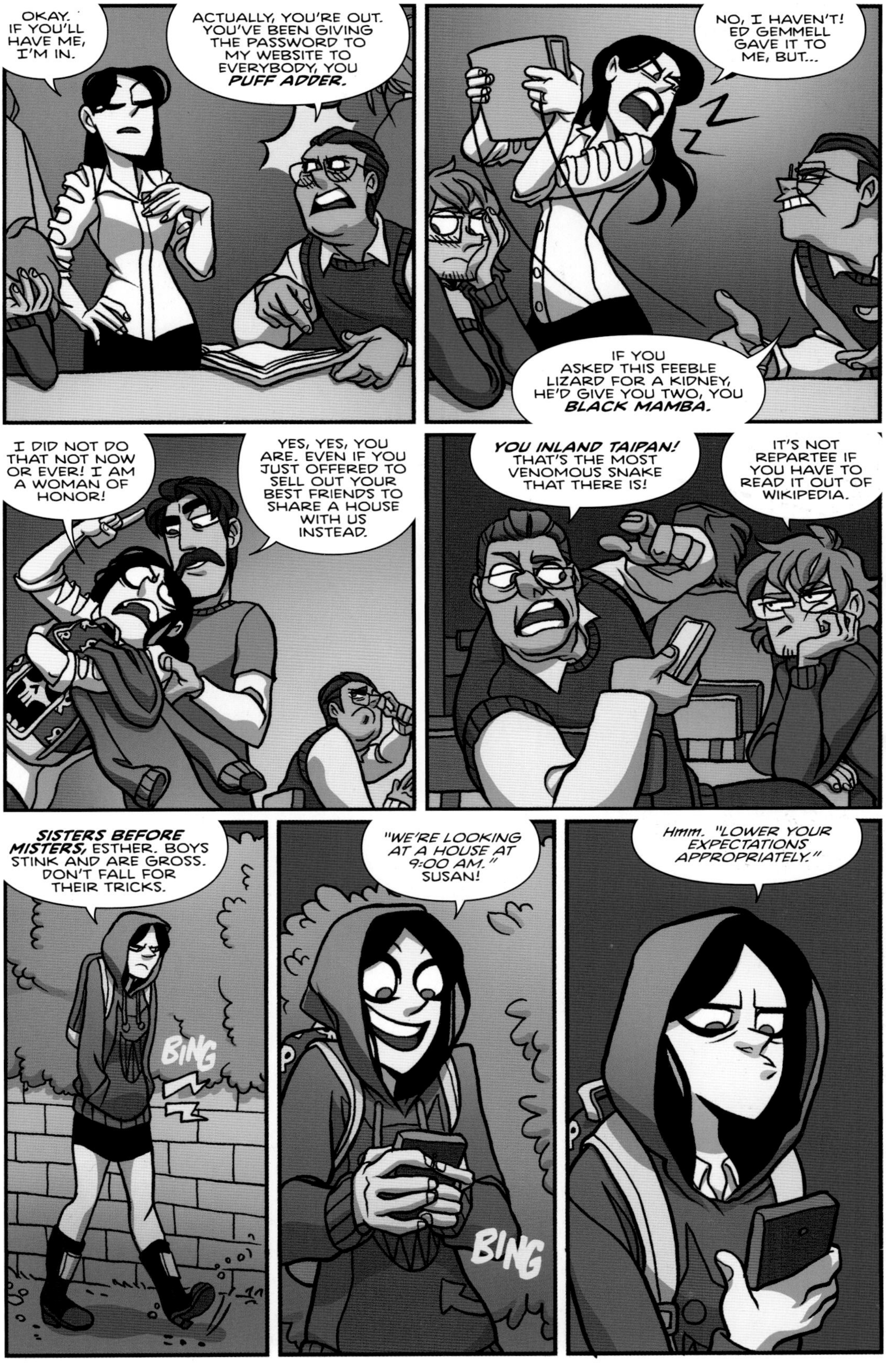
OKAY. IF YOU'LL HAVE ME, I'M IN.
ACTUALLY, YOU'RE OUT. YOU'VE BEEN GIVING THE PASSWORD TO MY WEBSITE TO EVERYBODY, YOU *PUFF ADDER.*
NO, I HAVEN'T! ED GEMMELL GAVE IT TO ME, BUT...
IF YOU ASKED THIS FEEBLE LIZARD FOR A KIDNEY, HE'D GIVE YOU TWO, YOU *BLACK MAMBA.*
I DID NOT DO THAT NOT NOW OR EVER! I AM A WOMAN OF HONOR!
YES, YES, YOU ARE. EVEN IF YOU JUST OFFERED TO SELL OUT YOUR BEST FRIENDS TO SHARE A HOUSE WITH US INSTEAD.
YOU INLAND TAIPAN! THAT'S THE MOST VENOMOUS SNAKE THAT THERE IS!
IT'S NOT REPARTEE IF YOU HAVE TO READ IT OUT OF WIKIPEDIA.
SISTERS BEFORE MISTERS, ESTHER. BOYS STINK AND ARE GROSS. DON'T FALL FOR THEIR TRICKS.
BING
"WE'RE LOOKING AT A HOUSE AT 9:00 AM." SUSAN!
BING
Hmm. "LOWER YOUR EXPECTATIONS APPROPRIATELY."

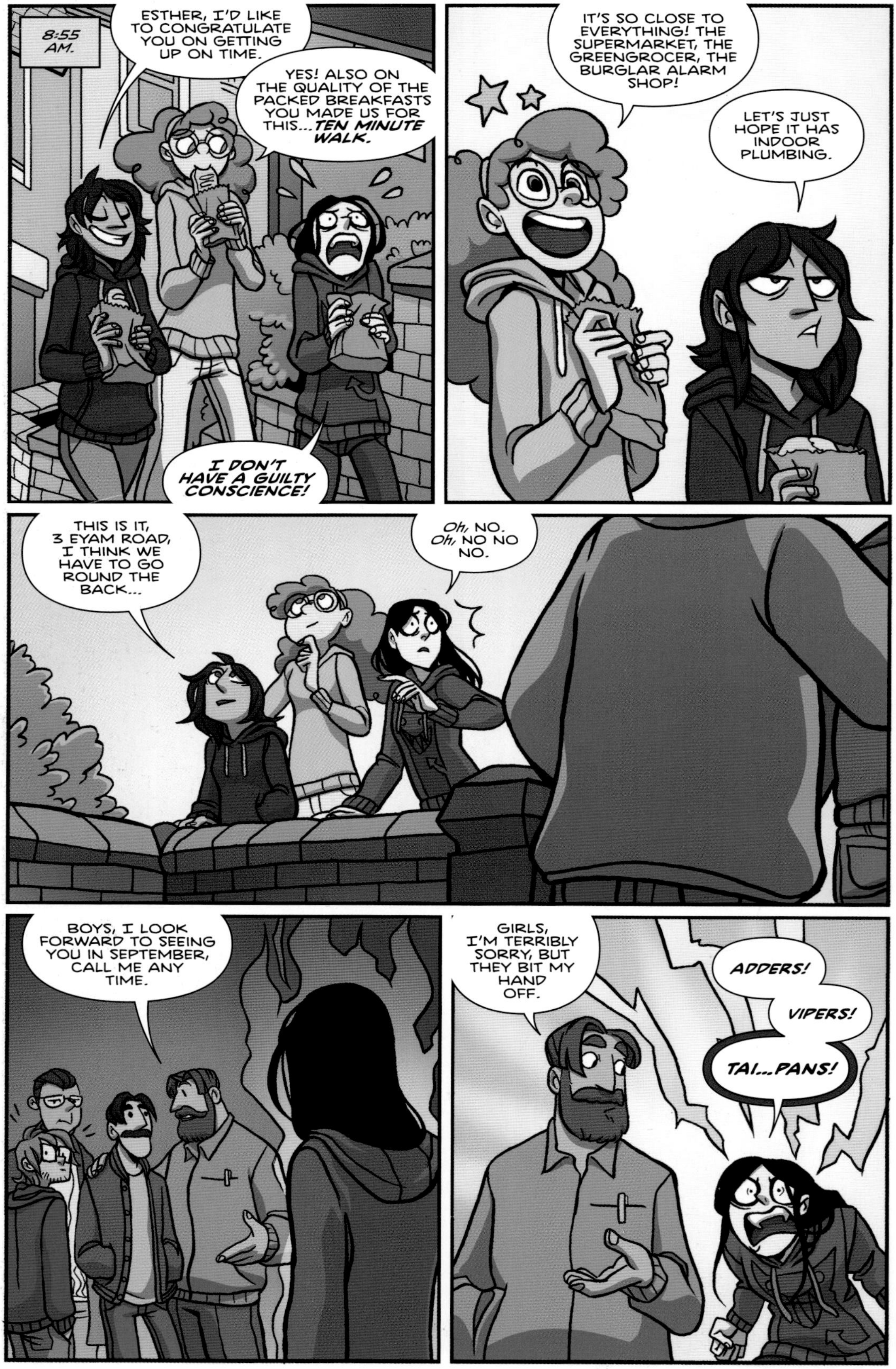
8:55 AM.
ESTHER, I'D LIKE TO CONGRATULATE YOU ON GETTING UP ON TIME.
YES! ALSO ON THE QUALITY OF THE PACKED BREAKFASTS YOU MADE US FOR THIS... TEN MINUTE WALK.
I DON'T HAVE A GUILTY CONSCIENCE!
IT'S SO CLOSE TO EVERYTHING! THE SUPERMARKET, THE GREENGROCER, THE BURGLAR ALARM SHOP!
LET'S JUST HOPE IT HAS INDOOR PLUMBING.
THIS IS IT, 3 EYAM ROAD, I THINK WE HAVE TO GO ROUND THE BACK...
Oh, NO. Oh, NO NO NO.
BOYS, I LOOK FORWARD TO SEEING YOU IN SEPTEMBER, CALL ME ANY TIME.
GIRLS, I'M TERRIBLY SORRY, BUT THEY BIT MY HAND OFF.
ADDERS!
VIPERS!
TAI...PANS!

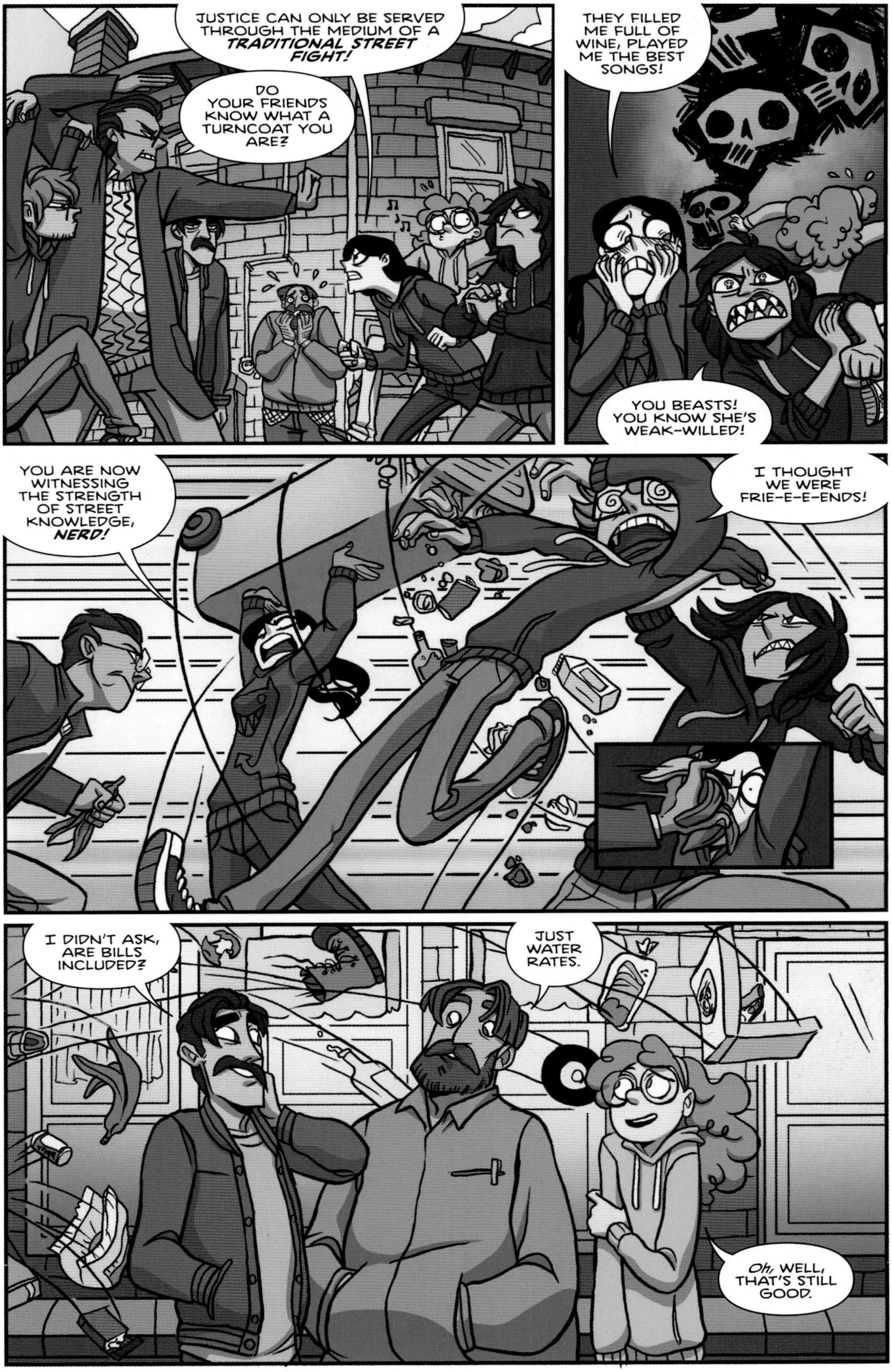
JUSTICE CAN ONLY BE SERVED THROUGH THE MEDIUM OF A TRADITIONAL STREET FIGHT!
DO YOUR FRIENDS KNOW WHAT A TURNCOAT YOU ARE?
THEY FILLED ME FULL OF WINE, PLAYED ME THE BEST SONGS!
YOU BEASTS! YOU KNOW SHE'S WEAK-WILLED!
YOU ARE NOW WITNESSING THE STRENGTH OF STREET KNOWLEDGE, NERD!
I THOUGHT WE WERE FRIE-E-E-ENDS!
I DIDN'T ASK, ARE BILLS INCLUDED?
JUST WATER RATES.
Oh, WELL, THAT'S STILL GOOD.

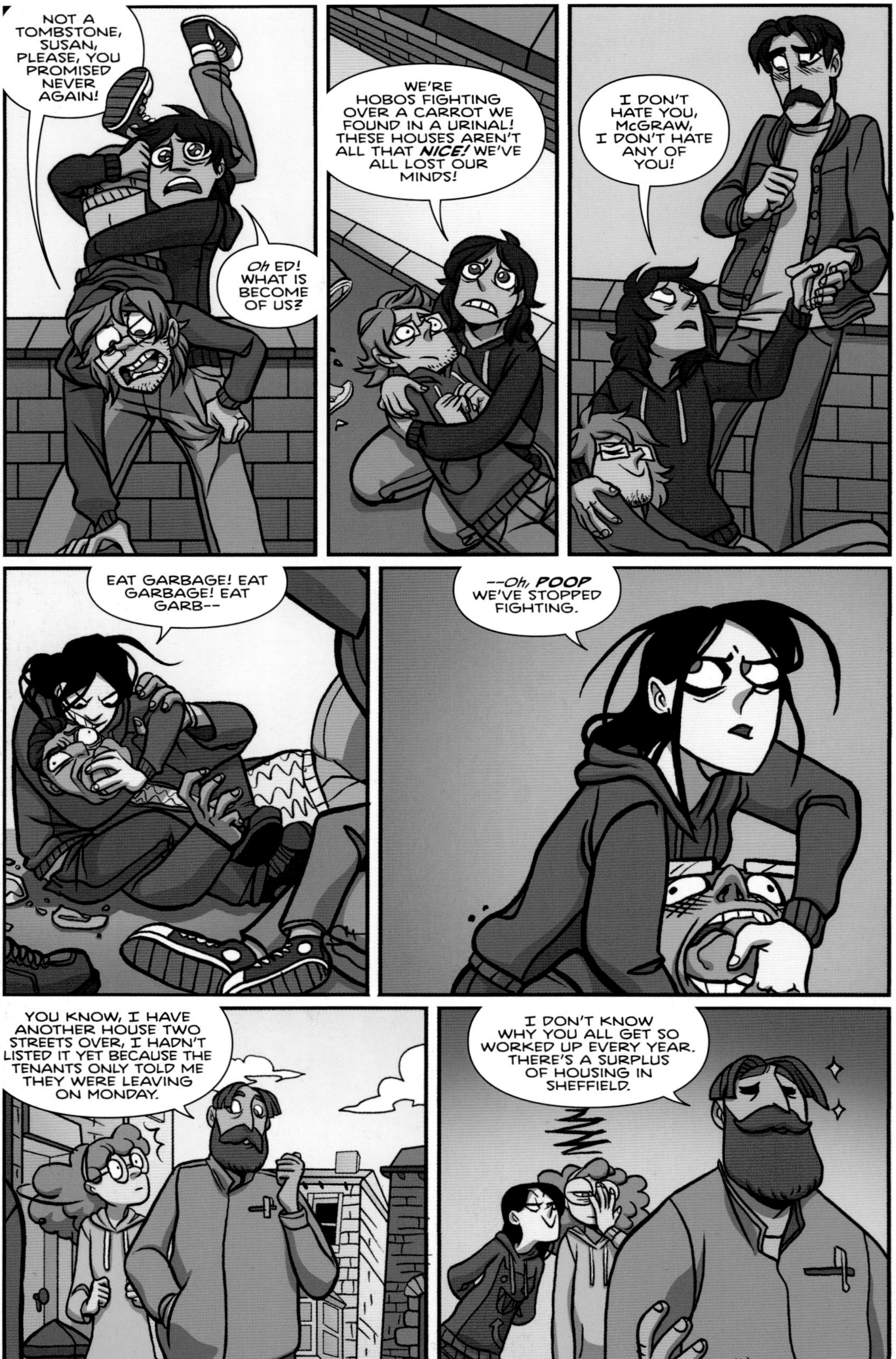
NOT A TOMBSTONE, SUSAN, PLEASE, YOU PROMISED NEVER AGAIN!
Oh ED! WHAT IS BECOME OF US?
WE'RE HOBOS FIGHTING OVER A CARROT WE FOUND IN A URINAL! THESE HOUSES AREN'T ALL THAT ***NICE!*** WE'VE ALL LOST OUR MINDS!
I DON'T HATE YOU, McGRAW, I DON'T HATE ANY OF YOU!
EAT GARBAGE! EAT GARBAGE! EAT GARB--
--*Oh*, ***POOP*** WE'VE STOPPED FIGHTING.
YOU KNOW, I HAVE ANOTHER HOUSE TWO STREETS OVER, I HADN'T LISTED IT YET BECAUSE THE TENANTS ONLY TOLD ME THEY WERE LEAVING ON MONDAY.
I DON'T KNOW WHY YOU ALL GET SO WORKED UP EVERY YEAR. THERE'S A SURPLUS OF HOUSING IN SHEFFIELD.

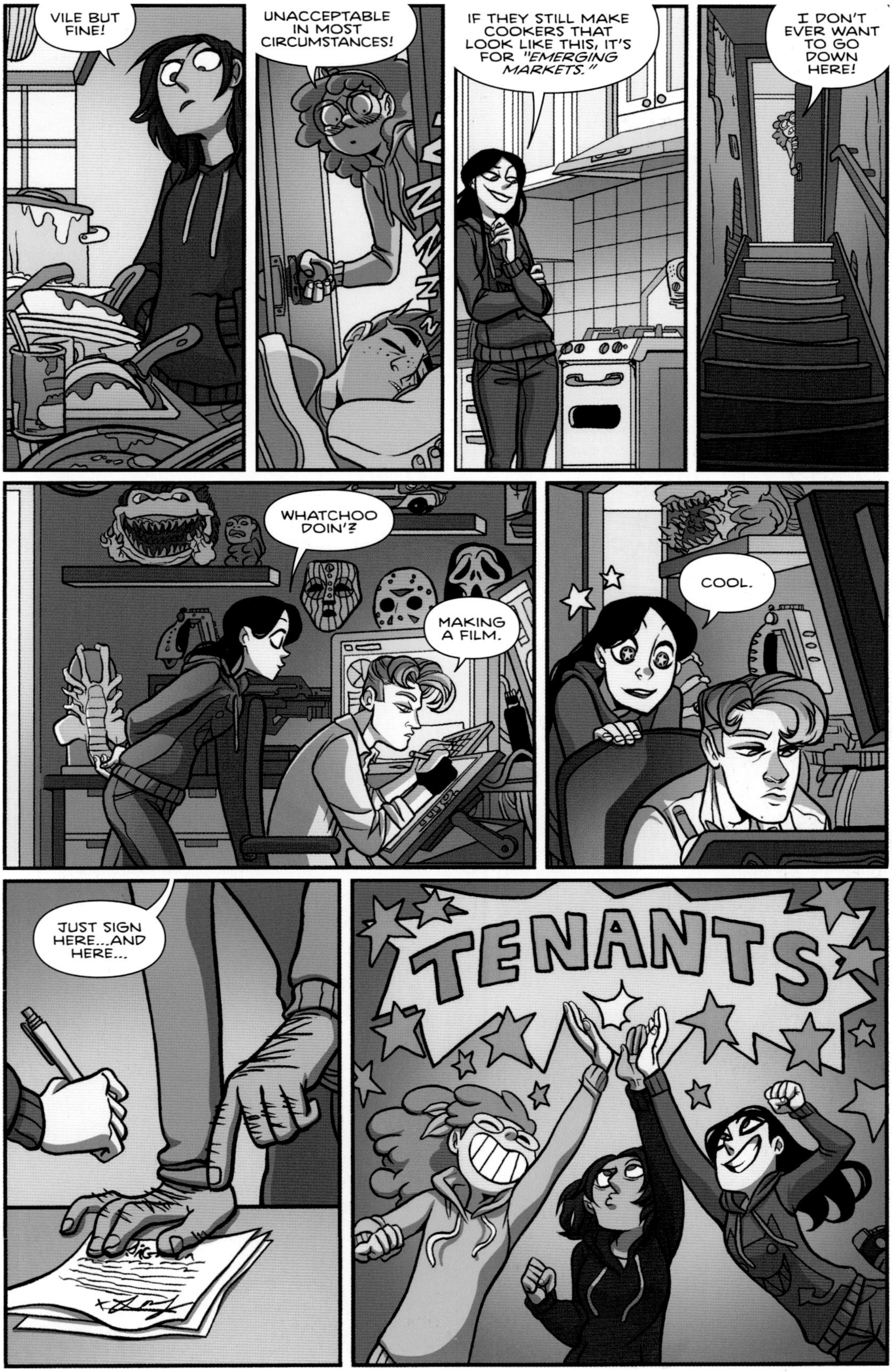
VILE BUT FINE!
UNACCEPTABLE IN MOST CIRCUMSTANCES!
IF THEY STILL MAKE COOKERS THAT LOOK LIKE THIS, IT'S FOR *"EMERGING MARKETS."*
I DON'T EVER WANT TO GO DOWN HERE!
WHATCHOO DOIN'?
MAKING A FILM.
COOL.
JUST SIGN HERE...AND HERE...
TENANTS

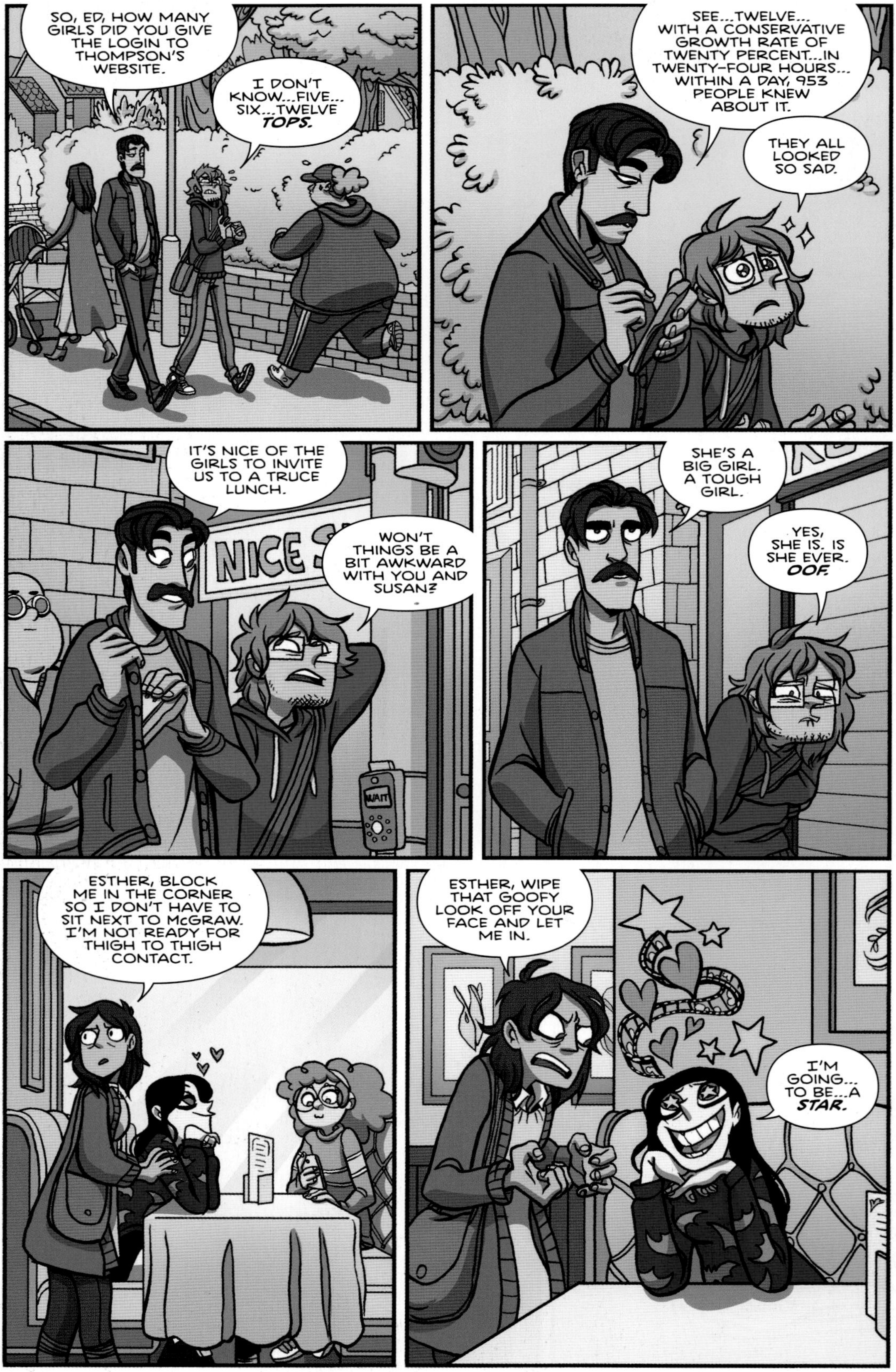
SO, ED, HOW MANY GIRLS DID YOU GIVE THE LOGIN TO THOMPSON'S WEBSITE.
I DON'T KNOW...FIVE... SIX...TWELVE *TOPS.*
SEE...TWELVE... WITH A CONSERVATIVE GROWTH RATE OF TWENTY PERCENT...IN TWENTY-FOUR HOURS... WITHIN A DAY, 953 PEOPLE KNEW ABOUT IT.
THEY ALL LOOKED SO SAD.
IT'S NICE OF THE GIRLS TO INVITE US TO A TRUCE LUNCH.
NICE
WON'T THINGS BE A BIT AWKWARD WITH YOU AND SUSAN?
WAIT
SHE'S A BIG GIRL. A TOUGH GIRL.
YES, SHE IS. IS SHE EVER. *OOF.*
ESTHER, BLOCK ME IN THE CORNER SO I DON'T HAVE TO SIT NEXT TO McGRAW. I'M NOT READY FOR THIGH TO THIGH CONTACT.
ESTHER, WIPE THAT GOOFY LOOK OFF YOUR FACE AND LET ME IN.
I'M GOING... TO BE...A *STAR.*

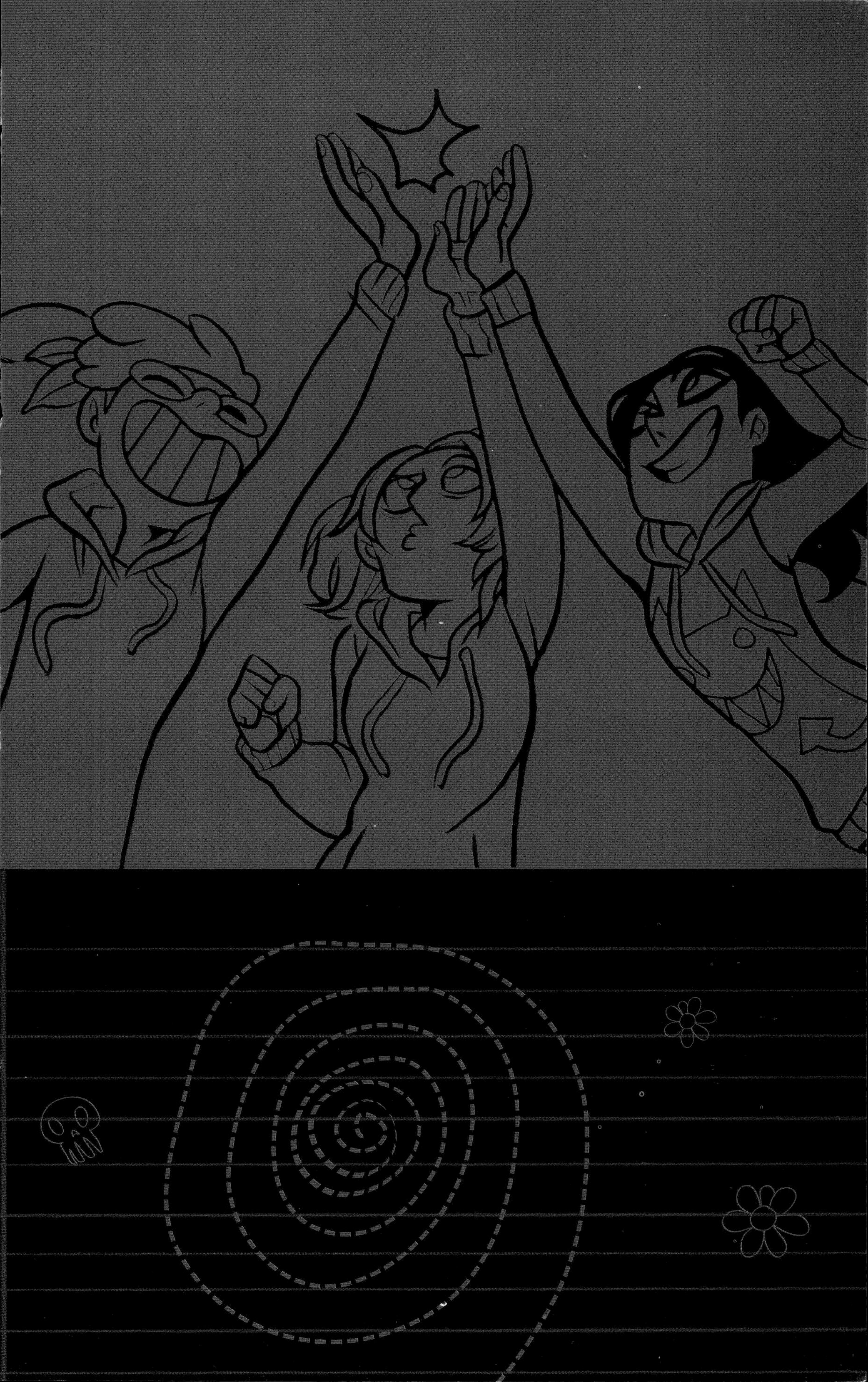

CHAPTER FIFTEEN

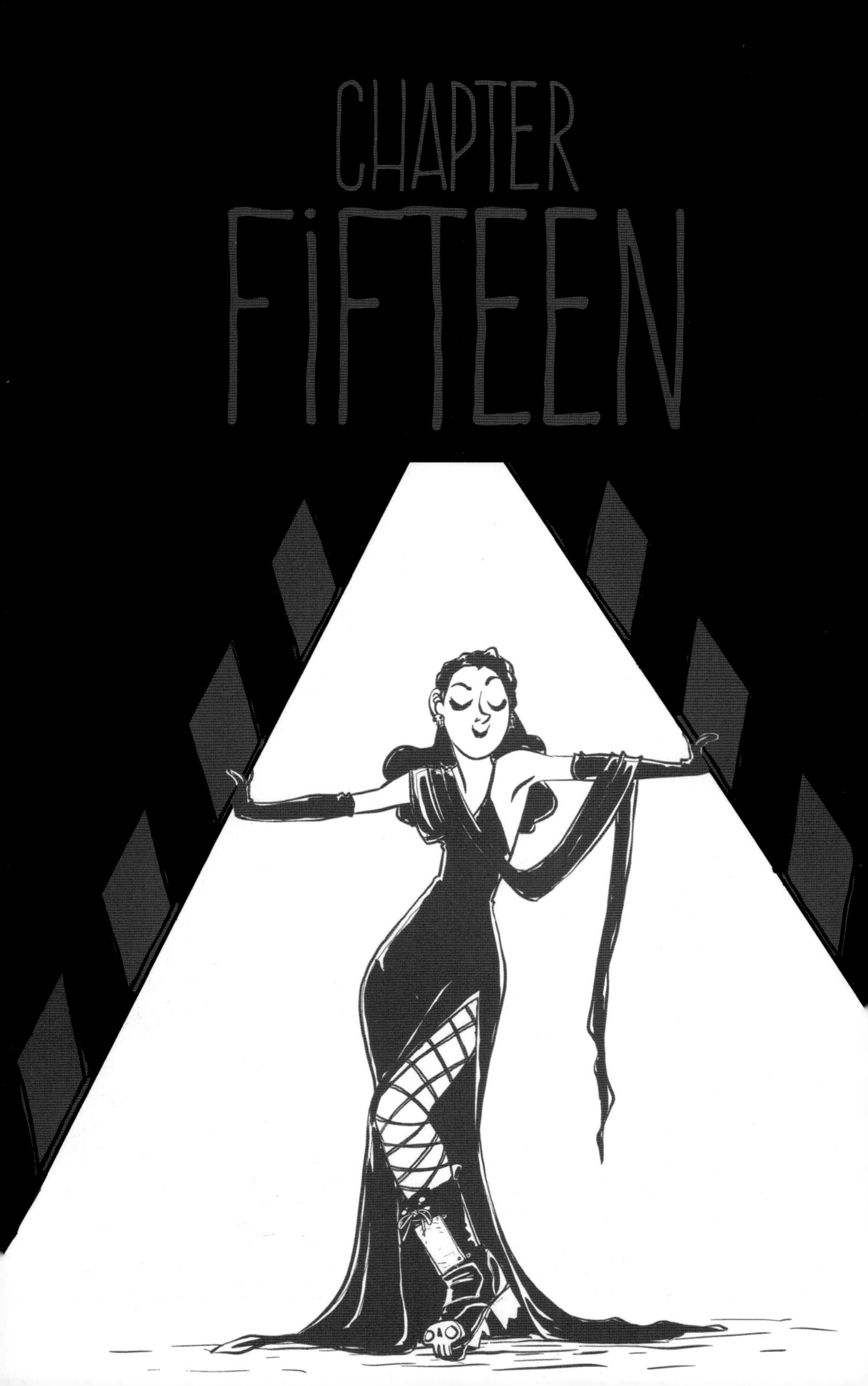

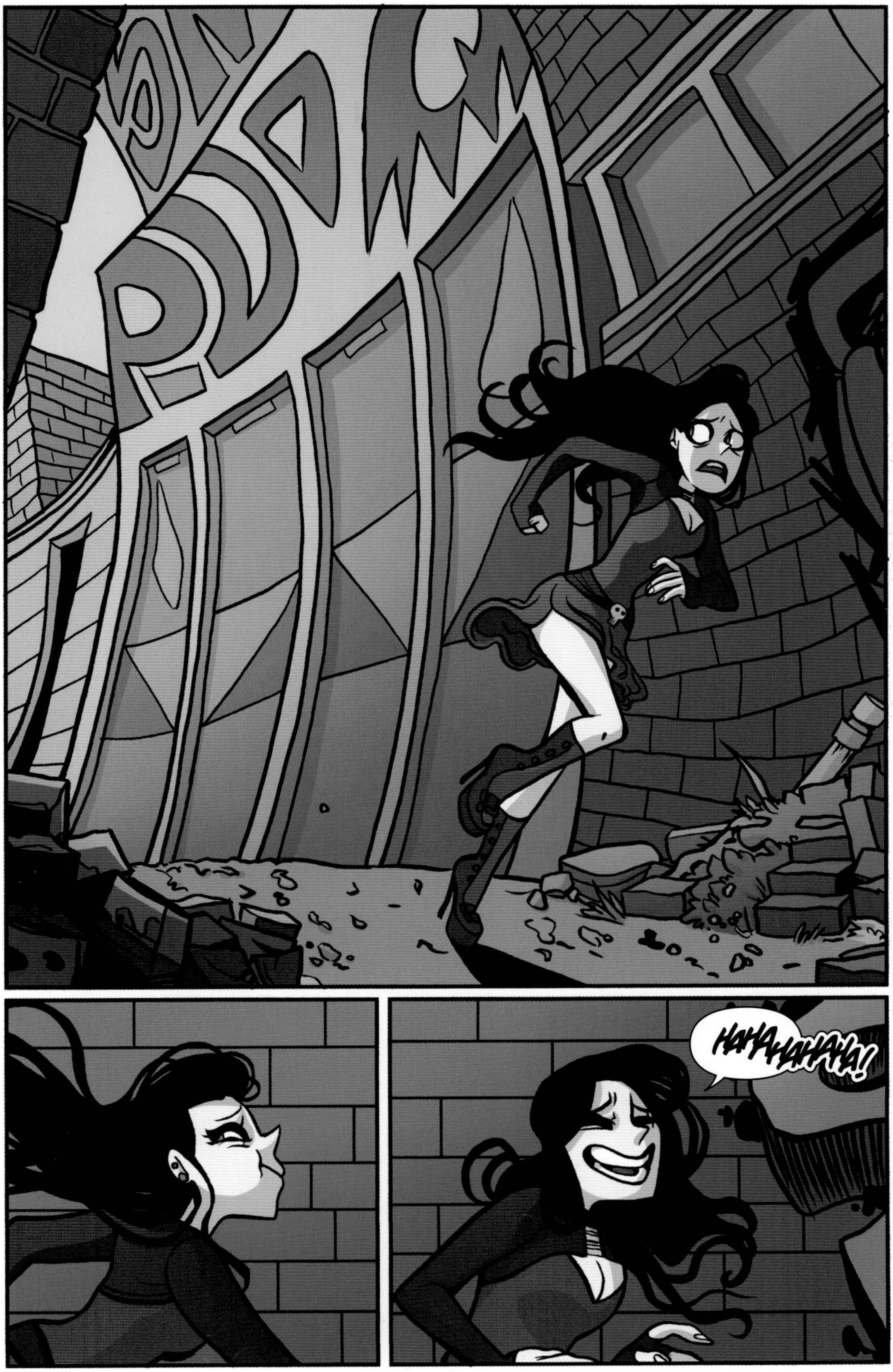
HAHAHAHAHAHA!

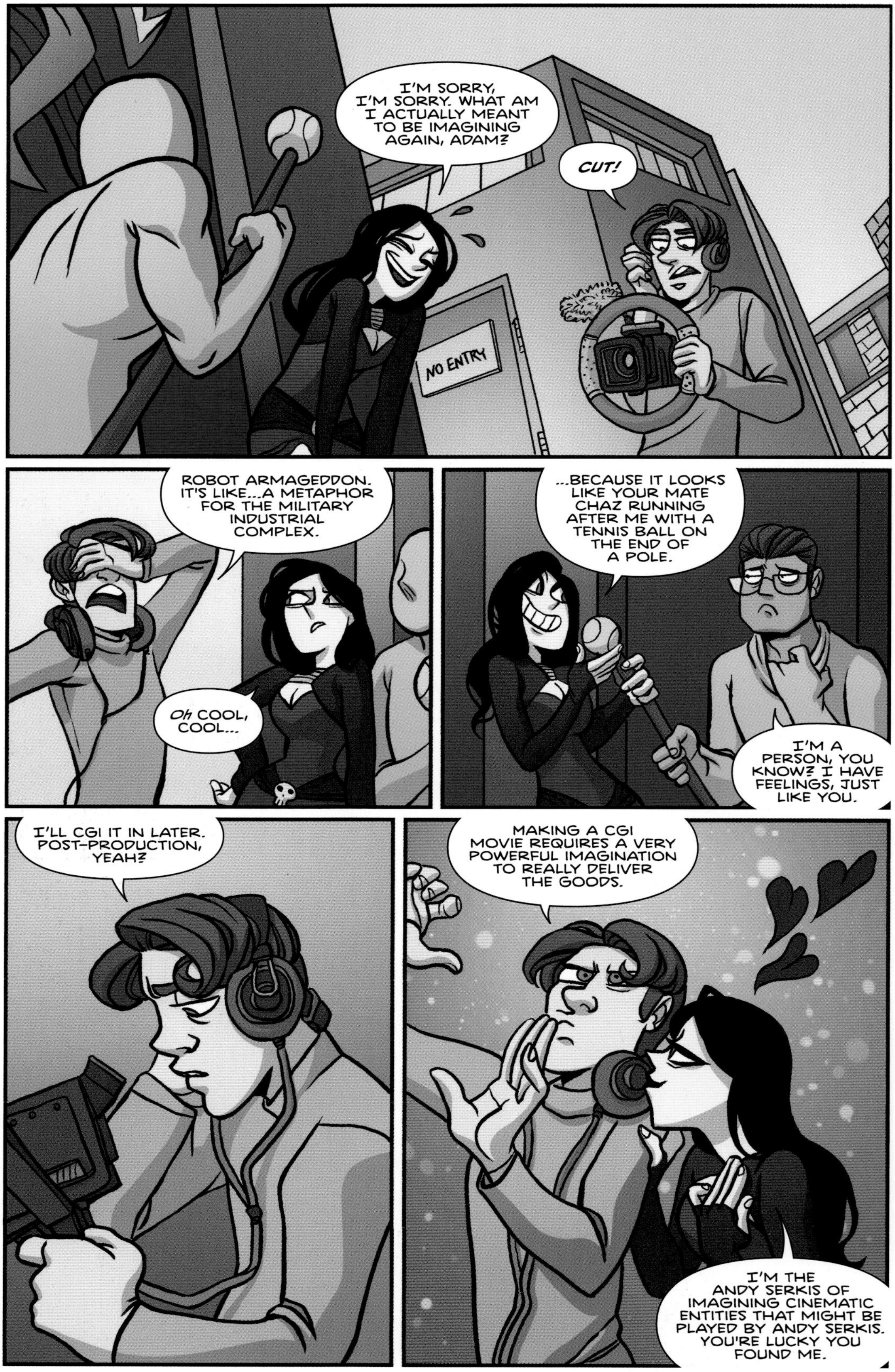

I'M SORRY, I'M SORRY. WHAT AM I ACTUALLY MEANT TO BE IMAGINING AGAIN, ADAM?
CUT!
NO ENTRY
ROBOT ARMAGEDDON. IT'S LIKE...A METAPHOR FOR THE MILITARY INDUSTRIAL COMPLEX.
Oh COOL, COOL...
...BECAUSE IT LOOKS LIKE YOUR MATE CHAZ RUNNING AFTER ME WITH A TENNIS BALL ON THE END OF A POLE.
I'M A PERSON, YOU KNOW? I HAVE FEELINGS, JUST LIKE YOU.
I'LL CGI IT IN LATER. POST-PRODUCTION, YEAH?
MAKING A CGI MOVIE REQUIRES A VERY POWERFUL IMAGINATION TO REALLY DELIVER THE GOODS.
I'M THE ANDY SERKIS OF IMAGINING CINEMATIC ENTITIES THAT MIGHT BE PLAYED BY ANDY SERKIS. YOU'RE LUCKY YOU FOUND ME.

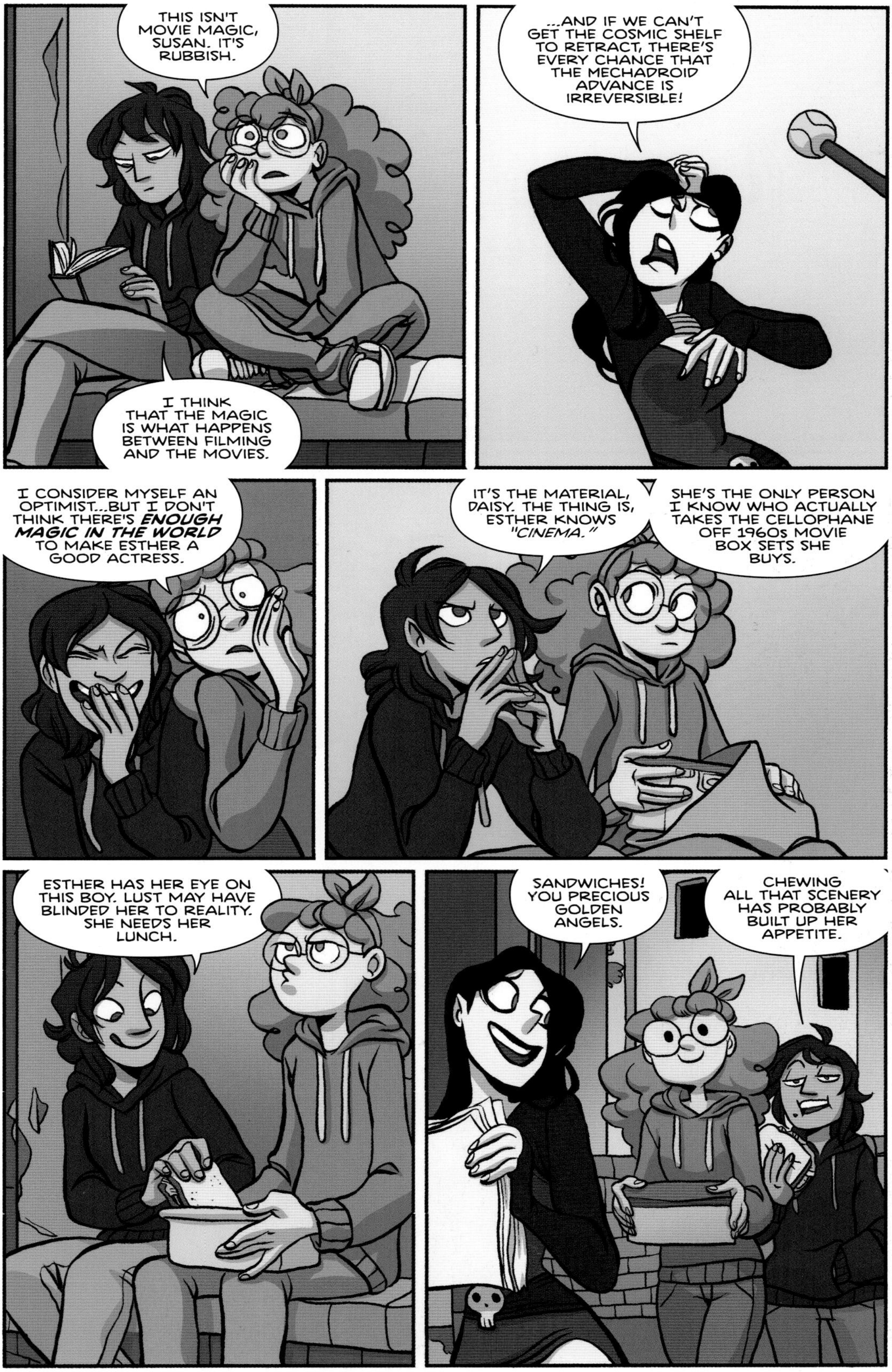
THIS ISN'T MOVIE MAGIC, SUSAN. IT'S RUBBISH.
I THINK THAT THE MAGIC IS WHAT HAPPENS BETWEEN FILMING AND THE MOVIES.
...AND IF WE CAN'T GET THE COSMIC SHELF TO RETRACT, THERE'S EVERY CHANCE THAT THE MECHADROID ADVANCE IS IRREVERSIBLE!
I CONSIDER MYSELF AN OPTIMIST...BUT I DON'T THINK THERE'S ENOUGH MAGIC IN THE WORLD TO MAKE ESTHER A GOOD ACTRESS.
IT'S THE MATERIAL, DAISY. THE THING IS, ESTHER KNOWS "CINEMA."
SHE'S THE ONLY PERSON I KNOW WHO ACTUALLY TAKES THE CELLOPHANE OFF 1960s MOVIE BOX SETS SHE BUYS.
ESTHER HAS HER EYE ON THIS BOY. LUST MAY HAVE BLINDED HER TO REALITY. SHE NEEDS HER LUNCH.
SANDWICHES! YOU PRECIOUS GOLDEN ANGELS.
CHEWING ALL THAT SCENERY HAS PROBABLY BUILT UP HER APPETITE.

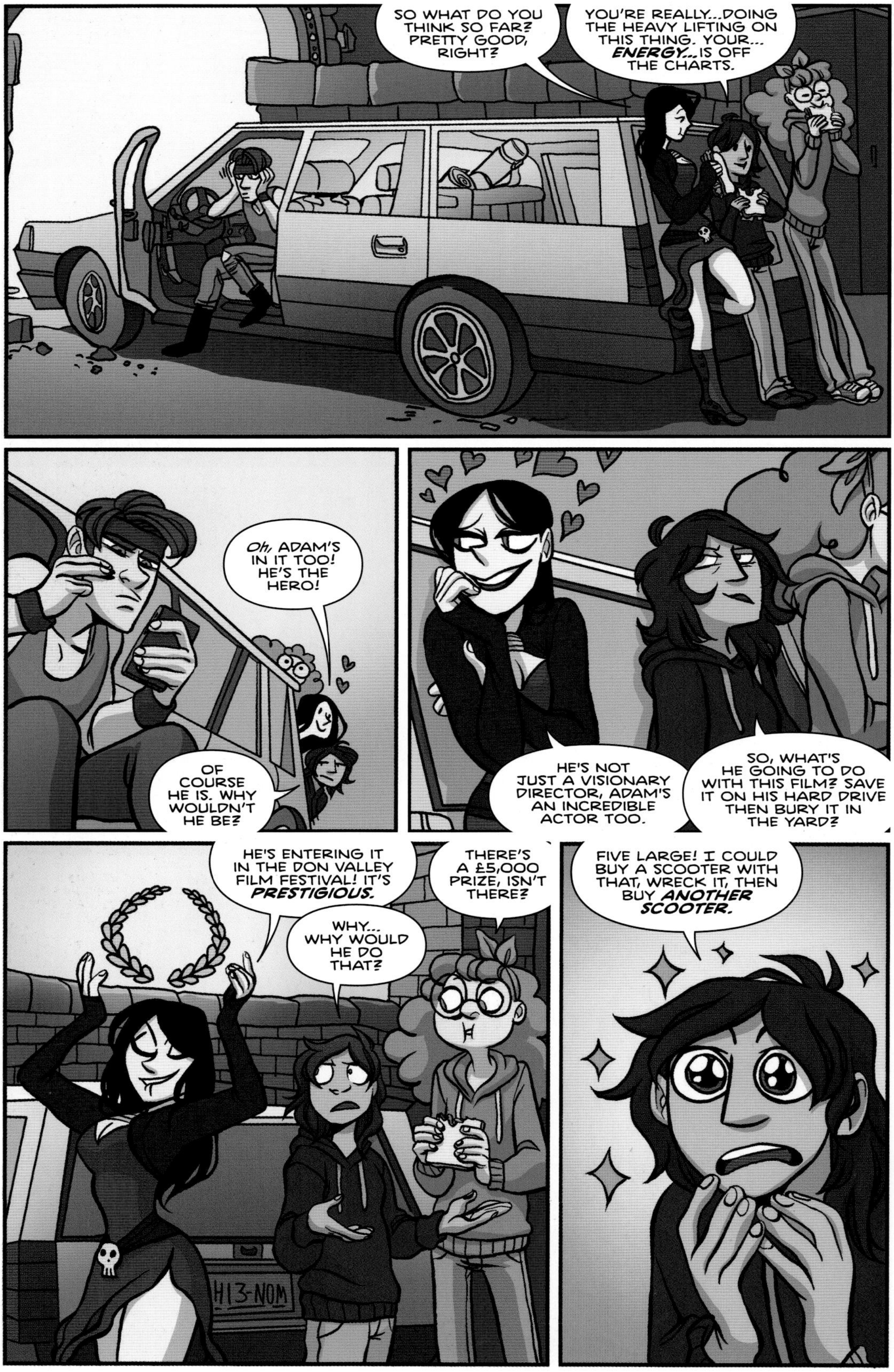

SO WHAT DO YOU THINK SO FAR? PRETTY GOOD, RIGHT?
YOU'RE REALLY...DOING THE HEAVY LIFTING ON THIS THING. YOUR... ENERGY... IS OFF THE CHARTS.
Oh, ADAM'S IN IT TOO! HE'S THE HERO!
OF COURSE HE IS. WHY WOULDN'T HE BE?
HE'S NOT JUST A VISIONARY DIRECTOR, ADAM'S AN INCREDIBLE ACTOR TOO.
SO, WHAT'S HE GOING TO DO WITH THIS FILM? SAVE IT ON HIS HARD DRIVE THEN BURY IT IN THE YARD?
HE'S ENTERING IT IN THE DON VALLEY FILM FESTIVAL! IT'S PRESTIGIOUS.
WHY... WHY WOULD HE DO THAT?
THERE'S A £5,000 PRIZE, ISN'T THERE?
H13-NOM
FIVE LARGE! I COULD BUY A SCOOTER WITH THAT, WRECK IT, THEN BUY ANOTHER SCOOTER.

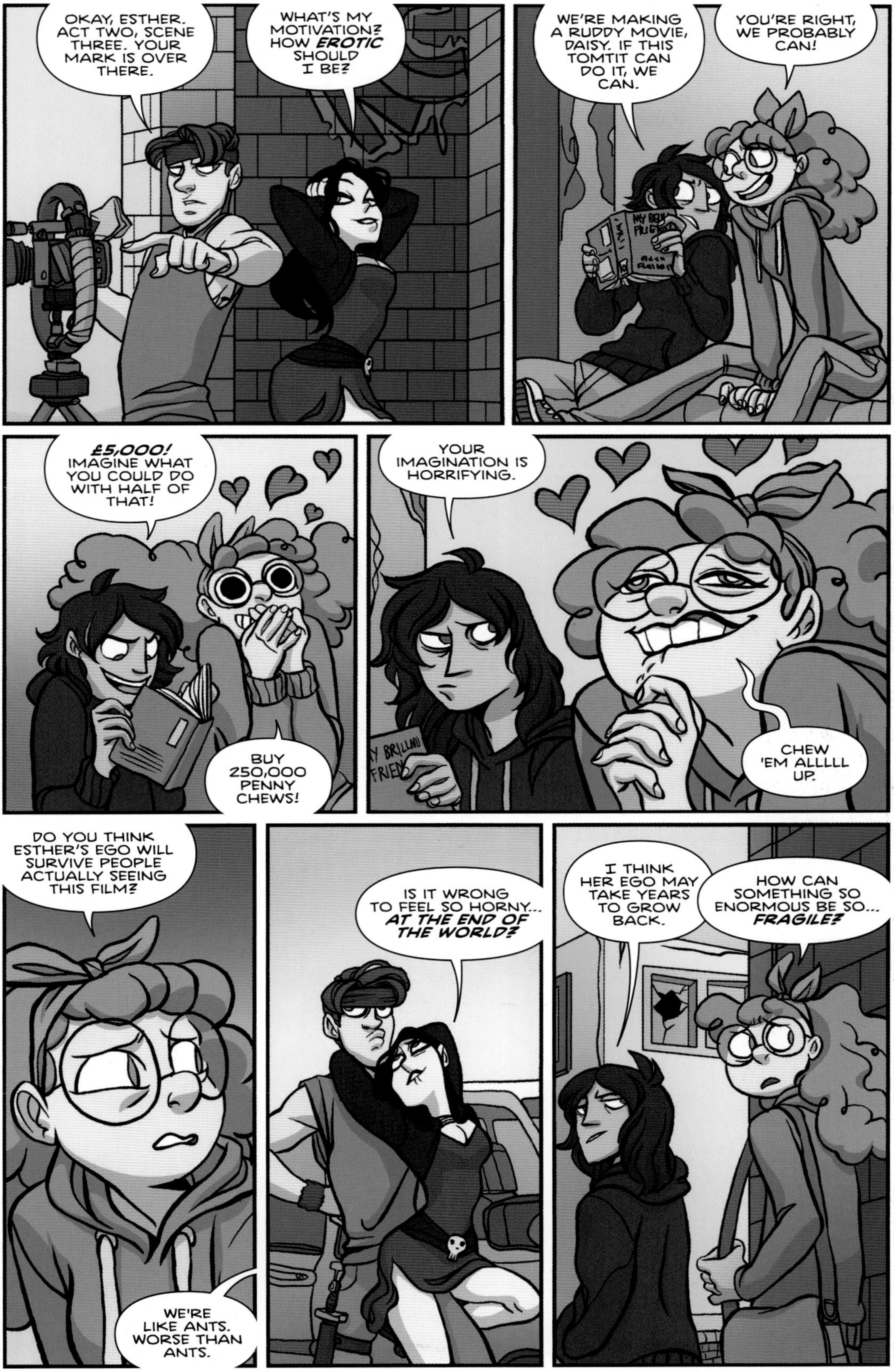
OKAY, ESTHER. ACT TWO, SCENE THREE. YOUR MARK IS OVER THERE.
WHAT'S MY MOTIVATION? HOW EROTIC SHOULD I BE?
WE'RE MAKING A RUDDY MOVIE, DAISY. IF THIS TOMTIT CAN DO IT, WE CAN.
YOU'RE RIGHT, WE PROBABLY CAN!
£5,000! IMAGINE WHAT YOU COULD DO WITH HALF OF THAT!
BUY 250,000 PENNY CHEWS!
YOUR IMAGINATION IS HORRIFYING.
CHEW 'EM ALLLLL UP.
DO YOU THINK ESTHER'S EGO WILL SURVIVE PEOPLE ACTUALLY SEEING THIS FILM?
WE'RE LIKE ANTS. WORSE THAN ANTS.
IS IT WRONG TO FEEL SO HORNY... AT THE END OF THE WORLD?
I THINK HER EGO MAY TAKE YEARS TO GROW BACK.
HOW CAN SOMETHING SO ENORMOUS BE SO... FRAGILE?

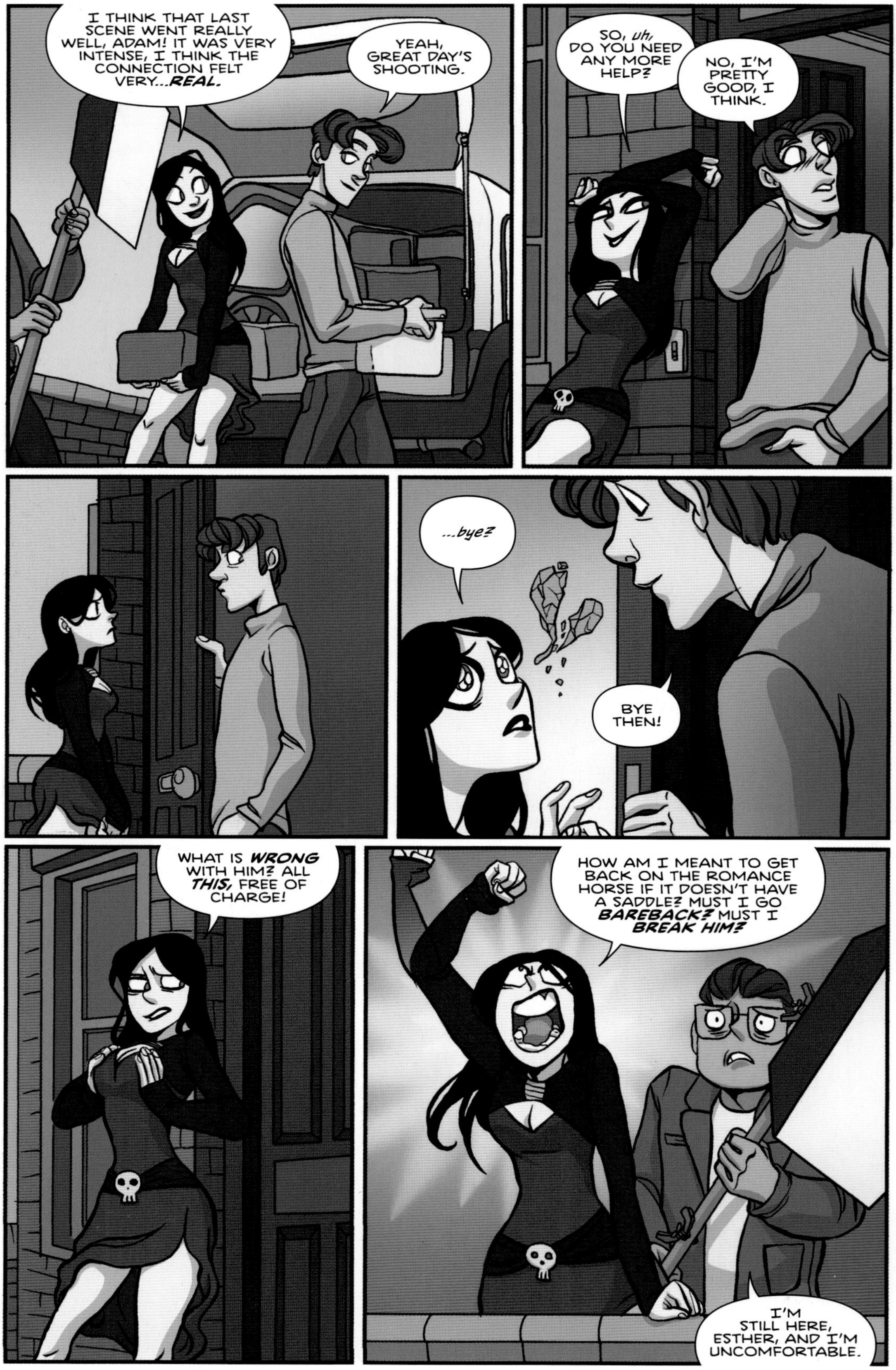
I THINK THAT LAST SCENE WENT REALLY WELL, ADAM! IT WAS VERY INTENSE, I THINK THE CONNECTION FELT VERY...REAL.
YEAH, GREAT DAY'S SHOOTING.
SO, uh, DO YOU NEED ANY MORE HELP?
NO, I'M PRETTY GOOD, I THINK.
...bye?
BYE THEN!
WHAT IS WRONG WITH HIM? ALL THIS, FREE OF CHARGE!
HOW AM I MEANT TO GET BACK ON THE ROMANCE HORSE IF IT DOESN'T HAVE A SADDLE? MUST I GO BAREBACK? MUST I BREAK HIM?
I'M STILL HERE, ESTHER, AND I'M UNCOMFORTABLE.

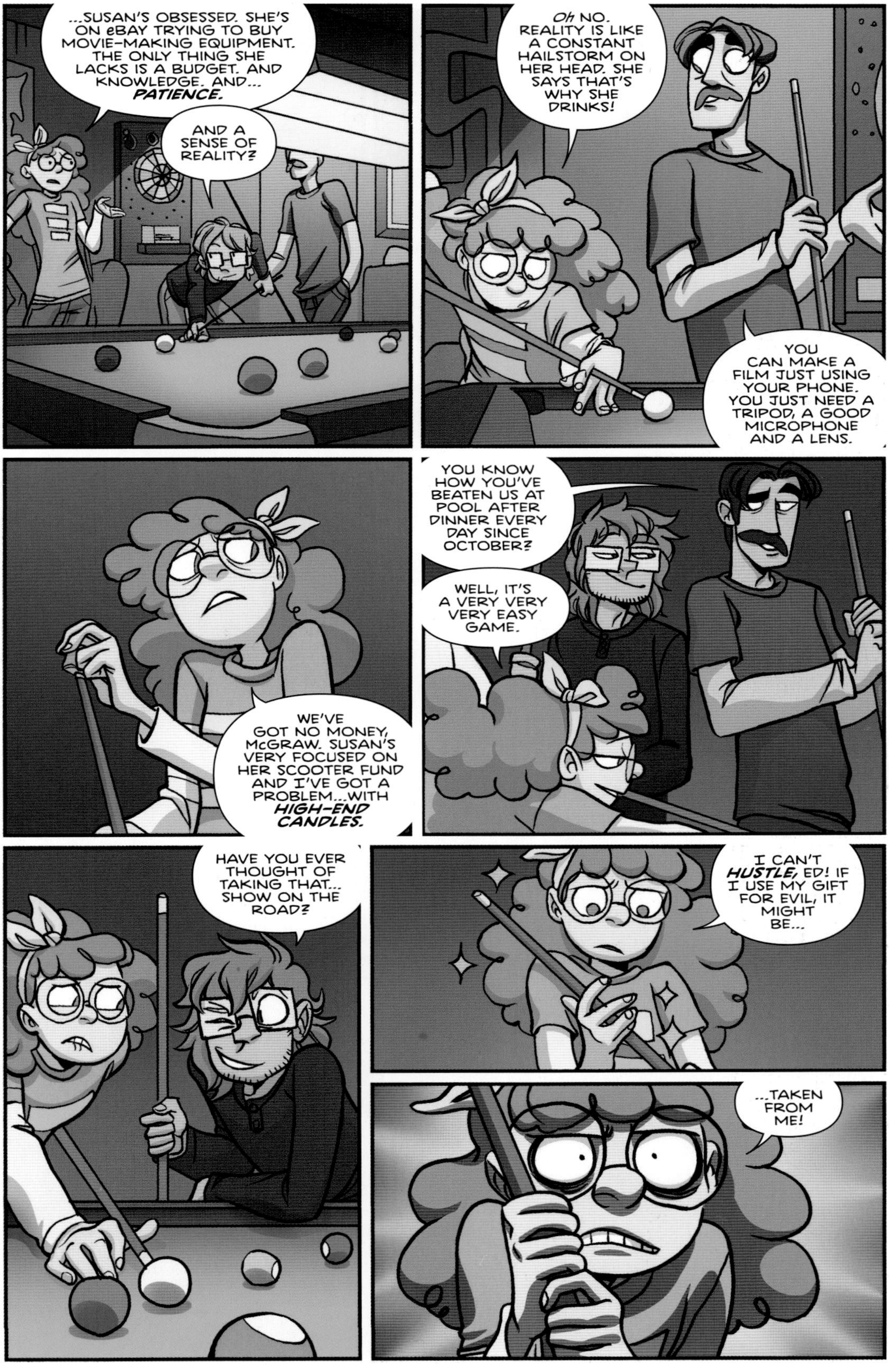
...SUSAN'S OBSESSED. SHE'S ON eBAY TRYING TO BUY MOVIE-MAKING EQUIPMENT. THE ONLY THING SHE LACKS IS A BUDGET. AND KNOWLEDGE. AND... PATIENCE.
AND A SENSE OF REALITY?
Oh NO. REALITY IS LIKE A CONSTANT HAILSTORM ON HER HEAD. SHE SAYS THAT'S WHY SHE DRINKS!
YOU CAN MAKE A FILM JUST USING YOUR PHONE. YOU JUST NEED A TRIPOD, A GOOD MICROPHONE AND A LENS.
WE'VE GOT NO MONEY, McGRAW. SUSAN'S VERY FOCUSED ON HER SCOOTER FUND AND I'VE GOT A PROBLEM...WITH HIGH-END CANDLES.
YOU KNOW HOW YOU'VE BEATEN US AT POOL AFTER DINNER EVERY DAY SINCE OCTOBER?
WELL, IT'S A VERY VERY VERY EASY GAME.
HAVE YOU EVER THOUGHT OF TAKING THAT... SHOW ON THE ROAD?
I CAN'T HUSTLE, ED! IF I USE MY GIFT FOR EVIL, IT MIGHT BE...
...TAKEN FROM ME!

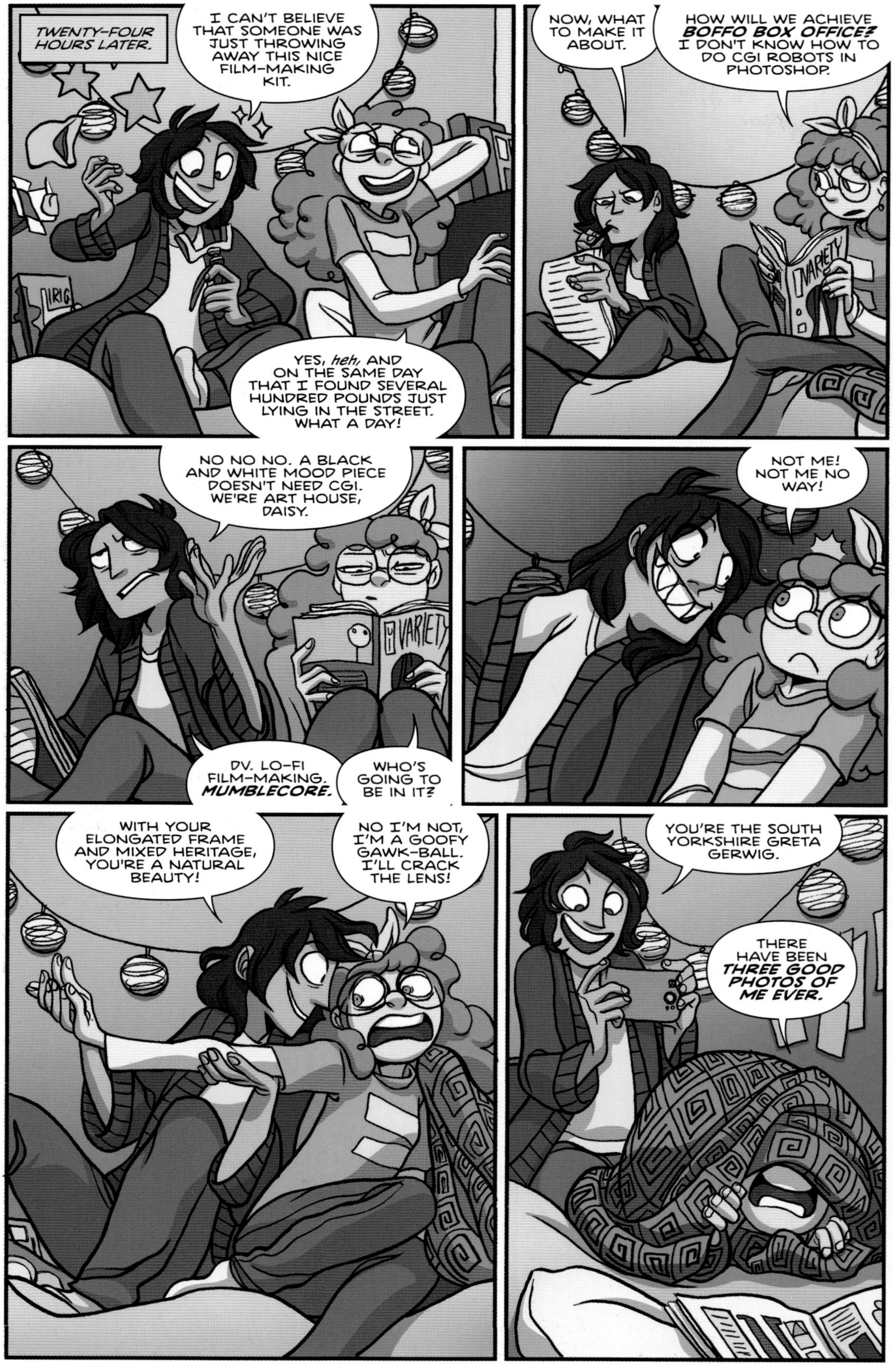
TWENTY-FOUR HOURS LATER.
I CAN'T BELIEVE THAT SOMEONE WAS JUST THROWING AWAY THIS NICE FILM-MAKING KIT.
YES, *heh*, AND ON THE SAME DAY THAT I FOUND SEVERAL HUNDRED POUNDS JUST LYING IN THE STREET. WHAT A DAY!
NOW, WHAT TO MAKE IT ABOUT.
HOW WILL WE ACHIEVE ***BOFFO BOX OFFICE?*** I DON'T KNOW HOW TO DO CGI ROBOTS IN PHOTOSHOP.
VARIETY
NO NO NO. A BLACK AND WHITE MOOD PIECE DOESN'T NEED CGI. WE'RE ART HOUSE, DAISY.
DV. LO-FI FILM-MAKING. ***MUMBLECORE.***
WHO'S GOING TO BE IN IT?
VARIETY
NOT ME! NOT ME NO WAY!
WITH YOUR ELONGATED FRAME AND MIXED HERITAGE, YOU'RE A NATURAL BEAUTY!
NO I'M NOT, I'M A GOOFY GAWK-BALL. I'LL CRACK THE LENS!
YOU'RE THE SOUTH YORKSHIRE GRETA GERWIG.
THERE HAVE BEEN ***THREE GOOD PHOTOS OF ME EVER.***

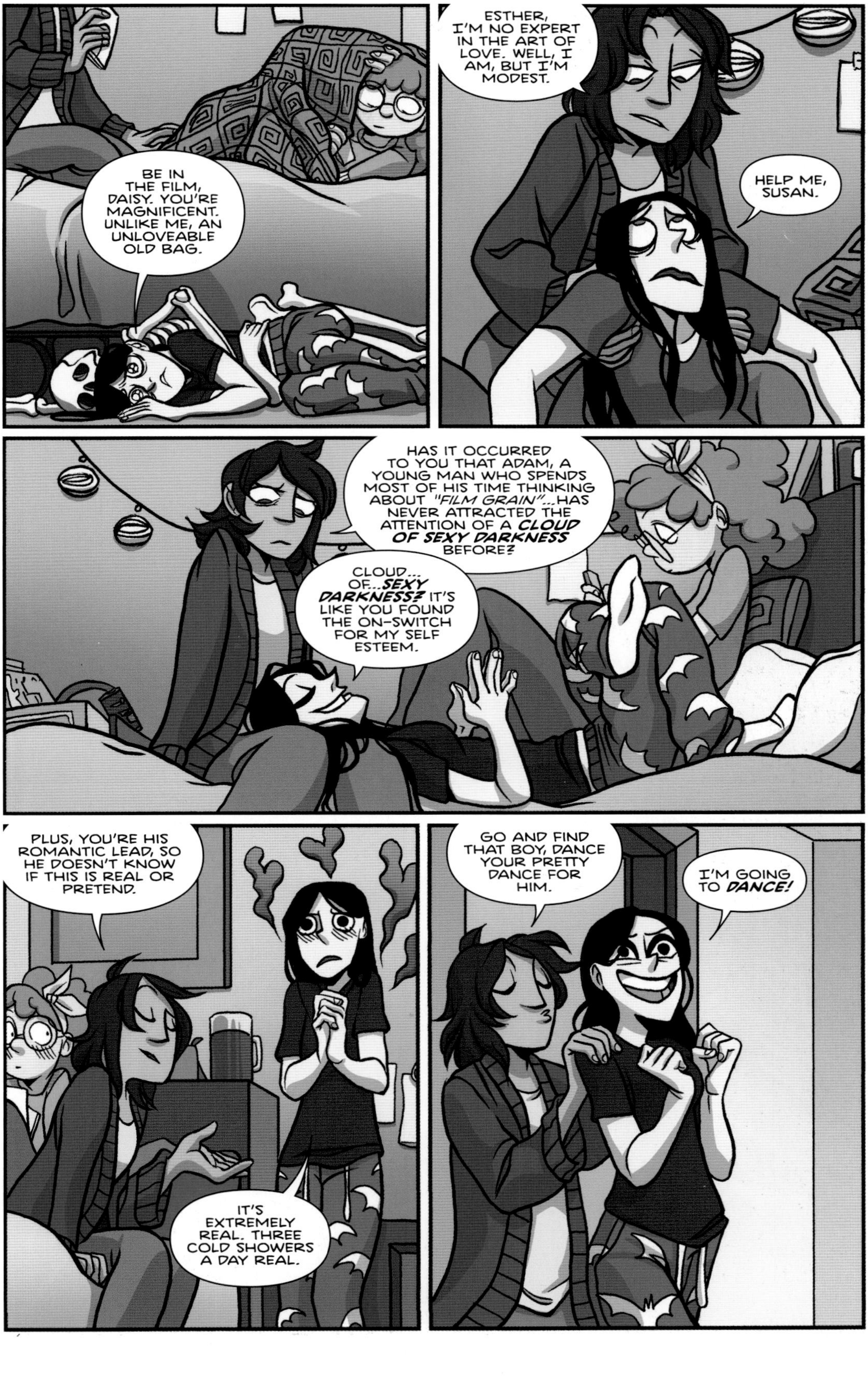
BE IN THE FILM, DAISY. YOU'RE MAGNIFICENT. UNLIKE ME, AN UNLOVEABLE OLD BAG.
ESTHER, I'M NO EXPERT IN THE ART OF LOVE. WELL, I AM, BUT I'M MODEST.
HELP ME, SUSAN.
HAS IT OCCURRED TO YOU THAT ADAM, A YOUNG MAN WHO SPENDS MOST OF HIS TIME THINKING ABOUT "FILM GRAIN"...HAS NEVER ATTRACTED THE ATTENTION OF A CLOUD OF SEXY DARKNESS BEFORE?
CLOUD... OF...SEXY DARKNESS? IT'S LIKE YOU FOUND THE ON-SWITCH FOR MY SELF ESTEEM.
PLUS, YOU'RE HIS ROMANTIC LEAD, SO HE DOESN'T KNOW IF THIS IS REAL OR PRETEND.
IT'S EXTREMELY REAL. THREE COLD SHOWERS A DAY REAL.
GO AND FIND THAT BOY, DANCE YOUR PRETTY DANCE FOR HIM.
I'M GOING TO DANCE!

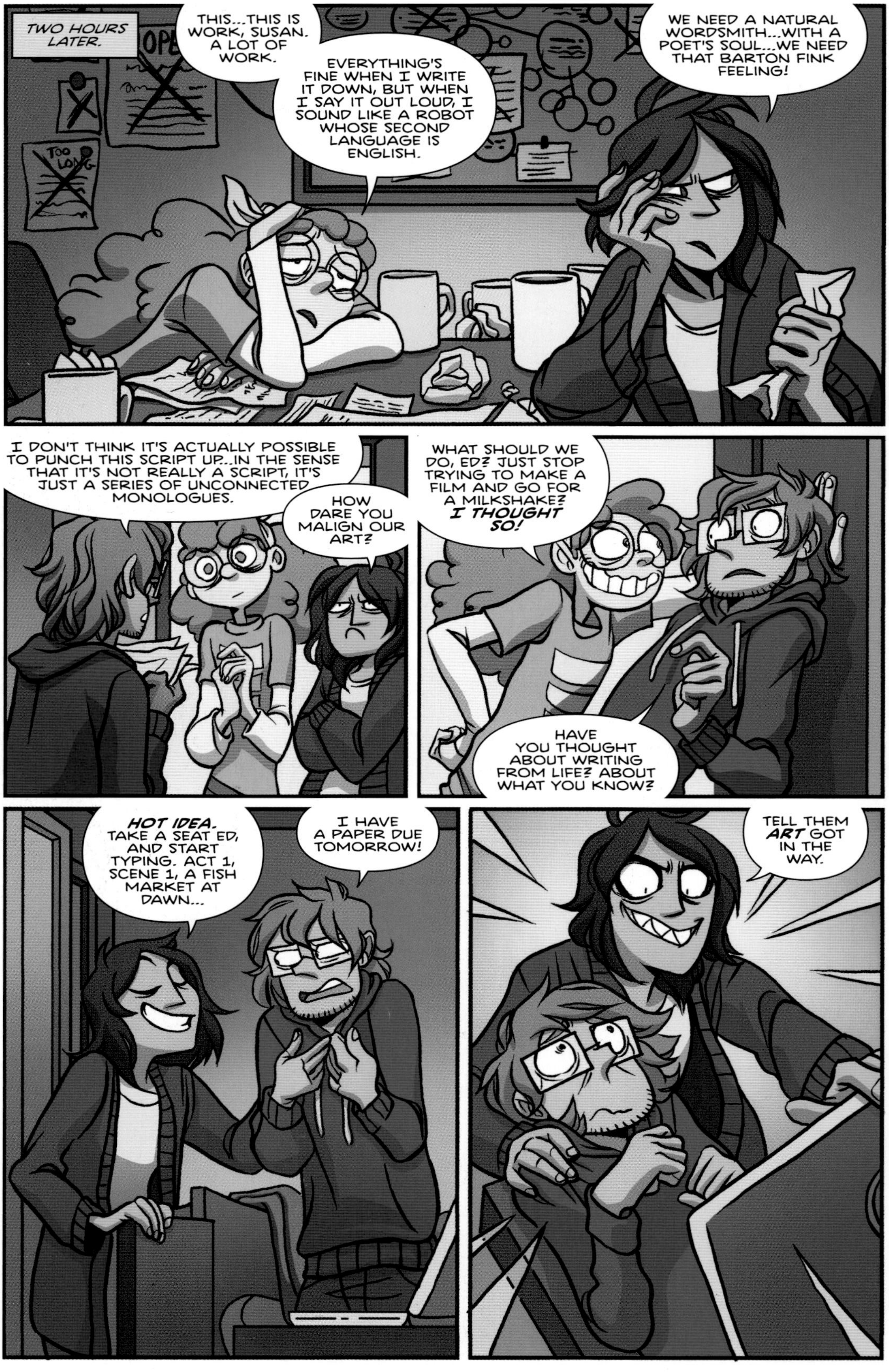
TWO HOURS LATER.
THIS...THIS IS WORK, SUSAN. A LOT OF WORK.
EVERYTHING'S FINE WHEN I WRITE IT DOWN, BUT WHEN I SAY IT OUT LOUD, I SOUND LIKE A ROBOT WHOSE SECOND LANGUAGE IS ENGLISH.
WE NEED A NATURAL WORDSMITH...WITH A POET'S SOUL...WE NEED THAT BARTON FINK FEELING!
I DON'T THINK IT'S ACTUALLY POSSIBLE TO PUNCH THIS SCRIPT UP...IN THE SENSE THAT IT'S NOT REALLY A SCRIPT, IT'S JUST A SERIES OF UNCONNECTED MONOLOGUES.
HOW DARE YOU MALIGN OUR ART?
WHAT SHOULD WE DO, ED? JUST STOP TRYING TO MAKE A FILM AND GO FOR A MILKSHAKE? I THOUGHT SO!
HAVE YOU THOUGHT ABOUT WRITING FROM LIFE? ABOUT WHAT YOU KNOW?
HOT IDEA. TAKE A SEAT ED, AND START TYPING. ACT 1, SCENE 1, A FISH MARKET AT DAWN...
I HAVE A PAPER DUE TOMORROW!
TELL THEM ART GOT IN THE WAY.

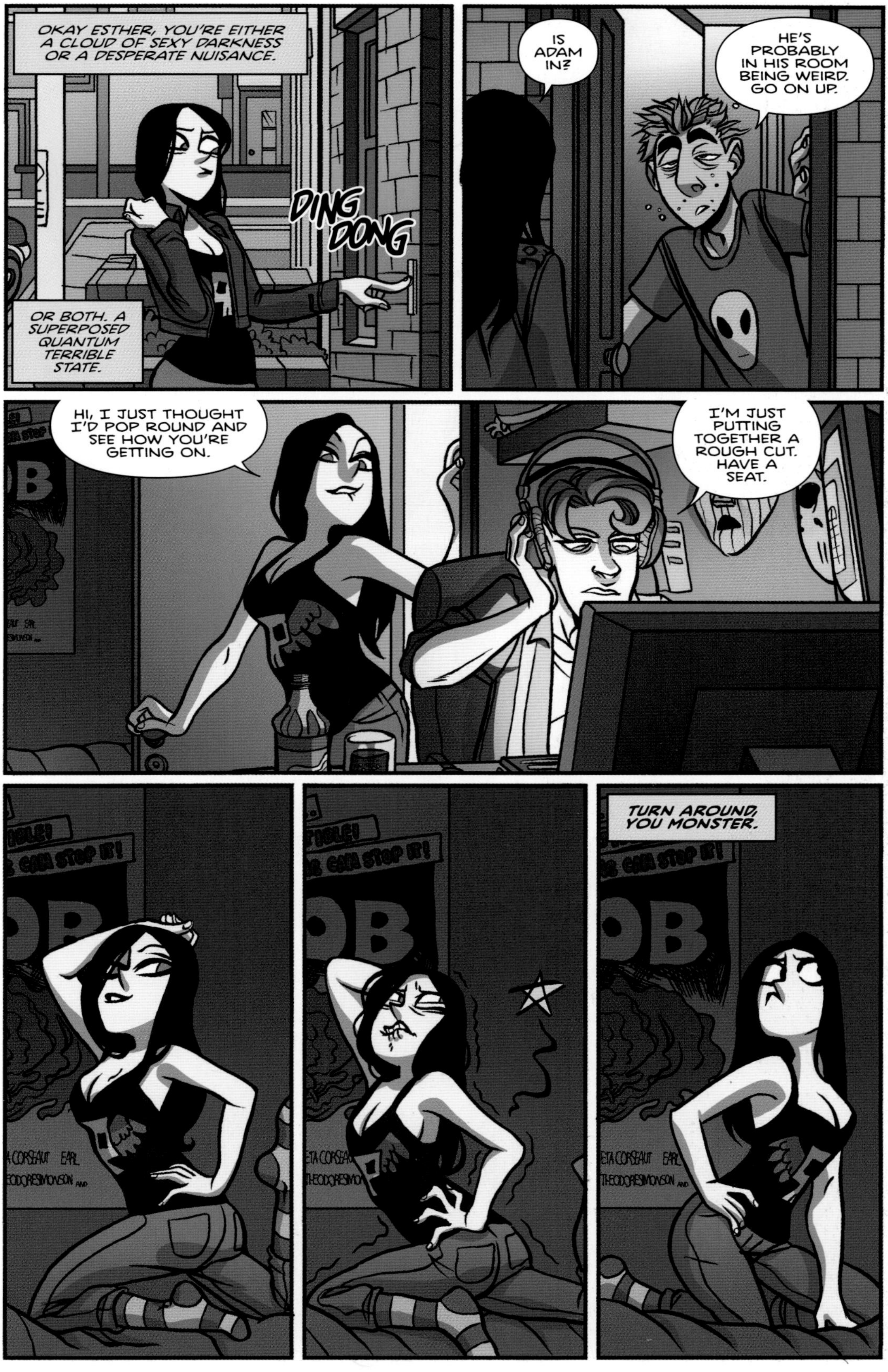
OKAY ESTHER, YOU'RE EITHER A CLOUD OF SEXY DARKNESS OR A DESPERATE NUISANCE.
DING DONG
OR BOTH. A SUPERPOSED QUANTUM TERRIBLE STATE.
IS ADAM IN?
HE'S PROBABLY IN HIS ROOM BEING WEIRD. GO ON UP.
HI, I JUST THOUGHT I'D POP ROUND AND SEE HOW YOU'RE GETTING ON.
I'M JUST PUTTING TOGETHER A ROUGH CUT. HAVE A SEAT.
TURN AROUND, YOU MONSTER.

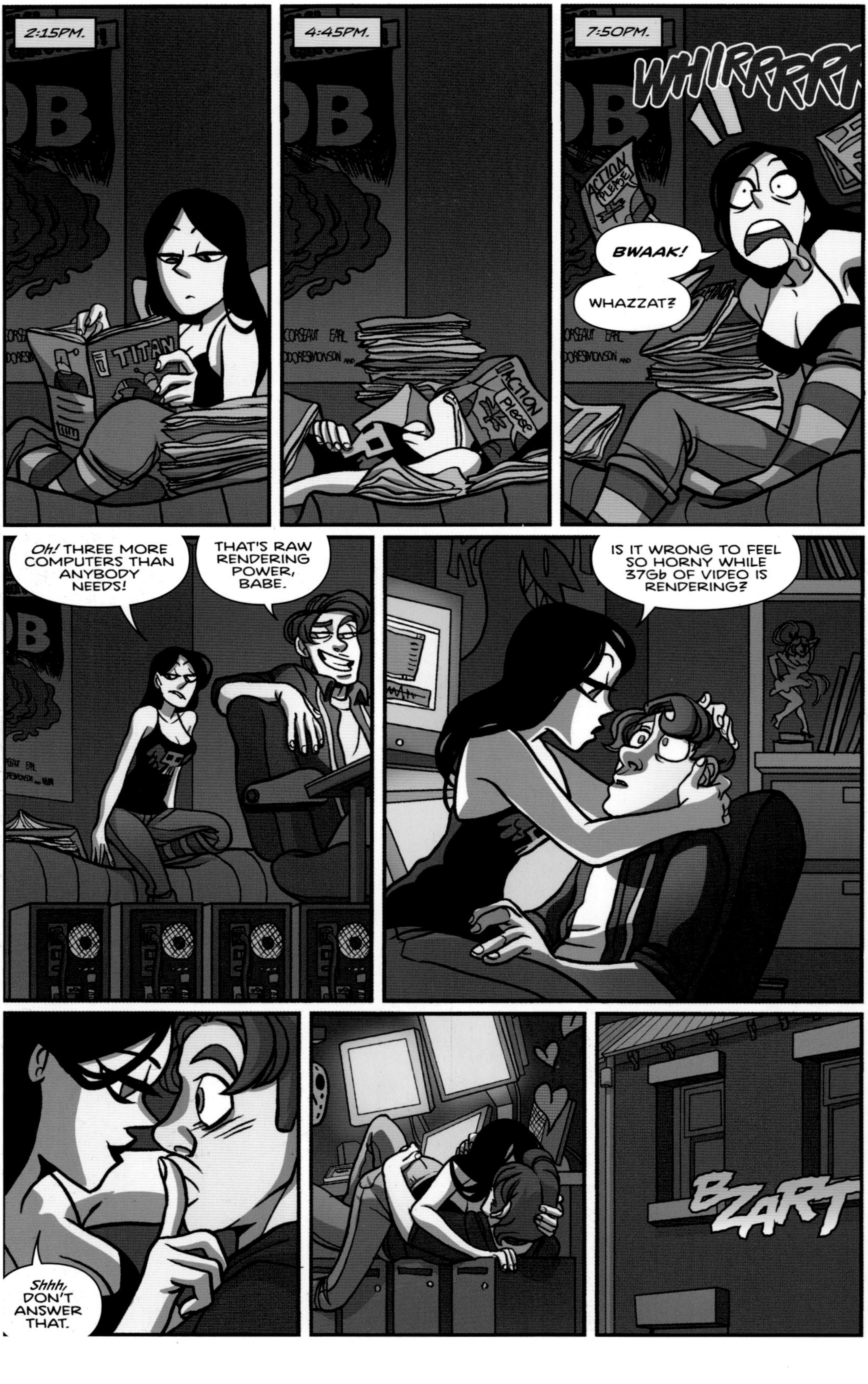
2:15PM.
TITAN
4:45PM.
ACTION Please
7:50PM.
WHIRRRRRR
BWAAK!
WHAZZAT?
Oh! THREE MORE COMPUTERS THAN ANYBODY NEEDS!
THAT'S RAW RENDERING POWER, BABE.
IS IT WRONG TO FEEL SO HORNY WHILE 37Gb OF VIDEO IS RENDERING?
Shhh, DON'T ANSWER THAT.
BZART

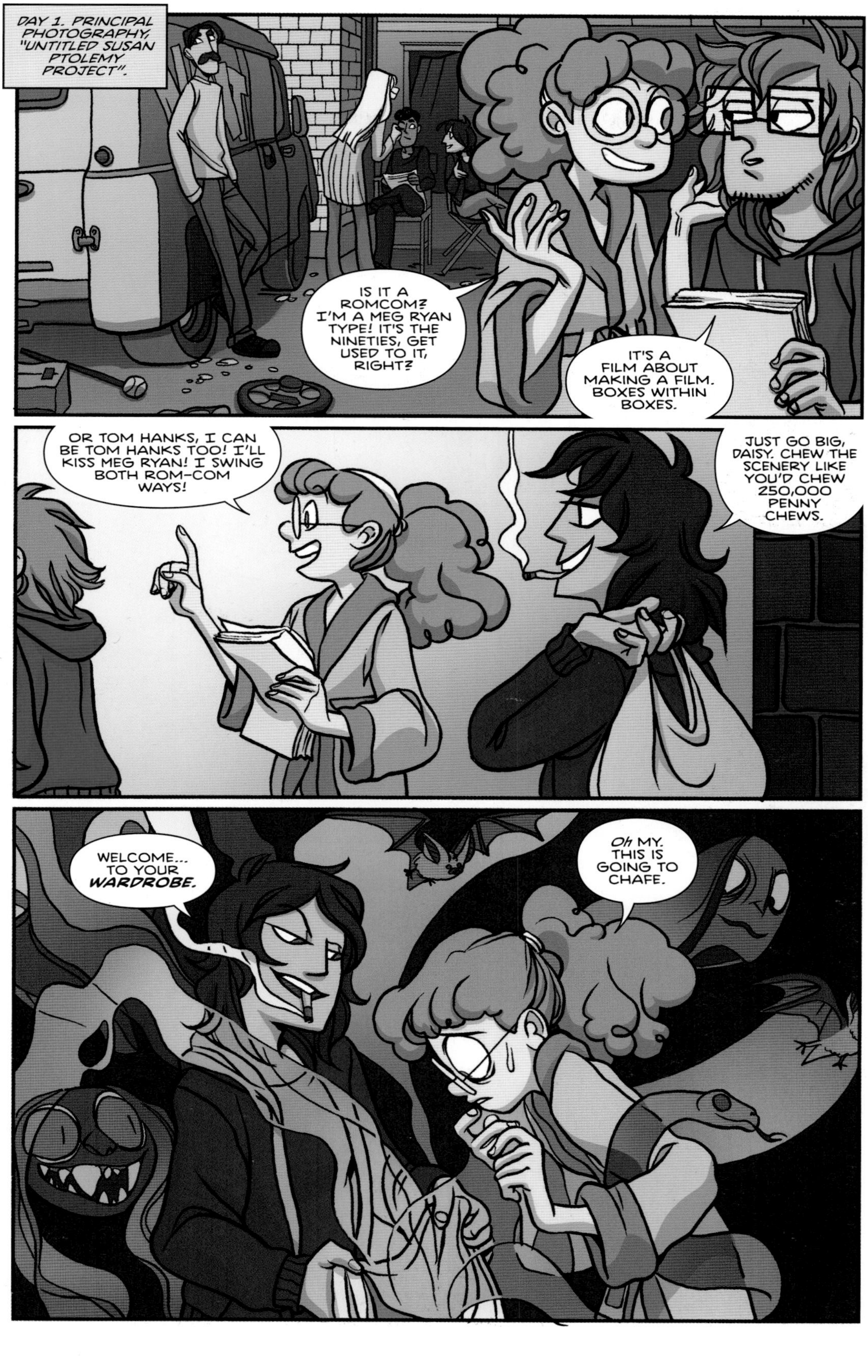
DAY 1. PRINCIPAL PHOTOGRAPHY, "UNTITLED SUSAN PTOLEMY PROJECT".
IS IT A ROMCOM? I'M A MEG RYAN TYPE! IT'S THE NINETIES, GET USED TO IT, RIGHT?
IT'S A FILM ABOUT MAKING A FILM. BOXES WITHIN BOXES.
OR TOM HANKS, I CAN BE TOM HANKS TOO! I'LL KISS MEG RYAN! I SWING BOTH ROM-COM WAYS!
JUST GO BIG, DAISY. CHEW THE SCENERY LIKE YOU'D CHEW 250,000 PENNY CHEWS.
WELCOME... TO YOUR ***WARDROBE.***
Oh MY. THIS IS GOING TO CHAFE.

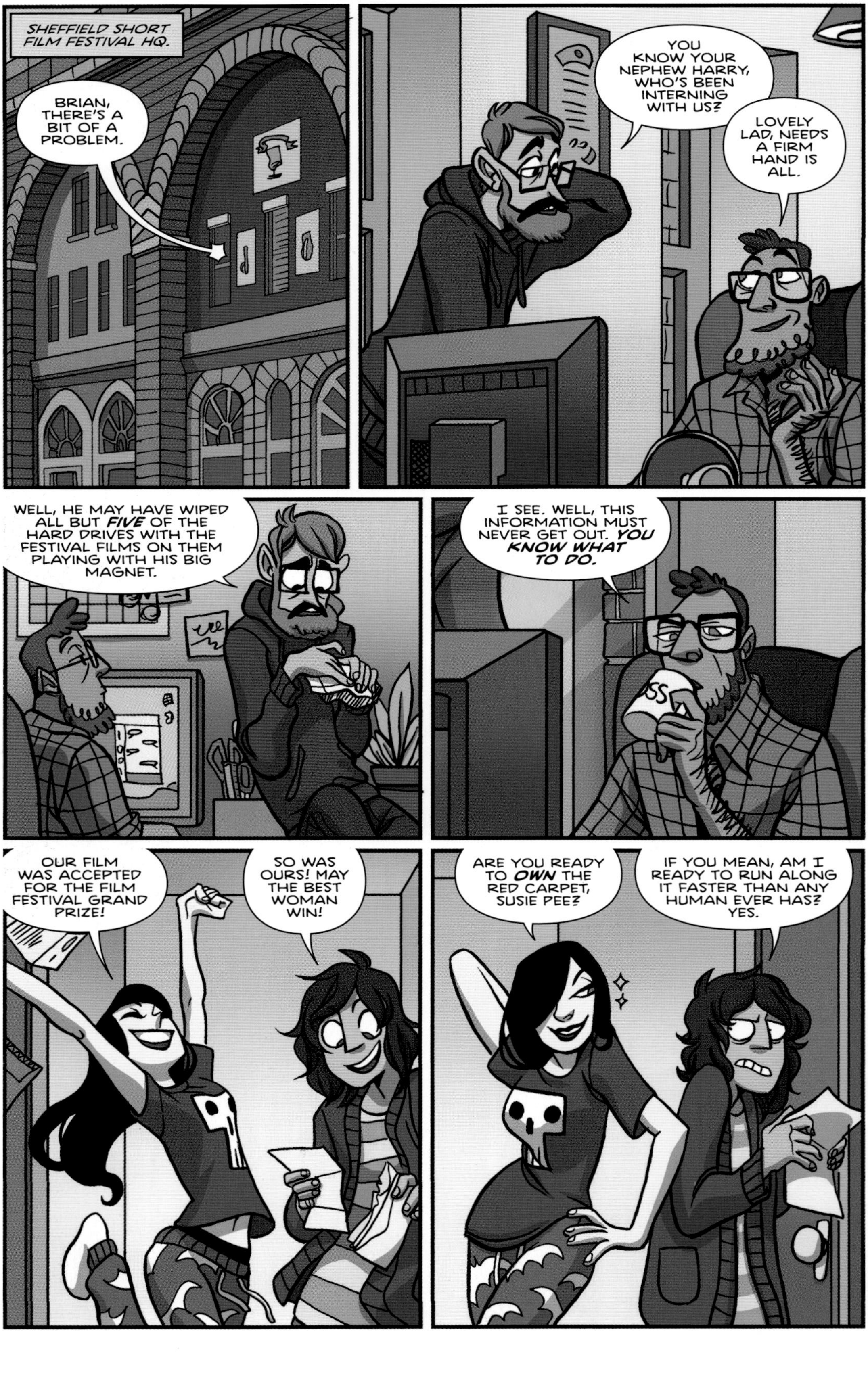

SHEFFIELD SHORT FILM FESTIVAL HQ.
BRIAN, THERE'S A BIT OF A PROBLEM.
YOU KNOW YOUR NEPHEW HARRY, WHO'S BEEN INTERNING WITH US?
LOVELY LAD, NEEDS A FIRM HAND IS ALL.
WELL, HE MAY HAVE WIPED ALL BUT FIVE OF THE HARD DRIVES WITH THE FESTIVAL FILMS ON THEM PLAYING WITH HIS BIG MAGNET.
I SEE. WELL, THIS INFORMATION MUST NEVER GET OUT. YOU KNOW WHAT TO DO.
OUR FILM WAS ACCEPTED FOR THE FILM FESTIVAL GRAND PRIZE!
SO WAS OURS! MAY THE BEST WOMAN WIN!
ARE YOU READY TO OWN THE RED CARPET, SUSIE PEE?
IF YOU MEAN, AM I READY TO RUN ALONG IT FASTER THAN ANY HUMAN EVER HAS? YES.

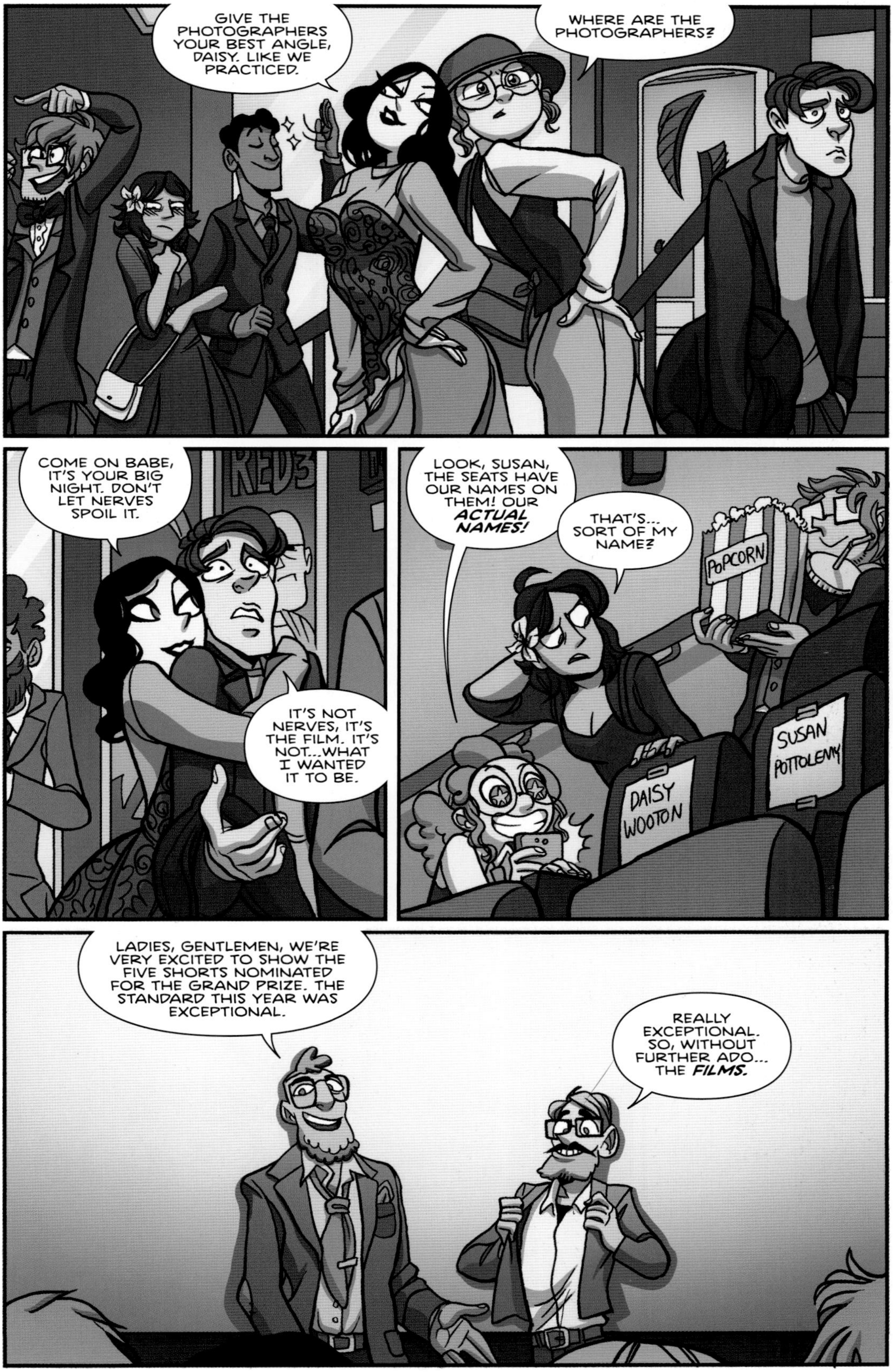
GIVE THE PHOTOGRAPHERS YOUR BEST ANGLE, DAISY. LIKE WE PRACTICED.
WHERE ARE THE PHOTOGRAPHERS?
COME ON BABE, IT'S YOUR BIG NIGHT. DON'T LET NERVES SPOIL IT.
IT'S NOT NERVES, IT'S THE FILM. IT'S NOT...WHAT I WANTED IT TO BE.
LOOK, SUSAN, THE SEATS HAVE OUR NAMES ON THEM! OUR ACTUAL NAMES!
THAT'S... SORT OF MY NAME?
POPCORN
DAISY WOOTON
SUSAN POTTOLENY
LADIES, GENTLEMEN, WE'RE VERY EXCITED TO SHOW THE FIVE SHORTS NOMINATED FOR THE GRAND PRIZE. THE STANDARD THIS YEAR WAS EXCEPTIONAL.
REALLY EXCEPTIONAL. SO, WITHOUT FURTHER ADO... THE FILMS.

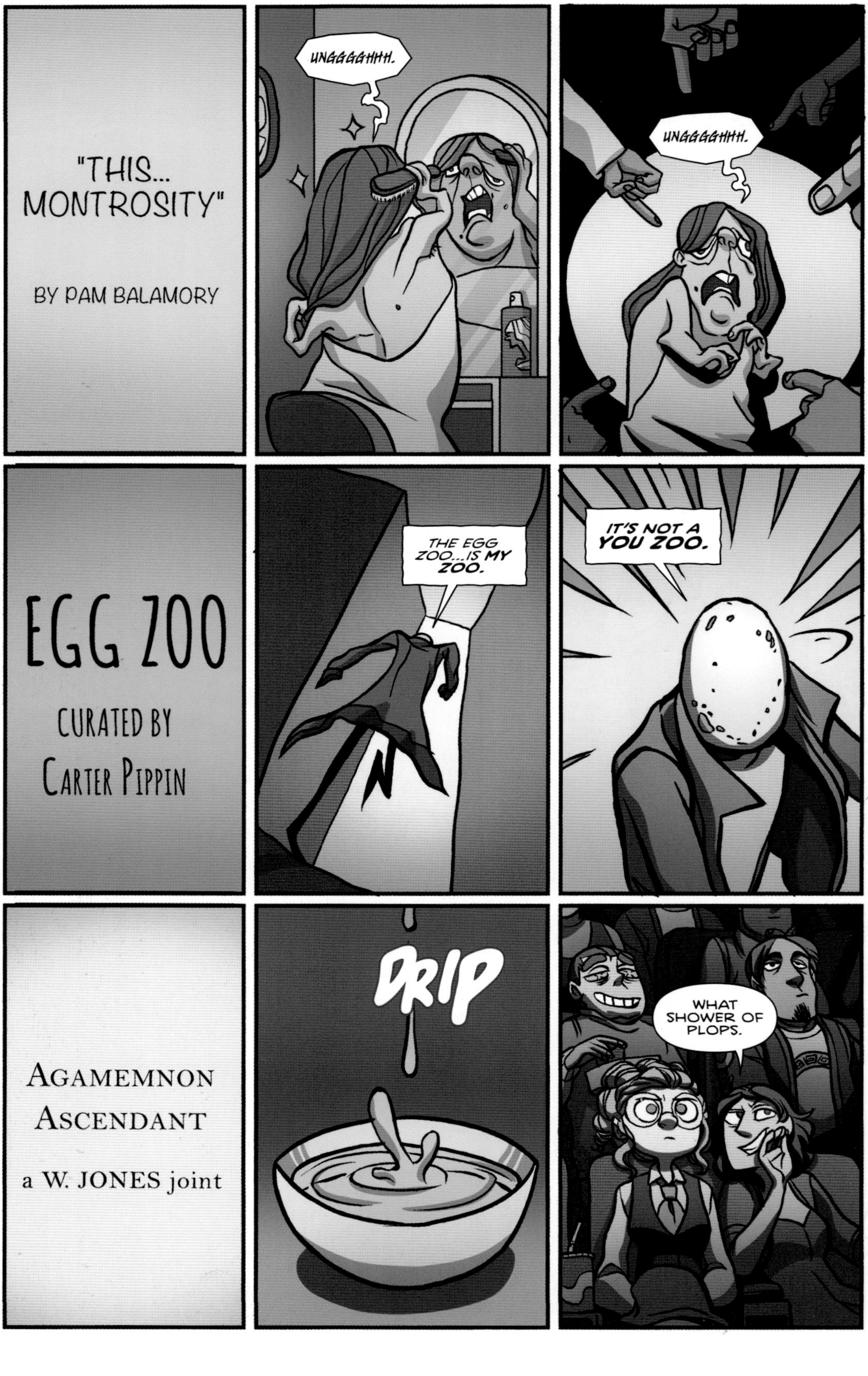
"THIS... MONTROSITY"
BY PAM BALAMORY
UNGGGGHHH.
UNGGGGHHH.
EGG ZOO
CURATED BY
CARTER PIPPIN
THE EGG ZOO... IS MY ZOO.
IT'S NOT A YOU ZOO.
AGAMEMNON ASCENDANT
a W. JONES joint
DRIP
WHAT SHOWER OF PLOPS.

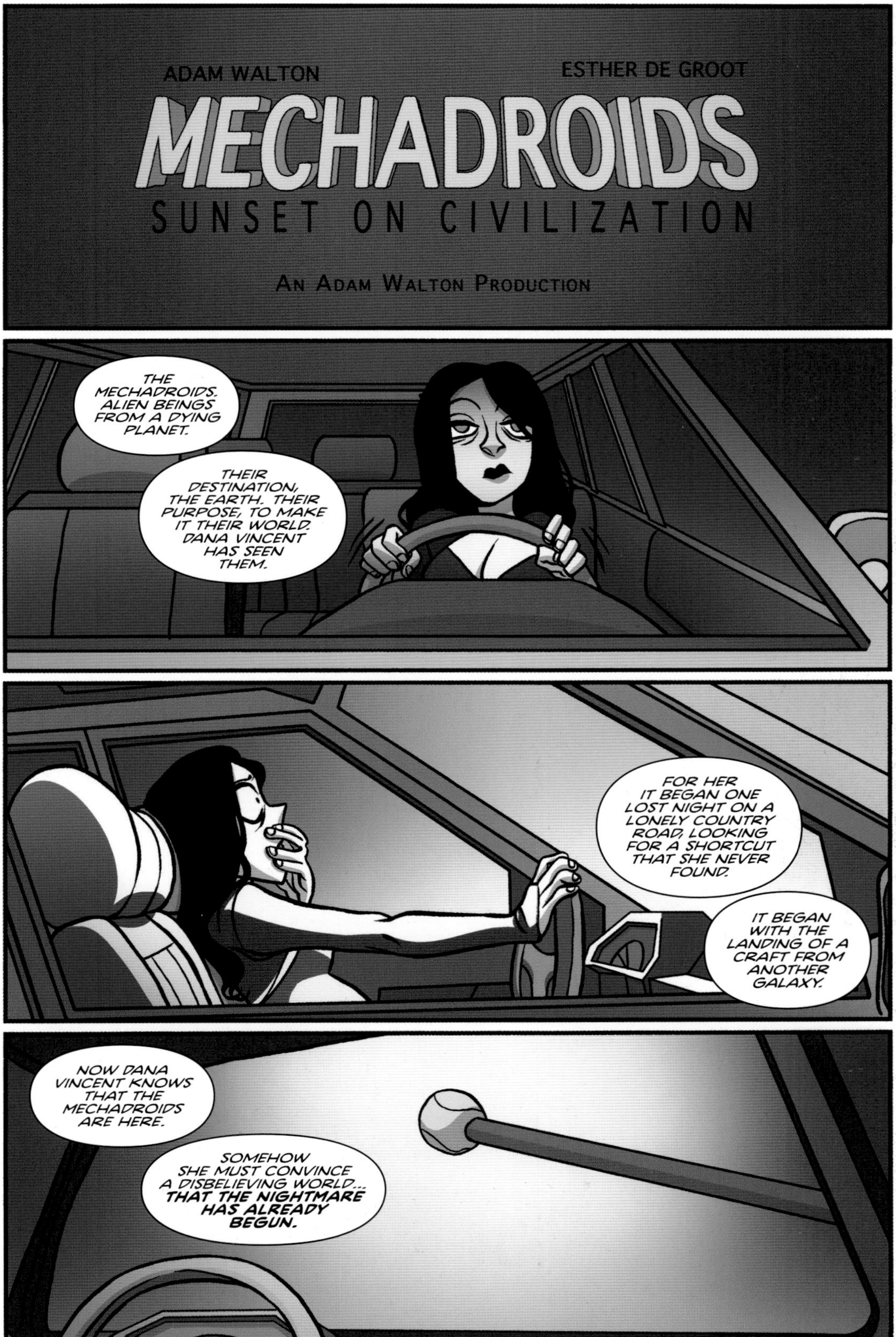
ADAM WALTON
ESTHER DE GROOT
MECHADROIDS
SUNSET ON CIVILIZATION
AN ADAM WALTON PRODUCTION
THE MECHADROIDS. ALIEN BEINGS FROM A DYING PLANET.
THEIR DESTINATION, THE EARTH. THEIR PURPOSE, TO MAKE IT THEIR WORLD. DANA VINCENT HAS SEEN THEM.
FOR HER IT BEGAN ONE LOST NIGHT ON A LONELY COUNTRY ROAD, LOOKING FOR A SHORTCUT THAT SHE NEVER FOUND.
IT BEGAN WITH THE LANDING OF A CRAFT FROM ANOTHER GALAXY.
NOW DANA VINCENT KNOWS THAT THE MECHADROIDS ARE HERE.
SOMEHOW SHE MUST CONVINCE A DISBELIEVING WORLD... THAT THE NIGHTMARE HAS ALREADY BEGUN.

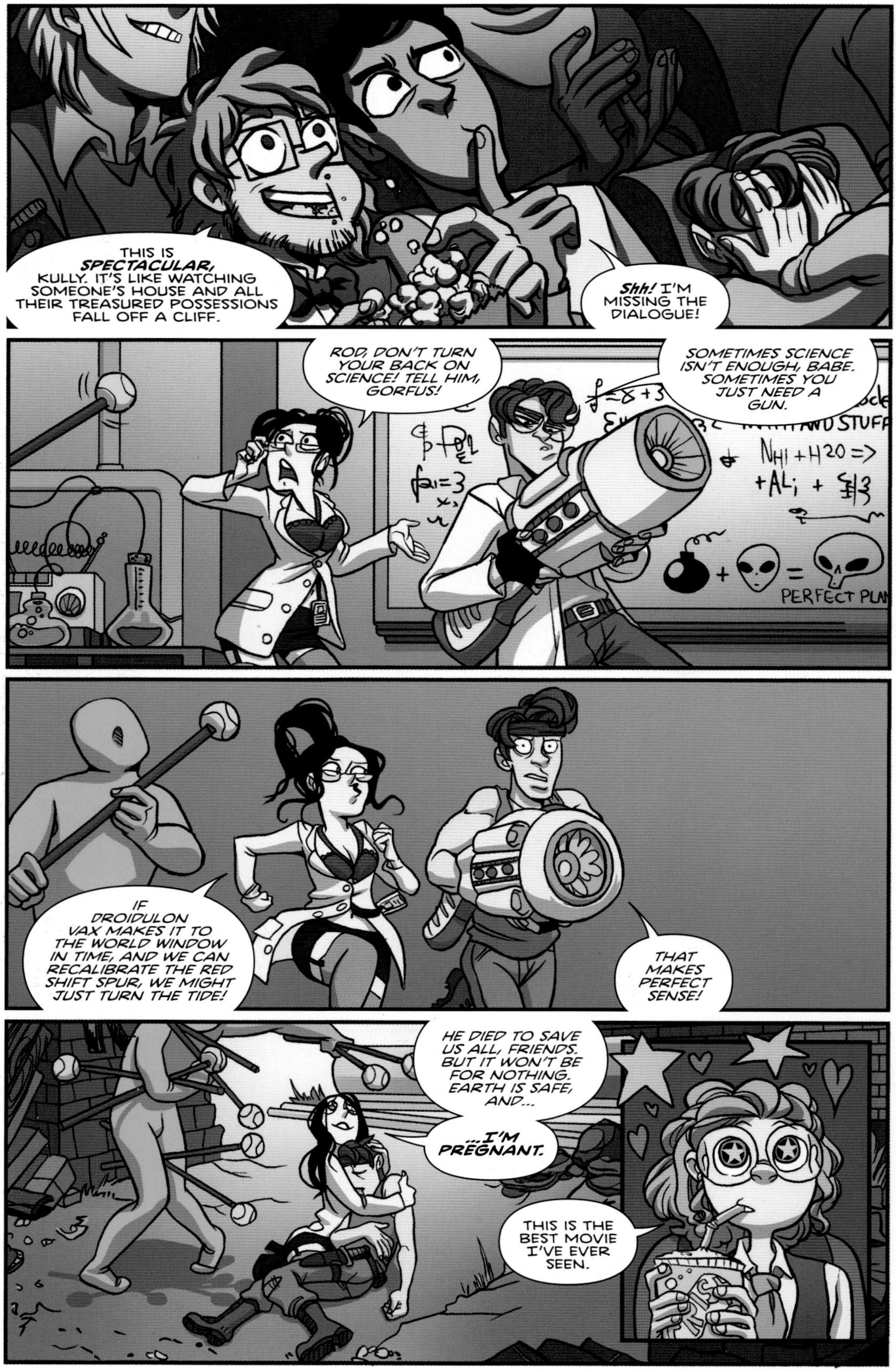
THIS IS SPECTACULAR, KULLY. IT'S LIKE WATCHING SOMEONE'S HOUSE AND ALL THEIR TREASURED POSSESSIONS FALL OFF A CLIFF.
Shh! I'M MISSING THE DIALOGUE!
ROD, DON'T TURN YOUR BACK ON SCIENCE! TELL HIM, GORFUS!
SOMETIMES SCIENCE ISN'T ENOUGH, BABE. SOMETIMES YOU JUST NEED A GUN.
PERFECT PLAN
IF DROIDULON VAX MAKES IT TO THE WORLD WINDOW IN TIME, AND WE CAN RECALIBRATE THE RED SHIFT SPUR, WE MIGHT JUST TURN THE TIDE!
THAT MAKES PERFECT SENSE!
HE DIED TO SAVE US ALL, FRIENDS. BUT IT WON'T BE FOR NOTHING. EARTH IS SAFE, AND...
...I'M PREGNANT.
THIS IS THE BEST MOVIE I'VE EVER SEEN.

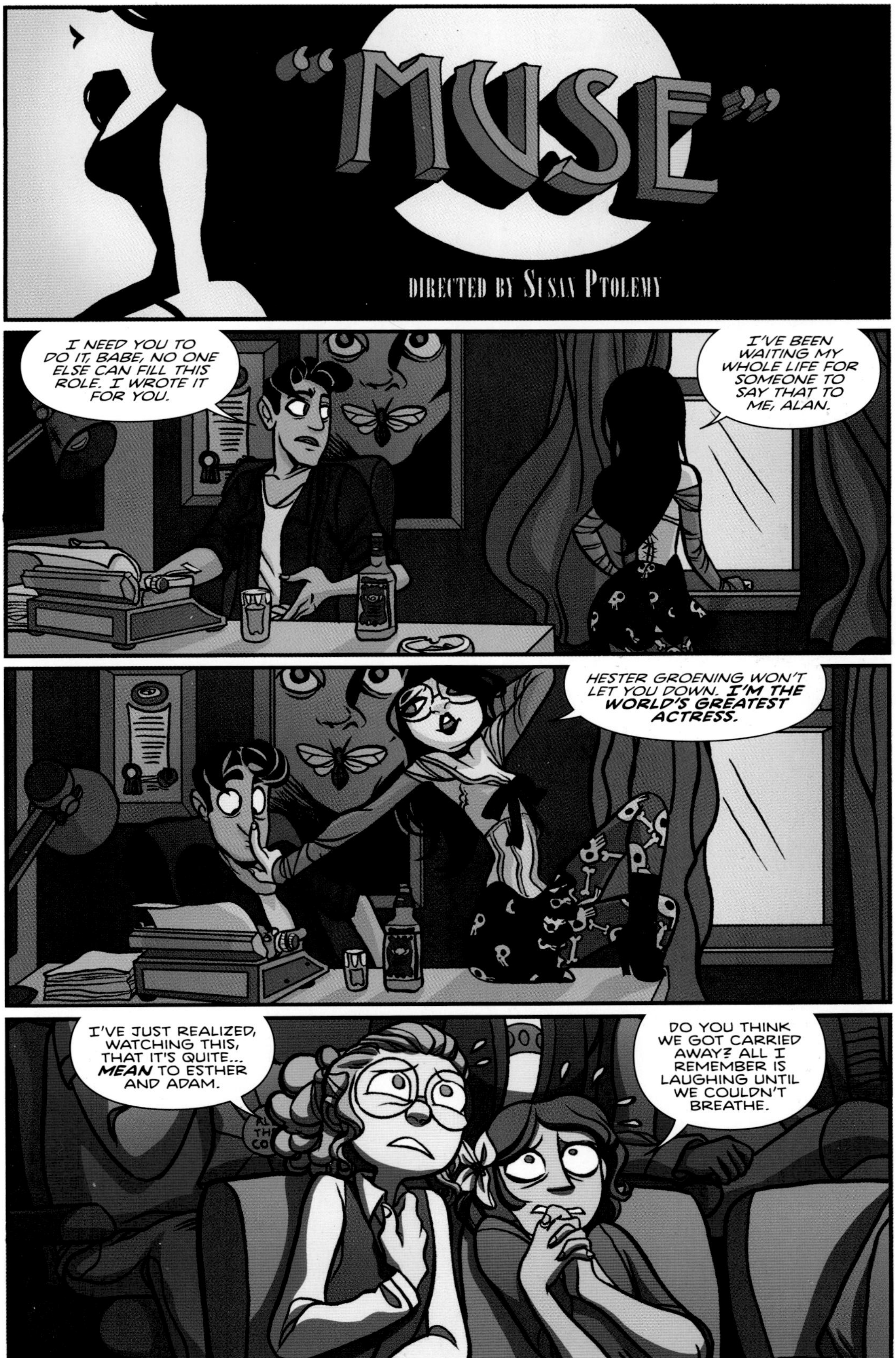
"MUSE"
DIRECTED BY SUSAN PTOLEMY
I NEED YOU TO DO IT, BABE, NO ONE ELSE CAN FILL THIS ROLE. I WROTE IT FOR YOU.
I'VE BEEN WAITING MY WHOLE LIFE FOR SOMEONE TO SAY THAT TO ME, ALAN.
HESTER GROENING WON'T LET YOU DOWN. **I'M THE WORLD'S GREATEST ACTRESS.**
I'VE JUST REALIZED, WATCHING THIS, THAT IT'S QUITE... **MEAN** TO ESTHER AND ADAM.
DO YOU THINK WE GOT CARRIED AWAY? ALL I REMEMBER IS LAUGHING UNTIL WE COULDN'T BREATHE.

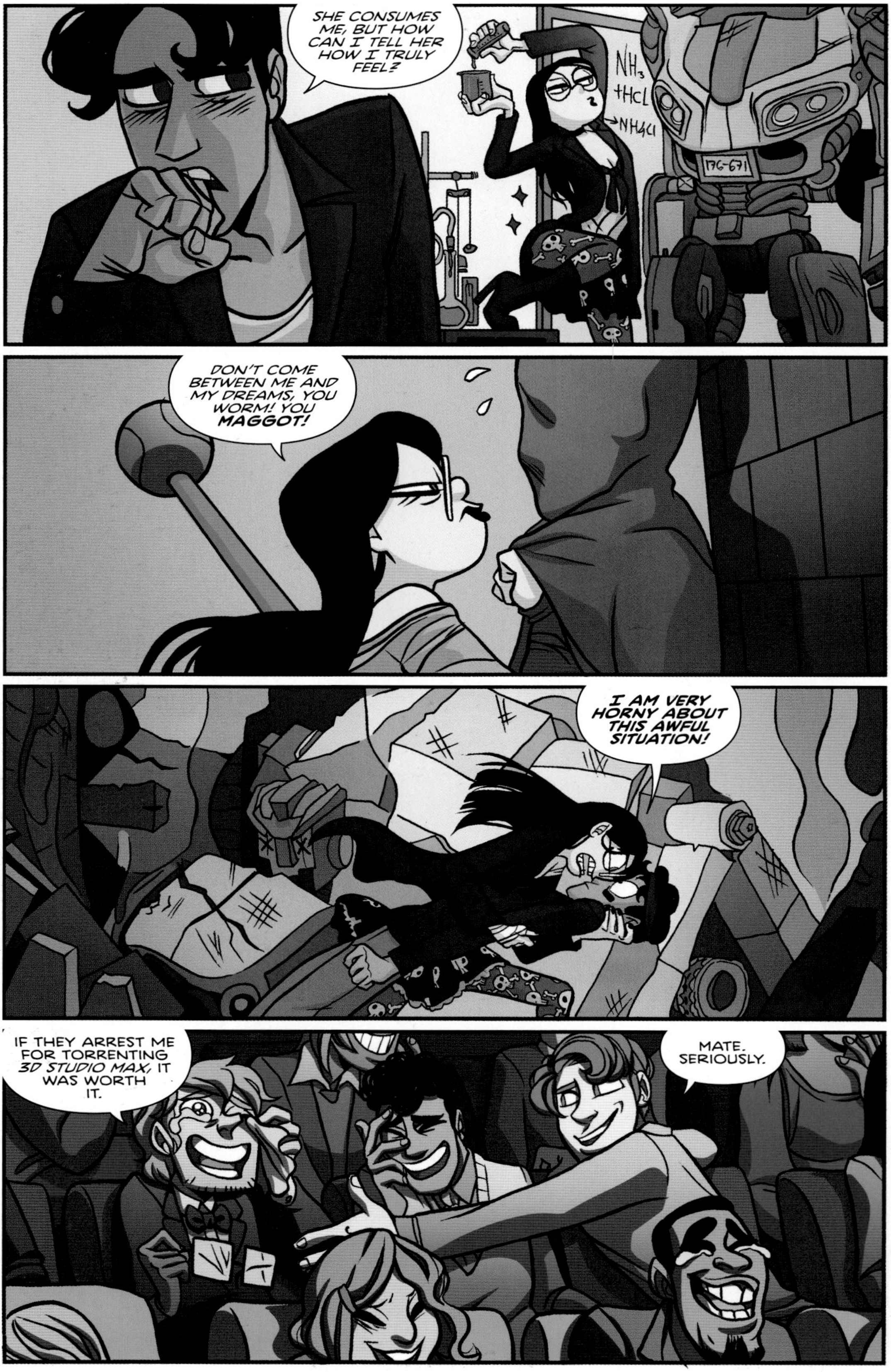
SHE CONSUMES ME, BUT HOW CAN I TELL HER HOW I TRULY FEEL?
NH3 +HCL → NH4Cl
176-671
DON'T COME BETWEEN ME AND MY DREAMS, YOU WORM! YOU **MAGGOT!**
I AM VERY HORNY ABOUT THIS AWFUL SITUATION!
IF THEY ARREST ME FOR TORRENTING *3D STUDIO MAX*, IT WAS WORTH IT.
MATE. SERIOUSLY.

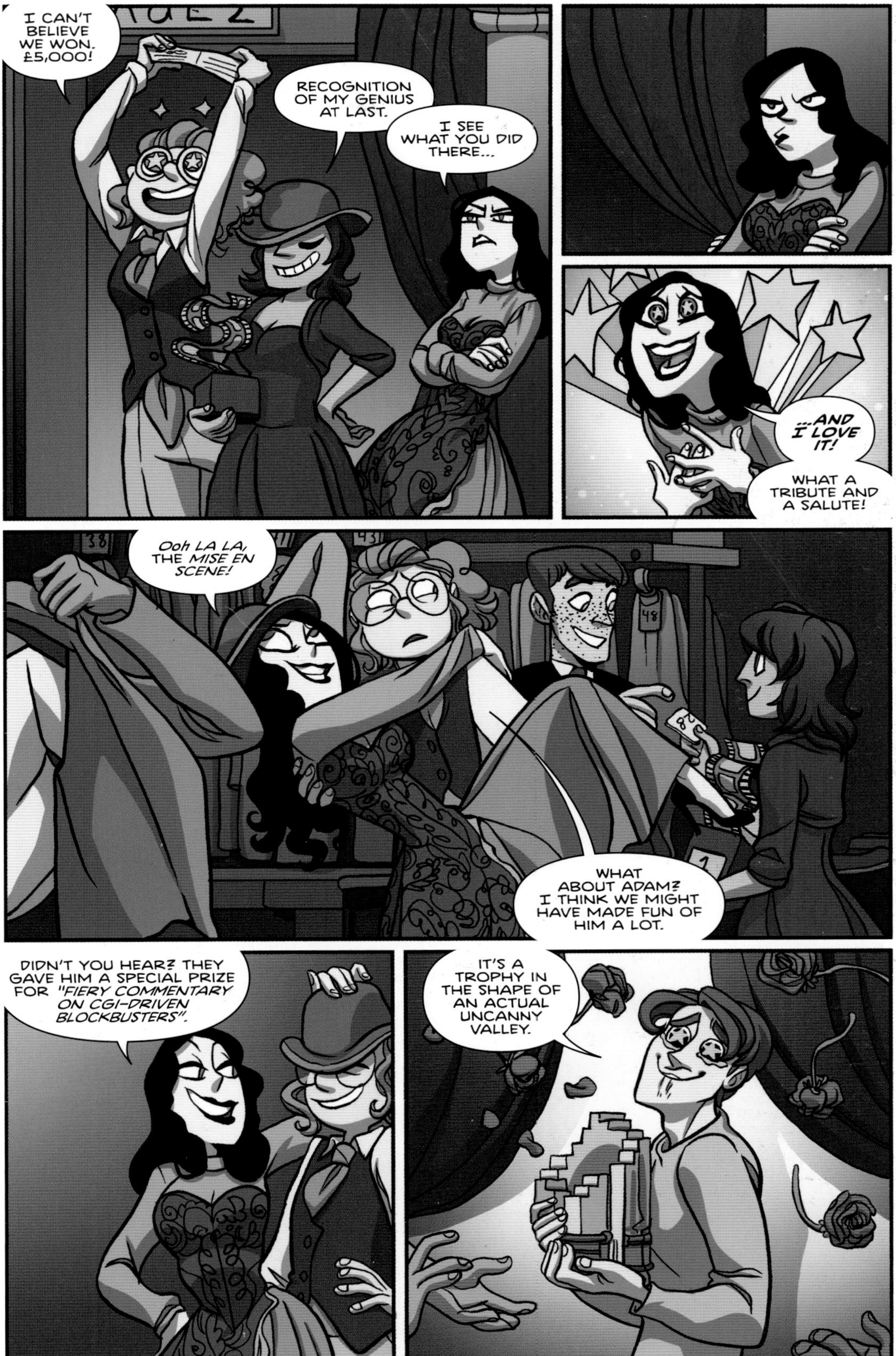
I CAN'T BELIEVE WE WON. £5,000!
RECOGNITION OF MY GENIUS AT LAST.
I SEE WHAT YOU DID THERE...
...AND I LOVE IT!
WHAT A TRIBUTE AND A SALUTE!
Ooh LA LA, THE MISE EN SCENE!
WHAT ABOUT ADAM? I THINK WE MIGHT HAVE MADE FUN OF HIM A LOT.
DIDN'T YOU HEAR? THEY GAVE HIM A SPECIAL PRIZE FOR "FIERY COMMENTARY ON CGI-DRIVEN BLOCKBUSTERS".
IT'S A TROPHY IN THE SHAPE OF AN ACTUAL UNCANNY VALLEY.

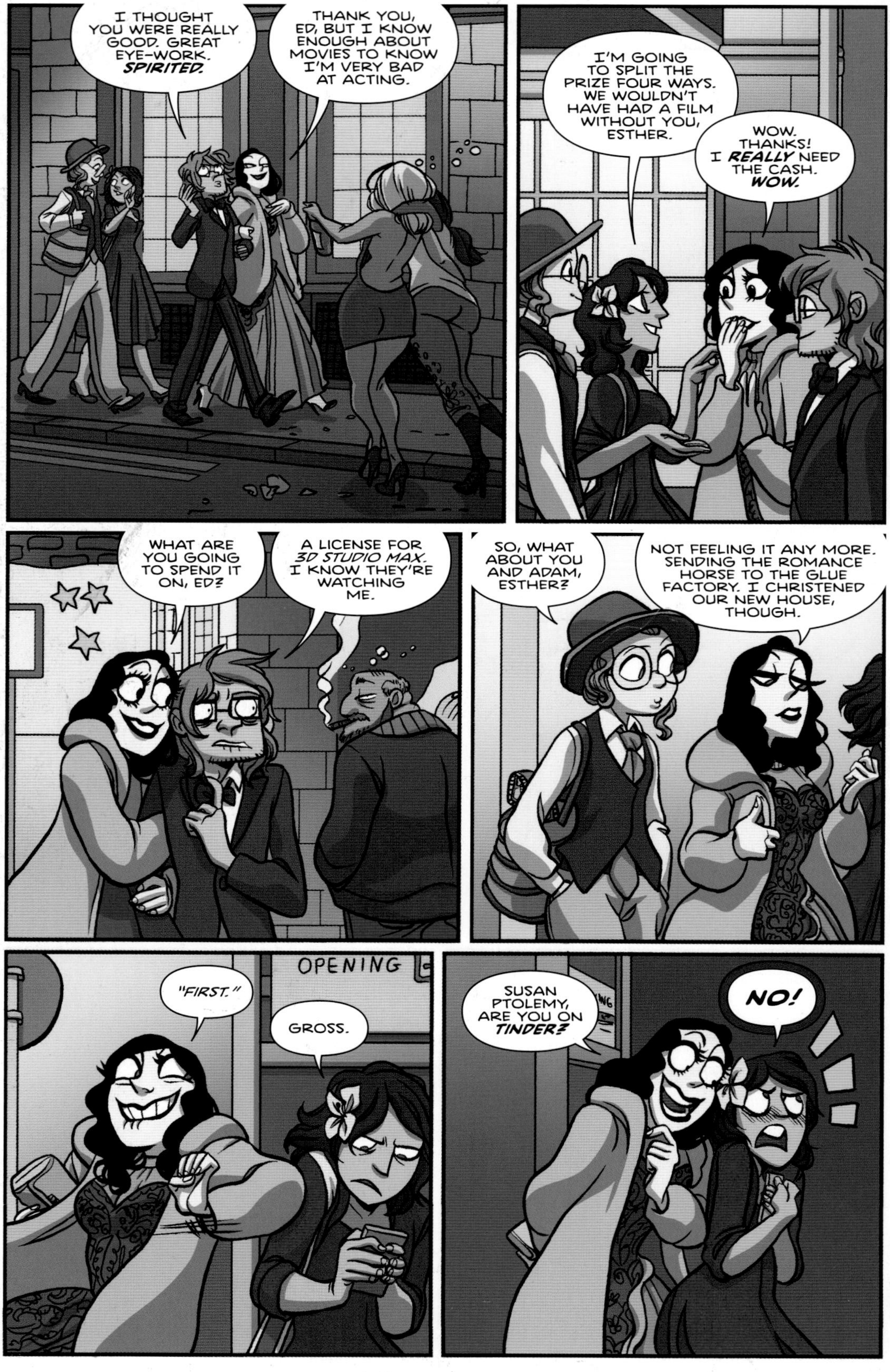
I THOUGHT YOU WERE REALLY GOOD. GREAT EYE-WORK. *SPIRITED.*
THANK YOU, ED, BUT I KNOW ENOUGH ABOUT MOVIES TO KNOW I'M VERY BAD AT ACTING.
I'M GOING TO SPLIT THE PRIZE FOUR WAYS. WE WOULDN'T HAVE HAD A FILM WITHOUT YOU, ESTHER.
WOW. THANKS! I *REALLY* NEED THE CASH. *WOW.*
WHAT ARE YOU GOING TO SPEND IT ON, ED?
A LICENSE FOR *3D STUDIO MAX.* I KNOW THEY'RE WATCHING ME.
SO, WHAT ABOUT YOU AND ADAM, ESTHER?
NOT FEELING IT ANY MORE. SENDING THE ROMANCE HORSE TO THE GLUE FACTORY. I CHRISTENED OUR NEW HOUSE, THOUGH.
OPENING
"FIRST."
GROSS.
SUSAN PTOLEMY, ARE YOU ON *TINDER?*
NO!

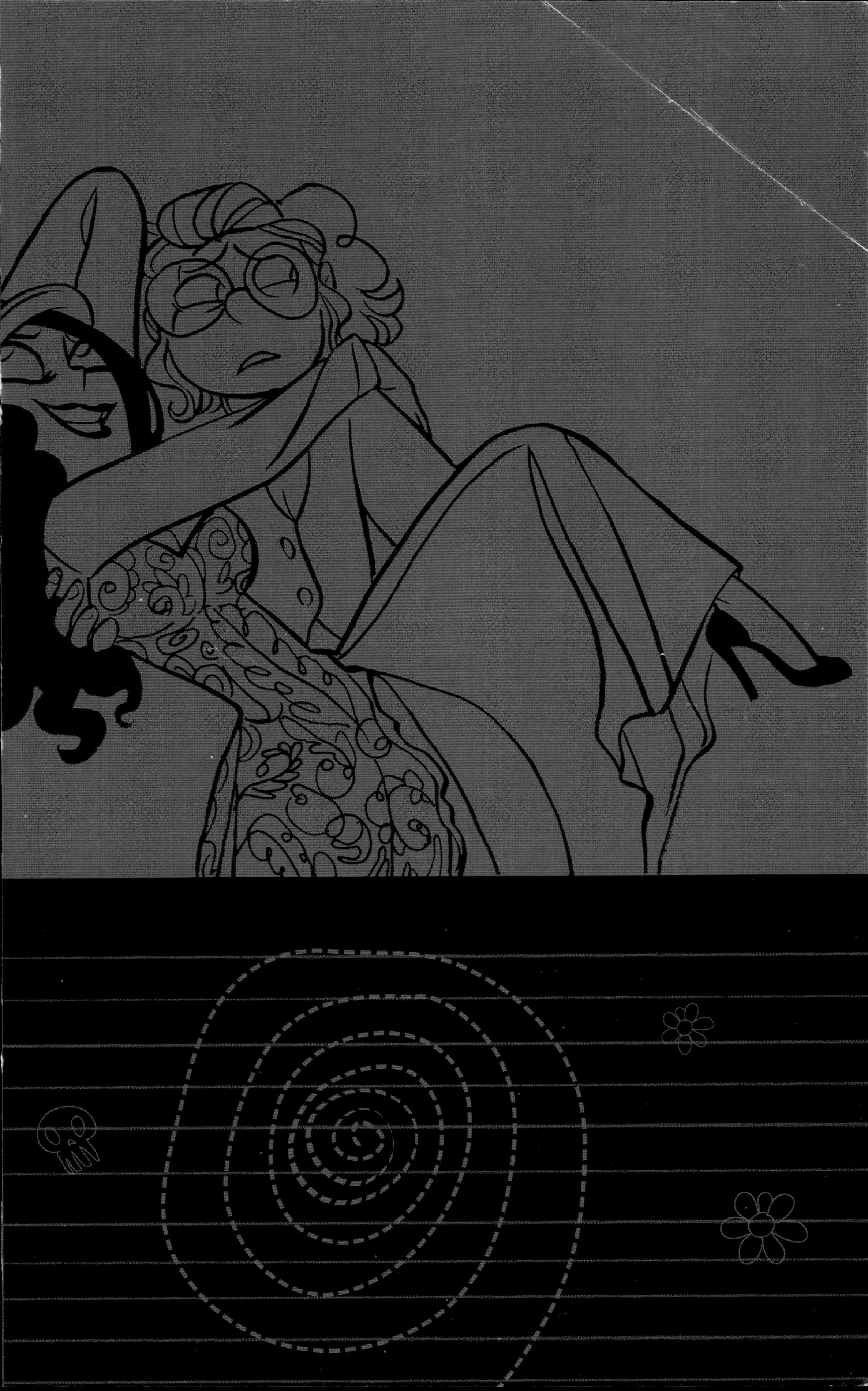

CHAPTER SIXTEEN

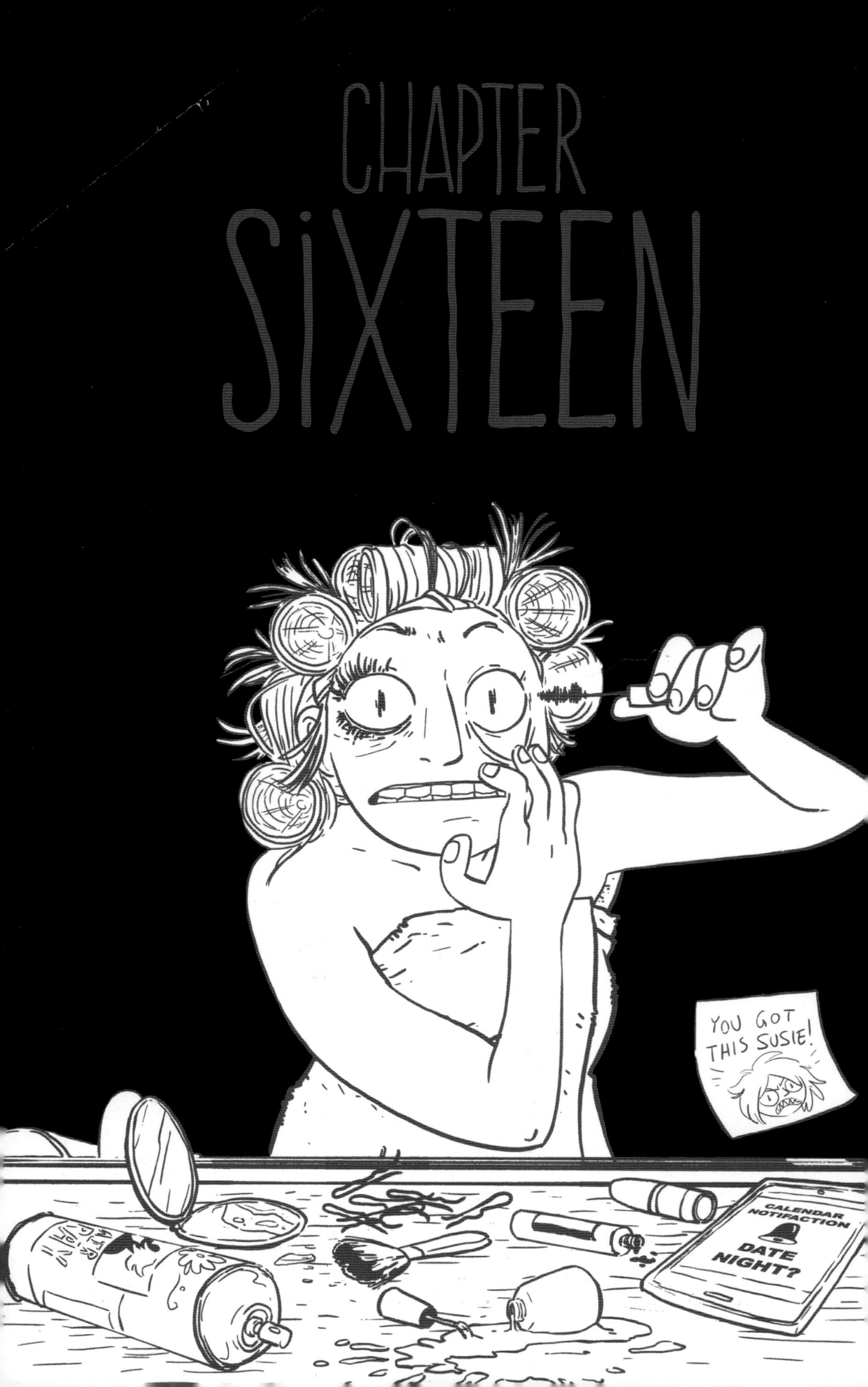
YOU GOT THIS SUSIE!
CALENDAR NOTIFACTION
DATE NIGHT?

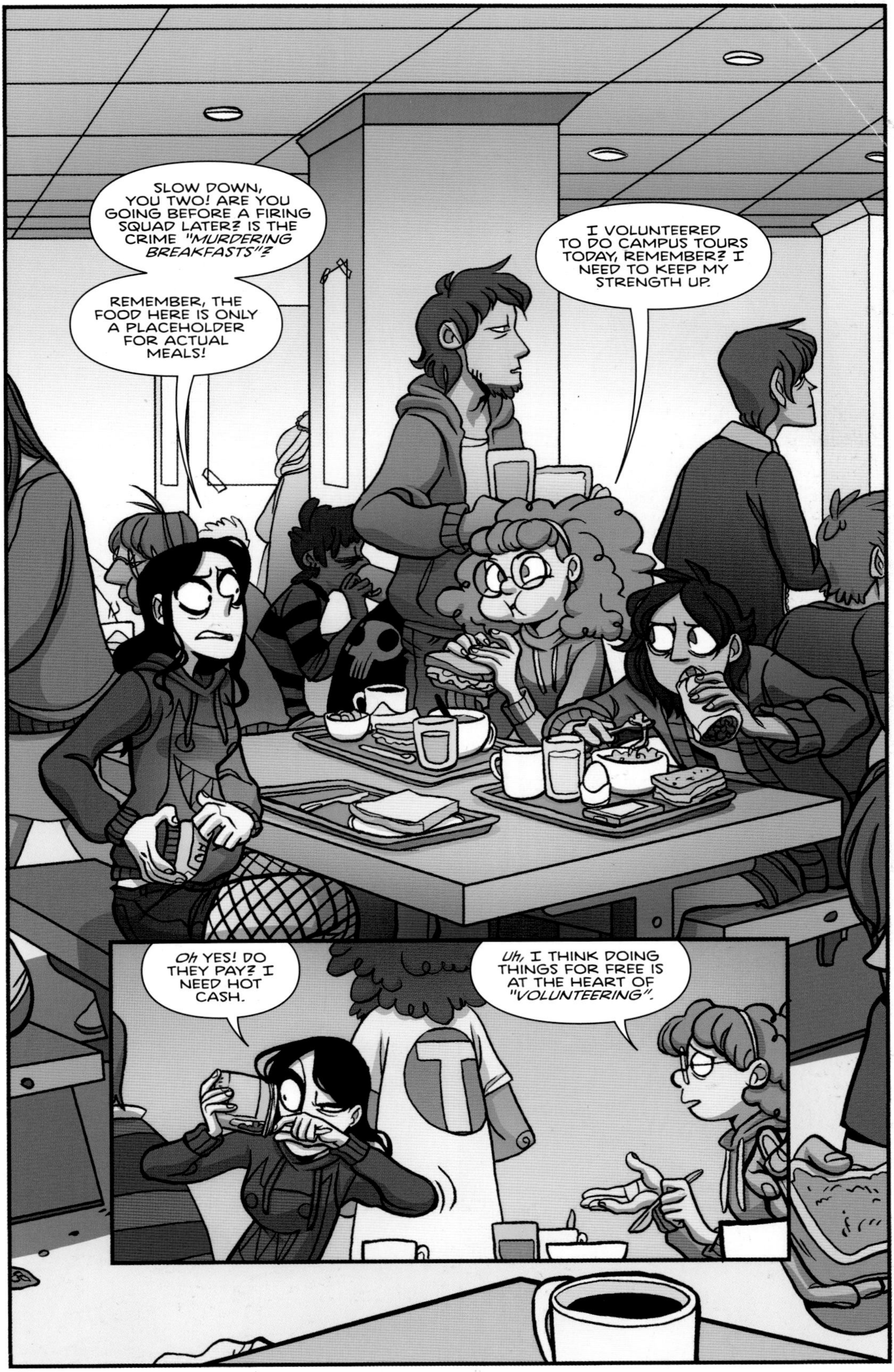
SLOW DOWN, YOU TWO! ARE YOU GOING BEFORE A FIRING SQUAD LATER? IS THE CRIME *"MURDERING BREAKFASTS"*?
REMEMBER, THE FOOD HERE IS ONLY A PLACEHOLDER FOR ACTUAL MEALS!
I VOLUNTEERED TO DO CAMPUS TOURS TODAY, REMEMBER? I NEED TO KEEP MY STRENGTH UP.
Oh YES! DO THEY PAY? I NEED HOT CASH.
Uh, I THINK DOING THINGS FOR FREE IS AT THE HEART OF *"VOLUNTEERING"*.

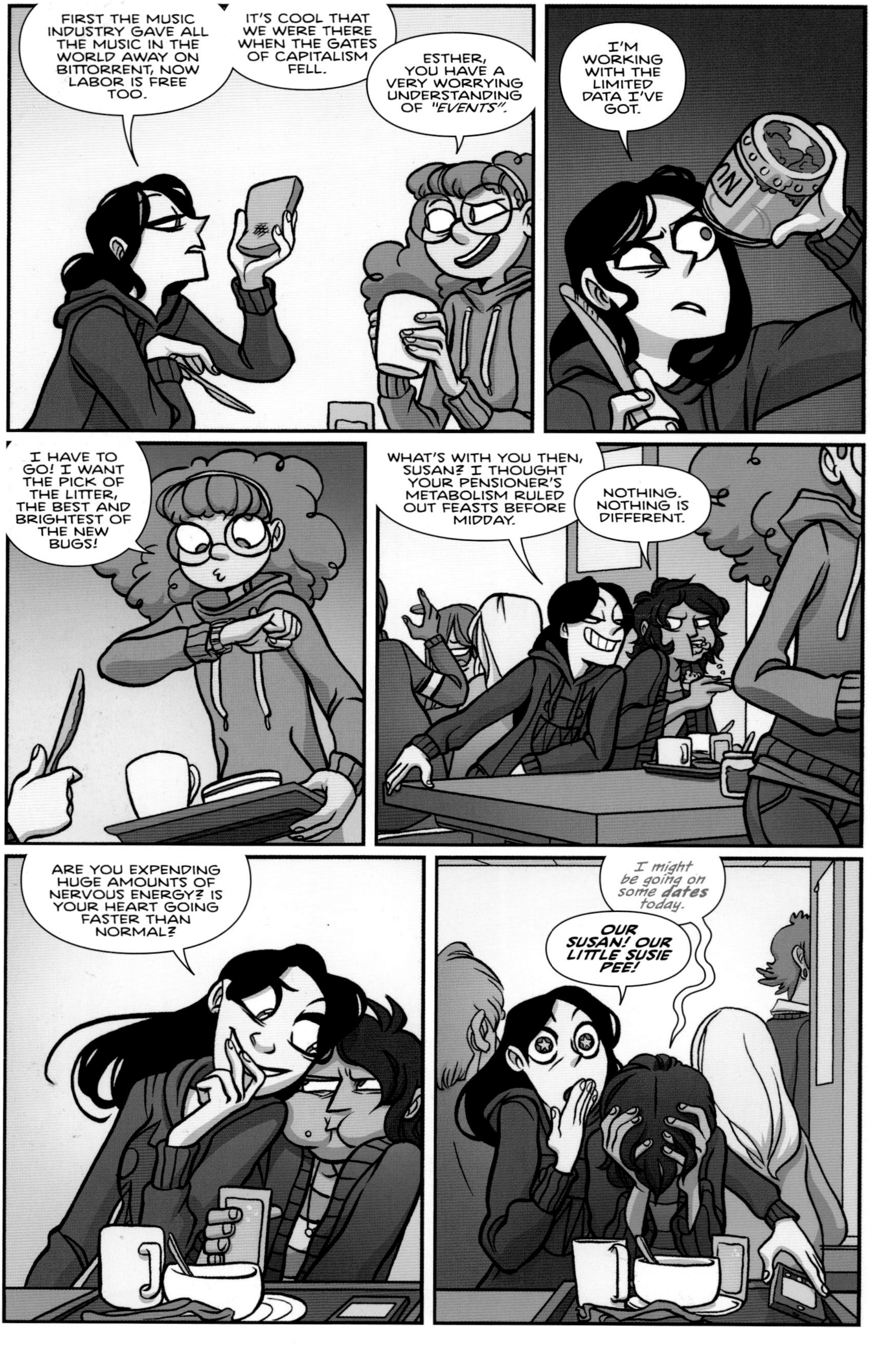
FIRST THE MUSIC INDUSTRY GAVE ALL THE MUSIC IN THE WORLD AWAY ON BITTORRENT, NOW LABOR IS FREE TOO.
IT'S COOL THAT WE WERE THERE WHEN THE GATES OF CAPITALISM FELL.
ESTHER, YOU HAVE A VERY WORRYING UNDERSTANDING OF "EVENTS".
I'M WORKING WITH THE LIMITED DATA I'VE GOT.
I HAVE TO GO! I WANT THE PICK OF THE LITTER, THE BEST AND BRIGHTEST OF THE NEW BUGS!
WHAT'S WITH YOU THEN, SUSAN? I THOUGHT YOUR PENSIONER'S METABOLISM RULED OUT FEASTS BEFORE MIDDAY.
NOTHING. NOTHING IS DIFFERENT.
ARE YOU EXPENDING HUGE AMOUNTS OF NERVOUS ENERGY? IS YOUR HEART GOING FASTER THAN NORMAL?
I might be going on some dates today.
OUR SUSAN! OUR LITTLE SUSIE PEE!

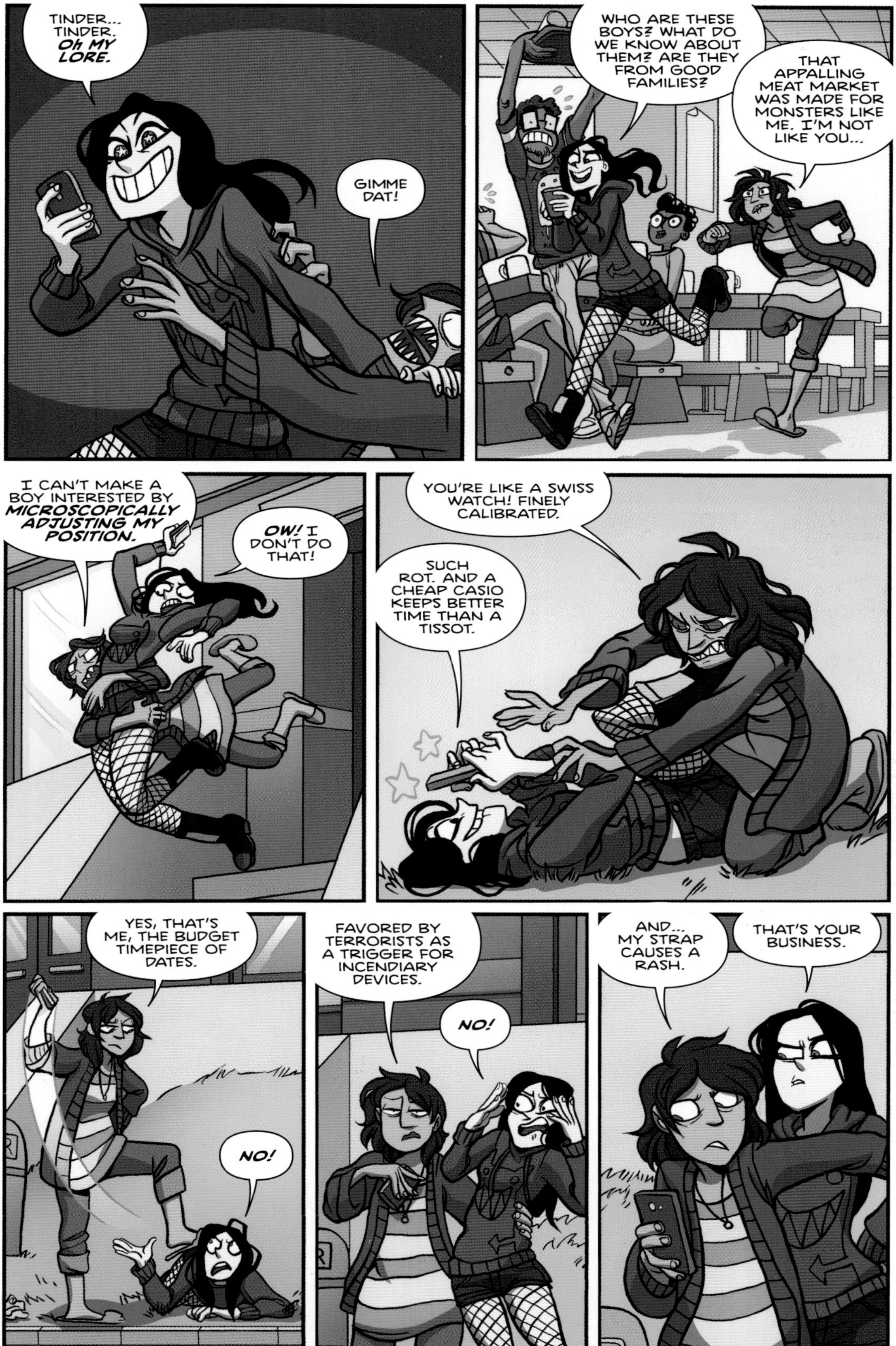
TINDER... TINDER. *OH MY LORE.*
GIMME DAT!
WHO ARE THESE BOYS? WHAT DO WE KNOW ABOUT THEM? ARE THEY FROM GOOD FAMILIES?
THAT APPALLING MEAT MARKET WAS MADE FOR MONSTERS LIKE ME. I'M NOT LIKE YOU...
I CAN'T MAKE A BOY INTERESTED BY *MICROSCOPICALLY ADJUSTING MY POSITION.*
OW! I DON'T DO THAT!
YOU'RE LIKE A SWISS WATCH! FINELY CALIBRATED.
SUCH ROT. AND A CHEAP CASIO KEEPS BETTER TIME THAN A TISSOT.
YES, THAT'S ME, THE BUDGET TIMEPIECE OF DATES.
NO!
FAVORED BY TERRORISTS AS A TRIGGER FOR INCENDIARY DEVICES.
NO!
AND... MY STRAP CAUSES A RASH.
THAT'S YOUR BUSINESS.

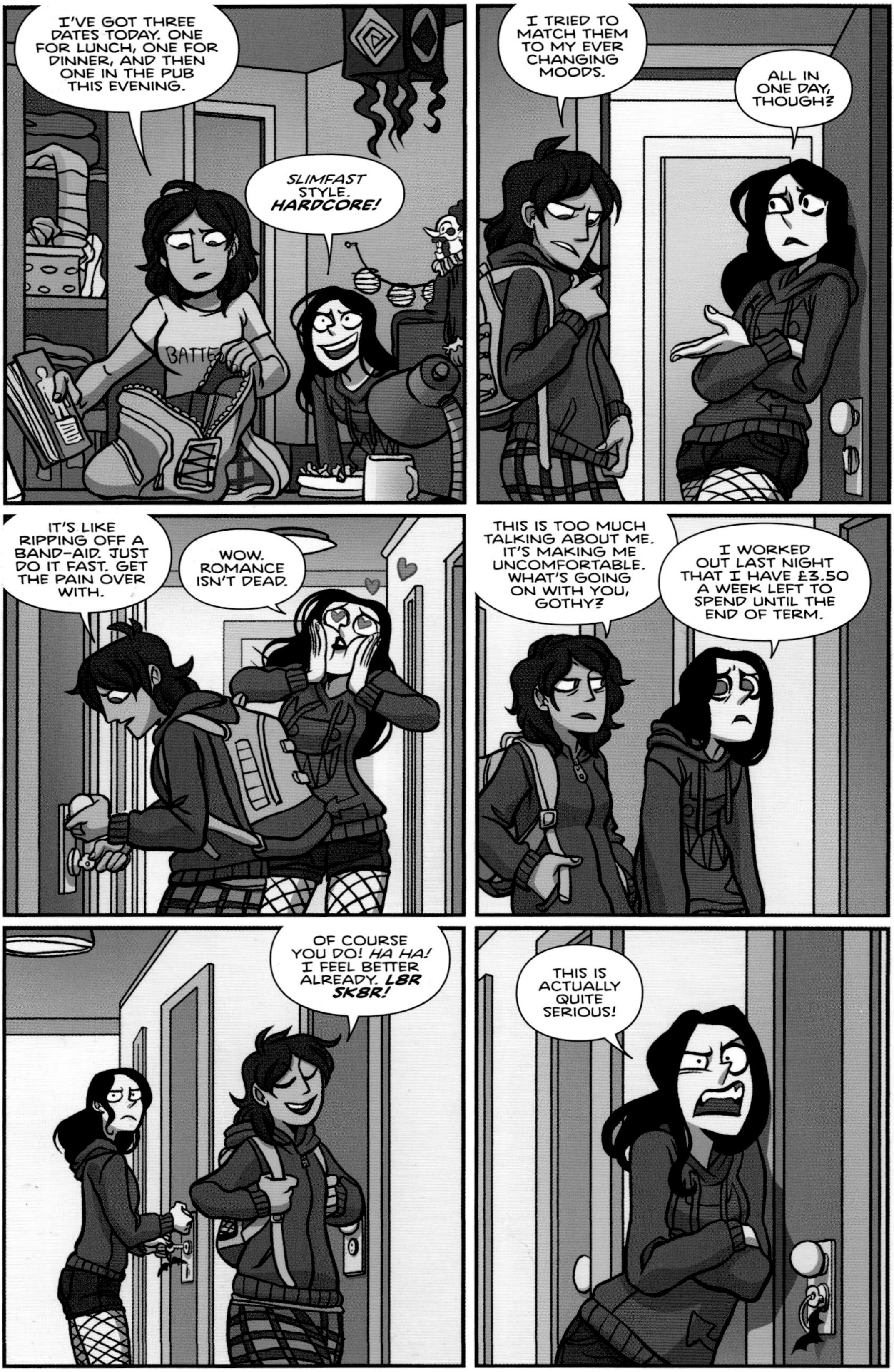
I'VE GOT THREE DATES TODAY. ONE FOR LUNCH, ONE FOR DINNER, AND THEN ONE IN THE PUB THIS EVENING.
SLIMFAST *STYLE.* ***HARDCORE!***
BATTE
I TRIED TO MATCH THEM TO MY EVER CHANGING MOODS.
ALL IN ONE DAY, THOUGH?
IT'S LIKE RIPPING OFF A BAND-AID. JUST DO IT FAST. GET THE PAIN OVER WITH.
WOW. ROMANCE ISN'T DEAD.
THIS IS TOO MUCH TALKING ABOUT ME. IT'S MAKING ME UNCOMFORTABLE. WHAT'S GOING ON WITH YOU, GOTHY?
I WORKED OUT LAST NIGHT THAT I HAVE £3.50 A WEEK LEFT TO SPEND UNTIL THE END OF TERM.
OF COURSE YOU DO! *HA HA!* I FEEL BETTER ALREADY. ***L8R SK8R!***
THIS IS ACTUALLY QUITE SERIOUS!

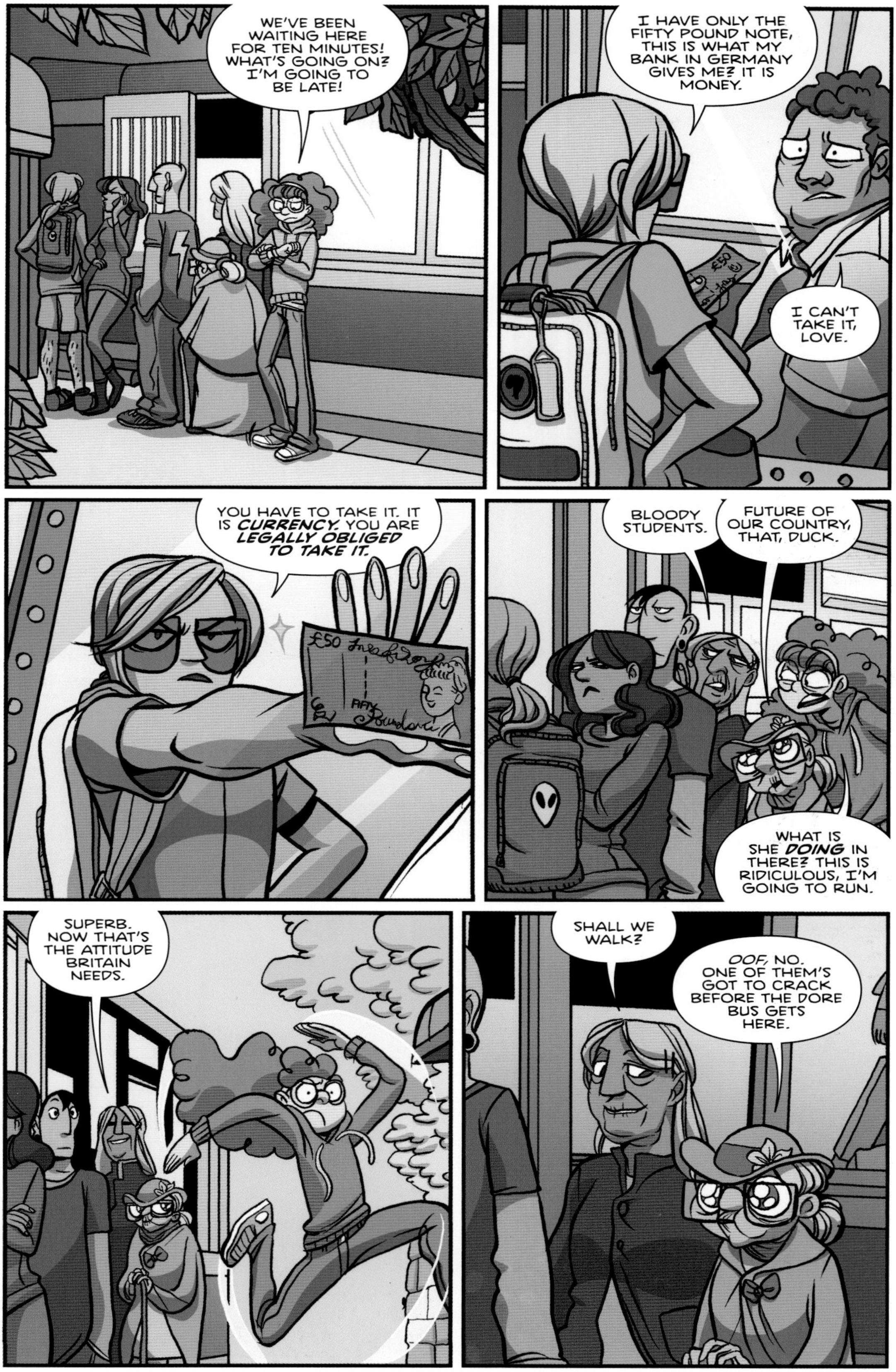
WE'VE BEEN WAITING HERE FOR TEN MINUTES! WHAT'S GOING ON? I'M GOING TO BE LATE!
I HAVE ONLY THE FIFTY POUND NOTE, THIS IS WHAT MY BANK IN GERMANY GIVES ME? IT IS MONEY.
I CAN'T TAKE IT, LOVE.
YOU HAVE TO TAKE IT. IT IS CURRENCY. YOU ARE LEGALLY OBLIGED TO TAKE IT.
BLOODY STUDENTS.
FUTURE OF OUR COUNTRY, THAT, DUCK.
WHAT IS SHE DOING IN THERE? THIS IS RIDICULOUS, I'M GOING TO RUN.
SUPERB. NOW THAT'S THE ATTITUDE BRITAIN NEEDS.
SHALL WE WALK?
OOF, NO. ONE OF THEM'S GOT TO CRACK BEFORE THE DORE BUS GETS HERE.

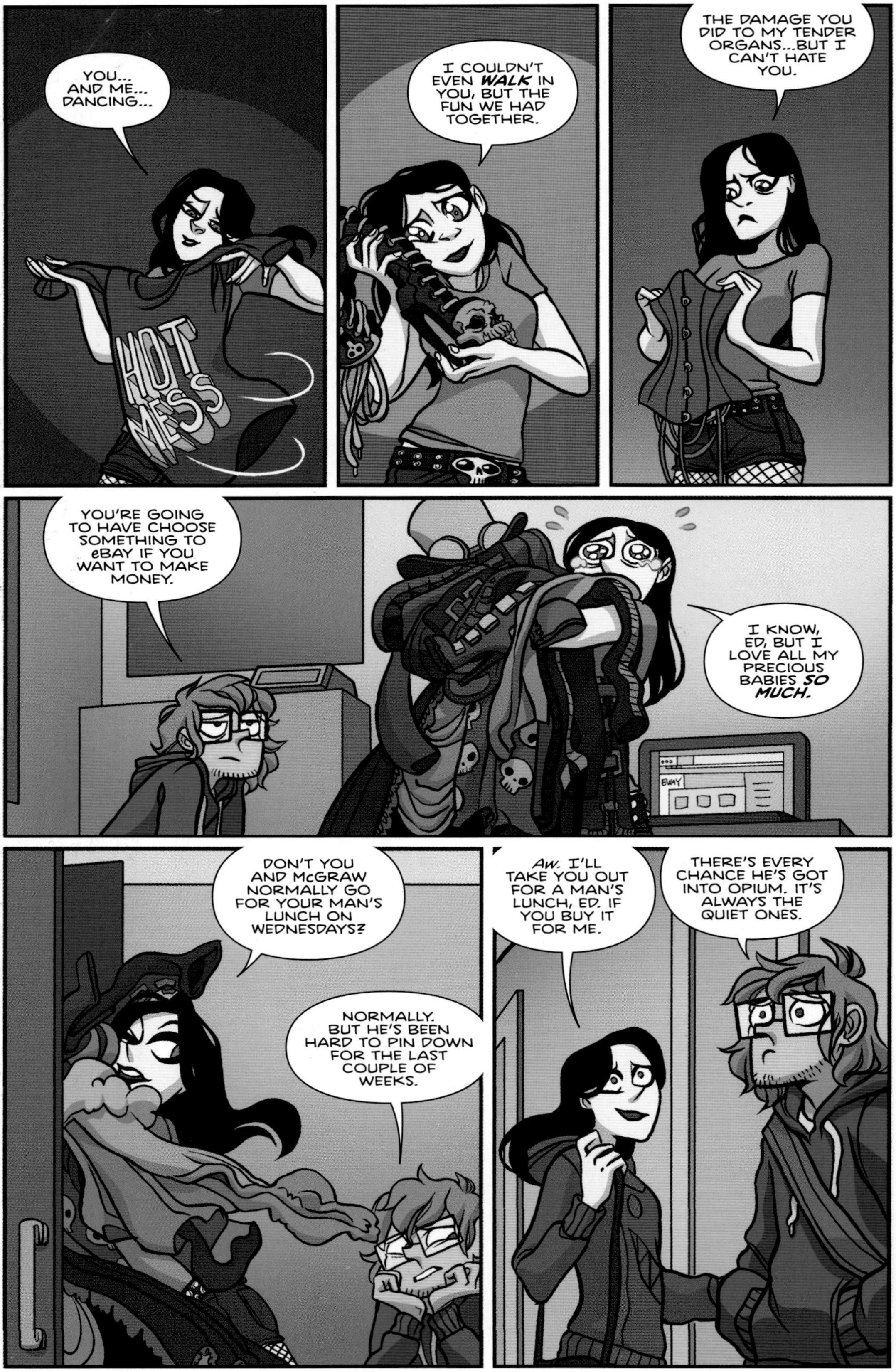
YOU... AND ME... DANCING...
HOT MESS
I COULDN'T EVEN WALK IN YOU, BUT THE FUN WE HAD TOGETHER.
THE DAMAGE YOU DID TO MY TENDER ORGANS...BUT I CAN'T HATE YOU.
YOU'RE GOING TO HAVE CHOOSE SOMETHING TO eBAY IF YOU WANT TO MAKE MONEY.
I KNOW, ED, BUT I LOVE ALL MY PRECIOUS BABIES SO MUCH.
EBAY
DON'T YOU AND McGRAW NORMALLY GO FOR YOUR MAN'S LUNCH ON WEDNESDAYS?
NORMALLY. BUT HE'S BEEN HARD TO PIN DOWN FOR THE LAST COUPLE OF WEEKS.
AW. I'LL TAKE YOU OUT FOR A MAN'S LUNCH, ED. IF YOU BUY IT FOR ME.
THERE'S EVERY CHANCE HE'S GOT INTO OPIUM. IT'S ALWAYS THE QUIET ONES.

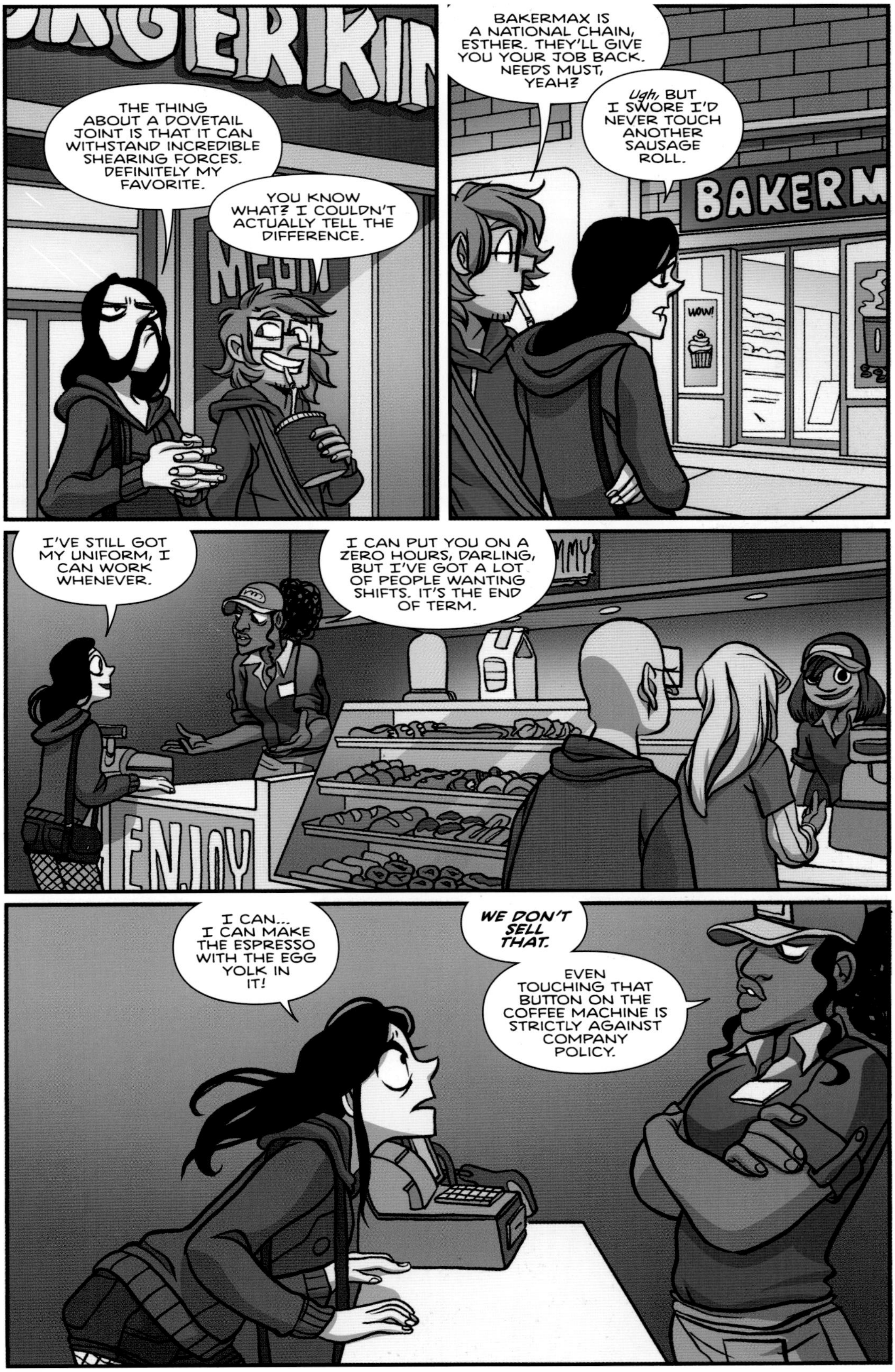

THE THING ABOUT A DOVETAIL JOINT IS THAT IT CAN WITHSTAND INCREDIBLE SHEARING FORCES. DEFINITELY MY FAVORITE.
YOU KNOW WHAT? I COULDN'T ACTUALLY TELL THE DIFFERENCE.
BAKERMAX IS A NATIONAL CHAIN, ESTHER. THEY'LL GIVE YOU YOUR JOB BACK. NEEDS MUST, YEAH?
Ugh, BUT I SWORE I'D NEVER TOUCH ANOTHER SAUSAGE ROLL.
BAKERM
WOW!
I'VE STILL GOT MY UNIFORM, I CAN WORK WHENEVER.
I CAN PUT YOU ON A ZERO HOURS, DARLING, BUT I'VE GOT A LOT OF PEOPLE WANTING SHIFTS. IT'S THE END OF TERM.
ENJOY
I CAN... I CAN MAKE THE ESPRESSO WITH THE EGG YOLK IN IT!
WE DON'T SELL THAT.
EVEN TOUCHING THAT BUTTON ON THE COFFEE MACHINE IS STRICTLY AGAINST COMPANY POLICY.

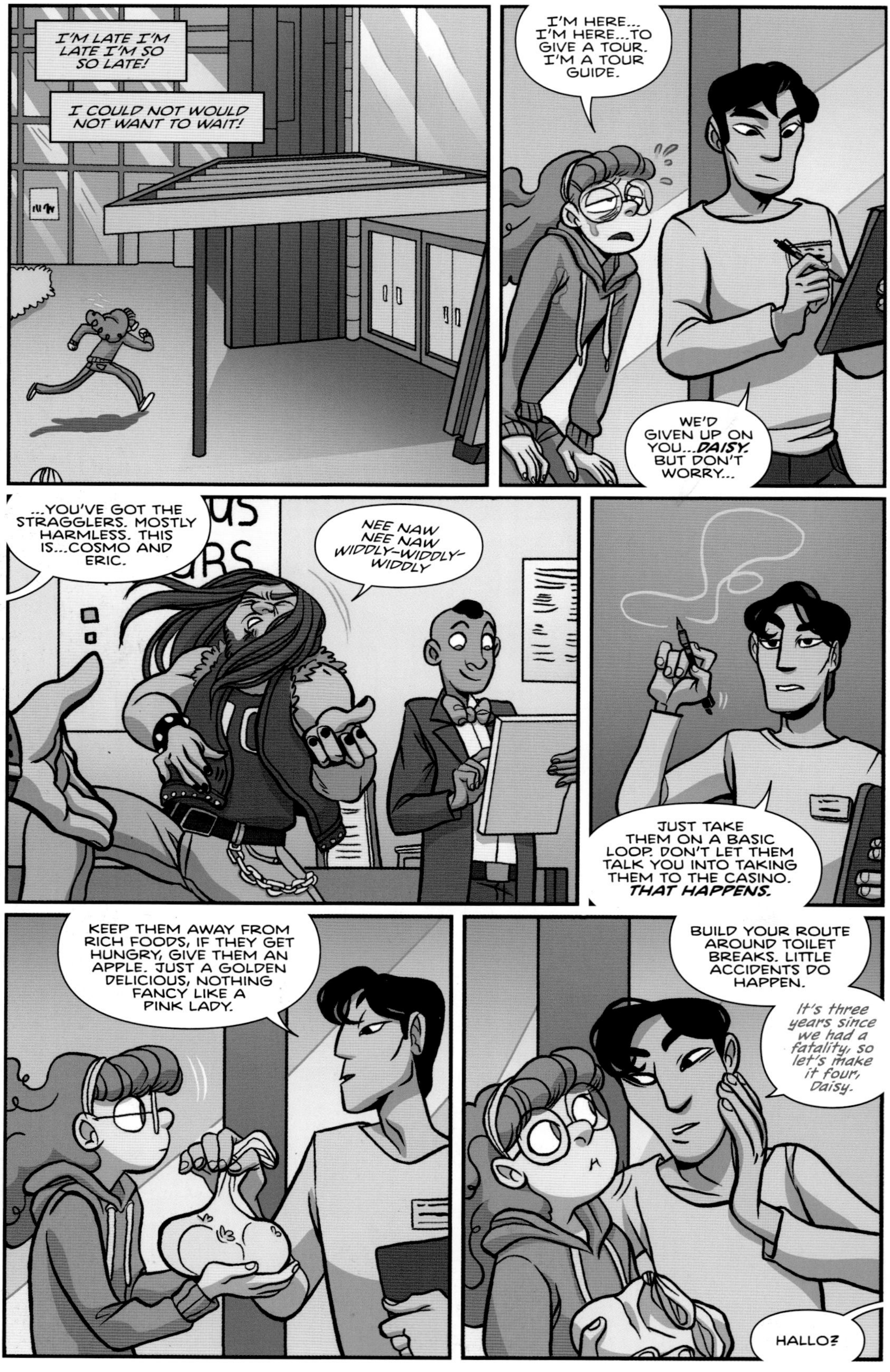
I'M LATE I'M LATE I'M SO SO LATE!
I COULD NOT WOULD NOT WANT TO WAIT!
I'M HERE... I'M HERE...TO GIVE A TOUR. I'M A TOUR GUIDE.
WE'D GIVEN UP ON YOU...DAISY. BUT DON'T WORRY...
...YOU'VE GOT THE STRAGGLERS. MOSTLY HARMLESS. THIS IS...COSMO AND ERIC.
NEE NAW NEE NAW WIDDLY-WIDDLY-WIDDLY
JUST TAKE THEM ON A BASIC LOOP. DON'T LET THEM TALK YOU INTO TAKING THEM TO THE CASINO. THAT HAPPENS.
KEEP THEM AWAY FROM RICH FOODS, IF THEY GET HUNGRY, GIVE THEM AN APPLE. JUST A GOLDEN DELICIOUS, NOTHING FANCY LIKE A PINK LADY.
BUILD YOUR ROUTE AROUND TOILET BREAKS. LITTLE ACCIDENTS DO HAPPEN.
It's three years since we had a fatality, so let's make it four, Daisy.
HALLO?

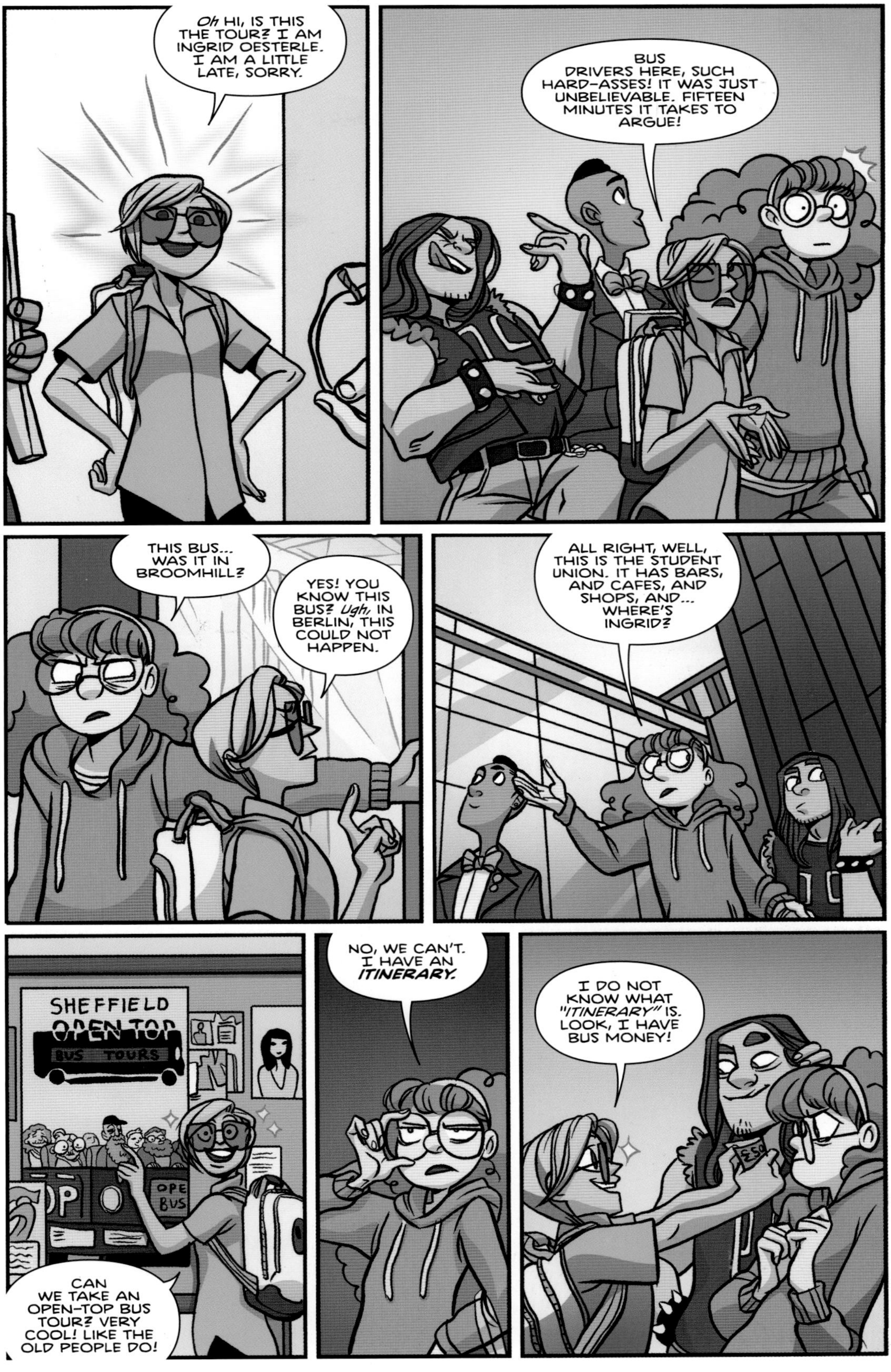
Oh HI, IS THIS THE TOUR? I AM INGRID OESTERLE. I AM A LITTLE LATE, SORRY.
BUS DRIVERS HERE, SUCH HARD-ASSES! IT WAS JUST UNBELIEVABLE. FIFTEEN MINUTES IT TAKES TO ARGUE!
THIS BUS... WAS IT IN BROOMHILL?
YES! YOU KNOW THIS BUS? Ugh, IN BERLIN, THIS COULD NOT HAPPEN.
ALL RIGHT, WELL, THIS IS THE STUDENT UNION. IT HAS BARS, AND CAFES, AND SHOPS, AND... WHERE'S INGRID?
SHEFFIELD OPEN TOP BUS TOURS
CAN WE TAKE AN OPEN-TOP BUS TOUR? VERY COOL! LIKE THE OLD PEOPLE DO!
NO, WE CAN'T. I HAVE AN ITINERARY.
I DO NOT KNOW WHAT "ITINERARY" IS. LOOK, I HAVE BUS MONEY!

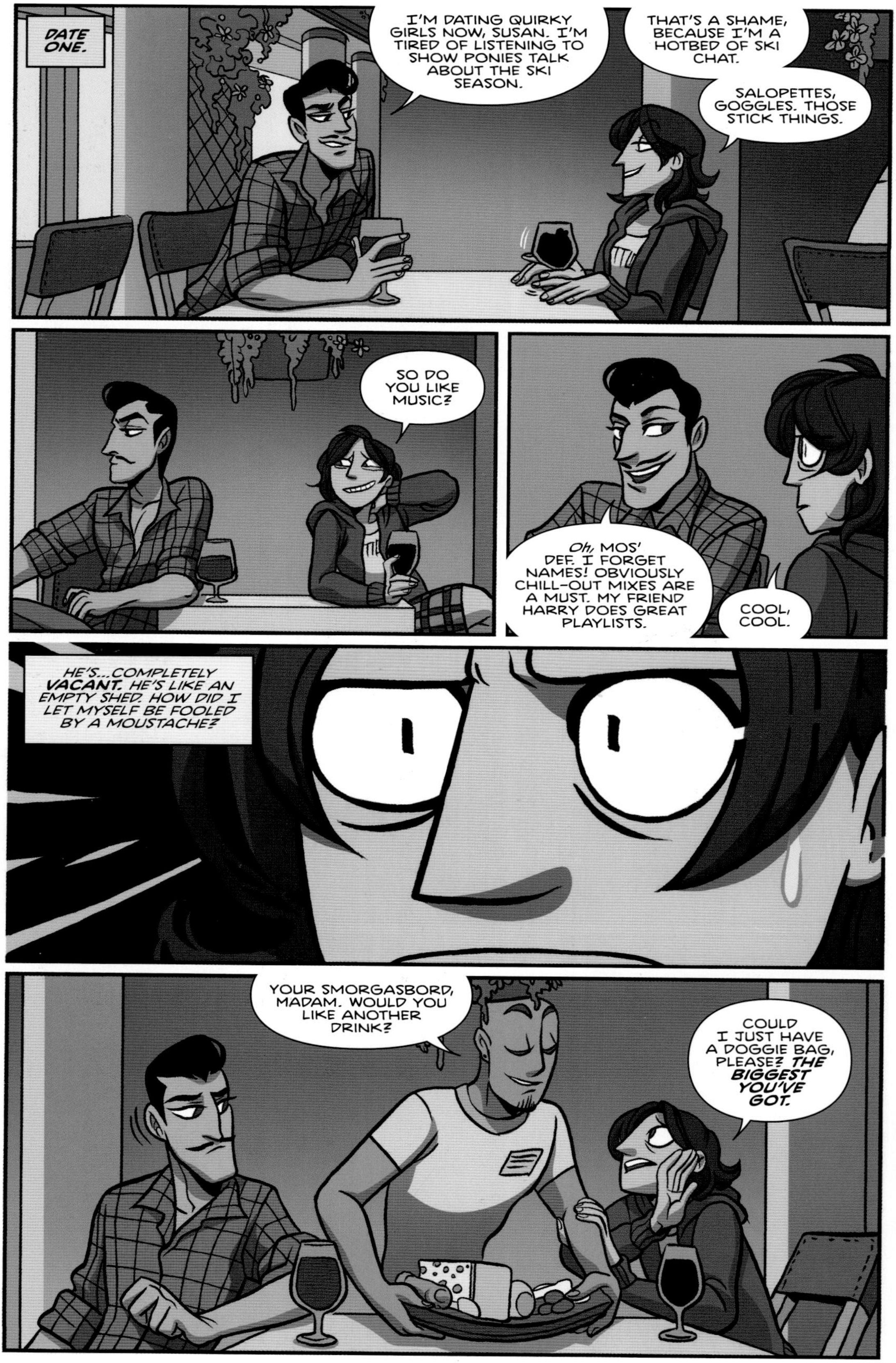
DATE ONE.
I'M DATING QUIRKY GIRLS NOW, SUSAN. I'M TIRED OF LISTENING TO SHOW PONIES TALK ABOUT THE SKI SEASON.
THAT'S A SHAME, BECAUSE I'M A HOTBED OF SKI CHAT.
SALOPETTES, GOGGLES. THOSE STICK THINGS.
SO DO YOU LIKE MUSIC?
Oh, MOS' DEF. I FORGET NAMES! OBVIOUSLY CHILL-OUT MIXES ARE A MUST. MY FRIEND HARRY DOES GREAT PLAYLISTS.
COOL, COOL.
HE'S...COMPLETELY **VACANT.** HE'S LIKE AN EMPTY SHED. HOW DID I LET MYSELF BE FOOLED BY A MOUSTACHE?
YOUR SMORGASBORD, MADAM. WOULD YOU LIKE ANOTHER DRINK?
COULD I JUST HAVE A DOGGIE BAG, PLEASE? ***THE BIGGEST YOU'VE GOT.***

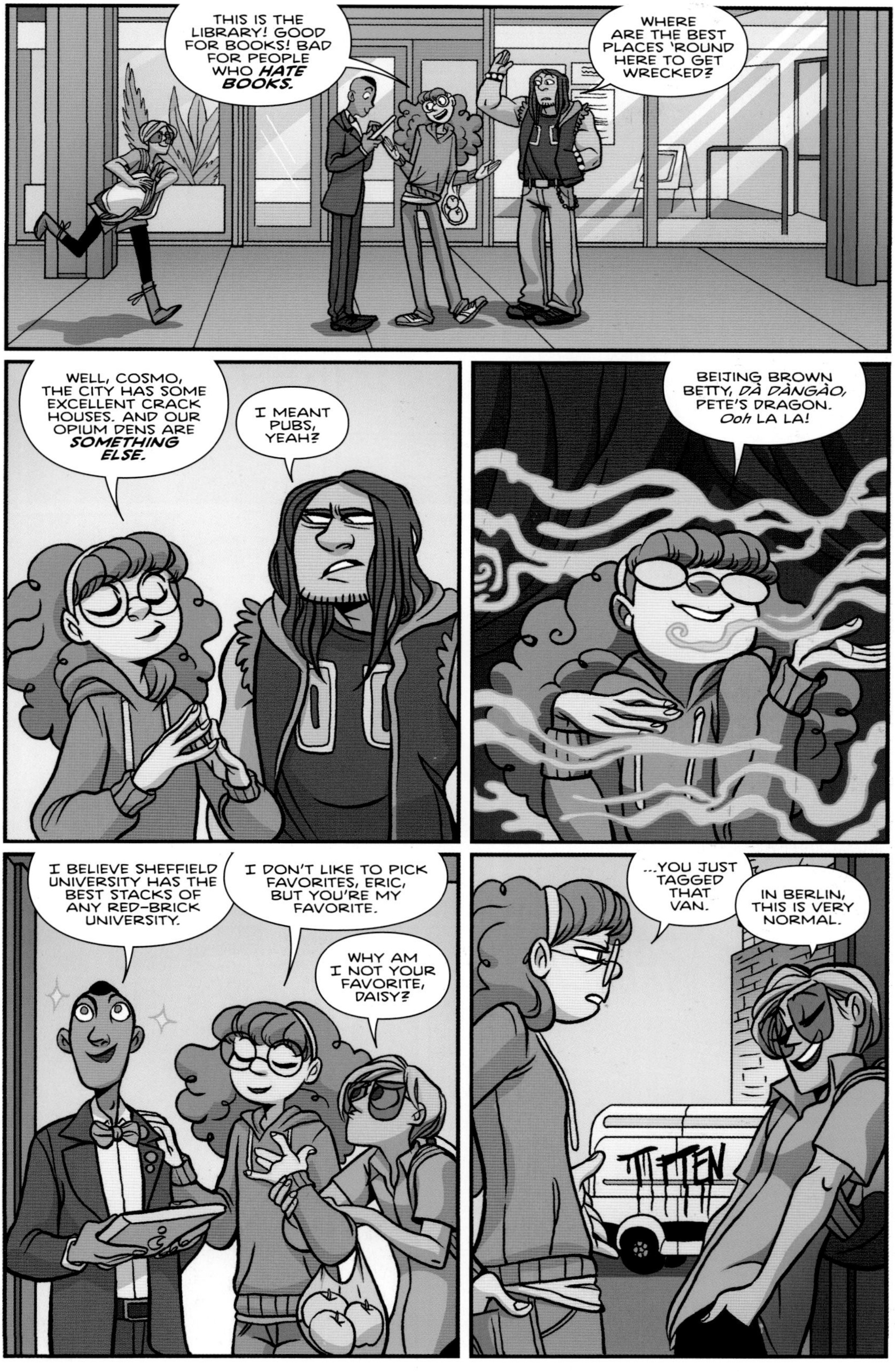
THIS IS THE LIBRARY! GOOD FOR BOOKS! BAD FOR PEOPLE WHO *HATE BOOKS.*
WHERE ARE THE BEST PLACES 'ROUND HERE TO GET WRECKED?
WELL, COSMO, THE CITY HAS SOME EXCELLENT CRACK HOUSES. AND OUR OPIUM DENS ARE *SOMETHING ELSE.*
I MEANT PUBS, YEAH?
BEIJING BROWN BETTY, *DÀ DÀNGÀO,* PETE'S DRAGON. *Ooh* LA LA!
I BELIEVE SHEFFIELD UNIVERSITY HAS THE BEST STACKS OF ANY RED-BRICK UNIVERSITY.
I DON'T LIKE TO PICK FAVORITES, ERIC, BUT YOU'RE MY FAVORITE.
WHY AM I NOT YOUR FAVORITE, DAISY?
...YOU JUST TAGGED THAT VAN.
IN BERLIN, THIS IS VERY NORMAL.
TITTEN

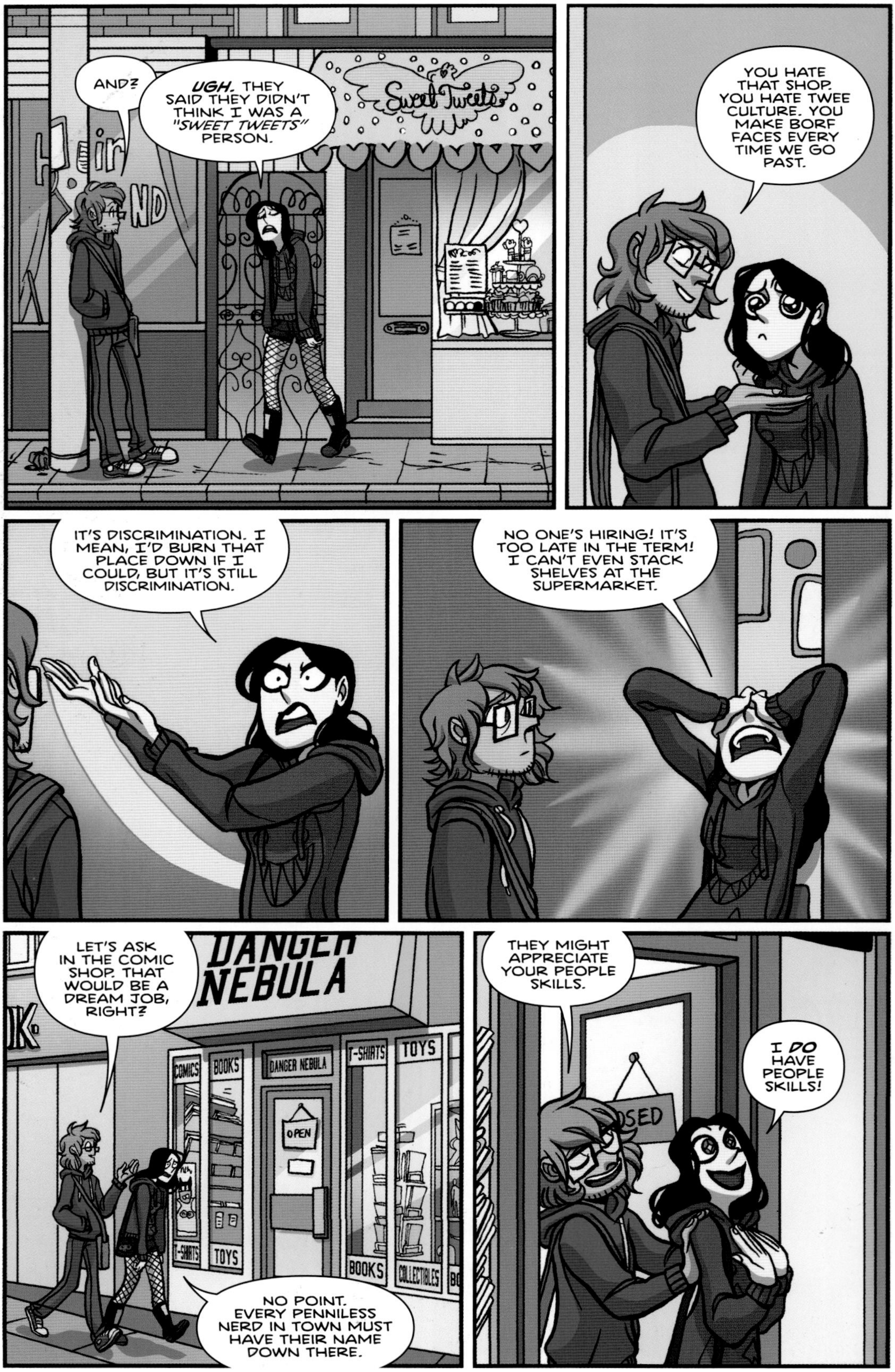
AND?
UGH. THEY SAID THEY DIDN'T THINK I WAS A "SWEET TWEETS" PERSON.
Sweet Tweets
YOU HATE THAT SHOP. YOU HATE TWEE CULTURE. YOU MAKE BORF FACES EVERY TIME WE GO PAST.
IT'S DISCRIMINATION. I MEAN, I'D BURN THAT PLACE DOWN IF I COULD, BUT IT'S STILL DISCRIMINATION.
NO ONE'S HIRING! IT'S TOO LATE IN THE TERM! I CAN'T EVEN STACK SHELVES AT THE SUPERMARKET.
DANGER NEBULA
LET'S ASK IN THE COMIC SHOP. THAT WOULD BE A DREAM JOB, RIGHT?
COMICS
BOOKS
DANGER NEBULA
T-SHIRTS
TOYS
OPEN
NO POINT. EVERY PENNILESS NERD IN TOWN MUST HAVE THEIR NAME DOWN THERE.
THEY MIGHT APPRECIATE YOUR PEOPLE SKILLS.
I DO HAVE PEOPLE SKILLS!

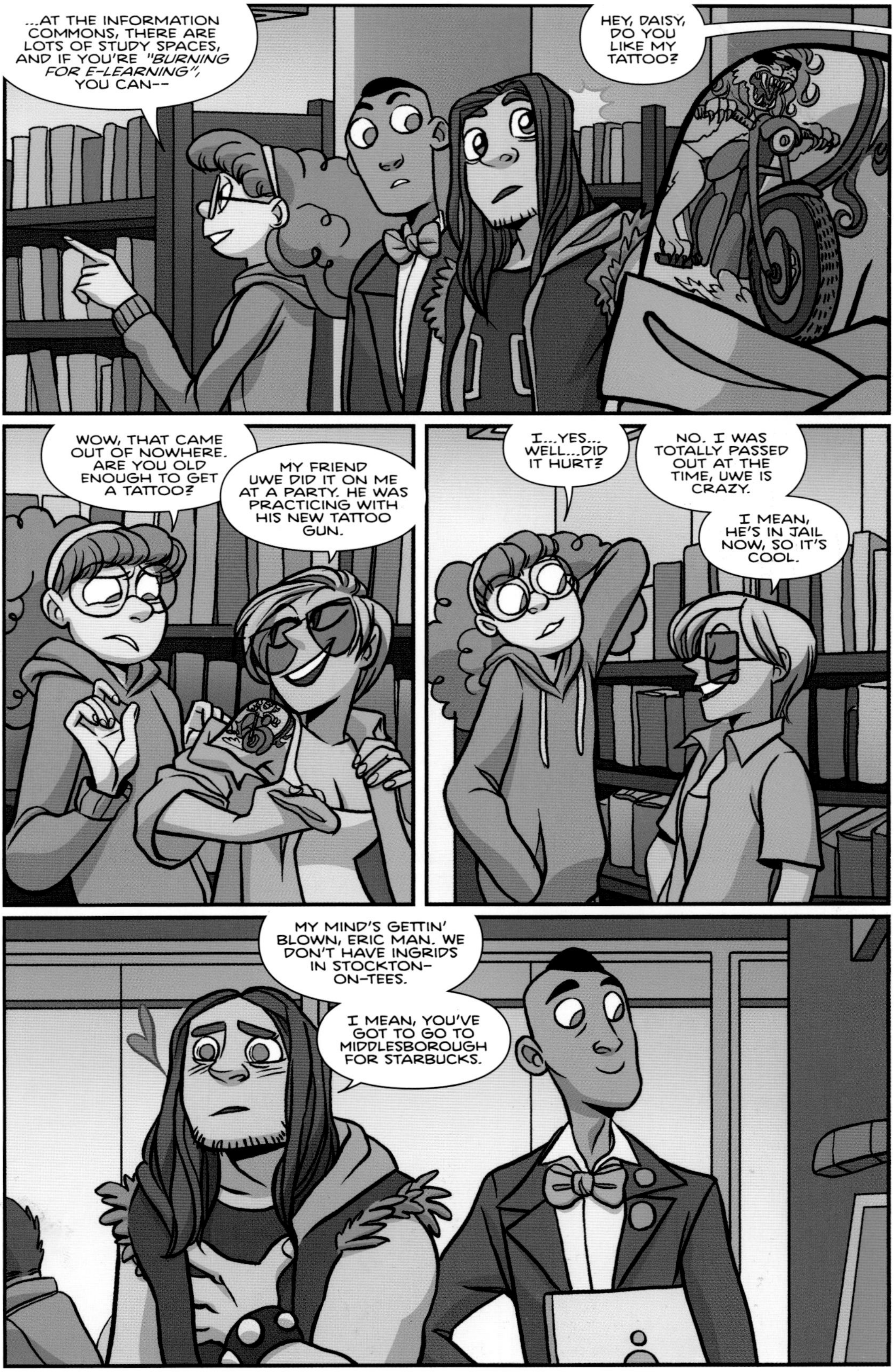
...AT THE INFORMATION COMMONS, THERE ARE LOTS OF STUDY SPACES, AND IF YOU'RE *"BURNING FOR E-LEARNING"*, YOU CAN--
HEY, DAISY, DO YOU LIKE MY TATTOO?
WOW, THAT CAME OUT OF NOWHERE. ARE YOU OLD ENOUGH TO GET A TATTOO?
MY FRIEND UWE DID IT ON ME AT A PARTY. HE WAS PRACTICING WITH HIS NEW TATTOO GUN.
I...YES... WELL...DID IT HURT?
NO. I WAS TOTALLY PASSED OUT AT THE TIME, UWE IS CRAZY.
I MEAN, HE'S IN JAIL NOW, SO IT'S COOL.
MY MIND'S GETTIN' BLOWN, ERIC MAN. WE DON'T HAVE INGRIDS IN STOCKTON-ON-TEES.
I MEAN, YOU'VE GOT TO GO TO MIDDLESBOROUGH FOR STARBUCKS.

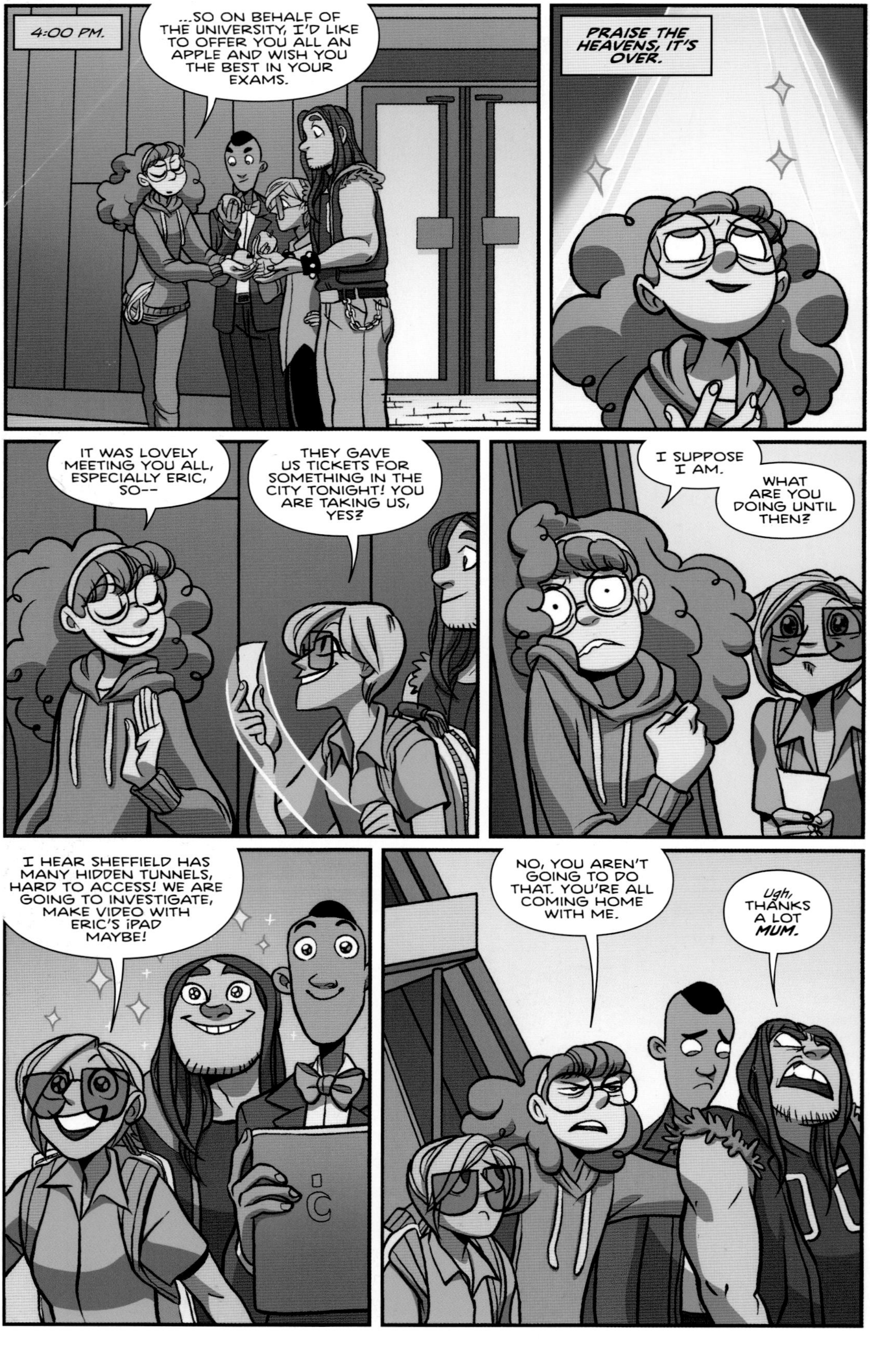
4:00 PM.
...SO ON BEHALF OF THE UNIVERSITY, I'D LIKE TO OFFER YOU ALL AN APPLE AND WISH YOU THE BEST IN YOUR EXAMS.
PRAISE THE HEAVENS, IT'S OVER.
IT WAS LOVELY MEETING YOU ALL, ESPECIALLY ERIC, SO--
THEY GAVE US TICKETS FOR SOMETHING IN THE CITY TONIGHT! YOU ARE TAKING US, YES?
I SUPPOSE I AM.
WHAT ARE YOU DOING UNTIL THEN?
I HEAR SHEFFIELD HAS MANY HIDDEN TUNNELS, HARD TO ACCESS! WE ARE GOING TO INVESTIGATE, MAKE VIDEO WITH ERIC'S iPAD MAYBE!
NO, YOU AREN'T GOING TO DO THAT. YOU'RE ALL COMING HOME WITH ME.
Ugh, THANKS A LOT MUM.

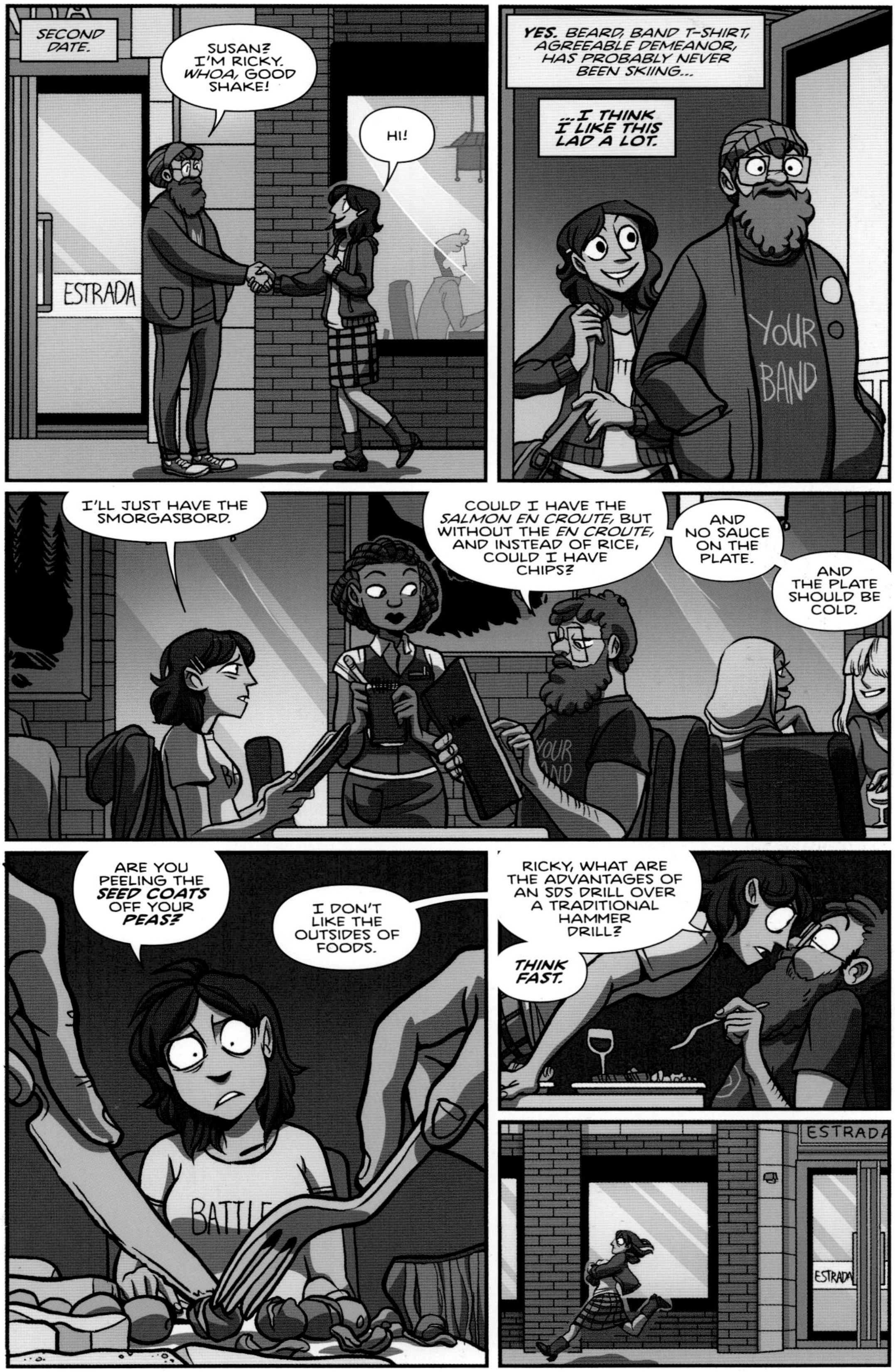
SECOND DATE.
SUSAN? I'M RICKY. WHOA, GOOD SHAKE!
HI!
ESTRADA
YES. BEARD, BAND T-SHIRT, AGREEABLE DEMEANOR, HAS PROBABLY NEVER BEEN SKIING...
...I THINK I LIKE THIS LAD A LOT.
YOUR BAND
I'LL JUST HAVE THE SMORGASBORD.
COULD I HAVE THE SALMON EN CROUTE, BUT WITHOUT THE EN CROUTE, AND INSTEAD OF RICE, COULD I HAVE CHIPS?
AND NO SAUCE ON THE PLATE.
AND THE PLATE SHOULD BE COLD.
ARE YOU PEELING THE SEED COATS OFF YOUR PEAS?
I DON'T LIKE THE OUTSIDES OF FOODS.
BATTLE
RICKY, WHAT ARE THE ADVANTAGES OF AN SDS DRILL OVER A TRADITIONAL HAMMER DRILL?
THINK FAST.
ESTRADA
ESTRADA

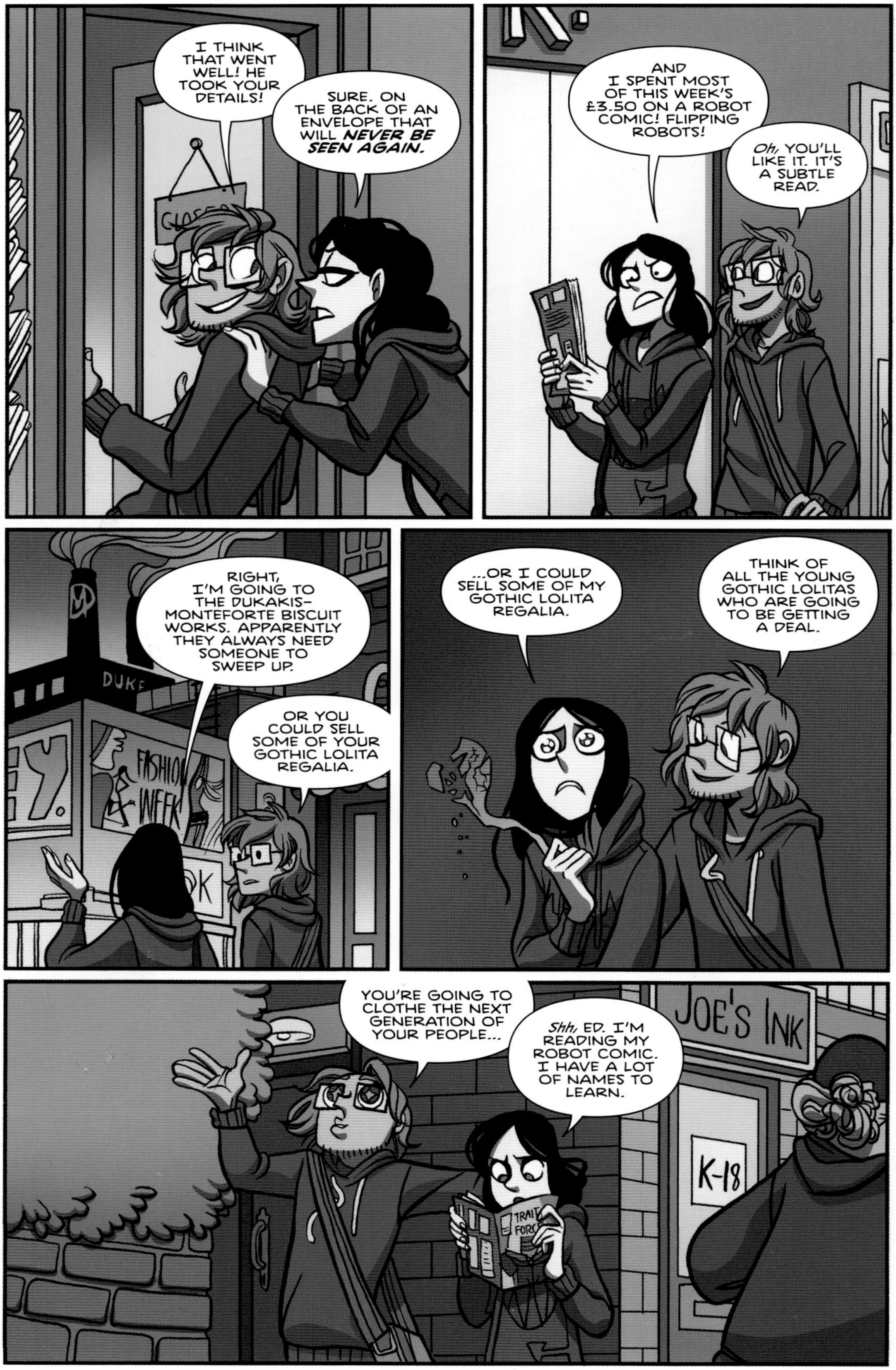
I THINK THAT WENT WELL! HE TOOK YOUR DETAILS!
SURE. ON THE BACK OF AN ENVELOPE THAT WILL ***NEVER BE SEEN AGAIN.***
CLOSED
AND I SPENT MOST OF THIS WEEK'S £3.50 ON A ROBOT COMIC! FLIPPING ROBOTS!
Oh, YOU'LL LIKE IT. IT'S A SUBTLE READ.
RIGHT, I'M GOING TO THE DUKAKIS-MONTEFORTE BISCUIT WORKS. APPARENTLY THEY ALWAYS NEED SOMEONE TO SWEEP UP.
OR YOU COULD SELL SOME OF YOUR GOTHIC LOLITA REGALIA.
DUKE
FASHION WEEK
...OR I COULD SELL SOME OF MY GOTHIC LOLITA REGALIA.
THINK OF ALL THE YOUNG GOTHIC LOLITAS WHO ARE GOING TO BE GETTING A DEAL.
YOU'RE GOING TO CLOTHE THE NEXT GENERATION OF YOUR PEOPLE...
Shh, ED. I'M READING MY ROBOT COMIC. I HAVE A LOT OF NAMES TO LEARN.
JOE'S INK
K-18

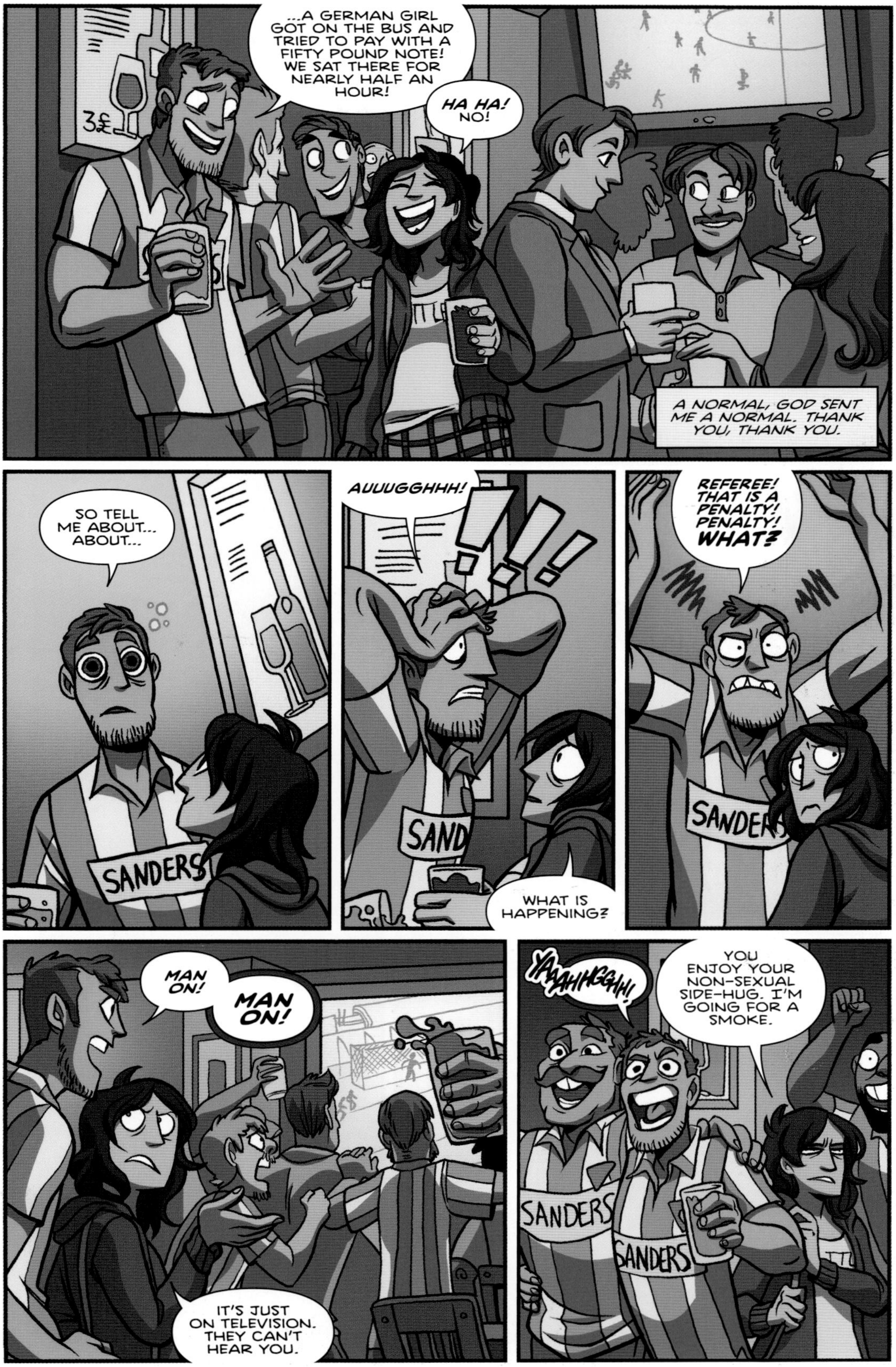
3£
...A GERMAN GIRL GOT ON THE BUS AND TRIED TO PAY WITH A FIFTY POUND NOTE! WE SAT THERE FOR NEARLY HALF AN HOUR!
HA HA! NO!
A NORMAL, GOD SENT ME A NORMAL. THANK YOU, THANK YOU.
SO TELL ME ABOUT... ABOUT...
SANDERS
AUUUGGHHH!
SAND
WHAT IS HAPPENING?
REFEREE! THAT IS A PENALTY! PENALTY! WHAT?
SANDERS
MAN ON!
MAN ON!
IT'S JUST ON TELEVISION. THEY CAN'T HEAR YOU.
YAAAHHGGHH!
YOU ENJOY YOUR NON-SEXUAL SIDE-HUG. I'M GOING FOR A SMOKE.
SANDERS
SANDERS

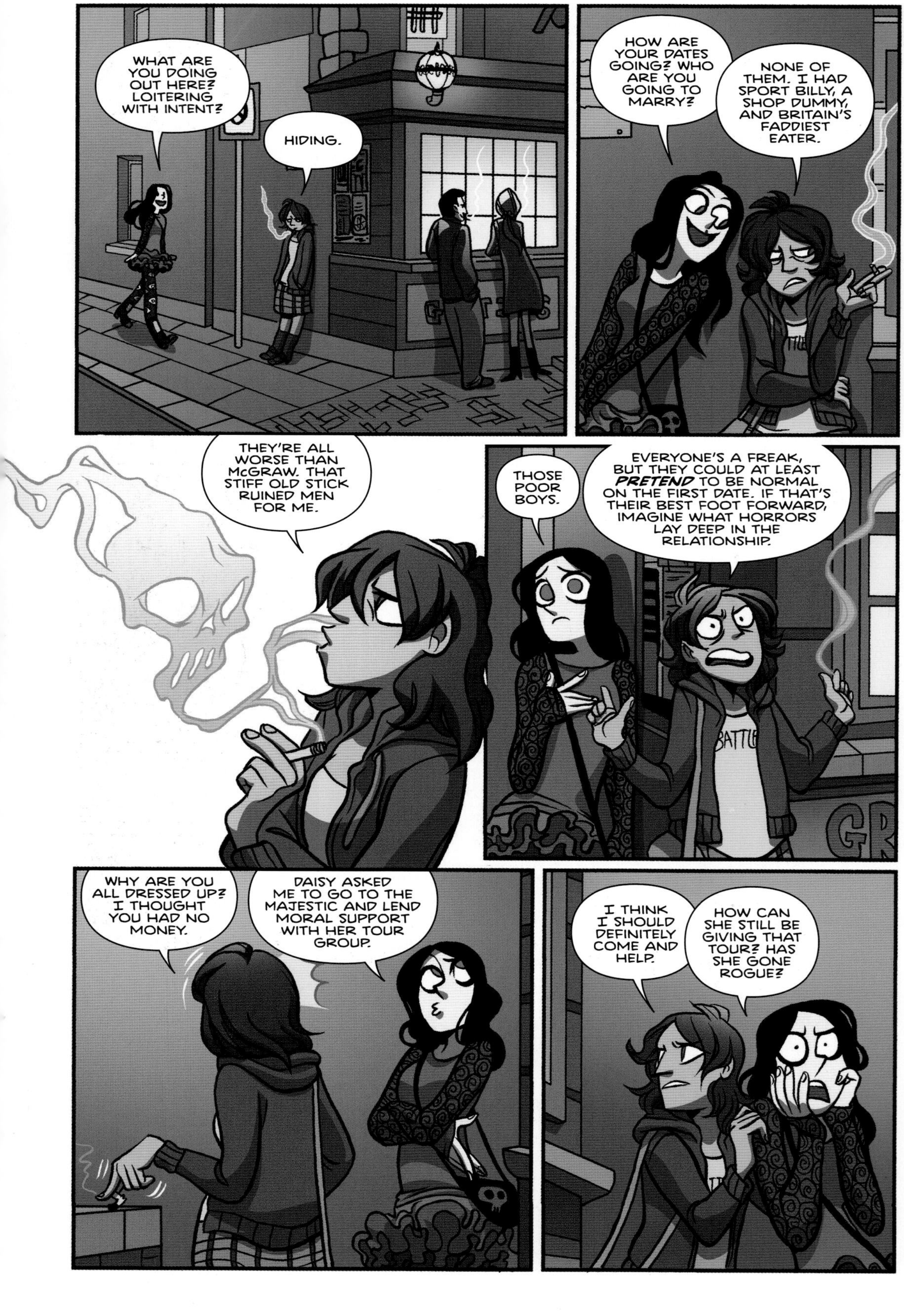
WHAT ARE YOU DOING OUT HERE? LOITERING WITH INTENT?
HIDING.
HOW ARE YOUR DATES GOING? WHO ARE YOU GOING TO MARRY?
NONE OF THEM. I HAD SPORT BILLY, A SHOP DUMMY, AND BRITAIN'S FADDIEST EATER.
THEY'RE ALL WORSE THAN McGRAW. THAT STIFF OLD STICK RUINED MEN FOR ME.
THOSE POOR BOYS.
EVERYONE'S A FREAK, BUT THEY COULD AT LEAST PRETEND TO BE NORMAL ON THE FIRST DATE. IF THAT'S THEIR BEST FOOT FORWARD, IMAGINE WHAT HORRORS LAY DEEP IN THE RELATIONSHIP.
WHY ARE YOU ALL DRESSED UP? I THOUGHT YOU HAD NO MONEY.
DAISY ASKED ME TO GO TO THE MAJESTIC AND LEND MORAL SUPPORT WITH HER TOUR GROUP.
I THINK I SHOULD DEFINITELY COME AND HELP.
HOW CAN SHE STILL BE GIVING THAT TOUR? HAS SHE GONE ROGUE?

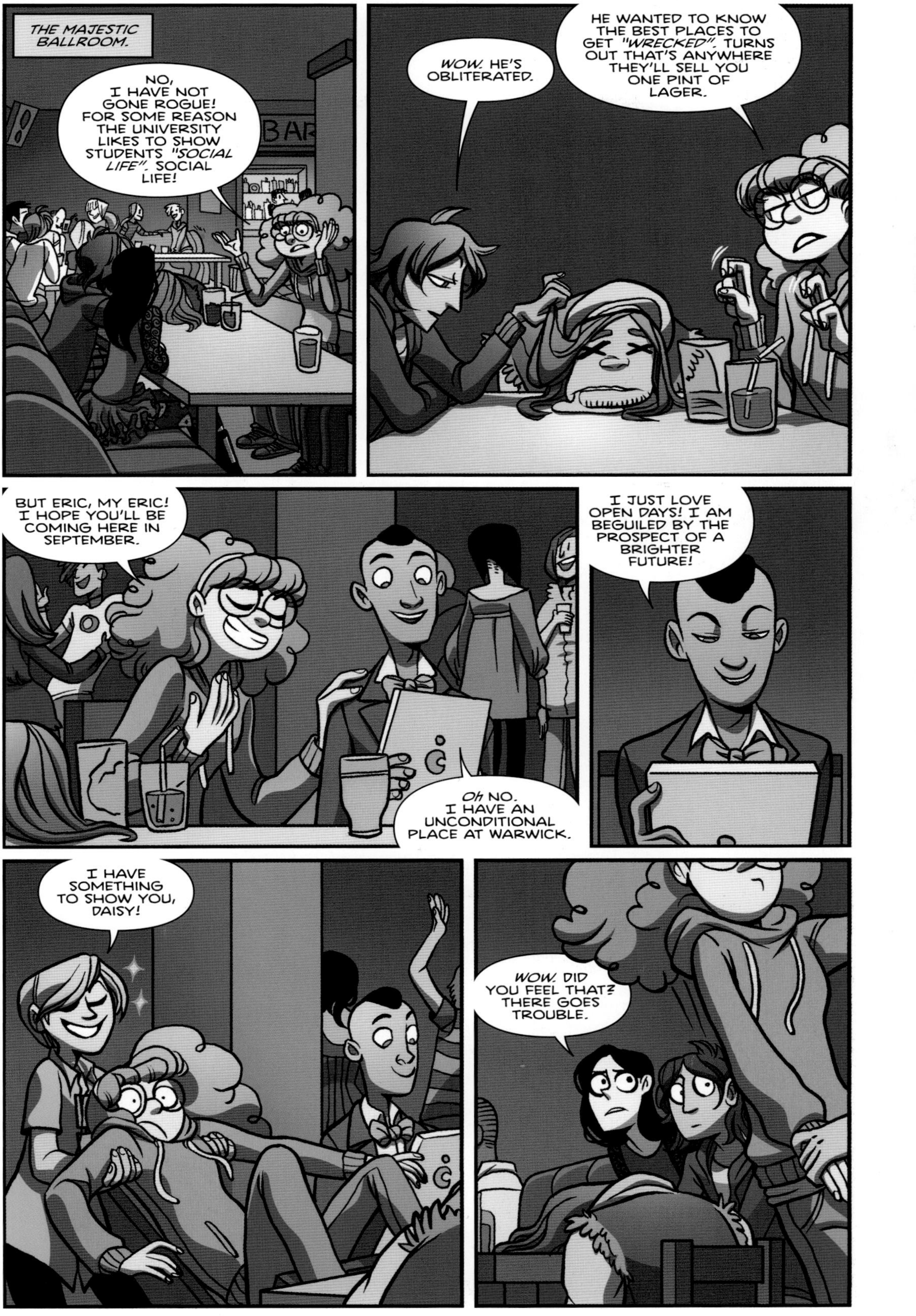
THE MAJESTIC BALLROOM.
NO, I HAVE NOT GONE ROGUE! FOR SOME REASON THE UNIVERSITY LIKES TO SHOW STUDENTS "SOCIAL LIFE". SOCIAL LIFE!
BAR
WOW. HE'S OBLITERATED.
HE WANTED TO KNOW THE BEST PLACES TO GET "WRECKED". TURNS OUT THAT'S ANYWHERE THEY'LL SELL YOU ONE PINT OF LAGER.
BUT ERIC, MY ERIC! I HOPE YOU'LL BE COMING HERE IN SEPTEMBER.
OH NO. I HAVE AN UNCONDITIONAL PLACE AT WARWICK.
I JUST LOVE OPEN DAYS! I AM BEGUILED BY THE PROSPECT OF A BRIGHTER FUTURE!
I HAVE SOMETHING TO SHOW YOU, DAISY!
WOW. DID YOU FEEL THAT? THERE GOES TROUBLE.

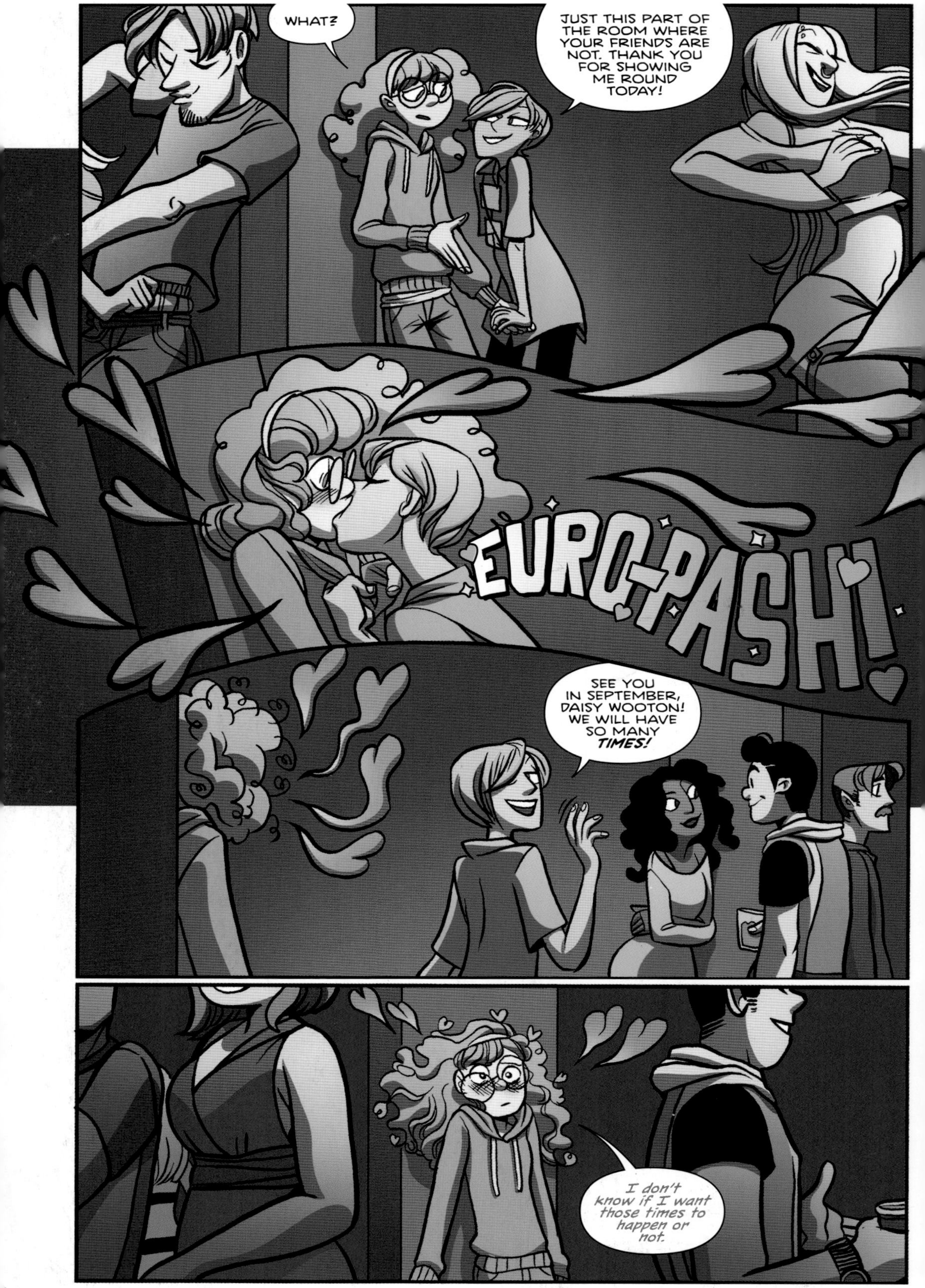
WHAT?
JUST THIS PART OF THE ROOM WHERE YOUR FRIENDS ARE NOT. THANK YOU FOR SHOWING ME ROUND TODAY!
EURO-PASH!
SEE YOU IN SEPTEMBER, DAISY WOOTON! WE WILL HAVE SO MANY *TIMES!*
I don't know if I want those times to happen or not.

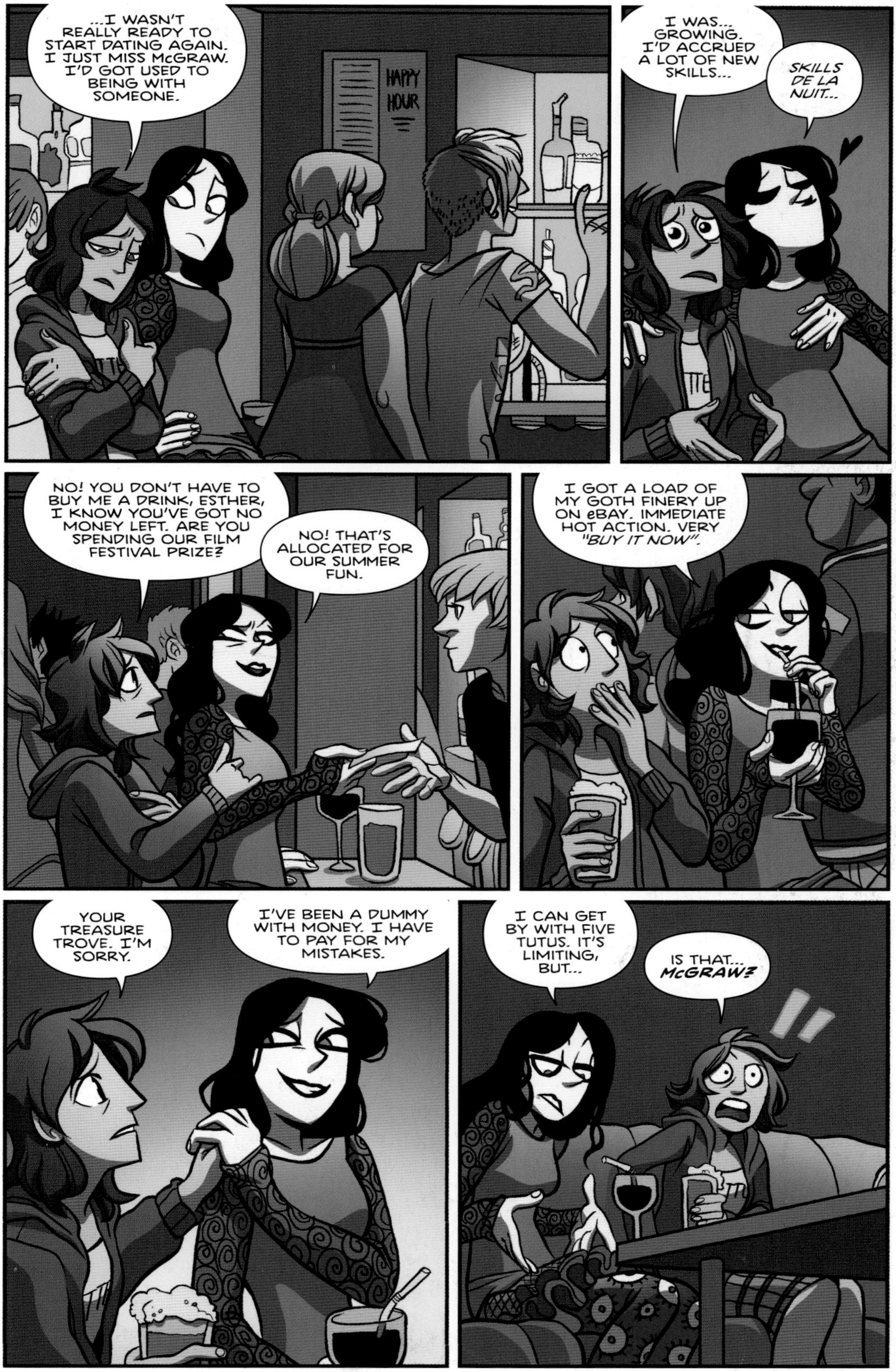
...I WASN'T REALLY READY TO START DATING AGAIN. I JUST MISS McGRAW. I'D GOT USED TO BEING WITH SOMEONE.
HAPPY HOUR
I WAS... GROWING. I'D ACCRUED A LOT OF NEW SKILLS...
SKILLS DE LA NUIT...
NO! YOU DON'T HAVE TO BUY ME A DRINK, ESTHER, I KNOW YOU'VE GOT NO MONEY LEFT. ARE YOU SPENDING OUR FILM FESTIVAL PRIZE?
NO! THAT'S ALLOCATED FOR OUR SUMMER FUN.
I GOT A LOAD OF MY GOTH FINERY UP ON eBAY. IMMEDIATE HOT ACTION. VERY "BUY IT NOW".
YOUR TREASURE TROVE. I'M SORRY.
I'VE BEEN A DUMMY WITH MONEY. I HAVE TO PAY FOR MY MISTAKES.
I CAN GET BY WITH FIVE TUTUS. IT'S LIMITING, BUT...
IS THAT... McGRAW?
!!

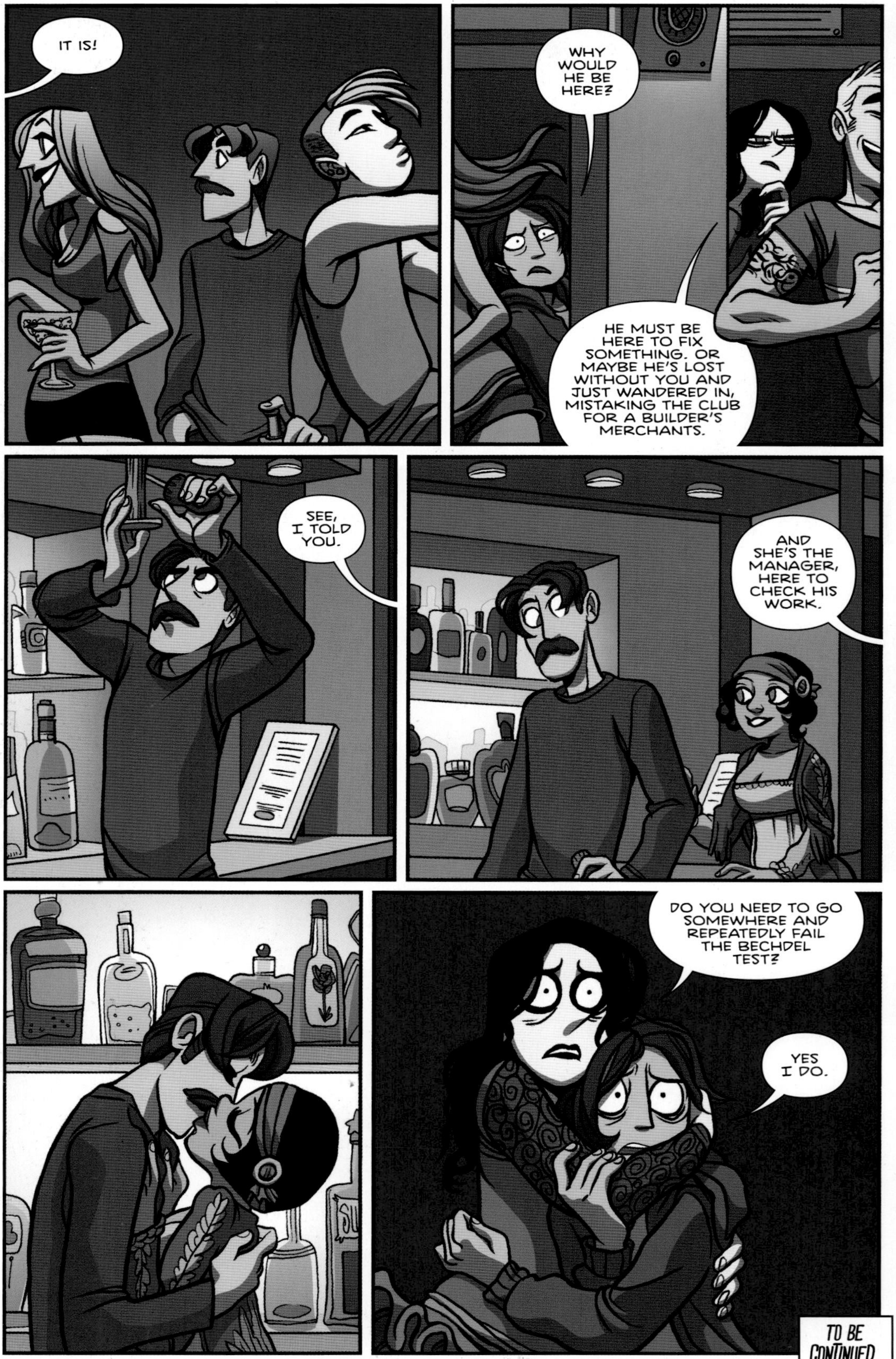

IT IS!
WHY WOULD HE BE HERE?
HE MUST BE HERE TO FIX SOMETHING. OR MAYBE HE'S LOST WITHOUT YOU AND JUST WANDERED IN, MISTAKING THE CLUB FOR A BUILDER'S MERCHANTS.
SEE, I TOLD YOU.
AND SHE'S THE MANAGER, HERE TO CHECK HIS WORK.
DO YOU NEED TO GO SOMEWHERE AND REPEATEDLY FAIL THE BECHDEL TEST?
YES I DO.
TO BE CONTINUED...

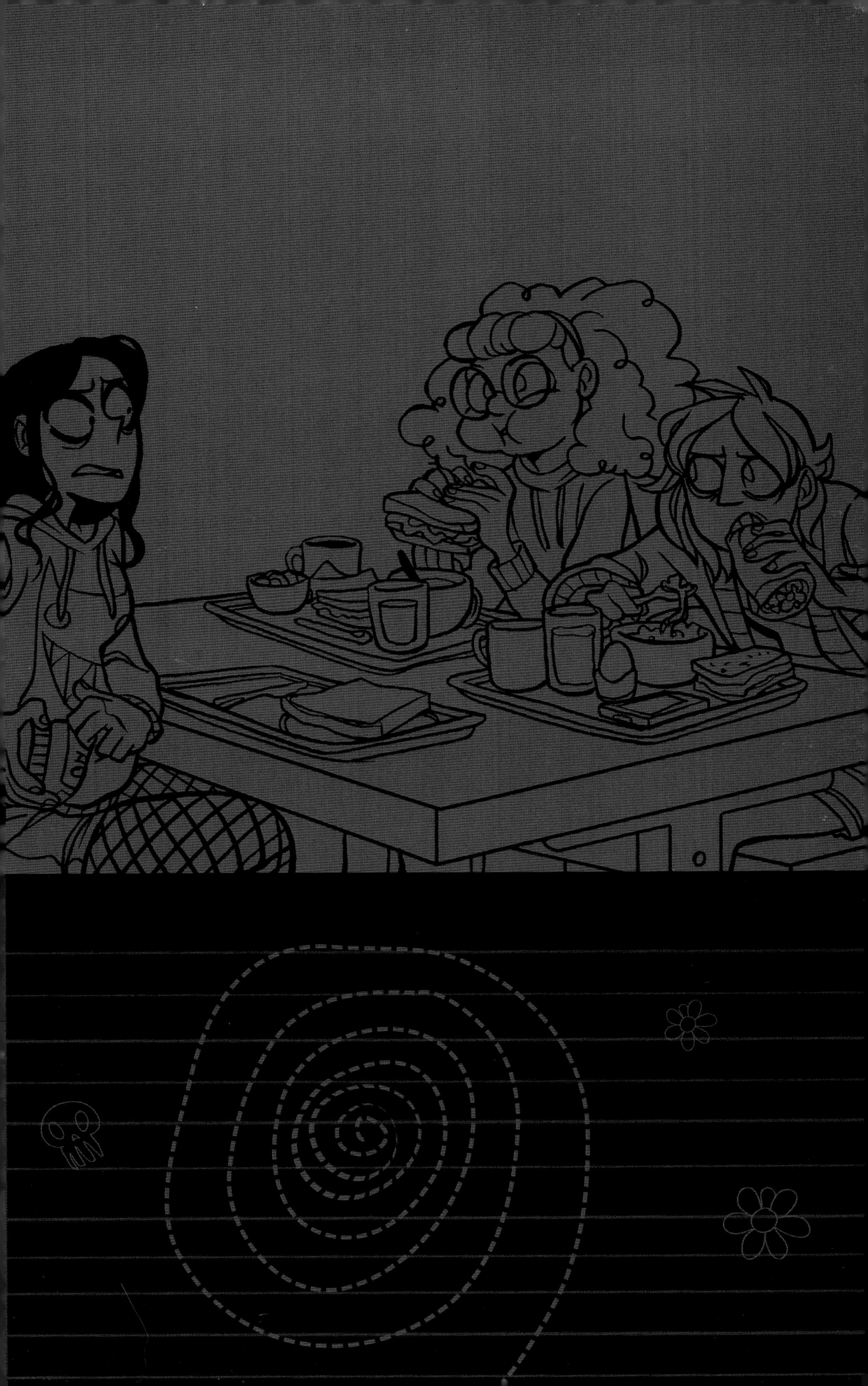

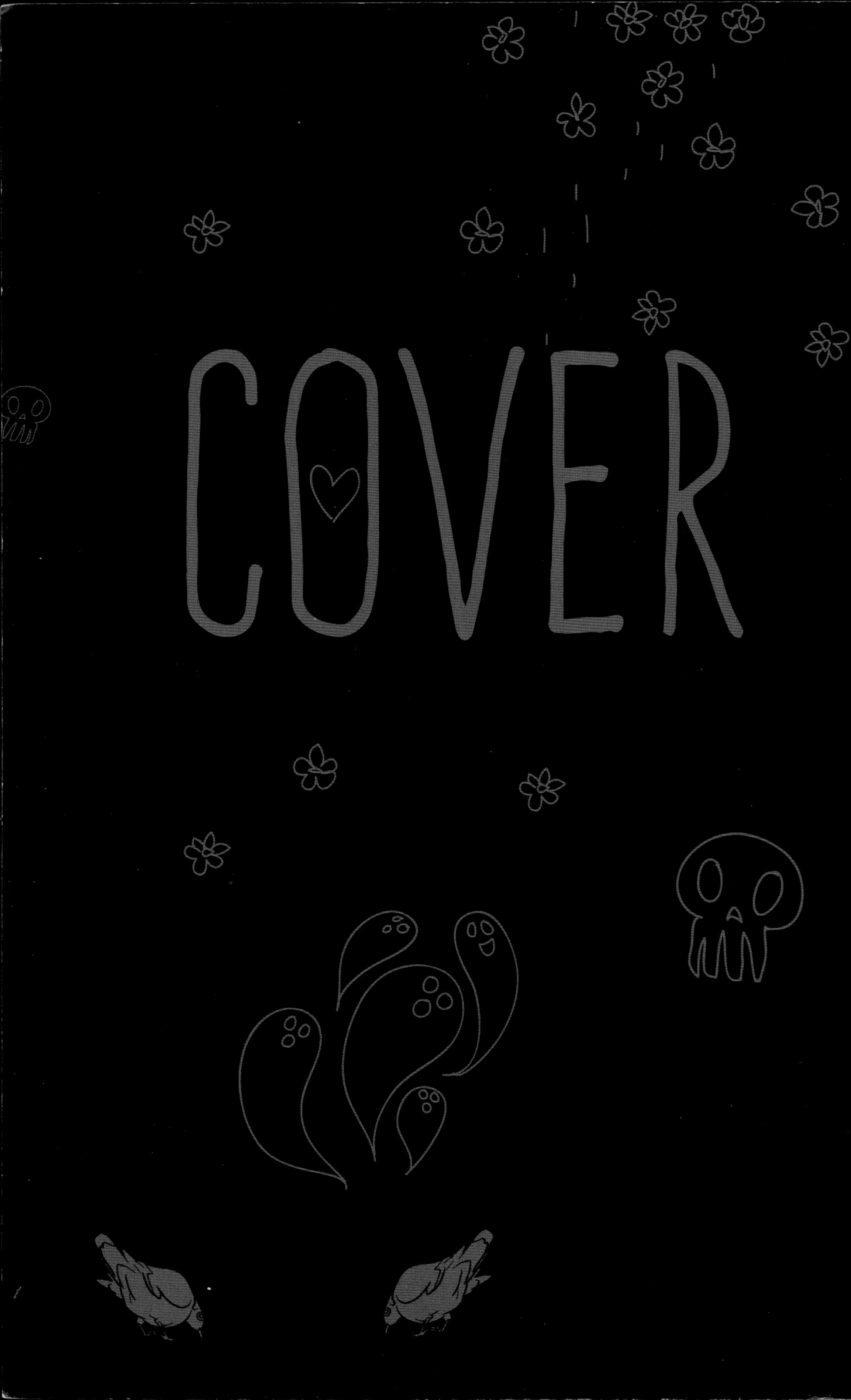
COVER

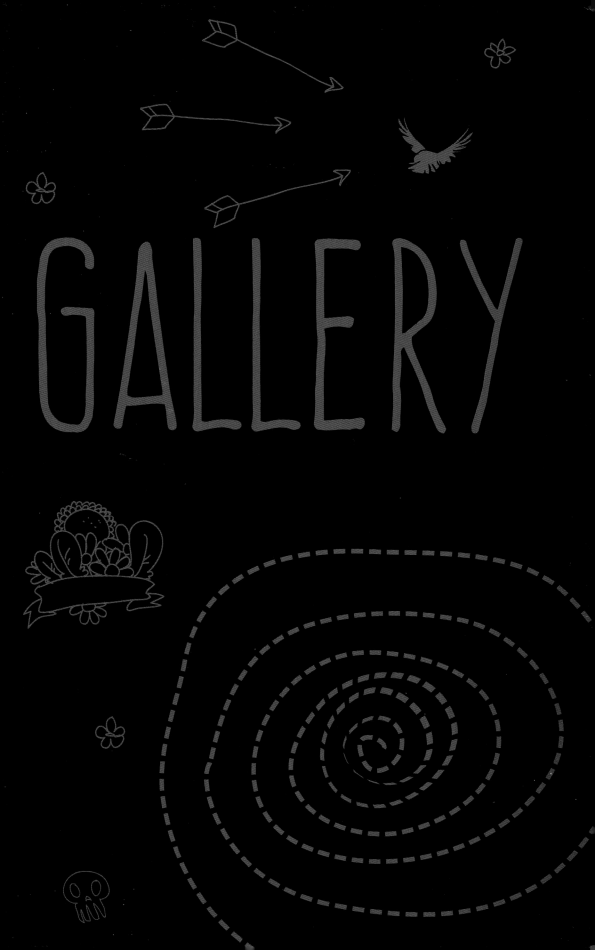

GALLERY

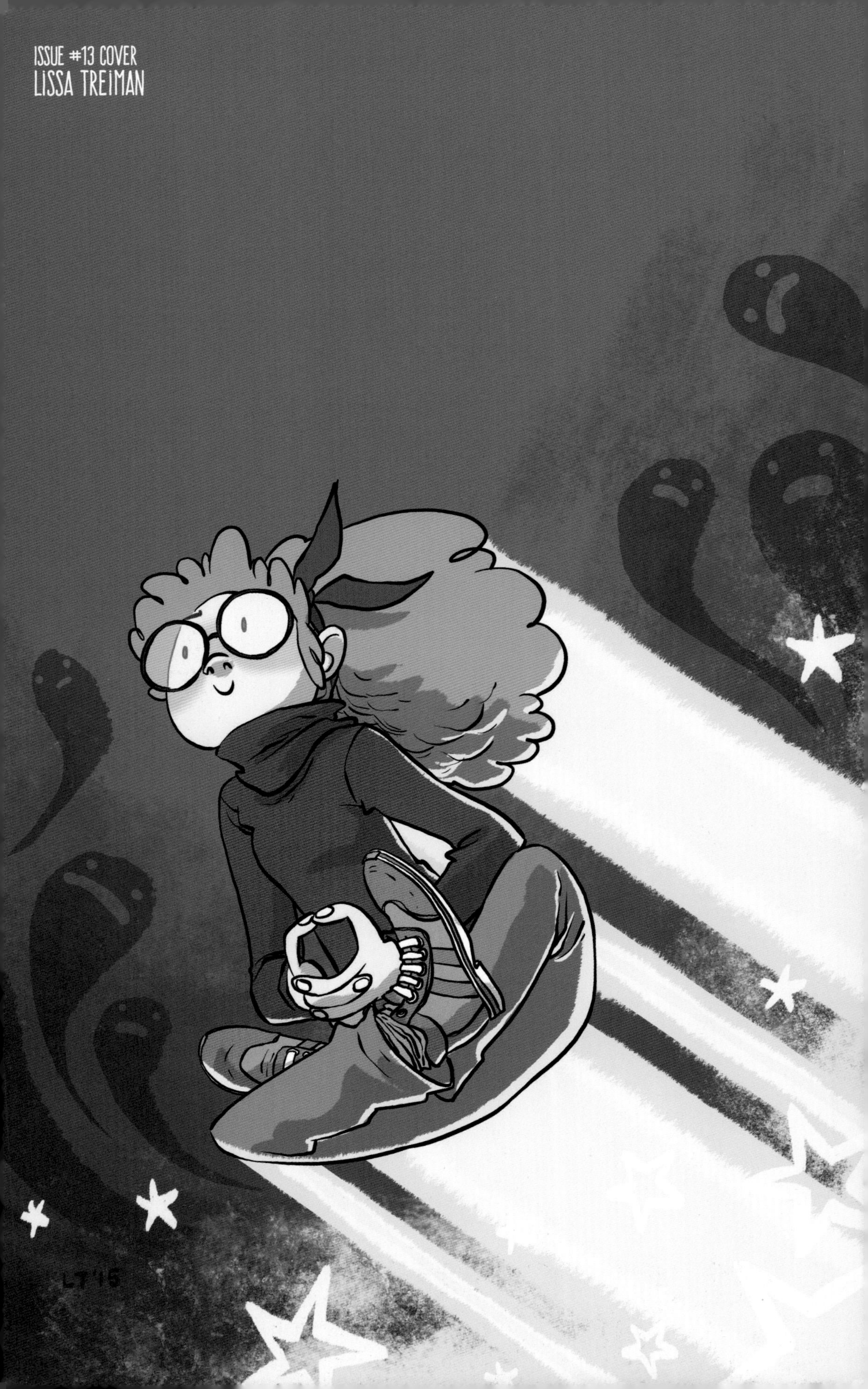
LT '15
ISSUE #13 COVER
LISSA TREIMAN

ISSUE #14 COVER
LISSA TREIMAN

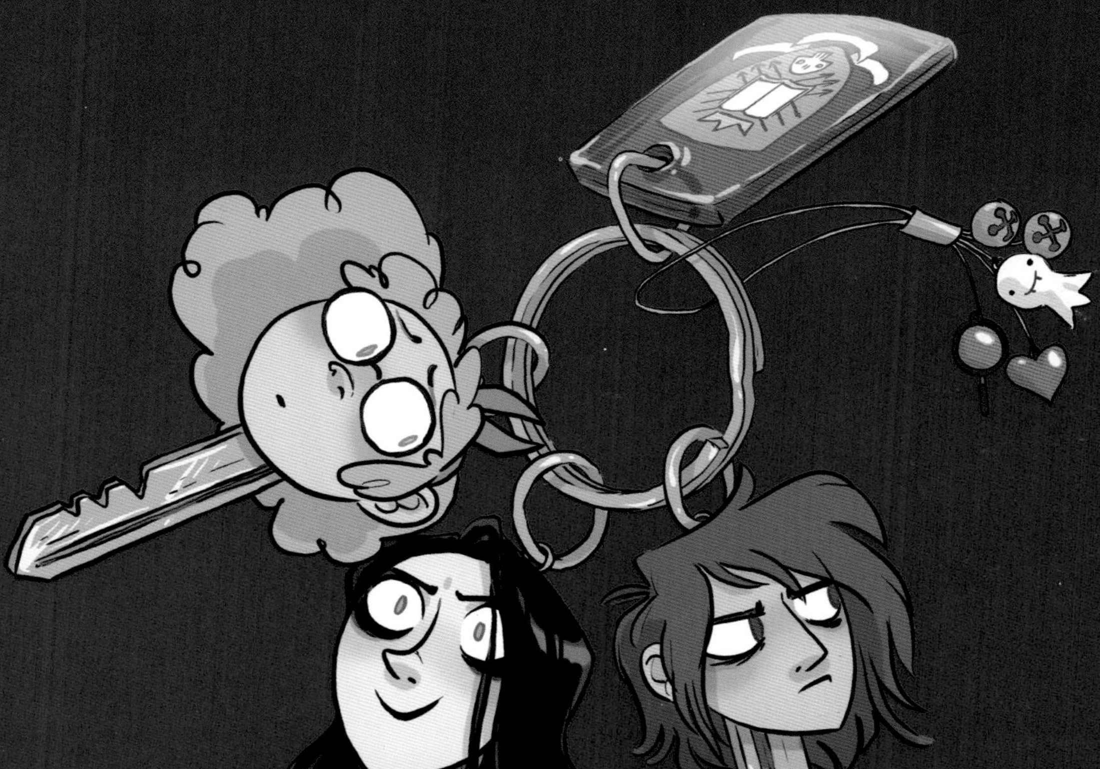

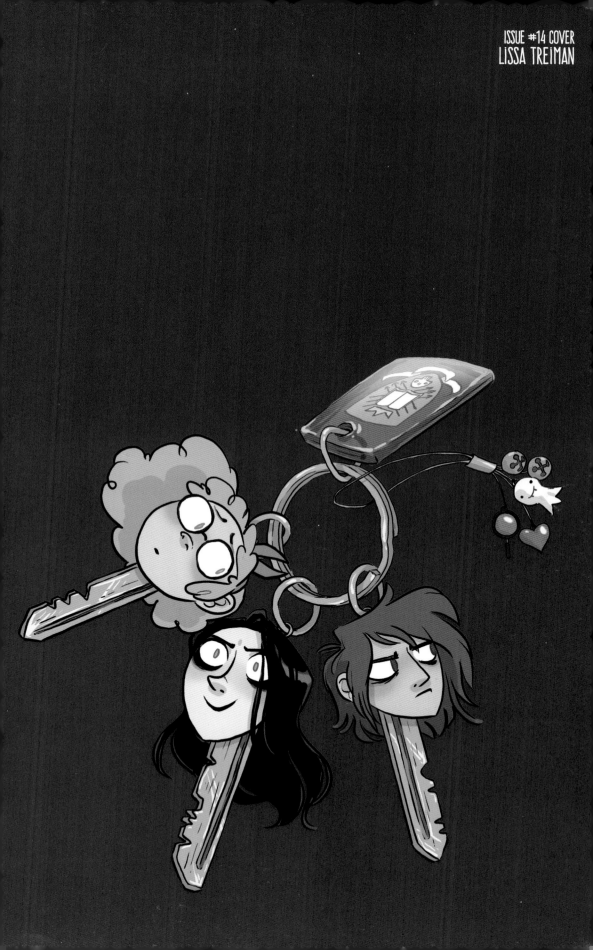

ISSUE #15 COVER
LISSA TREIMAN

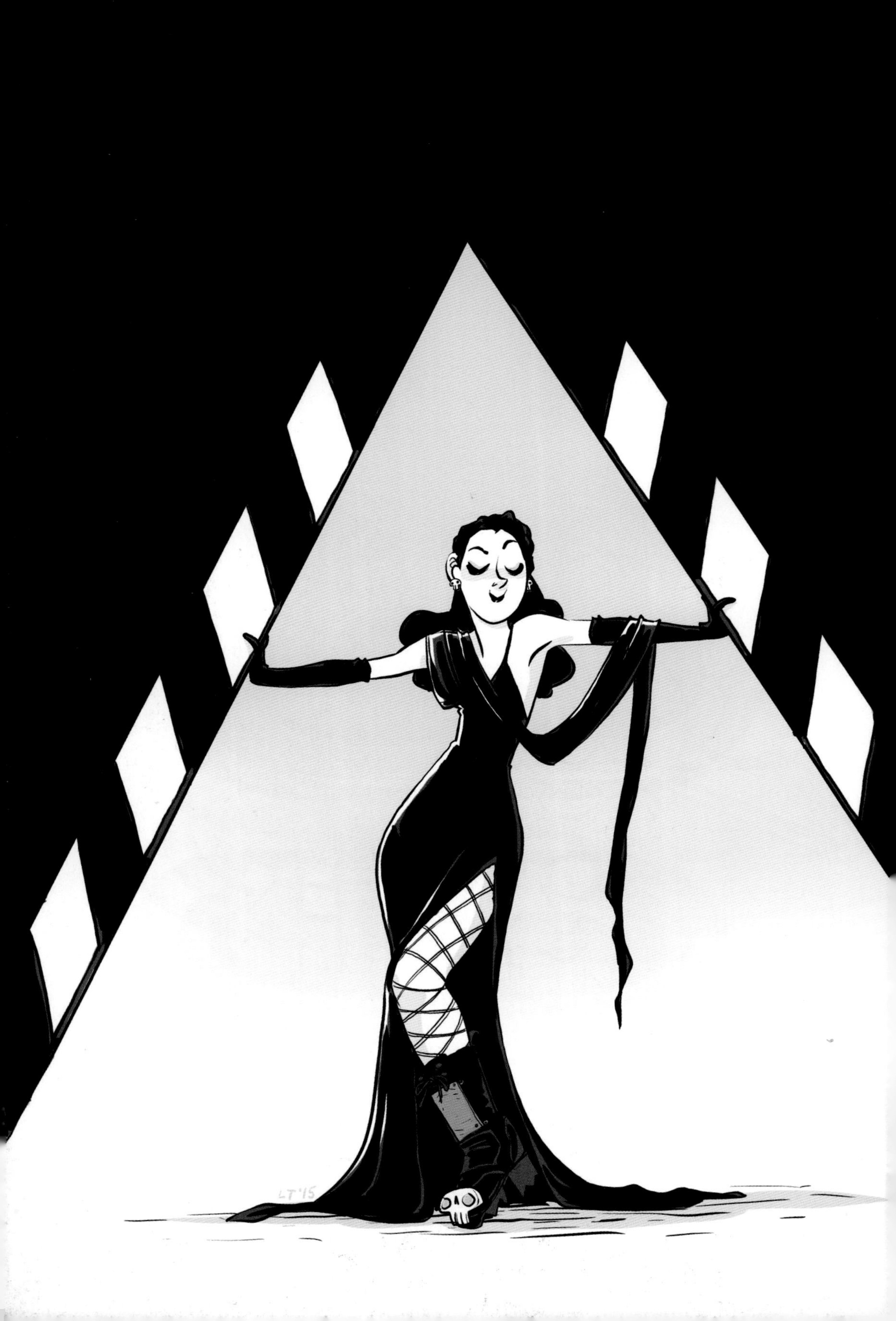
LT'15

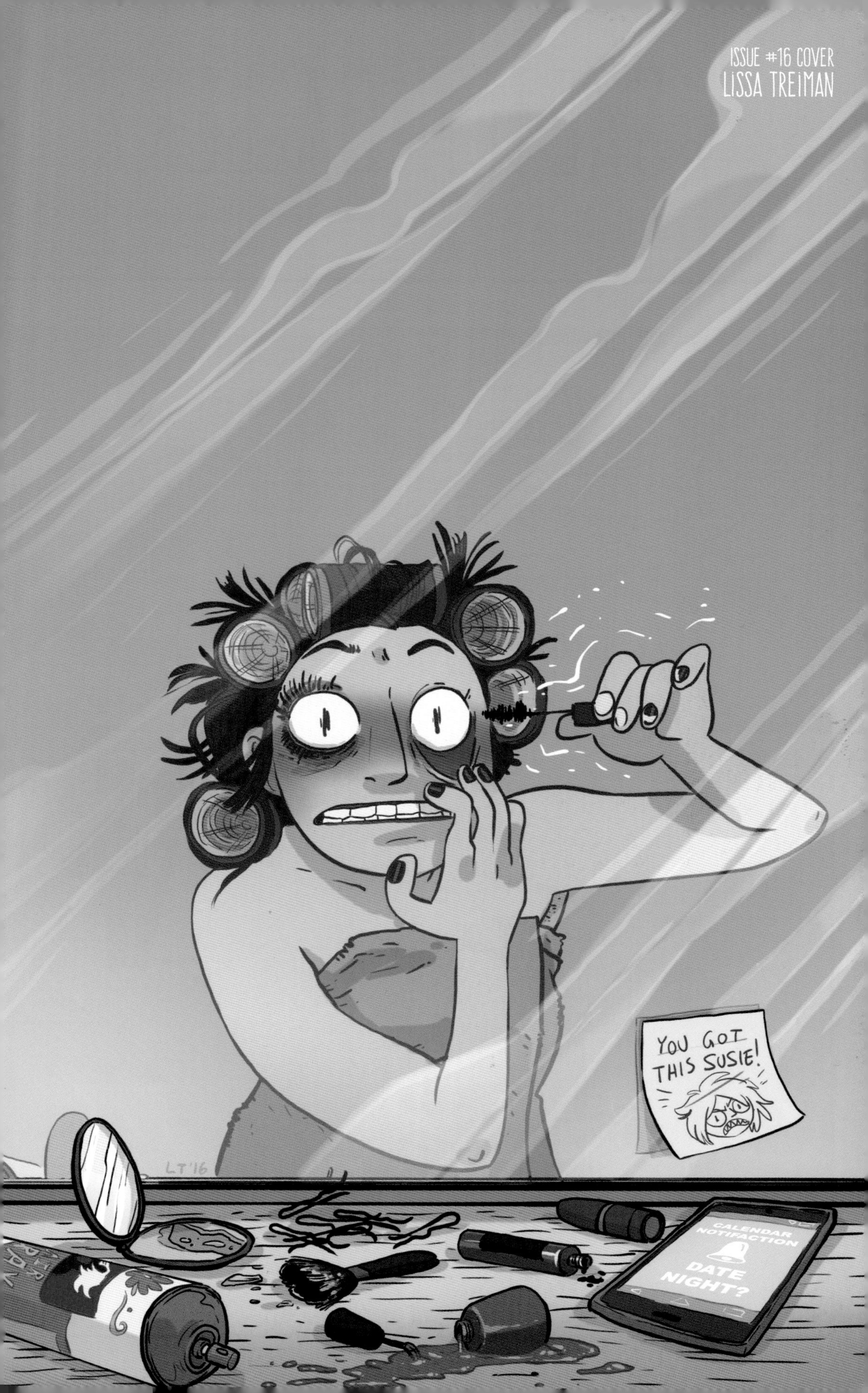
YOU GOT THIS SUSIE!
CALENDAR NOTIFACTION
DATE NIGHT?
LT '16
ISSUE #16 COVER
LISSA TREIMAN

SKETCH GALLERY

CHARACTER DESIGNS BY JOHN ALLISON

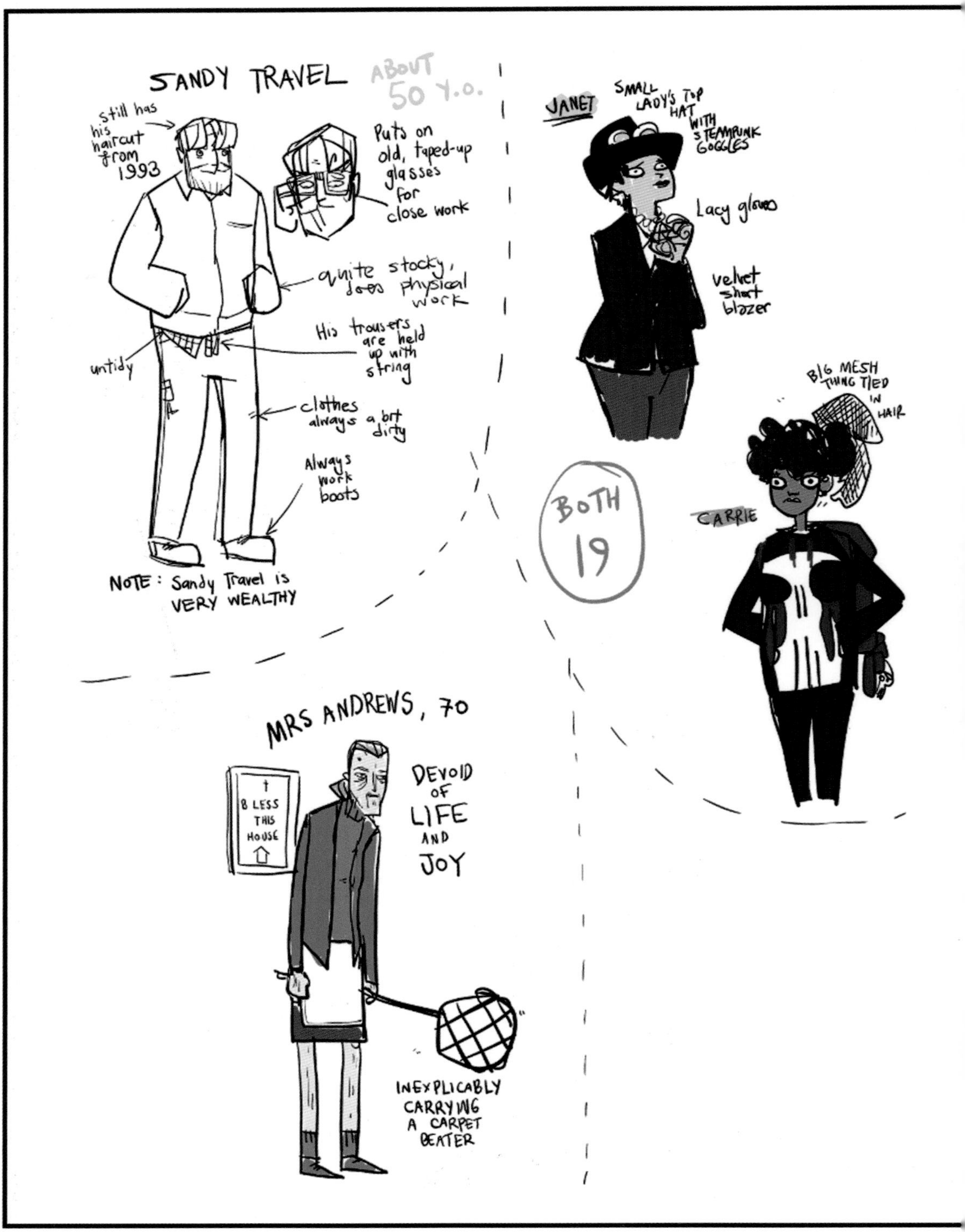

SANDY TRAVEL
ABOUT 50 Y.O.
Still has his haircut from 1993
Puts on old, taped-up glasses for close work
quite stocky, does physical work
His trousers are held up with string
untidy
clothes always a bit dirty
Always work boots
NOTE: Sandy Travel is VERY WEALTHY
JANET
SMALL LADY'S TOP HAT WITH STEAMPUNK GOGGLES
Lacy gloves
velvet short blazer
BOTH 19
BIG MESH THING TIED IN HAIR
CARRIE
MRS ANDREWS, 70
BLESS THIS HOUSE
DEVOID OF LIFE AND JOY
INEXPLICABLY CARRYING A CARPET BEATER

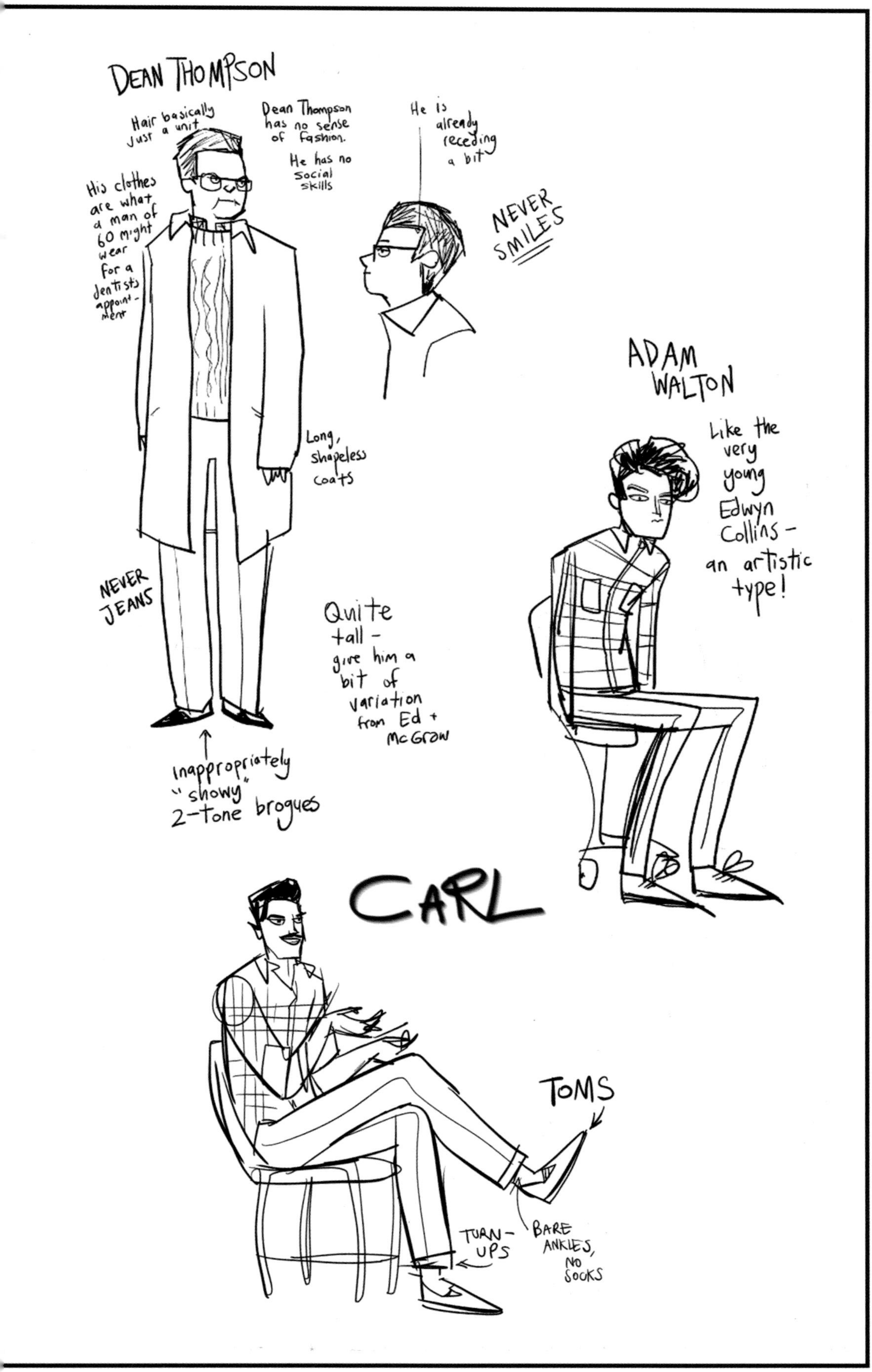

DEAN THOMPSON
Hair basically just a unit
Dean Thompson has no sense of fashion.
He has no social skills
He is already receding a bit
His clothes are what a man of 60 might wear for a dentist's appointment
NEVER SMILES
Long, shapeless coats
NEVER JEANS
Quite tall - give him a bit of variation from Ed + McGraw
Inappropriately "showy" 2-tone brogues
ADAM WALTON
Like the very young Edwyn Collins - an artistic type!
CARL
TOMS
TURN-UPS
BARE ANKLES, NO SOCKS

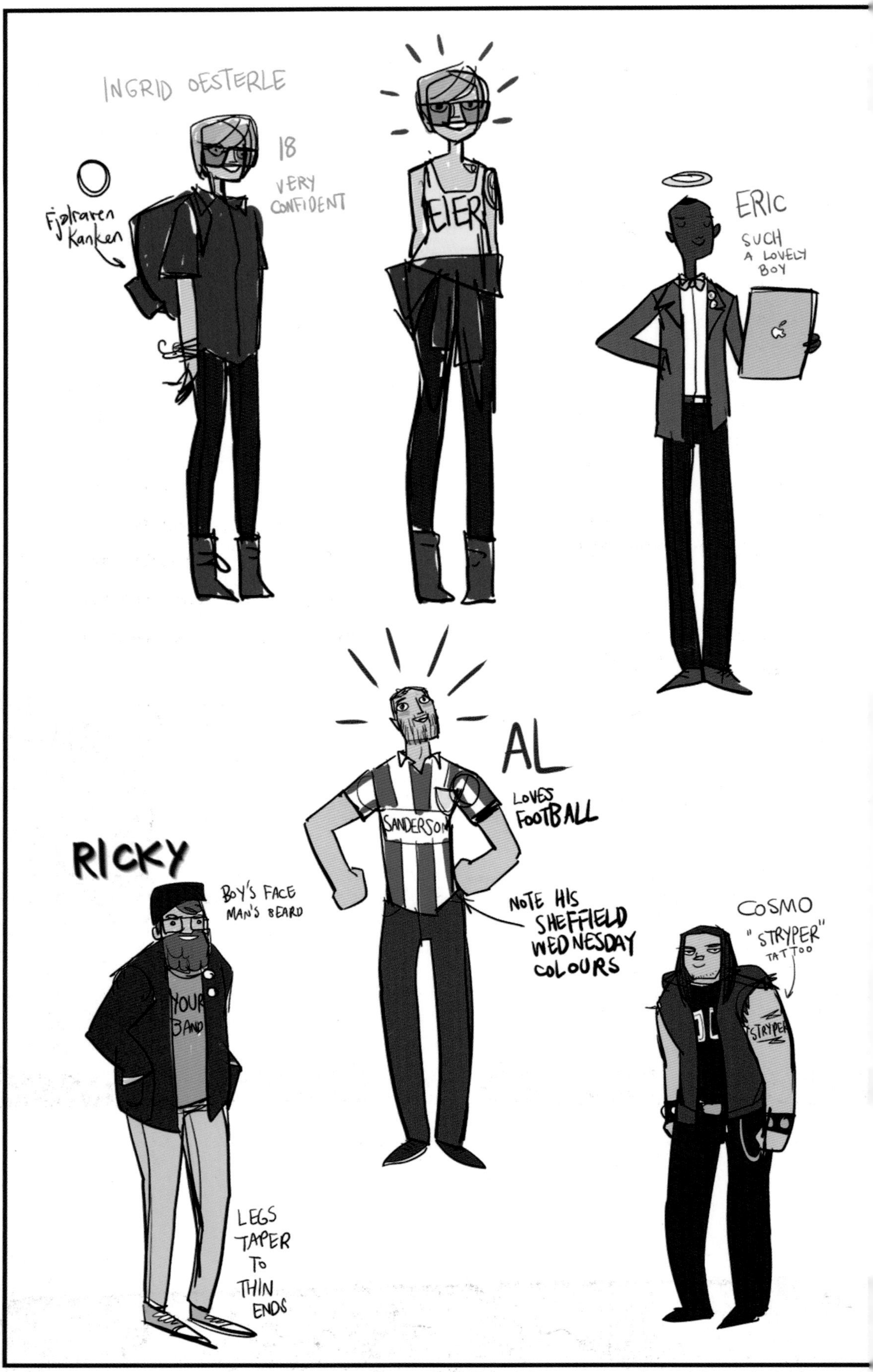
INGRID OESTERLE
18
VERY CONFIDENT
Fjølraven Kanken
EIER
ERIC
SUCH A LOVELY BOY
AL
LOVES FOOTBALL
SANDERSON
NOTE HIS SHEFFIELD WEDNESDAY COLOURS
RICKY
BOY'S FACE MAN'S BEARD
YOUR BAND
LEGS TAPER TO THIN ENDS
COSMO
"STRYPER" TATTOO
STRYPER

ALSO FROM BOOM! BOX™

FOR THE LOVE OF IT

STEVENSON · ELLIS · WATTERS · ALLEN
LUMBERJANES
BEWARE THE KITTEN HOLY

LUMBERJANES
Noelle Stevenson | Grace Ellis | Shannon Watters | Brooke Allen

Vol. 1: Beware the Kitten Holy TP
$14.99 US • $18.99 CA • £10.99 UK | ISBN: 978-1-60886-687-8

Vol. 2: Friendship to the Max TP
$14.99 US • $18.99 CA • £10.99 UK | ISBN: 978-1-60886-737-0

Vol. 3: A Terrible Plan TP
$14.99 US • $18.99 CA • £10.99 UK | ISBN: 978-1-60886-803-2

Vol. 4: Out of Time TP
$14.99 US • $18.99 CA • £10.99 UK | ISBN: 978-1-60886-860-5

Allison + Treiman + Cogar
GIANT DAYS
VOLUME ONE

GIANT DAYS
John Allison | Lissa Treiman | Max Sarin

Vol. 1 TP
$9.99 US • $11.99 CA • £7.50 UK | ISBN: 978-1-60886-789-9

Vol. 2 TP
$14.99 US • $18.99 CA • £10.99 UK | ISBN: 978-1-60886-804-9

Vol. 3 TP
$14.99 US • $18.99 CA • £10.99 UK | ISBN: 978-1-60886-851-3

JONESY
VOLUME ONE

JONESY
Sam Humphries | Caitlin Rose Boyle

Vol. 1 TP
$9.99 US • $11.99 CA • £7.50 UK
ISBN: 978-1-60886-883-4

Hope Larson · Brittney Williams · Sarah Stern
GOLDIE VANCE

GOLDIE VANCE
Hope Larson | Brittney Williams

Vol. 1 TP
$9.99 US • $11.99 CA • £7.50 UK
ISBN: 978-1-60886-898-8

TYSON HESSE'S
DIESEL

TYSON HESSE'S DIESEL: IGNITION
Available November 2017
$14.99 US • $18.99 CA • £10.99 UK
ISBN: 978-1-60886-907-7

ALSO AVAILABLE

HELP US! GREAT WARRIOR
Madeleine Flores
$19.99 US • $25.99 CA • £14.99 UK
ISBN: 978-1-60886-802-5

TEEN DOG
Jake Lawrence
$19.99 US • $25.99 CA • £14.99 UK
ISBN: 978-1-60886-729-5

THE MIDAS FLESH
Ryan North | Shelli Paroline | Braden Lamb

Vol. 1 TP
$14.99 US • $18.99 CA • £10.99 UK
ISBN 978-1-60886-455-3

Vol. 2 TP
$14.99 US • $18.99 CA • £10.99 UK
ISBN: 978-1-60886-727-1

POWER UP
Kate Leth | Matt Cummings
$19.99 US • $25.99 CA • £14.99 UK
ISBN: 978-1-60886-837-7

BOOM! BOX™

AVAILABLE AT YOUR LOCAL COMICS SHOP OR BOOKSTORE.
To find a comics shop in your area, call 1-888-266-4226.
Prices and availability subject to change without notice.

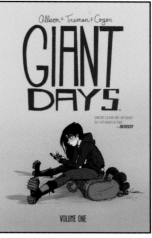

BOTTOM